A
HUMAN TRAFFICKING
THRILLER

MARION SCHERER

The Cage: a Human Trafficking Thriller © 2019 by Marion Scherer

Printed in the United States of America.

Cover Design by Damonza

First Edition: May 2019

ISBN: 978-1-7333735-0-0 - Paperback
ISBN: 978-1-7333735-1-7 - ebook

DEDICATION

To the most wonderful guy I know, my husband David.

ACKNOWLEDGEMENTS

Many thanks go out to the people who provided much valuable support and encouragement: Wendy Bowers, thank you for your unflappable belief in this book! Martha Waldman, you were a much-needed steady mind. Margaret Wilson you were a great first reader who helped me get through those icky first drafts, thank you all for your time, support, and comments! Dianne Rameriz, it was a blessing to have you for computer support. Debbie Gohlke and Soroptimist International of Oxnard thank you all for listening to excerpts and providing encouragement!

A special debt of gratitude for the professional assistance of Lieutenant Marc Evans and Sergeant Dante Reese of LAPD Human Trafficking Task Force Valley Bureau; Doctor Allison Santi-Richard, Emergency Medicine Physician at Los Robles Hospital, Thousand Oaks, California; and Detective Judith Porter, Human Trafficking Investigator for Ventura County Sheriff's Special Crimes Unit.

A huge salute to the many, many survivors out there who have been through hell and come out the other side. Sharing your stories to help educate others about this travesty helps more people understand that this is real, and it must end.

A well deserved thank you to my husband who has never stopped standing by my side.

And to my high school friend Betty Buckley who inspired the character Sandy—thanks, B, for the wonderful memories.

To the young who don't know they are
being manipulated until it's too late.

To the marginalized who fall prey to enslavement by others.

To all those who yearn to feel special, deserving of a unique status,

And who, in failing their ideal, collapse into
a world of despair and darkness.

This message is for you. Keep trying to
move up and out of the black.

It's the only shot you've got.

PROLOGUE

From the Pimp's Point of View:

The best victim is the one who doesn't know she's a victim.

My profits: $80,500 a week

Each girl: $1,500 per day

Method of approach:

Romeo: wines and dines and makes them believe he cares.

Gorilla: intimidates by threat or force.

Female Pimp: offers a better percentage.

Communication is by cell phone; booking is by internet. This is a 150-billion-dollar industry, second only to drug smuggling.

Drugs can be sold only once; humans can be sold over and over.

Advice to my flock:

> Don't look another pimp in the eye that's "out of pocket."
> Ask for permission to eat, sleep, or use the bathroom.

> I am your "everything" now. If you get to be my bottom bitch, then you will be my most trusted girl.

> If you cross me, I will kill you and your family, especially that cute little five-year-old sister of yours. I will fuck her until she ruptures what's between her little, itty, bitty legs!

> I can force you, coerce you, and terrorize you into doing whatever I want, whenever I want.

> I own you, bitch!

Julius

"Are you crazy? You can sell humans over and over, and drugs you peddle just once! I've never made more money in my life! Girls loved to be pimped! Money first, ass last! Make them beg for you to fuck them!

You don't understand—treating them like shit is what they beg for. Domination and control; they need this kind of discipline in their lives. I've discovered a gold mine, and there is no satisfaction in any other kind of life for me. I'm important, I'm rich, and my bitches love me. The johns are so grateful for my great-looking stable. Everybody's happy!

Selling body parts—hey that's for freaks! If you're stupid enough to be found or desperate enough to try and sell, you'll be killed. Nobody needs the weak ones. My world is defined by me!

Suzanne DeMarco

Suzanne is fifteen, a squeaky-clean kid who was a dead ringer (or so her grandfather said) for the actress Kim Novak. She guessed that she was sexy, but she didn't care. She seldom spoke to anyone unless they spoke first. She'd never had much luck with communication, even though she'd tried desperately as a child to make her feelings known. Her parents had never really cared, as they were too busy with things they considered important. So she learned early to shut it down and shut it up. Even when her feelings overwhelmed her she poignantly made attempts to communicate but the silence of others was deafening. Once, when with her little sister in a restaurant, a song came on the jukebox, and Bethy started crying and singing the words to everybody at the table: "I just gotta get a message to you!" Suzanne had known exactly what she meant. It's a pain so deep inside you, because the message is your soul crying out for help, and no one is listening, even if they do nod their head and say they understand. "You're being too emotional" they will say. It's really lost on people, so why try? It must have been that diaper that her mother pined on her when she came home from second grade, because she was still wetting the bed and would continue to for many more years to come. Sometimes she remembered this, but most times she forgot.

CHAPTER ONE

"Bark," a voice said in the cold, dark room. She tried to rise up on one arm, but a chain pulled her back down. Still suffering from some horrible taste in her mouth, she gagged and vomited on the floor—*on the what?* she thought. *I'm in a cage!*

It smelled like it had been used before—stale, slept in, peed in, and cried in many times before. She could see places where someone had tried to pry loose the wires. Bits of brown-looking stuff like dried blood clung to the hinges. She wondered if someone had died there; she thought she might.

Looking around beyond the cage, she saw a dimly lit room. It was putrid, with dirty navy-blue walls and a stained green-concrete floor. Not a garage. Maybe a room in a house? One small bulb burned faintly from an ancient wall sconce, offering just enough light to let her know that she was a prisoner in a cage, no more than an animal at the mercy of a monster.

The voice spoke again. "All you have to do now is listen. Do what I say and you'll be okay. There are two bowls on the floor in front of you. One's for food and the other for water. That's what you'll eat and drink when I give it to you. Do you understand?"

She tried to brush aside her growing panic. "Julius?"

"I told you to bark! That's how you answer me from now on. That's how you get permission to eat, go to the bathroom, or wear any clothes. You sleep on the floor naked until you earn the right to have a blanket. I am your world now. Do you understand?"

And from somewhere deep in her paralyzed soul, she answered with a tiny guttural sound, the sound of a wounded animal barking.

CHAPTER TWO

PAISLEY FALLS WAS not the kind of town anyone would call terrific or charming. It was a small suburb way out in the sticks of Northern California, blue collar people, tidy and conforming to the land, another Sierra Slope town carved out by miners foraging for gold. Suzanne often wished that she could live anywhere else, just not here. It was hot and tinderbox dry in the summer, cold and rainy in the winter. There was never anything to do. She and her only high-school friend, Sandy, would walk the country roads into town to the local McDonald's to have fries and a Coke. That was their big Saturday adventure! Neither one of them played sports or went to football games. Cheerleaders were a joke, and most of the boys were nerds. Sandy lived across the street from the weirdest one, Bruce Bonsford. The two girls constantly spied on Brucie Boy and laughed about his antics and his total avoidance of them.

"Doesn't he even walk with you to the school bus?" asked Suzanne one afternoon when they were looking through Sandy's binoculars pointed at Bruce's house.

"No!" Sandy replied, laughing. "He spies me coming and takes a detour! I feel like I'm a two-ton poisoned meatball rolling down the street at him!" They howled over this image of Sandy. Laughter was what helped them make the best of their lives. Each was questioning her own loneliness, however, unsure and hoping that a more exciting future would manifest itself.

Sandy was taller, bigger, and more practical than Suzanne. She got by well enough in school and, more importantly, connected with people. When they walked the halls before first period, Sandy would nudge Suzanne when people waved or said something to her. She knew that Suzanne had a hard time actually *looking* at people, sometimes not understanding others or situations right in front of her. Sandy was aware of this and frequently had to explain very basic things to her timid friend. She rescued her in many ways and would continue throughout her life to save Suzanne from herself and the trauma that she unknowingly attracted. Because Sandy had learned self-reliance early, she was more streetwise than Suzanne, and it was her strength that was the saving force behind the tragedy of Suzanne's life. However things went, Sandy would always believe in and staunchly support her friend. She would become the only candle in a dark night, to be remembered by Suzanne in her bleakest times as her guardian angel.

One day Sandy found a diary from some distant relative who had been in the Civil War, and Suzanne, who loved to read aloud, began reciting the annals of the journal after school. It became enthralling to hear the stories of the Confederate soldier who kept daily accounts of his duties. Somehow the dreariness of their own lives became enveloped in the life of the Confederate soldier, and each day they couldn't wait until they took up the story of the little man who had fought in a war so long ago. The journal ended abruptly one day, and then there was this entry:

Property of Private John Entron

died May 13, 1865, at the Battle of Palmito Ranch

Both girls were saddened, and Sandy said that she hadn't expected that to happen. They decided to visit the local cemeteries to look for people who had passed away during that time period, glancing at the headstones with tiny pictures of loved ones engraved on them.

"This is getting morbid, Suzanne," her mother, Rhonda, admonished one day. "Maybe you girls should try reading happier stories."

But Suzanne brushed her mother's suggestions aside. If Rhonda could find anything more boring for her to do, she would. They say life is what you make of it, and if the only thing to work with was the dinky little town she lived in, then her world had to become lit from within!

Sandy was eager to leave the Civil War journal and move on to more pressing interests, like boys, but Suzanne began studying the clothes and hairstyles that women wore during the Civil War era. She had long enjoyed reading the works of novelist Louisa May Alcott, but now she delved into the writings of Ralph Waldo Emerson, Henry David Thoreau, and Amos Bronson Alcott, as well as the work of the transcendentalists.

"What's a transcendentalist, Suz?" Sandy asked her friend one day as they walked the high school halls before first period.

"Oh, it's just something I'm very interested in right now. I wouldn't want to bore you with it."

"Oh yeah, okay. Hey look." Sandy gave Suzanne a nudge. "Ed Eastman just waved at you! What a dude! Wave back."

Sandy effusively waved back, smiling and giving Ed a big wink as they passed, but Suzanne was oblivious.

Transcendentalism was a philosophical movement that believed that people and nature were inherently good and pure and that both are corrupted by society and its institutions. Music became symphonies like *Death and Transfiguration*, which Suzanne described to herself as the inner awakenings of the spirit. She put a pitcher of water and a basin in her room and washed her face by candlelight. She became enmeshed in her beautiful world where illusion dominated and fantasy was real.

Her mother went crazy.

"What do you think you're doing? You can't walk around pretending you live in the past!"

But thankfully Suzanne had her own room, and a slam of the door was all she needed to protect herself, her thoughts and feelings, and her art! In her self-imposed isolation, her art blossomed.

Many late nights were spent writing poetry describing the cages she felt her life was in. Cages upon cages of stacked problems that weren't her fault, things she couldn't solve or escape. Living in this protected world was her only salvation. Sandy was becoming increasingly involved with Bruce Bonsford, and Suzanne thought they might have done something in the back seat of his car, but she didn't care. She was safe and happy and alone.

Suzanne thought her English teacher might be a friend. Miss Eirheart was everything she dreamed of becoming: beautiful, intelligent, and polished. Suzanne began giving her little bits of her poetry every day before class.

Texas coming in on his horse

Life on the open range

Is quite a sudden change

From the gangling, streaming strange

Closed planes of the insane

Miss Eirheart had loved it! *I've impressed her*, thought Suzanne. She started leaving little messages of poetry and wisdom daily, but sometimes she felt the interest was waning. One day she left a quote from a book by John Dos Passos. *Midcentury* was one of the books her father was constantly reading. The quote fit her so perfectly that she felt it was her own. Even at fifteen, it was what she had come to believe about her own existence. "One of the most galling disillusionments of our time is that we are." That had deeply impressed Miss Eirheart!

She had seen Miss Eirheart's eyes open wide as she read it. There was that wonderful smile as she quickly slipped the note into her desk drawer as she began the class. Suzanne never told her that the quote came from someone else.

Shortly thereafter, Miss Eirheart confided that she was submitting Suzanne's poetry to a publisher. Suzanne was thrilled! It didn't seem important to tell her that the one line she had given her that day wasn't her own. It didn't matter, reasoned Suzanne. It was her poetry that was important. That line was not poetry! She breathlessly awaited Miss E's response from the publisher. But Miss E had dropped out of the faculty at school. She'd abruptly gotten married and, even more suddenly, gotten pregnant. Suzanne never saw her again. When she finally summoned the nerve to filch her cell number from the faculty directory and call her, she received a cold, abrupt dismissal and vague explanation that Suzanne was fantasizing about her own importance. Miss E never said anything directly about the poetry, and still Suzanne never explained about the one line that wasn't hers. She felt ashamed and angry. Over and over again she rehashed the whole context of their conversation and her poetry. It had meant the world that Miss E had believed in her. Why hadn't she confronted her about her work? Why didn't Suzanne explain about the only discrepancy in her writings? Why, why, why bother?

And when she turned the corner in her head to embrace the confusion and despair of her own sad life, she ran right into the next person who would fill the void.

CHAPTER THREE

SUZANNE'S COURTSHIP WAS now in its final planning stages. She was so lovely she would bring good money, over and over again. Dino would be proud of him for scoring such a find! Julius had patiently stood in the same spot watching her from afar. It had taken her awhile to notice his gaze. At first she thought he was one of the seniors, a guy who played football, the epitome of tall dark and handsome. *What does he want with me?* she thought. *Why doesn't he go for a cheerleader or the prom-queen type?*

However, his glances became more and more intense, always promising more love and attention than she had ever known from anyone. She became transfixed, searching him out each afternoon after school, admiring the amazing red Corvette he stood next to on the street. She was hungry for his glance, and soon, he thought, his touch, his kiss, and his total possession and control.

He remembered the smell of her beautiful silky hair as he passed her one day in the shopping mall, oblivious to him then, but not for long. He had smiled in total anticipation of how good it would feel to have absolute control, not only of her body but also of her soul. *It's so sexy to use people,* he thought, and he got hard just thinking about that. How he wanted to fuck her and own her ass! It was just in his nature. He was born with it. Evil simply grew like it was meant to be harvested from his soul. He understood suffering and, in particular, what kinds of people needed to be used and punished merely by looking at them. Every feeling worth feeling resonated in the word *wicked*. All his entities—those weird little crippled hobbits that inhabited his being—quelled at the sound of that word. Wicked. It made him smile. Secretly, he knew he could never explain it to anyone. No one else really understood someone's inner life anyway, yet he felt that there were more people like him than anyone realized.

"Hi," he said. "It's time we met." He offered her his dazzling smile and opened his mouth slightly in a soft O shape, as though he was saying, "I wanna suck your nipples."

Suzanne looked up at him, confused about the signals he was sending. "Hi," was about all she could muster. *Oh my God*, she thought, *he is soooo cute!* Embarrassed because she knew she was turning bright red, she averted her face, which became Julius's cue to take her face in his hands and gently turn it back toward him.

"It's just 'hi, honey.' No need to be embarrassed." He laughed and gently brushed a strand of hair off her forehead. "Can I give you a ride home? You're looking at this shiny red car like you've never seen a car before. Here," he said and opened the door with a flourish like an attendant would do at a hotel, waving his hand as though to signal her inside. "Get in."

She couldn't believe he was finally talking to her. She had often envisioned kissing him. She would kiss her hand, then close her eyes, kiss the mirror, open her eyes, and pretend she saw her love!

"No, no. I don't even know you. Are you in senior class or something? I don't remember seeing you around in school."

Suzanne was a daydreamer, and there was nothing she wanted more than to get in that car and ride down the street hoping everyone would see them, but her mother had done much to make her afraid of everything and everybody. She hated that she wasn't more adventurous, so it was look but don't touch with the wonderful guy and his incredible car.

It was look but don't touch with Julius as well. *Take it easy with her*, he cautioned himself. *Back off a little. This baby's gonna take some time. Ease up, bro.*

"Well, I don't want to scare you, honey, but I would like to take you out for dinner some time. And I can assure you that no harm will come to you in my company." He leaned in. "You're stunning, you know that?" he whispered. "Any guy would love to be seen with you. I couldn't help noticing you coming out of school. I used to go here, and now I've got a business nearby. Whenever I have a minute, I drive by my alma mater for old time's sake. And today when I drove by, I spotted you and almost wrecked the car."

He gave her that dazzling smile again. All six feet of him smiled down on her, and all she wanted to do was melt into his arms. His strong, athletic, graceful body hovered near her as though he wanted to embrace her but didn't.

"Think about dinner, okay? And next time I drive by, maybe you'll let me take you home." With that, he got into the Corvette and sped off like some future Prince Lancelot.

"Who was that?" queried an amazed Sandy creeping out from the corner where she had been watching the whole scene. "I mean, who the fuck was that!"

"Oh, just a guy who used to go to school here. Maybe the

four of us can double date. You know, you, me, Bruce Bonsford and…" She had forgotten to ask him his name!

She rushed off, leaving a confused and dazed Sandy staring after her.

CHAPTER FOUR

"I THOUGHT I told you not to use the red Corvette. It attracts a lot of attention parked right in front of a fuckin' high school! Use the Camaro next time. It blends in better. We don't want no cop problems, pretty boy."

Dino Hu was a short, bullish, wannabe stud who was the brains behind the business; a guy who was made to order for trading in human slavery. All the intelligence he possessed was primed to spot a problem, whether it was a money transaction, a cop problem, or a bitch problem. Two years ago, he had set up a great business placing Asian girls in motels and moving them between locations in nine counties. The girls brought in about $350,000 a month. Julius fielded the calls from hundreds of men who answered sexually explicit ads on bluepage.com and directed them to motel rooms where the girls were kept. They were in this town to corral some local white girls to upgrade their business. The hierarchy, as Dino explained, was white, Asian, Hispanic, and then black. Even though Julius had his head stuck up his ass, Dino knew he had it in him to attract some awesome babes.

"Did you get her hooked yet?"

"Dino, things take time. We talked today. Just got acquainted, that's all."

Julius didn't feel the need to inform Dino that he had been tracking her for some time. He'd only get annoyed at the delay. He had no finesse. Dino was a numbers guy; the art of seduction eluded him.

"Shit, hurry it up. We've got to move soon. Did you get her cell number? I need pictures online right away."

"This is an old-fashioned girl, Dino. I can't rush this. She needs romancing."

"Don't get lost in all your charm, Romeo. Get a move on or flip to Gorilla. See her again tonight. Run into her somewhere."

"Should I take the blue Camaro for tonight? She'll think I have a stable full of cars."

"Don't be a smart ass; just get the job done. We're leaving this shit town in a few days. Gotta get back to LA. Don't lose track, bro. We need the money."

CHAPTER FIVE

"OH, THOSE LUSCIOUS lips," he said, making a sucking sound with his lips. "Oh, gimme some of those luscious lips. I wanna kiss."

He puckered up real close to her and began chasing her around the living room. He laughed as she looked disgusted and tried to shy away from him.

"Your father's just kidding, honey. He doesn't mean that the way it sounds." Her mother gave her dad a dirty look.

"Well, she locks herself up in that room of hers every night. She's gonna be an old maid. You're gonna be an old maid!" he shouted and was greeted with the sound of a door slamming. She pushed the lock on the door just in time, as she heard him come bounding down the hallway, and then his fists banging on the door. "Yeah, go on then. Lock yourself away. Who do you think is gonna take care of you? Me? You little bitch, open up this door!"

Suzanne and her father had been very close when she was a little girl. Her father could control and manipulate her then, and he worshipped her total dependence on him. In adolescence, she began to challenge him, not so much overtly, but by her physical changes that contributed to an alteration in her personality.

Going from child to woman was a threat to Evan, as he faced a double-edged sword with a jealous wife in tow. Also, an older Evan meant a less successful Evan—his alcoholism allowed him to wallow in his failures. Suzanne would inevitably grow up and leave home, as in marriage. He unconsciously struggled with the realization that the house would be minus another extension of him. How could he reconcile such a loss! His ego demanded that he bear down on her and force her to conform to the box their house had become.

The doorknob was being tested now. Her mother came down the hall after him.

"Evan, stop this right now. Leave her alone! Just stop it. You've had one beer too many! Come back and watch TV now. Let's just sit and watch…" The words drifted off as her mother led her father back down the hall to what was euphemistically referred to as the TV room. In reality it was a rapacious den where copious amounts of alcohol were consumed, mainly by her father, who toasted himself daily from five p.m. to the wee hours of the morning. Not that her mother was so sacrosanct—she belted them down occasionally just for communication's sake and, of course, to drown her own loneliness.

Suzanne didn't hate her parents; it was more that she felt nothing for them. As soon as she could find a way out of this prison, she would. In the meantime, she felt safe within the environs of her own room. It was the sanctuary she needed to have in order to survive in this house. The walls may have been paper thin and the door easily broken through, but it was her space to own and define. If she wanted basins and pitchers of water to wash her face in each morning, so be it. She felt like Jane Eyre anyway—orphaned, unloved, and unwanted, not to mention misunderstood. It was the cold starkness of existence that she felt empowered by. Jane survived by her own steady hand. She even found her own true love! *In spite of all odds*, she told herself. For there was no question, in her mind at least, that if she survived emotionally, it would be quite a longshot. Even at fifteen, Suzanne honestly didn't think she'd make it through her life.

Her phone rang. It was Sandy. "Hey, can you get out tonight? Bruce can get the car, and we're going to the mall and then maybe to a party after. Wanna come?"

"Oh, I guess Bruce doesn't think you look like a two-ton poisoned meatball anymore. I didn't know he had made it to boyfriend status," Suzanne said, laughing.

After an awkward silence, Sandy admitted that things had changed between her and Bruce.

"Yeah, I guess I forgot to mention that he thinks I'm kind of cute and we're sort of dating. Sort of, you know what I mean? But back to the question: are you coming with us tonight? It'll be fun!"

"Jeez, my dad's on a rampage. They'll never let me go out now."

"We'll be by in twenty minutes. He'll be shit-faced by then. Just sneak past him."

"Really? What about my mother? She's in there too."

"Well, think of something. Be dramatic! You'll know what to do. See ya. We'll honk. Bye."

Suzanne wanted to go. It was up to her now to figure out a way. She looked into her mirror and kissed her hand, feeling the warmth of her newfound lover, Mr. Wonderful with the red Corvette. Maybe she would see him at the mall. Glancing in the mirror again, she thought about adding lipstick. *No*, she thought, remembering her father's compulsion to blabber on about her lips. *Don't draw too much attention to your mouth.*

She grabbed her coat and made her way quietly down the narrow hall, preparing in her mind the lie that she would tell.

CHAPTER SIX

THE GIRL IN the cage picked her head up to see the dawn coming through the one dingy window in the room. The trees were swaying in the distance. *They seem to be waving*, she thinks, *smiling at me*. The swaying motion revealed the light of the sky showing through the bleary hole. She wasn't sure how long she had been there. Twenty-four hours for sure. She had peed in the corner like an animal and had drunk from the water bowl. Her arms were still chained, and she'd had to put her mouth in the bowl on the floor and lap water with her tongue. Sure of one thing, she had become a vessel for pouring emptiness into. Oddly enough, bits and pieces of her life began to make an appearance before her, as if to say, "remember us, for we define you and we are your saving grace." The doll she'd had when she was little. She hadn't saved it.

Night after night, she had put it outside the doorstep of her house where it would get rained on or covered with dirt that the wind had blown onto it. She would get the doll first thing in the morning, but she could see that it had suffered; it was wounded. Her father would bind the doll together with green tape, at first an arm, and then a leg. Every day she would take it inside and love it, but come each night, out it would go to the porch. Sometimes she forgot to retrieve it, and it would be left out there for days. Her father had questioned her about why she did this, but she had no answer. Eventually, the doll was so damaged it had to be thrown away. She had finally lost interest in it. She felt nothing as her mother threw it into the trash.

Well, you abandoned the most precious parts of yourself, didn't you? It's like you tried to forget what was important, thinking that if you just ignored it, it would go away. Instead, all the pain and sorrow you didn't want to feel just piled up outside the door of yourself. You were too undeserving to get any real happiness in life. And life fooled you once again, sucker! Now here you are in the middle of hell.

She went over and over in her mind the details of the night before. Her mother's harried look, for example, and the cynical reaction as she left the house to meet Sandy and Bruce Bonsford. "Where do you think you're going?" she had asked as Suzanne slithered past the family room where her father, in a state of stupor, stared absentmindedly toward the TV.

"Ah, Sandy called and we both have a biology test tomorrow. Thought two minds would be better than one concentrating on that stuff." She added a giggle as an acknowledgement that her mother might be in sync with this line of reasoning.

"I know what you're up to. Don't try to be coy with me. Just be home by ten or I'll let your father know," she whispered. "And that wouldn't be so good for Suzanne, would it?" She cackled to herself and turned her head back to the task that was much more important to her—watching mindless, trivial, ever-present sitcoms.

She'd been so excited as she jumped in the back seat of Bruce's old battered Ford Pinto. His ride, as he called it, was better than nothing at all, and the girls had laughed as they sputtered off toward the mall. What she hadn't known was that across the street the blue Camaro started up, and Julius began a discreet tail of their car. He had found Sandy earlier that afternoon and had given her a few bucks to set up a meeting with Suzanne at the mall. He had told her the story of being a love-struck guy who wanted a chance to hook up with the girl of his dreams, and Sandy had fallen for it, like the goofy little freak she was.

Why didn't he take her? Why didn't he want us both? What is he going to do with me?

And although she didn't think she had any more strength to cry, she started sobbing once again.

"I'm in here with you," said the voice.

"Julius?"

"Bark!"

"What happened? What did I do wrong? Please let me go and I'll be good. I promise!"

All she heard was the sound of a door slamming shut.

She rattled the chains around her fists and started howling.

CHAPTER SEVEN

THEY WERE SUPPOSED to meet by the yogurt kiosk at the mall. He would pass by them on the way to a movie and stop suddenly, surprised to see them, and ask what they were up to. He chuckled to himself as he made his way through the sad, dilapidated dinosaur anchored by the two most trustworthy and antiquated hallmarks of Americana—Sears and JCPenney. He couldn't wait to get out of this dumpy little town and back to LA where he could get lost in a sea of stupefied superficiality. He had chosen a shirt of light grey in a raw silk to go with his dark-grey gabardine slacks, simple loafers, a gold Gucci watch, and, of course, his dazzling white teeth. He knew his smile was his signature gesture. That smile, combined with his mesmerizing dark eyes, although they reflected only his emptiness, brought women to their knees begging to be possessed by him. He knew he was worth so much more than working for Dino and his lousy stable. He knew he could break into the big time. He was Vegas, he was LA, he was the world!

"Hi… hey you, hi!"

It was his little darlin' Suzanne, running up to him and tapping his shoulder.

"How funny... I mean, how great it is to see you here. Tonight!" she added.

She laughed, embarrassed that she was blushing and didn't even know his name. Sandy and Bruce paced themselves a little behind Suzanne, not wanting to ruin the first moment of contact between them. They each gave the other a knowing look and decided to play dumb about the chance encounter. Sandy spoke first.

"Oh, hi. Haven't I seen you around school? Don't you drive that incredible Corvette?" she gushed with proper teenage enthusiasm. Bruce awkwardly said nothing but stood back as though he wasn't interested.

"Yeah, I used to go to Paisley Falls High, and I love driving by the place sometimes, just to check it out and check *you* out."

He beamed down on both of the girls, and they giggled. Bruce coughed and turned away, checking out two babes going into a Forever 21 shop. Julius took up the slack and nonchalantly mentioned that he was on his way to a movie and that they had better not stay out too late on a school night. Suzanne didn't know what to say; she didn't want him to go.

Sandy nudged her and whispered, "Ask him if he wants to go to a party. Go on, ask him."

She gave Suzanne a gentle push. Julius had started to walk away, knowing the game being played. He hesitated and turned slowly back toward the girls. Suzanne saw the tip of his loafer turn, followed by the soft flow of the gabardine slacks as he moved back toward them. She thought he was so elegant, so charming, and he liked *her!* Boldly, she turned into him, almost colliding, and breathlessly asked, "Would you like to go to a party with us tonight?"

"Whoa, babe," he responded, "I'm a little old for your crowd."

I'd have to buy the beer, and later somebody's parents would call the cops, and where would that leave me?"

Bruce snickered at this but covered his sarcasm with a cough. Julius gave him a cold look, and then suggested that he'd like to drive Suzanne over to the party and drop her off, getting promises from Sandy and Bruce that they would drive Suzanne home at a decent hour. They agreed, and Bruce, who had had some time to glance at the movie arcade, noted to himself that all the movies playing were girly romances. Why, he wondered, would this slicker waste his money on that crap?

Once they were in his car, Suzanne couldn't wait for him to kiss her. He held her close for just a minute before he turned on the ignition, but she put her hand on his as if to say "not just yet." She turned her face up to him and closed her eyes in preparation. Julius gazed down at her, but not with lust or affection. The steely coldness of his being saw only a conquest to be mined and controlled to do his bidding, whenever and whatever he asked. *You can sell drugs only once*, he thought to himself, *but you can sell humans over and over*. And, like some Dracula figure of old, he sank his lips down over hers and kissed them.

"Oh," she moaned and opened her eyes to see him gazing down upon her. Interpreting his gaze to be one of passion, she uttered, "I think we've finally found each other."

As he started to speak, she held up her hand to gently cover his mouth and continued, "I've seen you watching me at school. That's not the first time you've been parked there with your red Corvette."

She could feel her heart beating so rapidly she thought she might faint. Her hand trembled as she withdrew it from his mouth. How she wanted him to kiss her again. But to her surprise, he didn't. He seemed almost detached from the encounter between them. *What's wrong?* she thought. *Did I say something wrong?*

"Oh, I'm embarrassed to ask this, but what's your name? I feel like I know everything about you, but I don't after all." She giggled with this newfound knowledge and hoped he didn't think she was just another airhead. Wait till she read him her poetry. Maybe they'd be sitting in his apartment by the fire, sipping wine while she read aloud and he listened adoringly. He would become spellbound by her passion and appreciate her dreams. Soon he would never want to be without her. Sandy and Bruce Bonsford would get married and have some dinky little small-town ceremony, but she and—

"It's Julius, little dreamer! Where did you drift off to? You looked like you were daydreaming up a storm." He smiled with those dazzling white teeth again, and Suzanne's heart melted. She squeezed his hand and, as if on cue, he brushed back a strand of hair on her forehead.

"Hey, beautiful green eyes, I better get you over to that party before I forget myself and take advantage of you." And with that he slid his fingers down her face to the tip of one breast.

"Oh, kiss me again. I could care less about that stupid party."

How he wanted to take her then and there. Dino would be expecting this prize tonight, but he knew he had to be cautious. Those two kids would be sure to accuse him of kidnapping her. He had to make it look like she left town of her own free will. That was the professional touch he needed. It was a lot classier than just taking off with her. That was a Dino move, and got you a felony for kidnapping if you were caught. No, he had a much bigger and better plan in mind.

"Hey, girl, where's that party goin' on?"

Right then, Sandy and Bruce drove by and Sandy hollered

out the window, "You coming or what?" while Bruce snickered in the driver's seat.

"We'll follow you." Julius lined up behind Bruce's pathetic Pinto, and they caravanned off to the party.

When they pulled up to a stylish home with lots of cars parked everywhere, Julius leaned in to plant a chaste kiss on her cheek. "Don't stay out late, ya hear? I wouldn't want my baby to get in any trouble."

At that, Suzanne's face lit up like a Christmas tree. She fell once more into Julius's arms, so wanting to feel him encircling her. A Katy Perry song wafted out into the street as sounds of laughter filtered out from the house.

"When will I see you again?" she asked.

"When you see me drive by, little girl."

Sandy and Bruce bounced up to the car laughing. "Come on, you two. Let's get going or it will be over!"

"Bye, sweetie," said Julius the wolf.

"Till tomorrow then," said Little Red Riding Hood.

CHAPTER EIGHT

THE MINUTE SHE walked into the party she regretted it. All she wanted to do was be with Julius. *What a beautiful name*, she thought. She pronounced all three syllables of his name in her head slowly, like it was the title of a new song. *Ju-li-us.* It flowed and spread out in her mind and consciousness like a misty fog enveloping all her senses. She only wanted to be in his arms. What was she doing at this dumb party!

All around her, kids she'd seen at school were drinking beer and getting drunk. Some were already pretty wasted. She wasn't sure whose house this was, but it was a wealthier home than hers and on the better side of town. Ethan-Allan-type furniture. Stylish, rich patterns of gold and green leaves adorned the beautiful, overstuffed couch, which looked now as if red wine had been spilled on it, staining some of the gold leaves a putrid brown. Popcorn and chips littered the elegant carpet, and somebody had puked in a corner.

Sandy and Bruce were nowhere to be found. Once they all had gone into the house, the two of them disappeared into the noisy crowd that was now belting out the chorus of that Katy Perry song, "Last Friday Night." Suzanne was so happy she started dancing in spite of herself. Suddenly, she felt hands grab her around the waist. Thinking Julius had come into the house, she turned around right into the arms of Dick Willis, a senior and the lead quarterback for Paisley Falls High.

"Hey, baby!" said Dick as he started grinding his hips toward her with a big shit-eating grin on his face. Blonde-haired and blue-eyed, tall and strong, he was every high school girl's dream of the perfect boyfriend. Rumor had it that he'd laid every cheerleader on the squad. Suzanne wondered if this were his parent's house.

"Oh, excuse me… ah… Dick, I didn't mean to—"

"I've seen you around school, sweet little thing. What year are you?"

"Whew, it's kinda hot in here," she responded. "Think I'll get some air." And with that she skirted around Dick and made her way to the front door.

Dick, not used to being rejected, took affront at this and quickly moved in front of her to block her way.

"What's your hurry, honey? Stick around, 'cause we're going to play some really nice games."

It was obvious that he had been drinking, and he definitely wasn't used to not having his way.

"Hey, Dick, is this your parent's house?" She was hoping to change the subject and get him off her.

Why had she even come here? Why hadn't she let Julius take her home? Why didn't she have his cell phone? Why hadn't he asked for her cell number? Trying to figure all this out while dealing with big Dick, as she now thought of him, had made her dizzy, and she felt that she would choke from all the loud noises and booze and grass. She had to get out of there, but she didn't even know where she was. And where were Sandy and Bruce?

Dick started closing in on her. He grabbed a beer from a nearby table and began sucking the nozzle as he moved toward her. The sound of the sucking noise started to make her sick, and as she grimaced, he chuckled and then taunted, "That's what I'm going to do to your pussy, baby. And it's gonna feel just great."

He had jammed hard up against her and pushed her against the door frame. A couple of guys had seen his move and began cheering him on.

"Go, Dick you prick!" they said laughing and toasting him. "Do your thing, buddy, that thing you do so well."

Suddenly the whole house was in total chaos. People were hanging on banisters and laughing and singing so loud she could barely hear herself think.

"Let's go all the way tonight, baby!"

No one seemed to be paying any attention to her. This had become a game like the lions and the gladiators.

Looking into Dick's grinning red face, bloated from one too many beers, she thought of her father's endless taunts about her lips, or her hips, or the size of her feet. *Hey, gunboat, bring your skis over here.*

She brought one knee up to his groin and shoved it in hard. His dumfounded look said it all. There was uproarious laughter and cheering all around. Dick staggered back, and then quickly lunged forward, furious for losing face to this nothing girl.

"Listen, you fucking cunt, I am gonna have your ass for this!"

She cowered backward into the screen of the front door, frantically pushing the lever to get it open, but it was stuck, and she was trapped. It was then that everybody heard the screams of the sirens and threw themselves into panic mode. The police were on their way. Suzanne quickly let herself out and scurried across the yard and onto the neighbor's lawn. She hid behind their garbage barrels until she could catch her breath. *Come on, Sandy, get out here!* But the police were already inside taking everybody's names and addresses. She heard sobbing from some of the girls, but except for them, the place had fallen silent. She waited. Should she get up and leave? She had absolutely no idea where she was!

From behind her, a voice called out, "Are you in some kind of trouble?"

A child of no more than five stood on the front porch looking down at her crouching behind his parents' garbage barrels. He was in pajamas with a green dinosaur print, holding a stuffed green dinosaur and looking very much like the king of the manor. Suzanne laughed in spite of herself and said no, that she was just looking for something. In fact, she had left her purse with her cell in it at the house, and now she couldn't even call Sandy without going inside and getting into trouble with the police.

"You wouldn't by chance have a cell phone, would you?" And then she heard, "Justin, get back inside. What are you doing out there?"

"Oops, gotta go. I don't want you to get in any trouble."

With that, she got up on her feet and looked around for any information that could tell her where she was. A blue Camaro drove by, hesitated, and then backed up to where she was standing.

"Get in."

"Oh, Julius, thank God it's you."

Sandy peered out from the bushes as the blue Camaro sped away. "Wait, Suzanne! I've got your purs—"

A hand quickly cupped over Sandy's mouth as Bruce Bonsford whispered, "Shut up! Do you want the police to hear you?"

Bruce and Sandy had headed to one of the bedrooms on the

first floor after they arrived at the party, planning to do what most teenagers do—make out on the bed. When they heard the sirens, they fled through one of the side windows, falling into a pile of prickly hedge. "Ouch!" cried Sandy, seeing the scratches on her leg.

"Hey, it could have been worse. The cops might have nailed us," muttered Bruce, bouncing on one foot as he tried without luck to get his other shoe on.

Sandy looked on, following the lights of the Camaro. *Boy, he sure is her Prince Charming,* she thought, *always there when you need him. Wonder why he's driving that old Camaro when he's got that awesome Corvette?* Staring out into the night, she thought that maybe she didn't like Mr. Wonderful after all. A sense of uneasiness crept over her as she still held Suzanne's purse in her hand. *She doesn't even have her cell phone to call anyone if she's in trouble.* She was shaken out of her reverie by Bruce's insistent nudging.

"For Christ's sake, Sandy, let's get the hell out of here before those cops find us. C'mon!"

They found the old Pinto that they had thankfully parked on one of the side streets and barreled off into the night.

CHAPTER NINE

SUZANNE WAS QUIET in the car, holding tightly to Julius's arm as they slowed down after getting a few miles away from the chaotic scene.

"Who was that guy anyway?" Julius slid her arm off of his as he shifted into neutral.

"Just some obnoxious senior that thinks he's God's gift to women."

"Does he have a name?"

"Oh, Julius, it's not important now that you're here."

Something in his tone made her a little uneasy. Did Julius have a violent temper? Dick had just been drunk; nothing had happened. Julius came to a stop and slowly turned to her. His face had contorted into a frightening grimace, and he seized her wrist as though he might snap it.

"Don't ever change the subject when I'm asking you a question, okay?"

His grimace quickly disappeared as suddenly as it had come, and without wasting an instant, he swept her into his arms and thrust his tongue into her innocent mouth, his lips taking over hers. Suzanne moaned and fell backward into the seat, amazed at the flurry of emotions that encapsulated her. For the first time she felt whole, complete, like someone had finished making her. Her fragile body vibrated with passion for him. *I feel so safe, so complete. I want to live in no other world but his. Julius is like kissing an angel!*

All Julius could think about was raping this bitch. He was going to have to teach her a lot of lessons. *You're just a worthless little slut*, he thought, *but you're a moneymaker. What a good bottom bitch you're gonna be!*

"Baby, you've got a luscious mouth," he cooed. He couldn't help noticing her engorged nipples poking through her thin, cheap blouse.

"How would you like me to take care of you? Buy you nice clothes and take you out of this dumpy little town."

He closed her eyes with his fingers and cupped one breast with his hand. Gently, he put his mouth on her nipple and sucked it through the cloth till it was wet with his saliva. He moved his hands down and pushed at her leggings until he could insert a finger into her panties and massage her soft pubis. She spread her legs lovingly and cradled his head as his mouth found what it needed to vanquish.

"Oh my God, that feels sooo good."

"Yeah, and there's a lot more where that came from." He pulled his head up suddenly, abruptly, stopped his passionate thrusts as though there was a more important priority at stake. "I'll be right back, baby. Something here that I gotta check into. Lock the door, and I'll be right back to finish what I started." He laughed and flashed that dazzling white smile as he wiped her wetness from his mouth.

Dino wanted the girl tonight. He had made that abundantly clear. "We haul tonight. Bring her in and let's move some ass."

It was late, around two a.m., and he should have been at the warehouse by now. There was a circle of girls that needed to be transported tonight, but Julius knew that Dino wanted to wait on Suzanne. What with the cops breaking that place up and him being seen at the mall with her and those two shmucks, it was too dangerous a haul. Besides, he wanted her for bigger business. Her pussy fit right into a high-class escort service. Big clientele needed beautiful, young, white chicks, even though he knew he would salt and pepper it with all breeds, a few boys, and even babies for those with more refined tastes. He grinned in anticipation of his growing business; it made his prick so hard, but he couldn't double-cross Dino just yet. Better check in and stall him about recruiting Suzanne. She was here in the car if he had to turn her over now. Dino was still the boss until he was out on his own.

Satisfied that he was on a roll, he walked up to the warehouse door and gave the signal knock. When there was no answer, he tried again. Nothing but silence.

He smiled back at the young thing in the Camaro and tried the lock. To his surprise, it was open. An eerie darkness confronted him, and there was a sickening smell he couldn't place.

"Dino?"

Something was wrong.

His hand fumbled for the light switch somewhere on the wall. He felt a sticky film on the switch, and when he finally turned on the light, he couldn't believe what he saw. He gasped at the bloodbath that was everywhere. "Oh my God," was all he managed before he threw up at the image before him.

Dino had been guillotined. His headless body lay sprawled out on the floor, while his head with eyes wide open sat propped up on a table. Julius staggered toward it. The head was displayed like some prize at an auction. Mesmerized by the look of the contorted corpse's face, he reached toward it as though he could make it speak.

Blood, a great deal of it, had been purposely spattered all across the four walls, and the words, "Stay out of Paisley Falls" had been scrawled for the next person to find. A riotous message meant for both of them? Had he been made? He had been so careful, keeping himself unconnected to Dino, never a partner to his comings and goings. The whole recruitment of off-the-street druggies had never been his idea anyway. And where were the girls? He looked at the cages, now empty, chains hanging like some old forgotten zoo where the petrified animals had finally been set free.

Every moment that passed put him in more danger. His mind screamed, *Get out, get out, get out!* even as he realized that he had left a gun in one of the drawers. Cautiously, he made his way to the wall where an old, tin, file cabinet stood. *Get the gun and get out!* But it wasn't there. He tore open all the drawers looking for what he knew he would never find. Was that a noise? How long ago had this happened? The air felt thick and warm. This was recent. Recoiling in horror, he forced himself to take one more look at Dino's face. It seemed to be grinning back at him. "You're next," it said. He heard laughter and wondered if it was his own. He was losing control.

He took a quick look around and realized all plans had to be changed pronto. He quickly found the place where they stashed their cash and the chloroform. He wasn't sure if Dino had crossed with gangs or police, but he figured if he stayed around he'd find out. Hands shaking, he wiped his fingerprints off the light switch and made his way back to the little bitch waiting for him in the car. *Time to be a gorilla and get the hell outta Dodge.*

Suzanne peered out from the car window to the dingy surroundings. It was awfully late, and where were they? She didn't recognize this neighborhood. A vacant lot and a dilapidated warehouse stood empty. It looked like they were miles away from anywhere. Hesitantly, she opened the Camaro's door and stepped out into the foggy night. She thought she'd heard a scream a while back. Maybe Julius had hurt himself.

"Julius?" she called softly as she walked over the concrete slabs that led up to the warehouse.

"I'm right here, honey," he said, slipping the rag with chloroform over her head.

CHAPTER TEN

"THIS IS SERGEANT Dormer calling in. I've got a situation, ten-four."

"Roger, go ahead, sergeant."

Sergeant Andy Dormer was a twenty-two-year veteran with the Paisley Falls Police Undercover Task Force. He had a wife and two girls, ages fourteen and sixteen, and a comfortable house with a mortgage in the suburbs of Paisley Falls. His sturdy build and positive attitude were great assets in the grisly world of undercover crime. All he ever wanted to do was fix the world so it would be right again. In his twenty-two years on the force, he had witnessed racial prejudices, bombings, and violent demonstrations, but going undercover had introduced him to the enigmatic world of the night. Still, he had never seen anything like what was unfolding before him.

"Request backup at northeast corner of Fourteenth Street and Delaware. Four females, three white, one Asian, look to be in their teens, walking toward me in a line, four across, with no clothing on at all."

"Ten-four, backup on its way. It's cold out there, Andy. Is there anyone around them?"

"Negative, the strange thing is, they don't appear to be cold. They look like they're in a trance, possible drug intoxication, lights, and sirens."

Andy was just ending a ten-hour shift and, at fifty-five, he was tired. In spite of his robust spirit, his soul was even wearier. Who had done what to these girls? The monsters that preyed on these children were the lowest form of human beings. He couldn't count the times he'd found young victims bound, gagged, and tortured into becoming somebody's ho. All because, in many instances, they had hooked up with someone on the internet. He and his wife, Dolores, had decided to police their own two girls after it was obvious that they knew more than their parents ever would about surfing the net. Every night before bed, the girls had to surrender their devices. Andy had laid down the law that there were to be no cell phones or laptops in the bedroom.

"But, Dad, no one else does that," Julia had complained.

"It's monstrous," whined the younger daughter, Catherine.

"You'll thank me when you're older," Andy had said. And looking at the sad quartet trudging before him, he thanked God for the street knowledge his profession had given him. He prayed that his own two daughters would never come to know how hideous this underside of life could be.

The young girls, who appeared to be in a trance, walked as if in step to a silent command.

"What the hell?" he said as he shone his flashlight on the first girl. "Looks like some kind of tattoo on her—No, wait a minute." He quickly moved the flashlight to the others.

"It's blood. All of them are marked with streaks of blood. Looks like it might spell out a name, and that's why they're in a line. Need ambulances, STAT!"

CHAPTER ELEVEN

JULIUS HAD BEEN born with a silver spoon of good looks. His mother declared upon first looking at his face that he was the most beautiful baby ever born. His father noted that boy babies were considered handsome not beautiful, but as he grew, his mother saw much of her own countenance in her son's face. Thick, luscious, mahogany hair; piercing, seductive, dark eyes; and a commonality of attributes that she knew he would learn to use for his own exploits, just as she had done. It had been unclear whether her current husband was truly the boy's father, and she had been so relieved when the child bore an almost exact resemblance to her.

Artfully, she groomed her son in eyes of elegance, at least the glitzy, superficial, tinsel elements that she could skillfully maneuver. She gave him the best of everything, showering him with gifts and clothes all the way into his twenties. Six feet plus by the time he was sixteen, his father, a pudgy five five, who had long since realized that the kid was not his own, struck him down with a club in a fit of rage. Large amounts of cash were missing, as mother and son had been discovered embezzling the old man. The clubbing had seriously damaged Julius's right foot, and despite numerous surgeries and physical therapies, Julius walked with a slight limp. He'd learned to camouflage the defect with perfectly tailored clothing, and he worked out diligently to carve a beautiful sculpted physique.

His mother, destroyed by this deliberate and tragic deformity of her child, drank herself into oblivion as Julius's presupposed father left them both in a state of poverty. In order to support his extravagant tastes, he set out on a road of petty theft, robbery, and burglary, stringing along a lengthy rap sheet that got him time in prison and sagacious underworld connections to the nefarious world of human trafficking. Prison had had its own dubious reward. It had made him tougher, thicker, and meaner. He learned to hide his lust for power and controlling people under his interpretation of elegance, just as his mother had taught him.

Leaving her to lick her own wounds—people begging for mercy bored him—Julius dreamed only of making enough money to support his empire. His only nod to her existence was a small tattoo he had inked around a small mole on his neck. The mole served as a spider's body that sat in a web of its own making with the word "mom" imbedded in the web as it waited for its prey. He didn't know that he was incapable of feeling anything. Nothingness was his shadow breathing for him. Nothingness felt real. He didn't know what genuine was or what it meant to anyone else. It seemed to him that his mother would be proud of the little prize he had captured. She was his connection to the wealth, the beginning of the empire that would soon be his.

The chloroform had taken effect almost immediately, and he quickly opened the trunk of the Camaro and shoved her in. As he took one last look around the place, he could see that the grounds were empty; the place looked desolate. Remembering Dino's grisly face and the urgency with which he must now move, he grabbed the steering wheel and peeled off into the night.

CHAPTER TWELVE

IT WAS TWO a.m. and Rhonda couldn't sleep. Suzanne was supposed to have been home by ten, eleven p.m. tops. She was going to be in so much trouble when she finally strolled in. Rhonda lit another cigarette as she restlessly paced the kitchen floor. The drinks she'd had earlier in the evening had lost their glow and were being replaced by a headache that was growing bigger every minute.

"Where's the damn Tylenol?" she muttered as she fished through the catch-all cabinet over the kitchen sink. The last thing she wanted to do was tell Suzanne's dad, but she figured he'd be out cold the rest of the night sleeping it off. *Snoring his way through life*, she thought. He's either drunk or asleep and not much good to anyone in the in-between times. He'd recently gotten into a snit over Suzanne, probably because she's turning into a very good-looking woman. A father being protective or a tyrant being possessive?

But at the moment neither one of those things mattered. Where in the hell was Suzanne? She'd tried her cell, but it just went to message. What was her friend Sandy's last name? She could try and find her in the phonebook. No, wait! People didn't use phonebooks anymore. Maybe Suzanne had her number written somewhere in her room. As she padded down the hall to her daughter's room, she heard Evan stir.

"Rhonda, when ya comin' to bed?"

"It's okay, Evan. Just go back to sleep." She was tired, hungover, angry, and worried. The little bitch had some nerve staying out this late. They were going to have it out when they finally met face to face.

Entering her daughter's room, she was struck again by the bizarre staging of the bedroom. Candles were placed on each nightstand on either side of her bed. The bed itself was covered with an old chenille bedspread and some of her grandmother's handmade quilts. Pictures of family life circa the Civil War era hung on the walls, and a pitcher of water next to a basin and a towel adorned her dresser.

It's like a stage setting for some kind of play, she thought. She knew Suzanne played some wild games with her younger sister, Bethy, too. At Christmas time she would redecorate her room with Bethy's Christmas presents, and drape fabrics over the furniture to make it look like someplace else. Suzanne would tell Bethy that they were going up to Fantasyland, using the sliding closet door as an elevator. "Up into the clouds, past the thirteenth floor, past the fourteenth floor," she would hear Suzanne tell her sister. The elevator would stop, and the door would open to reveal Fantasyland where all of Bethy's Christmas presents would be revealed. If Bethy remained a good girl till Christmas, Suzanne promised that all these presents would be hers.

Rhonda had almost choked outside the door when she overheard this scenario being played out. Later, when she had confronted Suzanne about doing this wild adventure, she had asked her how many Christmases this had gone on.

"Ever since she was about three," Suzanne had answered smugly. "It's just a little fun for the holidays," she had added.

Rhonda had become so mad she slapped Suzanne's face and told her it wouldn't be long before Bethy, now seven, would figure this out. "Presents cost money. They don't grow on trees in Fantasyland! If I catch you doing this again, I'll expect you to pay for every damn present she gets."

She didn't know what to make of Suzanne, and she was jealous of what she saw. Suzanne was becoming a beautiful girl, prettier than she had been. Now when Rhonda looked in the mirror, all she saw were more lines coming each day and tired, blood-shot eyes, but more than looks, Rhonda felt a soul weariness that she could not explain. She knew that she didn't understand her daughter one bit. It was like the girl came from a different planet. Rhonda knew that she resented her daughter's free spirit, but when she opened the door to her own inner feelings about her daughter, she realized that Suzanne was nothing like her. She didn't look like her or talk like her. She didn't want to be like her, and that was what she hated about Suzanne the most. What daughter doesn't want to be like her mother? Sometimes the rejection was more than she could bear. *If she disappeared, I wouldn't care*, she thought. It'd be one less worry and maybe she'd get Evan back. She was shocked by the revelation now that if Suzanne simply disappeared, her life would be so much simpler.

Standing in her daughter's room, she took one last look and shut her mind off. She didn't want to think about Suzanne anymore. She had to admit that she wanted her out of her life. Rhonda shut the door to her daughter's room and willed her to go away. *Please just continue on to wherever you went and don't come back.*

A knock at the door jolted her out of her reverie. She hurried to the door, hoping Evan hadn't heard it. She gathered up all her righteous anger for the dramatic tirade she was about to deliver and jerked open the door to find a hysterical Sandy quivering in tears on the doorstep.

"Oh, Mrs. DeMarco, I think Suzanne's run away with a tall dark stranger!"

"Sandy! Where have you girls been? It's two o'clock in the morning!"

"Oh, Mrs. DeMarco, I don't know how to explain exactly."

"What do you mean? Where's Suzanne?"

"Well she's… she ran out of the party."

"Party? What party? I thought you girls were going to study for a biology test!"

"Well we… uh… Mrs. DeMarco, you didn't really believe that, did you?" Sandy didn't wait for a response but gushed on, feeling more hysterical by the moment. "Suzanne and I and Bruce—"

"Bruce? Who's Bruce?"

"Oh gosh, Mrs. DeMarco, please let me finish. Bruce is my boyfriend, and that's his car parked outside. See?" She pointed outside to a sheepish Bruce Bonsford, slouched in the driver's seat of his Ford Pinto trying to look impervious to the situation. "Well, Bruce and Suzanne and I just stopped by for a minute to a friend's house for a little gathering, you know, about that big biology test tomorrow when—"

"Oh, cut the crap, Sandy. Where is Suzanne?"

"Rhonda, what the hell is all the goddamn noise in this house about?" Evan came staggering down the hall, struggling with his bathrobe as he walked, pajamas hanging slack.

"Button yourself up, honey," whispered Rhonda. "You're

showing." And she quickly moved to pull the string around his waist tighter.

"Oh, stop fiddling with me! What the hell is going on? What time is it, and where is Suzanne?"

"Well," gulped Sandy, "if everyone would just let me finish... she ran out of the party and the police came and Suzanne jumped in that guy's Camaro, the one who'd been watching her in the red Corvette, and they sped off before I could get to her and give her her purse. And her cell phone is in it, and now she can't call anyone if she's in trouble or what."

Everyone took a collective breath after that as Sandy produced the purse as evidence that her story was on the up and up.

Rhonda and Evan stood silently for a moment, as if they were absorbing a news story of a mass shooting. Evan spoke first.

"I need some Pepto Bismol, Rhonda, and then I think we'd better call the police."

"It gets worse, Mr. DeMarco."

"You say Suzanne ran off with some guy that's been stalking her, and the police have been involved in some raid on a party she's been at... how does this get worse?"

"Well, Bruce and I," she pointed again at Bruce outside at the curb, who then waved a weak hello to the growing group, "Bruce and I followed the blue Camaro."

"I thought you said he had a red Corvette?" demanded Evan, looking like he might puke at any moment.

"Oh my gosh this is hard. This guy—"

"What's his name?" asked Rhonda.

"Well, Julius I think, but—"

"Julius? What kind of a name is Julius? Is he Italian?" Evan knew he wasn't going to make it much longer standing up, and he irresolutely plopped down on the front doorstep from which no one had moved since the door had been opened.

"Oh Christ, Evan, get up! Sandy, come on inside and tell us please whatever it is you're trying to tell us." With that, Rhonda pushed Evan aside and shoved Sandy in the front door.

"Well, Mrs. DeMarco, we couldn't keep up with the Camaro, so we just drove off in that general direction. And there sure is a lot going on in town right now. The police have cordoned off downtown at Delaware Street. Apparently, a bunch of naked girls were walking all-together like, but in sort of a trance, with blood markings all over them. Then we heard there was a murder or something at that old abandoned factory that was shut down last year. We tried to keep up with the car, but we just couldn't! I'm so sorry, Mrs. DeMarco. I hope Suzanne isn't in any trouble. I was hoping she'd be here by the time we showed up." Sandy began to cry with righteous indignation, hoping this would signal her exit. "Well, Mr. and Mrs. DeMarco, I'd better be getting on home. It's almost three o'clock, and my parents will be worried. If they're up," she added.

"Yes," said Rhonda, "Evan, I think we'd better call—" But Evan had slid even further down to the floor and was clawing at his heart as though he'd had a heart attack. "Oh my God, Sandy, call an ambulance!" And with that Rhonda began to cry.

CHAPTER THIRTEEN

THE GIRL THOUGHT she was safe. She'd managed to escape from the cage by pretending she had to go to the bathroom. She said it was number two, because if she just had to pee, he would accompany her and watch as she sat on the toilet. But he hated the smell of shit, especially since she'd been having diarrhea as a result of the rotten, fetid food he'd been giving her. She knew the lock on the window was broken, and she'd jimmied it while moaning in pretend abdominal pain. *I've got to make it*, she kept telling herself, praying that he wouldn't get suspicious. *I've got to make it, or I'll die.*

She wondered why he wasn't banging on the door yelling at her to get out. It was strangely silent in the abandoned warehouse. She knew where they were being kept: in the old cotton mill on the outskirts of town. There were four other girls besides her, each kept in her own cage. *Like animals*, she thought. She'd been drunk when she met him sitting outside on the sidewalk of the Loosey Goosey Saloon. Too drunk to even care that he was trying to shove her into a car, she'd started waving her hands and yelling, but it was already too late. Then some smelly chemical rag he put over her face made her black out. By the time she woke up, she had vomited all over the car, and he was pulling her out by her hair. He hosed her down once inside the musty place, and that's when she started screaming.

"Won't do you any good to scream, baby. Just calm down and you won't get hurt."

The grimy little fat man looked like he was high on meth. His eyes were popping out of his head, his hands were puffy, and the foul odor of nervous sweat poured off him. He ripped off her clothes and dragged her over to what had looked like a large dog kennel. When she bit him, he backhanded her and she fell to her knees.

"Well, bitch, looks like you deserve to be treated just like a dog. Better not be rabid or I'll have to shoot ya." And with that, he lifted her up and flung her into the cage.

"Here's the rules," he advised, "no clothes, no cell phone, no blanket, and no food until you be good and keep quiet. You see this?" He brandished a cattle prod that had been lying on one of the long blank tables nearby. "You make one sound from now on, and every time you do, I'll have to give you some of this." He made a shoving motion with the instrument, as if he meant to imply that the prod would be going inside some orifice.

Nadine was only sixteen, underage, but friends at the Loosey Goosey often paid her way for certain favors. Now she was in for it, more trouble than she had ever been in in her life. She bowed her head. Mousy brown hair, sticky from the vomit, hung limply down her frail shoulders. She meekly drew a finger across her lips to show him that they would stay shut.

Now, sitting in the bathroom, she thought about the last two days. One by one, several other girls had been brought to the warehouse in various forms of bondage. They could not see each other, but Nadine was certain they were in cages much like the one she was in. During the night she could hear movement and some sobbing noises but couldn't make out words. Of course, like her, she knew they were sworn to silence or risk some terrible punishment. She wondered if they were all being drugged, because the water he put in the dog bowl for her to drink tasted funny. She'd been on enough highs to know that whatever he was giving her wasn't a fun time. She moaned even louder this time, just to see if he would respond, but there was no answer. *He's not even standing by the door!*

It was then that she heard a terrible roar coming from someplace deeper inside the warehouse. All hell was breaking loose!

She heard what sounded like a ripping, shredding noise, and a terrible, agonizing scream. Quickly, with all the courage she could muster, she crawled through the filthy window of the abandoned warehouse and ran for her life. Shards of glass had torn at her flesh as she pushed and shoved her way through the tiny opening. An old rusty nail pierced her left foot as she landed on the ground, forcing her to let out a yelp of pain. Quickly, she turned to see if she had been heard, but the inhuman shrieks going on inside the old abandoned warehouse were far more petrifying. Gasping for air at each painful step, she ran as though her abductors were right at her back.

Run, run, run, she kept telling herself. The horrifying sounds from the warehouse continued to follow her. What sounded like a grinding, sawing noise was the most frightening. She heard screams from a terrified man—must be the guy who had abducted her. Where were the girls? She didn't hear anything from them. She wondered if they were already dead. What craziness was happening? She saw two beat-up cars parked around back and figured more than one person was involved in whatever horror was taking place. She thought about the other girls. Once she was out of danger, she would call the police, tell them everything, but for now she needed to cover some serious ground.

Inside the warehouse, the two henchmen, their faces covered with masks, had surrounded a cowering Dino. Each had a heavy saw-toothed blade. They moved soundlessly toward him, tightening their circle as a terrified Dino tried to get away.

"Listen," pleaded a petrified Dino. "Am I into your territory? I'll get out. Tonight! Take the girls, they're yours!"

"The evil that your society produces is the end product we seek to vanquish. We are killing you in the name of Allah for the entire world to see your vile ways."

With that, one swift move extracted Dino's head from his body, and it fell unceremoniously to the ground. The other one picked it up as casually as if it had been a basketball and placed it in the center of a worktable in the musty cavernous warehouse.

"It is done. We are free now," Henchman number one said.

"Free the girls," said Henchman number two. "Tell them Allah awaits them, to cleanse them of their sins. Mark them with the blood of this infidel, to show the world that they have been purified and that they belong to us."

After being locked up against their will for two days, the girls were suddenly in no hurry to leave the cages after the awful scene they had just witnessed. Terrified and hysterical, they clung to the bars of their prisons as though this had become a welcome refuge from the monstrous men in masks that they saw before them. With lightning speed, the two terrorists broke open the cells with thick steel cutters and forcefully removed each girl. One by one, they took each horrified victim up to the grisly scene and took blood dripping from Dino's body to mark them with Arabic symbols as a sign of power and domination. Since their clothes had been taken from them, the men simply joined the girls' hands together with wire so that they stood four across in a straight line.

"Do not break this line or you will die," one of them instructed.

"We will set you free on the edge of town, and you will walk until someone notices you. You are not to utter one word, or you will be killed. We will be watching you from a distance and will shoot any one of you who breaks our commandments. Nod your head if you understand what I've just said."

By this time, the girls had seemed to merge into one unit. They ranged in age from fourteen to sixteen.

Kim Su, fourteen, had been abducted from the Happy Nails Salon in the Paisley Falls mall while waiting for her mother to finish giving a gel manicure and pedicure. Cindy B, fifteen, had met a very cool guy in a chat room who wanted to meet for real at the local Starbucks. He said he was sixteen; he was forty-six. Marissa and Shelby, both sixteen, had been following online dating sites and answered an ad to meet the guy of their dreams and be the star in a music video.

Oddly, these four girls were not all from Paisley Falls. They did not know each other from town, but they understood each other from fear. They nodded as one in a sinister fashion, not knowing where they would be taken next but grateful to be removed from this ghastly scene.

As each subject was anointed with the dead man's blood, the two henchmen bowed ceremoniously as if to commemorate a religious ceremony. And if the girls were relieved to have escaped the presumptive fate of their previous abductor, they were even more terrified to be standing naked in front of the two adherents of Islamic terrorism.

◆

Nadine couldn't believe the kindness the nurse in the emergency room gave her. No one in her life had ever cared much about what she was thinking or how she was feeling. If there were any tears left in her to shed, it would have been because of this wonderful moment when a total stranger seemed to sense that here was a tragedy, someone who was a total mess, a lost soul, someone to pity.

"Honey, what happened to you? Are you high on something? Where are your clothes?"

The words came out in big gulping sobs. She had been drunk. Some man had shoved her in a car and taken her to the vacant cotton mill on the outskirts of town. "But," cried Nadine, eyes wide and swollen from crying, "this wasn't just a sex-in-the-backseat kind of thing. This guy had a cage, big enough for a large dog or even a bear, and he took away my clothes and purse and threw me in it! And there are other girls! Something horrible is happening there right now!"

And with that, she groaned and began shaking from the cold and the shock. Nurse Powell covered her with a blanket and called in the ER doctor, who proceeded to examine her and prescribe a treatment.

"We'll need to call the police, Doctor. Sounds like she's had quite an experience tonight."

"She's been drinking, yes?" answered the young Dr. Wilson gazing deeply into Nadine's eyes. "Let's wait a minute on this. She sounds like she's deranged. Maybe it's just drugs and alcohol. No need to worry the police about this so soon."

"That's not all, Doctor. She's been traumatized by some awful experience."

"Yes, maybe hallucinating from a drug overdose. Wild night out on the town, young lady?"

Nadine should have known he'd be the one to examine her. She turned away from him, looking embarrassed and ashamed for so many things she could not explain.

"She's fine," declared Wilson. "Just a few cuts and bruises that will heal over time."

Nurse Powell couldn't believe the cavalier attitude Dr. Wilson had about Nadine's wounds and her incredible story. In all her years of training, she realized that while she'd been given training in domestic violence, there had been little emphasis given in identifying human trafficking victims.

"Of course, Dr. Wilson." And a curious Nurse Powell watched as he sauntered down the long corridor and left the building.

CHAPTER FOURTEEN

SUZANNE WAS SO groggy at first that she couldn't tell where she was. It smelled awful in there and was so confining that it was squeezing her insides out. She felt an old fear, the fear of others who had been locked inside this spooky old car before her. Or was it a van? No. She was in the trunk of his car. She shook her head to try and clear it and thought back to the last place she remembered being. There was that party, and then Julius showed up and they had driven off somewhere. Wasn't it the old, abandoned cotton mill? Why? That's when she started to get frightened. Being there out in the middle of nowhere so late at night. If her mother had waited up, she'd be in big, big trouble, but now in the bottom of a car trunk she felt a panic she had never known before.

"Help!" she screamed out to the blackness surrounding her. The coffin-like compression weighed heavily on her chest, and she was suffocating from the smell of vomit and sweat of others who had been in this trunk.

"Help! Why are you doing this, Julius?" she cried out again. Finally, she began to roll around and kick frantically at the lid and the taillights. She remembered hearing that kicking them out and sticking a foot through one of them could signal to someone, anyone at all, behind them. The car suddenly sped up. Was Julius driving? This couldn't be him. Where was he taking her? Why would he do this? She began to cry, fearing for herself. There had always been that feeling way in the back of her thoughts that her life would somehow come to a tragic end. Panic and a morbid sense of despair overtook her, and her sobs filled the trunk of Julius's Camaro with a hollow, engulfing sadness. Numbly, she realized that she would have gone with him willingly anywhere, if only to get out of the excruciating senility of a time and place that did not adhere to her needs. She remembered a saying that Sandy had taught her when she'd had one of her anxiety attacks: "Look around you. Find five things you can see, four things you can touch, three things you can hear, two things you can smell, and one thing you can taste."[1]

She felt a bit better, more grounded, and then the car suddenly lurched to a stop. Quickly, the door slammed. Julius knew that he had been speeding. There was a thump of a fist on the trunk and the sound of sirens in the distance. He cursed himself for losing control. He had to think fast. Now they were coming closer. They slowed down and came to a stop a few yards behind the Camaro.

He wondered if they had found Dino at the warehouse yet. If so, they would be on alert especially to an outsider like him. He knew this girl was panicked. Why shouldn't she be, he reasoned. If she made one sound it would be all over for him. *Best to stay out of the car and follow the cop's orders*, he thought. But he had to say something to throw this bitch off course, make her feel like he was on her side. Swiftly, he softened his demeanor to a stance

---

1   Emergency Action for Panic Attacks—Project LETS

that was soothing and solicitous, just like his mother had taught him. "Start with their name," she had said. "Everyone loves to hear the sound of their name."

Julius turned to the side of his car and bent down as though to check the tire. He whispered loudly enough for Suzanne to hear, "Suzanne, darling, I'm so sorry to put you through this. Don't make a sound. We're both in terrible danger! Do you hear me? Make a bump sound with your fist if you hear me."

Suzanne did as she was told, a ray of hope shining into the dark.

"You'll be all right. Honey, I'm sorry I had to put you in the trunk, but we had to get away from a terrible murder. I put you in there to protect you, so you wouldn't be seen. The police have stopped the car, but I don't know if they are in on the murder at the warehouse or not. Honey, can you trust me a little bit more? Just don't make a sound. I'll explain when I can get you safely out of here. That's my baby."

He stood up just in time to face the approaching officer.

"Well, you sure were in an awful hurry, mister. Got a fire you need to see? Just need your license, son. Have you had anything to drink tonight?"

"Sorry, officer, I'm just hurrying to oversee the delivery of some freight."

"Well slow down or you could kill somebody."

Julius smiled at the irony of that statement and agreed that safety mattered.

As the officer wrote out the ticket, Julius realized that overseeing the delivery of some freight wasn't a total lie.

The Port of Long Beach was a major hub for many forms of specialized services. It was the most accessible port for trans-loading and multi-modal distribution on the West Coast. And it was the vehicle that he and Dino had chosen to use for the international distribution of trafficking their merchandise.

As she heard Julius greeting the approaching officer, Suzanne felt an incredible sense of relief. There was a reason Julius had done this. He was protecting her. She felt so taken care of, so special. This sense of protectionism, the value he placed upon her life, was the sum of all her heart's desires. He did love and cherish her after all. There could be no other explanation for this bizarre behavior. The tone of his beautiful and soothing voice faded as he moved away from the car. She could hear the sounds of their conversation drifting off. And she herself fell into a dreamy blissful state of troubled sleep.

CHAPTER FIFTEEN

AFTER CALLING 911, Evan was quickly whisked off to Paisley Falls General with a frantic Rhonda clinging to his side.

"Do you have a list of his medications, ma'am?" the admitting nurse asked.

"Well, I don't have a list, but I know what he takes." She glanced down at the flaccid face of her husband, who kept trying to catch his breath.

"Just take it easy, honey," she said as the stretcher quickly became a hospital bed being rapidly wheeled down a corridor. She squeezed his hand as tears kept rolling down her face. The ER doctor ordered tests, and blood work was already being done.

"How long have you been having chest pain? What other symptoms have you had?" asked the ER doctor. As a pale Evan struggled to form the words, Rhonda took over.

"He's had terrible indigestion all night, and we've had an awful scare with our daughter who, according to her friends, has been abducted by some guy she just met. Sounds just like something she would do," scolded Rhonda, not wasting any time feeling much concern for her daughter. Evan picked up his head, evidently attempting to add to the conversation.

"Her friend Sandy... right, Rhonda? Her friend's name is Sandy. Came to the door tonight or this morning... what time was it, Rhonda, two or three a.m.? To tell us that she'd been taken by some guy in a Camaro or Corvette. I never did get that straight." He fell back exhausted with a team of nurses scurrying down the hall administering various services.

Rhonda begged him to stop talking, and the medical team took over. Something about the way that conversation went bothered Nurse Powell. Earlier tonight, that girl Nadine had talked about being abducted, and she had come in around two a.m. Nurse Powell watched the frantic husband and wife as they were being moved into a room and wondered if there was any connection at all. It had bothered her that Dr. Wilson hadn't wanted to inform the police. Paisley Falls was a pretty small town compared to LA. Two young girls being abducted just didn't sound right. She checked her watch. It was almost four a.m. now, three more hours before she was off. She was tired and her feet hurt. Maybe she'd call in to the station when she got off. She was friends with the policewoman who was on phone duty now. They shared the same twelve-hour shift. She and Evie had gone to high school together, and Evie would tell her if she had heard anything.

She turned around to go to the nurse's station for some coffee. *Might as well beef it up for the last three hours*, she thought, and as she did all hell broke loose.

❦

A squadron of police cars had arrived outside the emergency at Paisley Falls General. The cascade of sirens made a deafening sound against the quiet usually felt in this sleepy little town at four a.m. Sergeant Dormer came in first, followed by several of Paisley Falls' finest, and then the four beleaguered girls who were found walking naked in the streets in the early hours of the morning. Flanking each side of the moving troupe of young females were two female police officers. The girls were still connected to each other with wire bound around each wrist and then banded to each other so that they could only move in unison. The two female police officers had covered the girls loosely with blankets, being careful not to disturb the blood markings that appeared to be some kind of language rather than just random splotches. A superficial examination made by the two female police officers revealed that the blood was not coming from any wounds inflicted on the girls but was rather someone's effort to mark them in a certain way. The girls still were not speaking and were obviously in shock.

Nurse Powell moved quickly to usher them into the ER for an immediate perusal of the situation.

"Be careful not to disturb those blood markings on their bodies. They are a crime scene," shouted Dormer as the nurse waved them into the first empty room.

"You've got to be kidding me," snapped Nurse Powell. "These girls are in shock! What's your name, dear?" She whispered to the first one who stared blankly ahead not speaking. "What is this wire around them? Are they connected to each other? Why aren't they speaking? Andy, what the hell is going on?"

Nurse Powell thought she'd seen everything, but this took the cake. *Mercury must be in retrograde again*, she thought. She put in a STAT call to Dr. Wilson and was beginning to prepare to wash off the blood to determine its origin when Sergeant Dormer again insisted that she wait until a more-thorough investigation could take place.

"Well, why did you bring them in here first if you didn't expect the hospital to provide them with care?"

"I… I think… ," stuttered the first girl.

Nurse and sergeant both riveted themselves toward her.

"Yes?" said Sergeant Dormer. "We've been trying to get them to say something," he said to Nurse Powell, "but there's been no response until now. What were you going to say? Can you tell me your name?"

"I think we can speak now. He said until someone finds us," said a shaking Kim Su.

"No! They told us not to utter one word or we'd be killed!" Cindy B burst into tears, and the other three joined in.

"We've got to get these girls calmed down enough so that we can find out what's going on."

A concerned Sergeant Dormer shook his head and deferred to Nurse Powell, who reminded him that they were cold, in shock, and obviously traumatized by whatever had happened to them.

"And this isn't the only unusual thing that's happened tonight," she continued. "We've got a heart attack in room seven. A father who claims his daughter was either abducted or ran off with a stranger. And we have another girl who claims she was abducted and forced into a cage in that old cotton mill and—"

Nurse Powell barely got the words out of her mouth when the four teenagers cringed and started screaming. Suddenly, none of them could stop talking. It all came out in bursts of pent-up anxiety and terrifying fear. They had been in cages for days, thrown into them by a horrible man who had gotten his head cut off by two tall men covered in hoods and masks. The horrible man had taken away their clothes and their cell phones; they'd had little food, just funny-tasting water that made them sick.

The exhausted girls were trying to hold onto each other as if they couldn't even exist now without the other.

"Please, please cut these wires off us. I want to go home! I want this to be over," Marissa cried, suddenly opening her eyes to look around her. Lifting up her head and attempting to take control of the situation, she demanded that they call her parents. She offered her name, street address, and phone number. "We've all been missing for days," she told the growing group of concerned medical personnel and police. "Haven't there been any missing persons' reports?"

Suddenly, Sergeant Dormer felt exhausted. He looked down at this frightened and desperate group of terrified children and thought of his own two kids; they could have been right here suffering the horror these girls had endured, which was written all over their little faces. There were missing persons' reports, but only one locally, and he hadn't had the time to put it all together. He wanted them out of danger and off the street. He witnessed their traumatized looks as male photographers moved in for more police photographs. They covered themselves with the blankets they had been given; they didn't want to be photographed nude. They didn't want to be photographed period.

Sergeant Dormer made a decision. He ordered everyone out of the room except Nurse Powell. He then spoke to the girls as he hoped their own father would have. He told them that they were safe now and very important people, and their courage would help the police find whoever did this to them and bring them to justice. He promised to bring in one female policewoman to get all their addresses and phone numbers and call their parents right away. There would be one—and *only one*—police photographer to take pictures of the Arabic symbols written on each girl's body. He stressed that it was absolutely necessary to take pictures of what was written on them but promised that their faces wouldn't be in the pictures and that these photos were to be used as evidence only. Then he wanted each girl to tell him exactly what happened.

"Then can we have hot chocolate?" whimpered Kim Su.

Sergeant Dormer wanted to take her in his arms and hug her. There was so much pain and misery in the world, so much cruelty. His eyes filled with tears, as he knew he couldn't take care of everyone. He knew it wasn't his job to ease everyone's sorrow; it was too big a task, but he would never give up trying. He would somehow keep trying to make the world a better, safer place, especially for the young and so very vulnerable. He reached down to stroke her hair and told all the girls they were safe, that the wires would be cut off soon, their parents had been notified, and they could have all the hot chocolate they wanted.

Nurse Powell stood in the corner and watched her friend Andy comfort the girls. Tears came to her eyes as well. In the ER, you saw a great many tragedies every day, but there hadn't been any day that she could remember where four young children came in naked and wired together. *So much darkness and not enough light*, she thought. *What's happening to the world?* She had agonized over this question more times than she could count. It was as though desperation was taking everybody over, and little things like being polite and respecting your neighbor were taking a back seat to old, worn-out narratives that involved prejudice, entitlement, and bigotry. She knew values were changing, she just didn't know why. And how could some monster take innocent children for no other reason than monetary profit? *Was it for profit?* she wondered.

She had heard of human trafficking, but like most ordinary people in small-town communities, she thought it happened to someone else, not here, not to those she knew and loved. Sexual apartheids manifested themselves in faraway places, not some ambiguous little hamlet in the boondocks of Northern California. *Although fear has crept its way here*, she thought. The world isn't a safe place anymore, no matter where one lived. If the police were right and those markings on each girl's body were of Arabic descent, then who in hell lived in Paisley Falls anymore? Maybe the government was right to want to ban all Muslims from entering this country.

Nurse Powell did not consider herself bigoted or prejudiced in any way, but she felt her inner self closing down and tempering off any challenge to her and her loved ones' inalienable right to a free and loving life. She felt ashamed for even thinking that the right thing to do was ban a certain religious group from her country. Good and bad people existed everywhere; religious preference did not sanctify anyone. She knew better, but fear was taking control. Just like her father had said when he talked about World War II and the atrocities taking Europe by storm. "We must never forget the past," he had said. "Once you take an entire group of people and label them as bad, you're starting to play God, and that's not good. We are all equal to each other, and we should value each other as such. If we don't, we'll just annihilate each other."

Suddenly, she was shaken out of her reverie by Sergeant Dormer, who was asking about her previous reference to another ER patient earlier that night.

"Oh yes, Nadine. She didn't give a last name, but she was a local girl, sixteen, who's seen some hard times. She came in about two a.m. with some wild story about being abducted and thrown in a cage that was kept in the old cotton mill. You saw the reaction of these girls tonight when I barely mentioned this."

"Is Nadine still here?" Dormer asked impatiently.

"Well, I'm not sure. Sorry, Andy, but it's been quite a night. She was in room eight, but I can definitely see she's not there now. We can ask the discharge nurse when she was let go. She was traumatized and beat up, several contusions and psychologically very unstable. She wasn't on any drugs, however; we did the labs, so the level of anxiety was caused, in my opinion, by some real circumstances."

"Why didn't you notify us immediately?" asked Dormer.

"Well, I wanted to, and I asked Dr. Wilson for permission to do so."

"And?"

Nurse Powell thought carefully before she replied; she felt her first loyalty was to the hospital and its staff. "Dr. Wilson didn't think it was necessary to disturb you." As soon as the sentence was out of her mouth, she heard how phony it sounded.

"Get Dr. Wilson in here right away," demanded the sergeant. "He may have unknowingly hindered the investigation. And show me room eight, for Christ's sake!"

As Nurse Powell scurried to get things done, it was no surprise to see that no one remained in room eight, nor had Nadine Hines been officially discharged.

After a few minutes, a very flustered Nurse Powell appeared before a belligerent Sergeant Dormer and announced that Dr. Wilson had left the premises with a young girl in tow. It didn't take much for either to conclude that that young girl in question was none other than Nadine Hines.

CHAPTER SIXTEEN

JULIUS HEADED SOUTH toward Los Angeles, just in case the police wanted to follow him. He knew he was skating on thin ice now and needed to think of something quickly. Suzanne wouldn't be staying quiet too much longer, and it was a miracle that he had gotten away from that officer. Before long, Dino's body would be discovered, and Suzanne's parents would panic when she didn't come home. With any luck, things wouldn't spring until morning, but he couldn't take the chance that events weren't already in motion.

That stupid bitch Sandy had probably already contacted Suzanne's parents. His immediate thought was to kill Suzanne right then and there and leave her body in the woods. There was a heavily wooded area just off the highway; he could make it look like an accident. His mother had always told him that when things were at their very worst to always use his imagination to find the most creative way out. *No, that wouldn't work,* he told himself. Sandy knew that Suzanne had run off with him. She'd be blabbing that to everyone by now, and with Dino murdered back in that grubby little town, his goose was cooked.

Suddenly, with the dawn of the early rising sun glaring in his eyes as he barreled down the highway, an ingenious plan began forming itself. He touched the mole on his neck, the spider's body with the web tattooed around it, smiling as he thought of his mother's venomous nature. What a miracle of an idea. *Creative as hell*, he thought and thanked his hapless mother for her meaningless existence. At least once she had said something right, and he snickered to himself. *A brilliant scheme indeed, thanks, Mom!*

Early on in his drug-running days, he'd formed a relationship with a small-town pilot. John Toomey had a small, private plane and a jones for heroin and other luxurious variations thereof. They'd hidden the drugs in the wheel wells of the little Cessna 320C Skyknight. Mexican drug trafficking organizations normally controlled the market, but Little John (nicknamed for his 300-pound, six-foot-five persona) had found a small, off-the-beaten-path connection to it in Canada via some buddies who had buddies who had family ties to China.

"Gotta keep a low profile, bro; nobody here expects it from Canada."

Little John owed him a favor too. They'd almost got caught once when Little John couldn't resist snorting a sample just to make sure he had the real deal. He did it in front of a stool pigeon, and Julius had cut down the stoolie with his trusty little flick knife. They had ditched the body in Puget Sound as they flew out of a small airport on the Canadian border one foggy night. The plane had almost collided with the Sound as they maneuvered it low enough to make the dump without being seen. The fog had hidden them and, despite the control tower's stern warning that it was unsafe to fly (their excuse had been an emergency back home), they took off without a second thought. When they'd dropped the body into the water, they'd laughed uproariously, saying that eventually it would get to the Skagit River, a moveable feast for the predators of the deep.

Julius was just a hop, skip, and a jump from Leverton, where Little John led a perfectly solid, low-profile life, working part time at an electric company. His motto was, "Stay straight on the weekdays, fly high on the weekends." He amazed himself by his own discipline in this matter. Any risk of getting high on the job might cost him his life, with faulty wires and downed lines being what they were. So, Monday through Friday even beer was off limits, but come the weekend, he did himself up royally—shooting, snorting, and smoking himself into oblivion. It was early Saturday morning now, Julius realized as he changed course going southeast toward Leverton. Hopefully, Little John wouldn't be up yet or have started in on his weekend habit.

Julius pulled out his cell, found Little John's number, and called it, but there was no answer. Sleeping it off no doubt. He left his number with a "call me back, shithead" and chuckled to himself. *What fun it would be hooking up again with this asshole*, he thought. Maybe consider making him a partner for a while since Dino was out of the picture.

No, better not, his mind told him. The guy wasn't classy enough for the kind of business Julius was going to do. Plus, he was a stupid addict. He needed to use the guy and then lose the guy, just like his mother had so artfully taught him.

Contemplating his classy-but-disposable commodity, Suzanne had been awfully quiet in the back of his trunk. *Good little girl*, he told himself. He sure didn't need any more trouble right at the moment. Still, maybe he'd better check on her, make sure she didn't suffocate. What good would pimping a dead bitch be? He laughed at that. Well, maybe some people had a fetish for fucking dead bodies. Ha! His mind was creating more jokes than he could handle this morning, and he laughed out loud and marveled at his inventiveness. Slowing, he pulled the car over to the side of the road and got out of the car. Hesitating, he stood by the side door and whispered into the trunk.

"Suzanne, honey, you okay?"

No answer. He tapped on the trunk and asked again.

"Hey, darlin', it's just a few more miles till we're out of danger, and then I can get you out of there. Can you hear me, baby?"

Silence.

"What the fuck!" he muttered to himself as he got back in the car, started back up, and proceeded to find a road remote enough to turn onto. *What kind of shit is she pulling now?* His temper began to flare. He could feel it boiling up inside him, scalding his throat. His fingers tore savagely at the steering wheel as he jerked it back and forth, causing the car to sway wildly. He calmed himself down quickly, however, not wanting to attract any more police scrutiny, and drove till he could see a turn off down a dirt road.

At five a.m. he didn't expect anyone to be near this location, but he carefully slowed down, stopped the car, got out, and took a good look around. A few pastured cows stared at him between mouthfuls of grass, but he didn't see any humans around. Maybe it was time to put her in the front seat and tell her some comforting story, he reasoned. Right at the moment, he couldn't think of a goddamned thing to tell her, but he was sure he'd come up with something brilliant.

He straightened out his grey gabardine slacks that were bagging a bit at the knees from all the duress he'd been under and tucked in the raw silk shirt he'd been wearing since last night. He needed fresh clothes and a shower, but that would have to wait a while longer. He flashed his dazzling white smile in preparation for the one he would give her when he opened the trunk and arranged his face with an apologetic look. *So sorry, honey, but we were in danger, and I had to protect you,* he rehearsed.

As he opened the trunk, he began the hastily prepared speech, but only got the word "so" out before the trunk lid was kicked up and a tire iron was rammed into his face. Suzanne leaped out of the trunk with all the energy she could muster and started screaming for help and running as fast as she could. One of her legs had gone to sleep, and she struggled to move. Her entire body ached, and she felt that she would collapse at any minute. Her mind raced ahead, however, and every step she took gave her the courage to take yet another. All the strength and willpower and muscle that she owned she put in motion to get away from this monster or die trying. She looked up ahead as she ran, seeing cows and pasture, praying there was a farm nearby.

Julius staggered and fell to the ground but quickly recovered and desperately ran after her with blood streaming down his face. He clutched at her back as she ran. He came up behind her and tore her blouse, raking it off her. Getting hold of her hair, he jerked back her head, taking a fistful of hair as he tried to grab her. She barely escaped his grasp.

"I'll kill you, you fucking bitch! Wait till I get my hands on you!"

With a fury she didn't know she even possessed, she turned suddenly and hit his face again and simultaneously kicked him hard in the groin. He had gotten hold of her, but the kick took him by surprise and he crumpled up in pain. As he did, she was able to pick up her foot and sent it full force into his bleeding face.

And then she ran.

He thought she might have broken his jaw. She certainly

had loosened a couple of his front teeth. Blood spurted out all over his raw silk shirt, and he struggled to his feet, growling like a hound. He soon caught up with her and, as the cows looked on with indifference chewing their cud, Julius viciously rammed his fist into her face repeatedly with such force that the impact rendered her unconscious, and she fell backward in a limp heap onto the grass. He dragged her back to the car and threw her ragdoll body into the trunk. Grabbing masking tape from the front seat, he hurriedly taped her mouth and bound her hands and feet. Taking another furtive look around, he felt sure no one had seen them. Quickly, he grabbed the front door open, slid in, and took one look at his face in the front mirror. *Oh my god, she's ruined my face! The little bitch!* He wiped the blood off with his hand and some bottled water, cursed the growing bruises all over his face, and he jerked the car back onto the main highway, heading for Leverton. Little John and his plane better be ready for him, as they were taking off as soon as he got there.

Back at the pasture, a farmer who had been preparing his dairy cows for milking looked askance at what he thought he had seen in the distance. His eyes had been failing him, and he'd just had cataract surgery, but he was pretty sure he had seen some guy badly beat up a woman. Darn it, he didn't get the license plate. Still it was worth a call to 911. He took out his cell phone and placed the call, told them all he saw, and then looked after his cows, shaking his head at how violent the times were getting.

CHAPTER SEVENTEEN

JULIUS WAS OUT of control. In his world control meant power, and that power was his never-ending source of strength. How could he have let this disposable piece of garbage destroy his ability to remain in control of his world? As he kept driving in the early morning light, now just twenty miles outside of Leverton, he thought about what it felt like to keep running. The last twenty-four hours had been a horrendous sequence of events. It wearied him. Plans that seemed so easily accomplished had suddenly fallen apart. He hadn't had a moment to process Dino's murder.

Who had done this? Were they after him also? The cages they had been storing the girls in were empty. How had they gotten out, and who had taken them? He needed to be back in LA, back with his people—better to avoid Dino's friends, however. They'd want to know what happened, so he'd make up some story about how they went their separate ways after a disagreement. After all, that part was true! He didn't murder Dino!

Christ, his face had looked awful, he thought. The memory of Dino's face, bloodied and staring back at him as if to say "you're next, buddy," haunted him. He'd been having some annoying dreams too; dreams that challenged his sense of propriety.

He'd be in a house, but it wasn't his house; it was someone else's, and if the owner of the house discovered that he was camping out, then he'd be punished and exposed. So, he kept running to new hiding places in this strange house filled with odd-shaped rooms that didn't seem to have any purpose other than to be another place in which to escape, always narrowly evading the owner and being discovered. Just keeping himself together was a challenge, and the owner seemed always to know where he was but relished the game of chasing and subjugating him to the inevitable fate of being caught.

Julius checked his face in the car mirror again and cringed when he saw the damage she had done. It looked like his nose was broken, and both eyes were swollen and blackened. There was a gash across his left cheek where the tire iron had torn his flesh. His balls hurt too from the kick she had given them. *I could kill, maim, and destroy her!* his brain shouted. Glancing at the empty back seat, he wondered if he should have dumped her in there so he could keep an eye on her when she regained consciousness. He didn't want to risk being so assaulted again.

He was hungry and nauseous at the same time, but he didn't want to stop for food or coffee. He tried Little John's cell again, but there was still no answer. Christ, he needed this dopehead's help. Better be careful though. Little John might be a druggie, but he wasn't stupid. *Play it straight with him as long as you can, and then dump him.* He was happy with himself that he was forming a plan! *Gotta keep moving,* he told himself, and that made him remember the running dream. He pulled over to the side of the road, opened the door, and threw up.

The dispatcher who took the 911 call from farmer Stan Beaufort listened intently and took down all the information provided, promising to notify the proper authorities. When he hung up, he chuckled to himself and hollered over to his associate. "Stan Beaufort sounds like he's hallucinating again."

"Oh my God," answered the girl across from him. "I thought Edna was going to put him in a facility. That's the second time this week he's reported something. Last week it was a rainbow over the barn with one of his cows floating in it."

They grinned at one another, remembering how hard it was to talk Stan down after he became hysterical over his cows being stolen by God. "This time it's some girl being attacked by a monster and then driving off in a hearse. Honest to God, he keeps it real!" They both had another good laugh over that one, but the dispatcher put the call into the police department anyway. Maybe Stan had seen something after all. Better to be safe than sorry.

The officer who had stopped Julius Conaforte for speeding just outside the town of Paisley Falls still had an uneasy feeling about the incident. When he looked up the license number, it showed that Conaforte had quite a rap sheet: petty theft, burglary, and a little stint in prison. Still, there were no warrants out for him, and the car wasn't stolen—it was a rental. He looked up the rental accounts for the blue Camaro and found that it was rented to a Dino Hu. He put in a call to the Elite Car Rental Agency to ask about the vehicle and was assured that it was legit and wasn't expected back until tomorrow.

"The car was being driven," said the officer, "by a Julius Conaforte. Was that the registered customer?"

"No," answered the rental agent, "it was registered to a Dino Hu, and he was the only allowed driver. Say, wait a minute, there's been a murder out at the abandoned cotton mill, haven't you heard?"

But the conversation was suddenly interrupted by orders for emergency backup at the abandoned cotton mill in Paisley Falls. An all-points bulletin had been issued for two masked men, possibly of Middle Eastern descent, who had been seen at the plant. Four young females had been found wandering the streets nude in Paisley Falls and had been brought to the hospital by one Sergeant Dormer. They had Arabic writing on their naked bodies and claimed they had been held captive for days and had witnessed a brutal murder. There had been some delay while much valuable time was spent decoding the messages their bodies carried.

The messages had been translated. There was a possible terrorist attack of great magnitude about to happen in Paisley Falls.

Suzanne was slowly coming back to consciousness in the trunk. Beneath her, the bottom was sticky and wet with her blood. The masking tape was cutting into her wrists every time she tried to move, and breathing had become increasingly difficult. She struggled to get enough air through her nostrils, but what she smelled made her so nauseous that she thought she might heave and drown in her own vomit. She had never been in so much pain. Her head felt like it was in a vice, and blood was pouring out of somewhere. She wished she could do something to stop the blood. It worried her that she might bleed to death in the car and no one would ever know.

Every minute that went by was filled with terror and anxiety about what might happen the minute the car stopped. She was totally at his mercy now. She didn't think she would live. He would kill her the first chance he got; she was sure about that. The steady motion of the car on the road felt oddly comforting. The trunk, which had once been claustrophobic, was now a reassuring haven from this lunatic. Why had she ever gone for him? He was older and not from around town, of that she was sure. No, she had to admit that she knew why he had attracted her. He had made her feel special and courted her, driven a fancy car and worn nice clothes. Everything he was she wanted to possess for herself. Suzanne lamented that she had needed someone else to make her feel better about herself than she could accomplish on her own. It had a similar ring to the disappointment she felt from that English teacher. She'd fallen from grace, and now that seemed like a thousand years ago. Then she met Julius, and that empty well of loneliness got filled up again. She realized now, too late of course, that these fillers of people were very poor substitutes for a genuine belief in one's self.

She thought of the people in her life that did things to keep away their demons. Her parents drank too much to accommodate their emptiness. Sandy had Bruce to make her feel beautiful. Most kids she knew at school were addicted to their cell phones, computers, and, of course, drugs. Maybe everyone needed something to make them feel more whole. The lucky people were the ones who didn't even know they were depressed and lonely. She had almost lulled herself to sleep when the lack of motion made her heart jolt.

The car had stopped.

CHAPTER EIGHTEEN

SHE HELD HER breath and braced herself for the evitable. Since her hands and feet were bound, she really couldn't move or scream or claw her way to anywhere. *Oh, let's get it over with,* she implored. *Just open the trunk and do it!*

She cried and prayed that the God she knew would be merciful. But there was silence, only the sound of waiting going on in her brain. What was that? She heard the sound of a groan and of someone being sick. Good! She knew that she had hurt him and was glad that he felt pain, especially since she felt so miserable. For now, there was no Julius slamming his fist into her face. Not yet anyway, because after a few moments she heard the car start up again. She'd gotten a reprieve and a deceptive sense of peace overtook her. She quickly fell out of consciousness as the blue Camaro sped off heading to its intrepid destination.

❦

Julius struggled to remember the turnoff to Little John's place. His body had taken a beating from that little bitch, and his head wouldn't clear. He thought it was on the outskirts of town, some little shack no one would notice. That was Little John's game, to play at being as invisible to people as possible. Julius chuckled to himself. Everybody in this little shit town probably knew every move he made. The ones who liked him didn't care; his enemies probably just waited till the right time to bust him on something. Wasn't that the way it was for everyone? Lots of road out here between houses, and Julius liked that aspect of rural Northern California. The backroads were quiet and a good cover up for what he was going to propose.

After a few wrong turns, he finally found the place Little John called home. It had been years since he'd been here. It looked the same as always: run-down but not down and out. A large black lab barked his welcome. The old one-story house had a small front porch with a little rocker in front like a welcoming sign. A battered old Folgers coffee can, now used as an ash tray, sat beside the rocker on an ancient TV tray. The front porch faced a field lying fallow for the season; Julius wondered if Little John sat in the rocker contemplating growing pot. *He would if he could,* thought Julius, snickering to himself.

He pulled up into the long dirt driveway expecting the dog's barking to have awakened his buddy, but the house was silent. He got out of the car, thought about opening the trunk, but decided against it. He'd leave her till after he'd talked with Little John. He approached the door with caution and shooed away the barking dog with his foot.

"You better watch yourself, Old Yeller, 'cause I hate dogs!"

The dog snarled back a response, and Julius wondered if there would be a problem with the damned thing. He'd kill it in a minute if he had to. A few knocks on the door were met only with silence, despite the ever-growling presence of the dog that had now become ferocious in his delivery and effort to make his master aware of the danger. He kicked the dog savagely with his foot, forcing his boot well into the dog's mouth until the pup cried in agony. Then Julius opened the unlocked door. The dog immediately retreated in defeat, and Julius stepped inside the tiny living room. Little John stood in a corner armed with a shotgun ready to fire. He lowered it immediately when he saw his friend.

"What the hell! I almost shot you, boy! What the fuck are you doin' here? Or I should rephrase that," he said, laughing. "What is it you need for me to do for you? 'Cause you look like you just got hit by a Mack truck. I thought you burned up all your baggage out here and headed out to LA to get lost in a sea of crime and degradation. Hand me my pipe, will ya? I need a toke first thing. Better than coffee, my man."

He stepped forward to shake Julius's hand, and the two men hugged, that brief bro hug that was typical of two grown men. Then Little John stepped back to take a better look at his friend's torn and battered face. LJ might have been a doper, but he wasn't stupid. Far from it. He had a passionate love of great literature, and when he wasn't high, he would be re-reading Dante and Proust to stimulate his intellect, and Somerset Maugham, JD Salinger, and Saroyan when he felt a love for humanity. He'd educated himself when young by skating classes at Yale for free until he was caught. His love for education and no money to acquire it had inspired a great sense of shrewdness, which had saved him from many a mistake with adventures and people. It wasn't that he disliked people, it was that he distrusted them. And there were many advantages to that perspective on life. The disadvantages, like loneliness, he solved with drugs.

"Okay, buddy, I need to know what's up. Are the cops following you?"

"No, but I've got a problem."

"Tell me what."

"Well, for starters, you got any Band-aids or ice I can use? Doesn't it look like I need it?" Julius looked menacing and took a step closer to him.

"What do you want, Jules?" Little John knew he hated to be called Jules and only did it to aggravate him.

"Hey, LJ, we've been pals a long time." Julius was getting weaker by the minute and thought he might pass out.

"That we have. So tell me your trouble, plain and simple." He put a hand on Julius's shoulder. It was not a comforting gesture.

Julius staggered. This wasn't going the way he'd planned. "You still play poker?" He laughed as he slid unceremoniously to the floor.

"Why not? I usually win."

"I'll raise you a thousand if you do me a favor."

"Winner takes all. What's the favor, bro?"

"I need you and that plane of yours to fly me and a friend to LA tonight."

"Sounds like the flop is a rainbow, pal. I thought you said the cop's weren't involved."

Julius pulled himself up from the floor and tried to focus on the blur before him. "Well they aren't... yet. But," he faltered, "there's a girl in the trunk. I need you to get her out of the trunk. She tried to kill me, and I—"

At this point Julius could no long hold onto consciousness and collided abruptly with the floor.

Little John looked at his friend for a long moment before he walked into the bedroom to get a blanket to put over him. Julius wasn't someone he remembered trusting. They'd done a few jobs together—lucky they didn't get caught. They went their separate ways without much fanfare. The fact that he had come here and laid this mess on him really pissed him off. There was no room in his life for becoming an accessory to murder. If this girl in the trunk was dead and he helped this sucker, then he'd be responsible for her death as well.

Shit, he thought. *I'd better go see what's up with this asshole's load.* He opened the screen door, peered out to make sure the road was clear, and ambled over to the trunk.

"Hello, anybody in there?" There was no answer.

He wasn't sure why, but suddenly he felt afraid. Maybe he shouldn't open the trunk. Let whoever was in there, if there was anybody in there, just rot, make sure they were dead before he opened the trunk. But he had no idea how long that would take. And there would be police, of that he was sure. He could take the car over to the junkyard and have it crushed; his buddy there owed him a favor anyway. If he never opened the trunk, he could legitimately claim that he had no idea what or who was in it. He couldn't call the police himself, he reasoned. Never raise a flag on yourself when you've already got so much to hide.

"Oh, what the fuck," he said as he opened the car's left front door and popped the lid. As he did, he took in the acrid smell of blood mixed with urine and feces, and he gagged. "Oh my God, maybe she's already dead."

As he leaned in to get a closer look at what was inside the trunk, he was horrified to find such a young girl. She was desperately trying to move. Her bound feet were making a dragging movement across the trunk floor. Was she writing a message of some kind? Her head had been split open and she looked to be drowning in her own blood.

"Jesus," said Little John, and he scurried to lift her up in his arms. Her eyes flashed a sign of pure terror at him, quickly replaced by a glimmer of hope. He could see that her mouth and hands were also bound with tape.

"You're just a kid," he said, gently pushing aside a clump of her hair covering her eyes that had been infused with dried blood. "What kind of trouble did you get yourself into with this animal?"

Immediately, Suzanne began to cry; a flood of tears overtook her. She wasn't sure she would last much longer, but here at last was someone who seemed to be taking pity on her. Little John carried her quickly into the house and, after placing her carefully on the sofa, went to get a blanket. When he came back, she was moaning for him to take off the tape over her mouth. He looked down at her and hesitated. What should he do? Unbinding her gave her the freedom he wasn't sure he wanted her to possess. Finally, he bent down and abruptly tore off the tape from her mouth and then the tape that bound her hands and feet.

As she lay sobbing on his couch clutching the blanket he had given her, she mouthed the words "thank you." Her eyes said even more. She felt a sublime sense of relief and gratitude all at once. It overtook her whole being. Here finally was someone who could help her, save her. A feeling of relief washed over her like some sacred balm. With prayers answered and a full heart, she looked up at this new savior with an inspired sense of redemption, only to be met with eyes that were full of lust.

He stood up abruptly and cowered over her. His hands touched her mouth, lingered on her breasts, stroked his growing cock, and then he said, "I'll clean you up, and afterwards I'll feed you, but now all I want to do is fuck you. That's what you're here for, isn't it?"

At that moment, something in Suzanne's mind snapped and then relaxed, like a coil suddenly being released from its duty to support something. It was as if she had bounded into perihelion and was then catapulted to the other side of the sun in some other universe. She had suddenly become the eponymous heroine of her newfound planet, and it was here that she felt safe.

And it was here that she would remain for a very long time.

CHAPTER NINETEEN

At five a.m. in Paisley Falls, a Code 3 had been issued to all police personnel within a three-county radius. This was an emergency response that transcended multi-agency, multi-jurisdiction, and multi-discipline events. Tactical force units from all three counties had surrounded the old abandoned cotton mill east of Paisley Falls, and national law enforcement units had been requested. Several cryptographers had been summoned to decipher the messages written on the four girls who had been abducted by two men, allegedly Muslim, who had covered each girl's body with Arabic symbols written with the dead victim's blood.

Each girl's parents had been contacted, and four sets of hysterical yet relived parents had arrived at Paisley Falls General. There was a bit of an uproar when the parents, at first, had to wait until the questioning and reports were finished. Sergeant Dormer had his work cut out for him as he assuaged the fears of the anxious parents that their daughters were all right but needed to be questioned further. He was giving them information layers at a time. They knew their children had been abducted but were now safe and unharmed. Telling them the details of this horrendous night was going to have to wait a little bit longer.

Kim Su's mother was weeping and begging for just a sight of her fourteen-year-old daughter. She had been cursing herself for leaving her alone to fend for herself in the mall while she finished a manicure for a client.

"No place in America safe anymore. It crazy here now. Safer in Viet Nam," she cried in her broken English. The other groups of parents nodded their heads in agreement.

Cindy B's mom looked exhausted at five a.m. A single parent, she had two jobs and worked hard to support herself and her daughter. She couldn't control her fifteen-year-old who spent endless hours surfing the net and meeting up with strangers she had met online. She wondered who her daughter had met this time. If she had a gun, she would hunt him down and kill him herself!

The hospital was crawling with reporters and police detectives. The body of the decapitated man had yet to be identified, and the police were hoping one or more of the young girls could provide them with more information about what had occurred. Sergeant Dormer was concentrating on Marissa and Shelby, both sixteen, the two oldest girls. He hoped that they could provide more clues as to the identity of the two men.

"You girls say you were picked up by a middle-aged, heavy-set man and put into cages. Can you remember what day this was?"

"For me it was the day before yesterday," sobbed Marissa.

"How did you meet him? What did he look like?"

"Well…" Marissa hesitated, not knowing how much she should reveal. Her mom would kill her if she knew. "I was in… Kik when—"

"What's Kik?" interrupted Dormer.

"It's an app… uh… application for instant messaging." She

saw the puzzled look on the sergeant's face. She knew he wasn't getting it. She hoped this wouldn't take all night.

"Kind of like Facebook for you old—" She figured she'd better stop.

"Okay, go on," ordered Dormer. "You downloaded an app called Kik, and... ?"

"Well, I started chatting with this really cool guy, and we exchanged selfies and he thought I was beautiful and perfect for a video he was doing and was I available. I mean, he was *really* cool. I thought it was legit! I really did." The valley of tears started up once again, but Sergeant Dormer persisted.

"So you went to meet this guy. When you saw him, didn't you realize that he wasn't the guy in the selfie he sent you? Or was he?"

"Oh no," wailed Marissa. "He for sure wasn't this dude I saw in the pictures. He was this old, creepy, fat dude, the one that I saw get his head cut off!"

Ignoring her tears, Sergeant Dormer pressed on.

"When you saw that it wasn't the guy in the selfie, why didn't you leave?"

"I didn't have a chance; he grabbed me so quick and put a rag close up to my face with some heavy smell. We were still outside the club and no one saw us. His van pulled up right next to me, and he grabbed me and pushed me into it. That's all I remember."

The sergeant knew he had to end this interview soon; this poor child had had enough.

"Well, I remember something more."

Shelby was the other sixteen-year-old and, from Dormer's estimation, a bit more streetwise than the other girls.

"My girlfriend dropped me off at the mall, and I was supposed to meet this guy for coffee at Starbucks. He wasn't the guy I was texting, but he came up to me and said he was the talent scout for the guy I was supposed to meet and asked me to accompany him—yeah, that's what he said, like I was some really important person—to the music studio where he wanted me to try out for the video."

Dormer wanted to say *how could you have been so stupid,* but he didn't. Finally, here was someone who might be able to give a description of this assailant.

"Shelby, what did he look like?"

"Well, he was the guy who took us to the warehouse and got his head cut off by these two big, very bad guys."

"Short, tall? Help me out, Shelby."

"Just a fat ugly guy with no hair. Ain't you seen him yet at the warehouse?"

"You're very brave, Shelby and Marissa, and the questions you answer tonight may help save lives. So just a few more, okay?" He longed to give the girls a reassuring hug, but times being what they were, even the slightest touch could be misinterpreted. "How did this man put you in cages and remove your clothes?"

"I was completely drugged out by the time I got there," said Shelby.

"Me too," echoed Marissa.

"Was anyone else there when you woke up?"

"Yes, the Chinese girl was already in one of the cages," offered Marissa.

"She's Vietnamese," corrected Dormer. "Did she say anything to you?"

"No, she was crying, and she started screaming when she saw me. Can I go now? My parents will be worried about me."

"Your parents are already here at the hospital, girls, and they know you are safe, but we really need your help in solving this case; everything you can tell me is of tremendous help."

"Well, all I know is that it was a nightmare," cried Marissa. "I know my mom hates it when I go to online dating sights, but that's how everybody meets up now. It's so boring around here; there's never anything to do. This guy sounded so cool. I was gonna be the star in a music video!"

As fresh tears cascaded down her cheeks, Sergeant Dormer could see that she was exhausted. They all were. After a few more questions, he was able to let the girls go. Forensics had gotten everything they needed from the girls at this point, but the warehouse was another matter. None of the girls were able to give a description of the two masked men who freed them from the cages and painted their bodies with gruesome messages written in a dead man's blood. They said they were big and spoke with a foreign accent. They were all so traumatized by their ordeals and witnessing an execution that Dormer knew they had to rest, immediately.

He thought of his own two girls and what they would be feeling if this had happened to them. *God*, he thought, *this must never happen to them or to any other child!* His heart was pounding as he swore an oath to himself that he would find whoever had done this. These monsters had to be stopped, but he realized that in order to stop them he had to think like them! What did they have to gain by publicizing a murder and freeing these girls so that the message they wanted to give to the world was seen on their naked bodies? Nothing made sense about this. The messages written on the body of each girl were basic phrases of fundamentalist Islamic philosophy, generalized principals condemning Western ways, etc. *Why such pageantry?* thought

Dormer. It wasn't until he got the call from the cryptographer at the warehouse that things started to fall into place.

"Hey, Andy, these messages, the ones written on the girls, they're encrypted. It's all a code for something else."

"What?"

"These guys aren't Muslim; they're part of a transnational criminal organization. They're essentially a nationally organized street gang. This guy they creamed was interfering with their territory, and they wanted to make it clear that they're the only ones in control of this territory."

"What territory?" demanded Dormer, who was starting to lose his patience.

"Paisley Falls. Andy, there is a human trafficking ring being run right here in Paisley Falls."

Sergeant Dormer should have been exhausted. As he hung up the phone and shook his head as if to clear it, he observed the sun coming up just outside the front door of Paisley Falls General. The coldness of the night was evaporating, and a slight wind picked up a few fallen petals from the snowball bushes that lined the hospital's front walk, promising a lovely spring day. It might be a lovely spring day for some people, he thought, but for him it continued to be the night that would not end. There were too many missing pieces in this puzzle, and a million questions still hammered in his brain.

He asked Nurse Powell where the couple was who said they had a daughter who had been abducted. At this point he knew he had to continue somewhere, and it was with them that he pursued the journey. Something told him that the series of events that had happened this night were all connected. How, he didn't know, but he was sure that he would soon find out.

Rhonda was still holding Evan's hand as though she thought he might die at any minute, when Nurse Powell introduced Sergeant Dormer to the couple.

"I understand that you have a daughter that's gone missing tonight," started the sergeant, only to be shushed by a hysterical Rhonda.

"Right now, my only concern is my husband, Lieutenant! Can't you see he's dangerously stressed?"

Sergeant Dormer had received Nurse Powell's permission to question the couple and was assured that he posed no problem to Mr. DeMarco who had fallen and had an anxiety attack. Dormer was struck by the fact that the wife seemed to have no concern for her missing daughter.

"It's Sergeant, Mrs. DeMarco, and I apologize for the lateness—or I should say the earliness—of the hour. Is your daughter in fact missing?"

"Well, she didn't come home last night. Not that that means anything."

"Rhonda, for God's sake, her friend Sandy rang our doorbell at two this morning to tell us that Suzanne had been abducted!"

Evan started in on a coughing fit, and Rhonda fidgeted, grabbing his hands to try and comfort him. Evan pushed her away and looked directly at Sergeant Dormer.

"This Sandy girl said someone named Julius—Italian I think—had run off with her. Please find our daughter, Sergeant!"

Well, at least one parent cares about this child, he thought. Dormer carefully made notes, getting a description of Suzanne, asking if they knew of her cell phone activities and the last name and address of her friend Sandy, then he took his leave of the couple and told them that he would be seeing them soon.

Rhonda laughed when he mentioned their daughter's cell phone activity.

"Our daughter never left the nineteenth century, Sergeant. You should see her bedroom; you'd think she lived during the Civil War."

"Well, I'd definitely like to take a look at her room, ma'am; it could provide some important clues."

As he turned to leave, Evan grunted out a thank you with pleading eyes while Rhonda abruptly shut the hospital room door.

CHAPTER TWENTY

As a twenty-two-year veteran of the Paisley Falls Police Undercover Task Force, the scourge of human trafficking was nothing new to Andy. He'd seen it quietly creep up on the streets and outside of seedy motels that advertised vibrating beds and free TV. He knew that some of the local grocery stores had late-night labor of dubious origins, and they'd busted a local hotel that had "hired" a string of girls from Thailand for housekeeping that were obviously slave labor. These things were going on in little rural towns all over America. That was nothing new. But he never expected to hear of a "transnational gang" existing in Paisley Falls.

After a few hours of sleep, he began once again to follow the trail of Suzanne DeMarco and the four girls, persisting in the hope that something or someone could tie all the events of the last twenty-four hours together. And then there was the question of what had happened to Nadine Hines, purportedly another victim of the warehouse cage episode. As a number of detectives were examining the evidence left at the cotton mill, Sergeant Dormer returned to Paisley Falls General to question

Nurse Powell further about the disappearance of Nadine and Dr. Wilson.

"He's not here, Andy, and this would be his day off anyway."

"This girl was last seen with him last night, is that correct?"

"Well, he was treating her for superficial injuries—"

"I think you know what I mean, Helen."

Nurse Powell avoided his eyes; she didn't want to think anything was going on between Dr. Wilson and a teenage girl. She'd heard things but dismissed them as hurtful gossip. What she didn't comprehend, however, was how complicated and pervasive teenage sex and the selling of bodies were. She had no idea, and neither did Sergeant Dormer, of everything that contributed to the desire for more and more porn, hard-core porn, the addictive desire for violence and the profits that were made from selling bodies for it.

It's not that Sergeant Dormer and Nurse Powell were naïve or stupid people. The ugliness of human trafficking hadn't become a standard reality for them. Not yet. It doesn't really hit you until it happens in your family, as they say. Everybody has his or her own version of perversion, but sometimes the horror of what some people desire is so revolting it defies acknowledgement. And both Sergeant Dormer and Nurse Powell would have their limits tested when they found out what Dr. Wilson was doing with Nadine.

There was nothing that Max Hardcore and his Gonzo super-hard-core porn-film industry wouldn't sell to their eight million salivating customers. Max's motto: "I force girls to drink my piss, fist fuck them, ream their asses, and drill their throats until they puke."[2] Gonzo films in no way resembled the feature soft-core

2   Victor Malarek, *The Johns: Sex for Sale and the Men Who Buy It* (New York: Arcade Publishing, 2009).

porn of the past. The only message was to degrade, punish, and humiliate girls. "Gaping," the use of dental and medical instruments, such as a speculum, to spread open the vagina or anus to the camera and give the viewer a look inside, was a current favorite. "Cherry Poppers" are instructional tapes for pedophiles on how to rape a child. They help the pedophile get ready to season the victim.[3] They normalize pedophilia and provide ideas. Max Hardcore has a tremendous following, including Nurse Powell's eleven-year-old son who discovered Max on the internet and hasn't closed his eyes yet. After stumbling onto Sex Cams 101 where he could order up a real woman anywhere in the world and order her to perform sex acts in real time, the kid spent almost all his spare time on the net. Private sessions were billed by the minute, from ninety-nine cents to $5.99. It was a whole new world for Johnny Powell, who used his weekly allowance to feed his growing obsession. His mother worked long hours, and his father could not care less what he did in the privacy of his room.

Somewhere in the back of Johnny's mind was the feeling that these films or these girls weren't about real relationships, but he didn't care. He understood that if the real girls he knew were aware of what he wanted to do to them, they would freak. This was the way the world was now, he reasoned. Even if you didn't watch hard core, you could game it. He loved the one where you could torture and kill a prostitute and then get your money back.

And it was with this knowledge—or lack of it—that Sergeant Dormer began his search, not only for Nadine Hines, but eventually for the soul of Suzanne DeMarco.

≈

Dr. Wilson was an accomplished physician, a married man with

---

3   Ibid

three beautiful children and a lovely house in the wealthy section of Paisley Falls. His trophy wife, Stephanie, spent her days attending charity lunches, playing tennis, and buying more and more stuff for their overly decorated and ostentatious mansion. Beautifully situated near the man-made river in Brook View Manor, the house, the family, and the two new BMWs appeared to be an idyllic replica of the American dream. But, like most post-card pictures depicting domestic tranquility, what you saw was not a lot of what you got.

Dr. Wilson, a tall, strikingly handsome man, hid much behind his gentle bedside manner. Anger and resentment sharpened his features and gestures, casting a pallor over his skin and cloudy eyes. Everything in his life had been geared to getting ahead, and he had acquired the trophy wife and children like he was collecting houses in a Monopoly game. He and his wife led two separate lives, and their sex had dwindled into a monotonous routine, which he performed regularly as his façade would dictate. In his mind, he divided himself into two separate entities. There was Dr. Wilson, devoted father, husband and physician, and then there was Dr. Wilson, fuck master of the universe. Sometimes he'd chuckle to himself that he was truly the Jekyll and Hyde of Paisley Falls, and he wondered how many others there might be. He couldn't remember when he first turned to the net for information on having a little fun on the side, but it was a big, big world filled with all kinds of opportunities. Soon, he discovered that any fantasy he had could and would be fulfilled. And he wasn't some kook. Millions of people were living out their sexual fantasies. Those who weren't were jealous of those who were.

After his first encounter with a young teenybopper, he couldn't get enough. It was pay4play, as those in the know called it, and he had the money and the lust for more. To whet his appetite when he wasn't fucking a luscious tween, he watched porn. But soon it wasn't enough. He felt such hostility towards his wife that he often thought about how great it would feel just to slam her head against the wall until it cracked. She was a cunt who ate up all his money! Hard core filled that need to pulverize her, reasoned the sensible Dr. Wilson. He'd never want to harm his wife or his children. His job was to protect and provide for them—and he was damn good at it too! He became an aficionado of Max Hardcore and Gonzo! He devoured the films over and over, jerking off over ATMs (ass to mouth, with the penis rammed in the ass then thrust into the mouth with the cry "eat shit.") Harder, ram it harder! He would groan as he watched the guy fuck the bitch. Often, the girls would be crying, mascara running down their cheeks. He didn't care. He wanted to punch them, fuck them. It wasn't enough! He had to find one for real and make fantasy a reality!

Then he found Nadine Hines.

Wilson had been frequenting the Loosey Goosey Saloon out of sheer boredom after work. He was contemptuous of the ER division of the hospital and felt that, despite his young age, he should be running the place. He had married up—his wife's family provided the larger share of income to the household budget. Stephanie's father was a well-known steel magnate, and his daughter's well-being meant everything to him. He hadn't approved of her choice in marriage candidates, but at least she had picked a doctor. Maybe he would make something of himself, reasoned the old man. The startup couple had received one million dollars as a wedding gift, and each child born to the couple brought individual trusts running into the millions.

Dr. Wilson didn't even have to work. After getting his

degree, he'd settled into Paisley Falls General like it was an old shoe, a smelly old shoe, worn and begging to be trashed. Their lavish honeymoon had given him a taste for the high life. Settling down and becoming a family man was and always had been just a ruse for Frederick Wilson. The internet activity had offered some escape, as had the porn, but now, he admitted, he wanted a personal connection. Someone he could call at will, a girlfriend or mistress, if you will, that he could dominate, control, and punish. Someone just like the pathetic loser he observed night after night grousing for drinks at the Loosey Goosey. He had to be careful, though, very careful. Being seen at a bar with an underage girl in a small town meant gossip. Just when he thought it would be impossible to pull it off without being noticed, Nadine had crept up to him one night as he was getting out of his car.

"Hi, I seen you around here a couple of times. I could be real friendly if you'd come outside with a couple of beers." She giggled and flipped her stringy brown hair back as if to be flirting with him, but her eyes had a distracted foggy look; this was a routine for her.

On your way to becoming a pro, thought Dr. Wilson. *Well let me help you along, little girl.*

"Why don't we go someplace where we can have some real fun, and I can treat you to a lot of drinks and a fabulous dinner? What do you say, honey?"

He stroked her hair back from her face, a gesture that most women took as a sign of real affection. Being gentle with them was step one in controlling them. They always mistook gentle for being in love. Lust and desire were just byproducts most of them merely put up with. The real clincher was being soft and gentle… at first. Nadine and Dr. Wilson started a relationship that very night. Tentatively at first, Nadine fell into the routine.

It wasn't long before she wanted out of it, but by that time it was too late. As she begged to be excused from any further activity with him, he slammed her against the wall of a Motel 6 one night, and with each slap across her thin face, he reminded her that she was nothing, just a tramp, a nobody, and without him she had no future.

"Do you think I would have wasted my time on a slut like you if I didn't think there was something you needed from me?" he taunted. "Do you think you can go crawling back to your family? I'm all you've got in this world right now. I control you, and you'll do as I say."

It was all he could do to not laugh at her pathetic, anxious face. He reveled in her frailty and marveled at his ability to make her sit, stand, and rollover. It was Nadine's first experience with a john and an unofficial pimp combined. She, like so many lost souls in the sex trade, began to believe she was worthless and evil. The drinks and trinkets she got from her suitor didn't make her feel special. They only contributed to the ever-growing feeling of worthlessness. She felt greyer and greyer every day, and she began fading into the landscape like one of the hedges lining the highways. Passing by in a car, one never really saw them, but they were part of a necessary reality. She didn't know Suzanne DeMarco, but they were both traveling the same murky passageway, a different course at a different speed, but the same journey into darkness nonetheless.

CHAPTER TWENTY-ONE

JULIUS WATCHED LITTLE John take Suzanne right there on the couch. She remained limp the whole time, said nothing, and did not cry out. As Julius looked on, he wondered if she was feeling anything. He knew this was probably her first time, and he cared little that he wasn't the one to have her. She was a business acquisition now, and it was easy for him to see her in this way.

Little John had gotten a beauty this time around, although she looked far from anything appetizing. Her clothes, what was left of them, were in tatters around her waist. Her face was a mass of bruises; he hoped half-heartedly that her nose wasn't broken—that would devalue her somewhat. Little John had hiked up her skirt to get at her and torn her panties to get in her. As he grunted in satisfaction and pulled away from her, it was clear that she was bleeding between her legs. Suzanne lay motionless, staring at the ceiling, glassy-eyed.

"Hey, bro, you shoulda told me. I didn't mean to horn in on your time with her. I popped her cherry, you know that." Little John grinned like he had just caught a big catfish and was showing it to his friend.

"Nah. that's okay. You deserved it."

They high-fived each other as Little John put himself back together. He glanced back at the girl he'd just had and, out of some erroneous show of concern, went to get a blanket to put over her. She didn't move when he returned and made no attempt to fix her clothes or cover herself. He half-heartedly straightened her skirt and sheepishly offered a towel for clean-up. When she didn't take it, he tossed it on her stomach and offered a bit of advice.

"Hey, darlin', it's best to get used to cleaning up after." He thought he saw her turn her head slightly, as though she hadn't quite heard what he said. He waited but she said nothing. Little John backed away from the couch where she still lay motionless. Julius motioned him over, and the two sat down in two chairs some distance away from Suzanne.

"Hey, bro, I think this chick might be going into shock. Why did you have to beat her up so bad?"

"Well, asshole," taunted Julius, "why'd you have to fuck her?"

"Hey, man, she was already banged up when you got here. Do you think she's gonna die?"

"No. Let's give her some water. Maybe make some tea or something. Oh hell, I'll do it. Then I want you to shoot her up with some smack, and we'll put her in the back room. Then we're gonna talk, my man, because I've got a plan."

Finally, Julius felt alive. All the trauma and anxiety of the last day had started to lift itself away. He no longer felt tired; his head didn't hurt. He'd had a couple of shots of whiskey from Little John's tiny makeshift bar, which gave him back his courage and refreshed his intent. Suzanne was moaning, and he brought her some water, helping her to sit up as she feebly took a few sips. Julius was kind and gentle with her, as if she were once again that cute little high schooler he had just met. He brought her the tea and gave her a sandwich he'd made of lunchmeat from the fridge. She gobbled her meal hunched over it like a hungry animal. He motioned for Little John to get his junk and do her up.

"Let's do her with chocolate rock or bars, whatever you got. I need her out while we plan this thing."

Little John got up like an obedient little boy and got his playthings. When Suzanne saw what they were about to do, she screamed and tried to get off the couch. Her legs were so weak she couldn't even stand. She fell back down on the couch in despair and curled up in a fetal position. Her body was suddenly racking with sobs. She felt with utter certainty that she had nowhere to go and that no one would come to save her.

Julius placed his hand on her head to steady her as Little John administered the dose that would take her to Never Neverland. They waited until she was out, and then carried her into the bedroom and dropped her on the bed. They taped her mouth as a precaution and tied up her hands and feet. Then they left her, both feeling like satisfied fathers who had put a spoiled child to bed.

It was now nine o'clock in the morning. In just a few hours, everything in Suzanne's life would be changed irreparably forever. For Julius and Little John, their world had just begun to blossom. Full of ideas, plans, and promises, Julius unleashed his ideas like some artist unveiling a new portrait with ghastly flair. Of course, there would be twists and turns he couldn't anticipate.

As Little John listened, he couldn't help a silent chuckle now and then. The literary scholar in him couldn't help but make a connection to Oscar Wilde's brooding novel *The Picture of Dorian Grey*, a torrid tale of the excesses of a debauched man's life. While Dorian's face and body remained young, his sins were etched into his portrait hidden in the attic. Except Little John didn't think that Julius had any soul, and he wasn't sure he had much of one himself. Besides, if there were any scars making a scratch that he could feel, there was always the soothing balm of oblivion an easy reach away.

Julius was exuberant. Flushed from the whiskey, his adrenaline pumped into overtime, and he couldn't wait to tell Little John of his plans and all that had taken place in the last twenty-four hours. In the back of some corner of his aggravated mind, exhaustion threatened to overtake him, but he pressed on; he had to. They had to get moving, as there was really no more than a few hours before all hell broke loose in Northern California. He needed Little John's plane now, and he needed a partner. The situation being what it was with Dino's death and the cop who stopped him, he had to act fast. Little John was smart and shrewd, but when Julius checked his feelings, there was nothing but distain for the crudeness that was an innate part of Little John's identity. He wasn't a classy guy, but then neither was Dino. Dino, however, had been a terrific businessman. He had a knack for sex trafficking and knew the money involved was big.

"Look," said Julius after they had settled onto the couch, beers in hand, "I'm right on the top of a very big transaction, and there's no reason why you can't be a part of it."

"Cut the bullshit, Jules. You're in trouble. How much are you gonna pay me to help get you out of it." He leaned back to take another draw from the bottle and smiled sarcastically at his narcissistic buddy.

"Listen, a business associate of mine met an unfortunate end…"

This elicited a huge yawn and a chuckle from Little John, who got up to get another beer. "Hey, cut to the chase, but wait till I get another one. You good?"

As he struggled to get his heavy frame up off the couch, Julius grew impatient. *Damn this asshole*, he thought to himself. He had to make this jerk understand the importance of what he was about to say.

"I've been running an international trafficking ring out of the Port of Long Beach. My headquarters is in LA. My partner has been... ah, disposed of. I'd like to make you the new partner, bro. It's a gig that could make you millions. Bring me another beer, and we'll discuss logistics. I'll need you to fly me and blondie in there to LA tonight. I also need your friend at the junkyard pronto. You're gonna love the deal I'm making with you, pal. This is gonna change your life forever."

Little John came back from the kitchen and shook his head, laughing at Julius while he handed him the next beer.

"You are one crazy dude, Jules. The fuckin Port of Long Beach? What'd you do, ship them in cargo containers?"

"All the way from Thailand, my friend, and then we transfer 'em in trucks to service the johns all across California."

They both howled at this. Clinking their beer bottles together, as old buddies often do, Julius began to tell Little John all about the way this would transform both their lives.

There was a huge market for illegal immigrants being imported to America. They wanted the American dream and they were willing to pay for it. Fees were extracted for everything: their smuggled transports, food, lodging, and once they got here, their clothes. Everything they needed cost them money. They were indentured servants; a lifetime for them wasn't enough to pay back their costs. Prostitutes earned more money simply because they could be sold over and over again.

"We've got a small stable now, but each chick can bring in about fifteen hundred a day. That's eighty grand a week and about three hundred twenty thousand a month. Dudes call in from ads we place on the internet. We drive the girls from Long Beach to LA to Sacramento and then to San Francisco. We keep them rotated. You know your shit can only be sold once, LJ, but people can be sold over and over again."

"Recyclable like plastic bags, brother," said LJ. "Dude, you're saving the environment."

This elicited another howl of laughter, as the two of them were getting wasted.

"I can go over more of the details of our fantastic dream of a business, but we gotta move, bro!"

Julius felt the need to communicate to his buddy an offering of true friendship, which was a ruse but something he needed to do to close the deal. Always at the back of his mind was the need to move quickly. He wished he could shoot up with his buddy to seal the deal, but he needed him sober to make the transaction. Plus, he hated addicts. Their addiction slowed them up. He could never understand why their fuckups always cost him money. *Clean up your act or get out of my world*, he often thought when things weren't going his way.

"Well, buddy, I got about a thousand questions for you." Little John stared at his friend as though he thought Julius was losing his marbles. "Why this chick? There are a million pretty girls out there. Sounds like you're in serious trouble with her. Why not put her back in the trunk of the car, take it to the junkyard, and have Eddie there crush it? She's out and won't feel anything. And more importantly, man, how much are you going to pay me now—right now—to get this done for you? Fly her out to LA with you or dump the whole lot at the junkyard. And what about your cargo at the Port? There's a whole lot of questions I don't hear any answers for, Julius."

"We need white girls, LJ. They bring more money, and I can't very well take her home and knock on her parents' door and say, 'I'm returning your sweet little daughter to you safe and unharmed'! What I can do with her now is train her, and when I'm done with her, she'll never leave, bro, and we'll have ourselves a great bottom bitch, I guarantee you."

Julius smiled remembering his first contact with one of the Asian girls in his stable. He'd learned a technique that trainers used on elephants to teach them submission. First, they're torn from their mothers at an early age and kept in a small dark cage or hole and beaten or tortured with bull hooks until their spirit is broken. Julius based his training on these principals when first breaking the girls in. The elephants are first kept in chains, then ropes, then strings, and finally they are not tied up at all but left free. They don't try to escape. They are entrapped and emotionally dependent, just like Julius's stable. If there were any problems after this point, threatening to kill their family always worked.

Ah, little Bethy, thought Julius, remembering that Suzanne had a little sister who would surely be some pedophile's fantasy fuck. There was a fuck for everybody's fetish under the sun, and Julius aimed to fill the need for all.

As he explained the ins and outs of the business to LJ, he felt a tremendous sense of pride. He didn't really need Dino Hu, although he wasn't sure how he could maintain Dino's connections in Thailand. That was another matter not to be discussed tonight.

Little John knew his own ass was in a sling and that now, at this very moment, he was in as much trouble as Julius, but a poker player never shows his hand, and LJ was a master poker player. He set his beer down with a deliberate bang and turned to look directly into his friend's eyes.

"How much money can you give me tonight?"

"Fly me to LA, and I'll give you ten thousand dollars, and from then on we're partners. You'll have all the money you'll ever need and more. Let's get moving, bro."

There was a look of utter panic in Julius's eyes. The tension and fatigue were catching up, and he knew time was running out. Between waves of excitement and exhaustion, he wasn't sure of himself anymore. He hated feeling weak; his mother had taught him better than that. "Stand up and be strong," she had told him, and he touched the spider tattoo on his neck as if to get some needed strength from her.

"Whaddaya say, man? Let's get going, okay?"

LJ could tell that Julius was at his wit's end. His pleading look said it all. LJ had him now. "Okay, I'll do it for a hundred thousand up front. Right now, we drive to the junkyard and get rid of the car. The Cessna will need refueling. Where are we flying to in LA?"

"To a little town near LA called Oxford. From there we'll rent a car and drive to my location. A hundred thousand dollars? Where do you think I can get that kind of money?"

"You get it somehow, bro. I have faith in you. Otherwise, I'll kill you, plain and simple. Once I get my money, I'm out of the picture. I don't want anything to do with your 'business.'" he chuckled.

"Do you think you can come back here and pretend nothing happened?" countered Julius. "What happens when the police catch up with you? The first thing you'll do is turn me in."

"Well, you'll just have to take that chance, won't you, Jules? If you're smart, you and Little Bo Peep will set up your stable in an unknown location. I don't think you have much choice now.

From the sound of it, your Port of Long Beach deal is going to be blown too, if you've knocked off your partner—"

"I didn't kill him," Julius interrupted, "but you're right, things are different now. All right," he said reluctantly, "I'll give you fifty grand now and fifty when we land."

Julius held his head in his hands trying to think through all that LJ was saying. It looked as if he would have to start over, but he was inventive, and he still had connections. A clean slate would be a good thing. He didn't need a partner. He could run a stable, and he could make Suzanne his bottom bitch. She'd be a better recruiter than he would. It would be a high-class stable too. He knew she had potential. He smiled to himself, proud once again of his ability to make a bad situation a profitable one. Reluctantly, he offered his hand in agreement.

"Let's do it now, LJ. Let's move fast."

Julius got up from the living room and walked back to the bedroom where Suzanne lay unconscious. He went into the adjoining bathroom to get a towel and washcloth. He wet the cloth and brought the towels into her room. Gently, he washed her face and removed her clothes to wash her body. He repeatedly went back and forth to the bathroom to rinse the washcloth, wiping each area clean of all the grime, blood, and semen. Like some newly found, life-size Barbie doll, she was his property now.

When he had finished washing her, he found a shirt of LJ's to put her in, and then put her back in the skirt she had worn. He carefully put all the rest of her clothes in a large plastic garbage bag that he would take with him. LJ was busy wiping down every surface they had touched. He washed the all utensils and gathered the blanket and towels they had used. He knew her DNA would be on the couch and the bed, but there was still hope that the police would have no reason to suspect Julius of coming here. There had never been any overt ties to each other.

He left his bewildered dog some food and water, and they set off for the junkyard. Julius drove the Camaro, and LJ drove his pickup truck. It was now eleven o'clock in the morning, a very special day for Suzanne. It was her birthday. She turned sixteen as she slept in a treacherous fog, dreaming of happiness in some parallel universe.

CHAPTER TWENTY-TWO

"Sergeant Dormer, I'm Detective Woodard with the California State Police. Thank you for your service in this investigation. We believe at this time that the entrapment of the four young girls is directly related to the homicide at the abandoned cotton mill and the two unknown assailants. We're going to be taking over this investigation, so your services in this matter are no longer needed. Thank you for your initial handling of this investigation. We would appreciate any additional material that you've gathered," he added as an afterthought, a bone for the sergeant's wounded ego.

Dormer was stunned. Just like that he was off the investigation. This was his home territory. He knew this town better than anybody at the state level. Ever the consummate professional, he accepted this decision but decided to toss in a few questions anyway.

"I believe there's a possible connection between one of the girls who is missing now and a Dr. Wilson, the ER doctor at the hospital. She was seen leaving the hospital with him late last—"

"Yes, we've interviewed Wilson, and the girl, Nadine Hines, is being questioned now at the station."

"And?" questioned Dormer.

"I'm not at liberty to discuss the findings, Sergeant. I'm sure you understand that."

"Well, there's another hitch in this whole thing: A young girl, Suzanne DeMarco, is missing as well."

"Yes, we've checked into that, and her parents at this time have not filed a missing person's report. Miss DeMarco was last seen at a high school party and apparently drove off with her boyfriend. Until the parents file a missing person's report, there's really nothing we can do. You know how these young kids are today," he said, "always flying off somewhere forgetting that anyone else exists."

"But I don't think—"

"Like I said, Dormer, thanks and that's all."

Jesus Christ, thought Dormer, *everything by the book, inside the box, and by the numbers.*

There was no question in his mind that the DeMarco case was connected to all these events. He knew he couldn't prove it, yet his instincts told him so. He recalled his meeting with the parents. The father was worried, but the mother was so obviously not. And the father had mentioned a friend, Sandy, that had rung their doorbell at two a.m. to tell them that Suzanne had been abducted. Well, Detective Woodard hadn't told him to stay away from the DeMarcos. Until he was informed otherwise, he was going to pursue every possible lead in this his own private investigation. Something they had said, or the way they had acted, he couldn't remember what exactly, but finding this lost girl was something he felt he had to do. Protecting her would be like protecting his own daughters, who he cherished. Somehow, he felt that Mrs. DeMarco didn't care if her daughter was lost or stolen. The way she had talked about her made the girl sound like she was disposable. Lonely, lost girls often ran into another's arms looking for validation. His heart went out to this girl who he didn't know but felt he understood. One thing he knew for sure, if he could find her friend Sandy, he'd eventually find Suzanne.

CHAPTER TWENTY-THREE

JULIUS TOLD LJ to get Suzanne jacked up with a little bit more speed while he checked the trunk to make sure it was clean. Actually, that was where the stash was hidden. He didn't want LJ to know he had more than a hundred grand on him, just to make it seem like he had to scrounge for every last dollar to pay him. He figured the stash he'd grabbed at the warehouse should total out to Dino's and his monthly usual, something around three hundred fifty thousand, but when he lifted the pouch from under the trunk's protective lid, he coiled back in disgust while simultaneously registering in his brain that this felt considerably lighter than it should have been.

Shit! She's peed on it! How in the hell did it get wet sitting in the wheel bed of the spare tire? he cried out to himself as he gingerly held the saturated pouch. There was no way he was going to keep the money in this disgusting container. He quickly distributed it as best he could between his coat and pants pockets. Finally, he put the rest in the waist band of his shirt, painfully aware that the three hundred fifty thousand felt more like two hundred fifty thousand and grateful for the moment that he didn't have to hide the one hundred thousand he was giving away as a bribe to his friend.

Little John appeared carrying a limp Suzanne in his arms.

"I don't think she's doin' so hot, Jules."

"Why is that?"

"Well her pulse is high as hell, and she's out."

"Ha ha ha," laughed Julius. "Aren't you the one who put her out? Why don't you give her some smelling salts?"

Little John's sporadic concern for Suzanne mixed with lust is touching, thought Julius. He himself had no such meandering of feeling.

"Just load her in the car, please. And prop her up so she looks like she's just drunk and we're going on a holiday. We don't want your friend in the junkyard to think there's anything wrong with her."

"Speaking of which, buddy, I'm going to need the hundred grand right now."

Julius turned sharply and pointed his finger in LJ's face, deliberately parsing his words.

"I told you fifty grand now and fifty gees when we get there."

Little John looked down at his friend's bulging shirt and sneered. "Looks like you gained a little weight there, bro." He touched the shirt, which made a crinkly sound, and Julius instinctively stepped back. "Just give me my money, Jules, and then I want to be done with you."

Julius wanted to kick him in the balls, but he knew that wouldn't get him anywhere good. He pulled the fifty grand from his pants pockets and handed it to LJ without another word. The two were silent a moment; an even draw. Then LJ plopped Suzanne in the front passenger seat of his Ford 150 and arranged her like a drunken nobody on a trip to nowhere. He came back over to stand directly in front of Julius, who was straightening up the trunk of the battered Camaro. Julius cowered a bit but stood up full force in front of any bullshit LJ would try to impose on him.

"Did you clean up everything that we left behind?"

"Well yes, asshole. I did everything I could to clean up your mess in my territory. In fact, I should charge you more than a hundred grand for my trouble."

"Ah well," Julius countered. "Become a partner and we can talk."

LJ's look was so grim that Julius wanted to be done with it.

"Okay, this is it. Now let's ride and get this over with."

"Then there's the matter of Eddie," said LJ, grinning. "And Junkyard Eddie's gonna want his share."

Sergeant Dormer was trying to think of a way to successfully find his way back into the DeMarco household without raising any red flags about his connection to this case. There were so many loose ends at this point that he wasn't sure he even understood the perimeters of it. Why the powers that be wanted him out of their hair he didn't know. He was a twenty-two-year veteran heading the undercover task force, for Christ's sake. No one knew Paisley Falls better than he did. Instinctively, he felt there was a connection between the abduction and release of the four young girls, the subterfuge of Dr. Wilson and Nadine Hines, and the disappearance of Suzanne DeMarco. He recalled Mrs. DeMarco's lack of concern over her daughter's disappearance. It would be interesting to see her reaction today. For all he knew, she might have even heard from Suzanne. He doubted that, however. He was most interested in the girl's room. What had Rhonda DeMarco said about her daughter's room? Something about it being in the nineteen century.

As he drove up to the house, he saw two cars in the driveway, so he figured they were both home. Obviously, Evan DeMarco wouldn't be driving anywhere, and she was probably taking care of him. He pulled up in front and went to ring the front doorbell. The door was abruptly opened before he even reached it, and an anxious Rhonda DeMarco peered out from the corner of the doorway as though she was afraid of what he was about to say.

"Did you find her? No, I guess if you had you'd be bringing her with you. Do you have any news?"

"May I come in, Mrs. DeMarco? I'd like to have a word with you and your husband."

Reluctantly, she opened the door just wide enough to let him in and ushered him into the kitchen, cigarette in hand, where she appeared to be making a sandwich.

Wonder Bread, bologna, and processed cheese. Yuck, thought Dormer as he watched her spread a glob of mayonnaise on the bread. She didn't appear to be as agitated as the night before; maybe it was because of the beer sitting on the kitchen counter.

"How is your husband doing today, Mrs. DeMarco?"

"Oh please, call me Rhonda," she said, taking a sip and a drag while she finished making the sandwich. "This is his lunch. We had quite a scare last night. My stupid daughter has upset her father to no end."

"Rhonda, who's that out there? Is someone here about Suzanne?"

"Don't get up, Evan. It's just the sergeant from last night here to talk to me. No, there's no news on Suzanne. The little slut," she muttered under her breath. "Sergeant, let me take this in to Evan, and then I can answer your questions." And with that, she sashayed out of the kitchen and down the hall.

Sergeant Dormer looked around the room: not the cleanest

place, but not filthy. Dishes in the sink were probably going to be loaded into the dishwasher. There were white, greasy-looking wooden cabinets and an old linoleum floor that had seen better days. A couple of ashtrays filled with butts told him she and possibly her husband were heavy smokers. The air in the place had a grimy, stale smell. It didn't feel like a very happy place to him. He hoped that seeing Suzanne's room would provide him with information that was more positive. He could understand that her room might well be an isolationist cave, a place of retreat, the getaway she needed to protect herself.

"Don't, Rhonda. I want to get up and talk.... Is Suzanne back? Have they found that guy who took her?"

There was the sound of a thud as Evan, evidently trying to get up, had fallen back onto the bed.

"Damn it, Rhonda! Help me up!"

"Jesus, Evan, I'll handle it. Eat your sandwich, and I'll bring the sergeant back to talk to you. There, there," she said cooingly, "don't overexert yourself. They'll find our Suzanne, don't worry."

"Well I miss my little girl. I love my little girl."

Sergeant Dormer thought he heard the quiet sobbing of a troubled father, and he knew how devastated he would be if something happened to his little girls. Catherine and Julia were young teenagers growing up in what he considered a violent world. He couldn't stand to think about how much danger they could be in. One of his driving forces was to protect those two girls who were the love of his life. He knew his wife, Dolores, felt the same. They lived to protect their daughters, shield them from harm, while at the same time realizing that they could only do so much, and that overprotecting would only lead to dependent and fearful children ill-equipped to handle the stress, anxiety, and challenges of the twenty-first century.

Damned if you do, damned if you don't, thought Dormer as he listened to the two parents who seemed to have two very different agendas.

Rhonda came back into the kitchen a few minutes later looking apologetic. "Can I get you some coffee, Sergeant?"

All of a sudden, she was brimming with hospitality. A concerned and worried look had adjusted itself onto her face as she became most conciliatory, almost cordial in her demeanor.

"Oh, Sergeant, we've been up almost all night what with the hospital visit, and then the continuous worry about our older daughter.

"Oh, I didn't know you had a younger daughter."

"Bethy. Yes, she's away at camp right now. Frankly, I'm glad she's not here to deal with all of this drama."

"Drama, Mrs. DeMarco? Your daughter Suzanne has been missing now for over—"

"Over?" Rhonda abruptly cut him off. "Yes, Sergeant. Overnight. Isn't it the police that say we don't regard persons as missing until it's been *over* twenty-four hours? Don't think I'm not concerned, I am, but right now my husband is the thing that's concerning me the most. Now, what can I do for you, and would you like some coffee?"

Sergeant Dormer thought the shift in her attitude was ominous. She wasn't even making any attempt to hide the contempt she felt for her daughter. He could chalk it up to her anxiety over her husband's condition, but any attempt she made to sound concerned about her daughter sounded like a lot of hot air, the kind she'd been full of for quite a while when it came to her true feelings about her daughter.

"I'd like to see Suzanne's room, Mrs. DeMarco. Even though she hasn't yet been missing for over twenty-four hours, there are a number of unexplained happenings in Paisley Falls in the time that your daughter has been… uh… has been absent," he corrected himself. "There may well be some connection to the murder at the abandoned cotton mill and the abduction of four teenage girls. All of these events took place during the same time period that your daughter, according to her friend Sandy, was seen driving off with a strange man that neither you nor your husband has ever met. Doesn't that seem odd to you?"

"What seems strange to me is that you're not out there looking for her, Sergeant!"

"Rhonda! Show the sergeant her room!" Evan had managed to get up out of bed and was leaning against the door frame of the kitchen, trying to prop himself up.

"Evan, you shouldn't be up! Sergeant, it's down the hall, last door to your left. Honey, come on, let's get you back in bed." And with that, the two of them started cooing at each other again, with Rhonda trying to comfort her distressed and weakened husband. Both had totally forgotten about him.

As Dormer opened the door to Suzanne's room, he first noticed the smell. It was either lilac or rose perfume that cloyingly filled the room and invaded his senses. He was struck by how staged the room seemed. Rhonda DeMarco had said that her daughter lived in the nineteenth century, and Sergeant Dormer could see that her room had a subdued, nostalgic look.

Candles were placed on either side of her bed on the night tables. There were no lamps. On her dresser was a basin and water pitcher. Dormer walked over to see if the pitcher was filled with water. It was. Pictures on the wall were of the Civil War era—women and men of that time as far as he could tell.

What a strange environment for a young girl, he thought. *She must have been so lonely.* He would have never let his own daughters become so isolated. This girl was turning inward to protect herself; it was no wonder that she might have fallen for someone who promised to take her away from all this. Dormer vowed to talk to her friend Sandy, the last person to have seen her last night and who had come over to Suzanne's house to warn her parents of her disappearance. He had to be careful not to step on the state's current intervention of the murder and the abduction of four girls. It was possible that they didn't see any connection between Suzanne's disappearance and these incidents, but he did.

Somehow, Sergeant Dormer was shaken by the presence of despair that filled this room. He opened a few drawers and looked in the closet, but nothing was there of importance. Her clothes were hung neatly on hangers, and everything seemed to have that staged effect rather than being actually used or lived in. As he turned to leave, his eye caught a small book lying on the floor by her bed. He picked it up and saw that it was tied with a purple ribbon—it was her diary. Inside the cover was a pocket containing a pamphlet that read: "How to Die a Beautiful Death Like Elvira Madigan." The little pamphlet appeared to be well worn, obviously much read and pondered. It was the story of a Danish tightrope walker, Elvira Madigan, whose illicit affair and dramatic death in 1889 were the subject of a Swedish film made in 1967.

"Oh my God," said Dormer." This girl is living a fantasy life from another era."

He tucked the book into his jacket and quietly made his way out of the room, down the hall, and out the front door, unnoticed by the DeMarcos, who were obviously much more concerned with themselves than anything he might have to say to them.

CHAPTER TWENTY-FOUR

SANDY MCKINNON WAS relatively easy to find even without the help of the DeMarcos. Sergeant Dormer had only to check at the local high school, questioning the concerned principal, and telling him that one of his high school students might have gone off on a holiday fling (spring break was the following week, and she may have left early). After joking about the hormonal impulses of the young teen years, Sergeant Dormer just wanted to check up on a possible disappearance of the young girl, and did the principal know of any friends she had, etc. Of course, Mr. Parsons, a jolly pink-faced fellow, insisted on confidentiality; he wasn't in the business of giving out names, but this was the police after all. With assurances that nothing was really wrong, the congenial principal was more than ready to oblige. Suzanne DeMarco and Sandy McKinnon were the best of friends. They were seldom apart and always left school together. Mr. Parsons didn't know the extent of their activities, but it did seem like the two didn't really participate in the usual high school extra curriculum.

"Well, I know that neither one of them is on the cheerleading team. Certainly pretty enough, but neither one of them is particularly outgoing. Um, let's see, not on the debate team either. Two of our quieter students, but that doesn't mean they don't have college potential. Now that I think of it, one of our students, a Cheryl Schwartzfeger—I think that's her name— passed away last year from leukemia. She and Suzanne were very close. The entire faculty was aware that Cheryl was dying, but I guess none of us knew how to prepare Suzanne for the possibility that this might occur."

"So, you're saying that she and Suzanne were friends before her death?"

"Oh yes, her English teacher was in here several times talking about how Cheryl's mother was taking her daughter on world-wide tours of Europe and paring her off with lovers... at the age of fifteen, for heaven's sake."

"And was Suzanne aware of this?"

"Well, I think she was—at least her English teacher thought so. Suzanne was apparently very depressed, withdrawn, and angry during this time."

"Did she receive counseling?"

"Well, we're not a hospital, Officer, and kids go through a lot in high school, all of them. It was just a miracle that Sandy showed up when she did."

"Did Sandy know Cheryl as well?"

"Oh no. Cheryl died, and it was a few months before Sandy showed up."

"Showed up? It sounds like a movie script."

"Sandy came into school mid-term sophomore year from Albuquerque, New Mexico. I remember that she stood out like a bandit—barn-door-red hair, skinny as a whip, and her mother was a dead ringer for Marilyn Monroe. I guess I remember Sandy because of the profound," he laughed self-consciously, "effect her mother had upon me."

"Well, I guess she made quite an impression."

Giggling at the memory made the principal's round pudgy face turn even pinker under the office light.

At least he's into adult women, thought Dormer.

"Sounds like the two girls clicked because they both had something to beef about."

"Well, Sergeant, that does just about sum it up. The two girls clicked because I think they felt they had no one else to turn to, and maybe that's as good a reason as any."

Sergeant Dormer soon took his leave of the obsequious Mr. Parsons and made his way down the walks of the high school he once attended himself. *Ah, those were the days*, he thought. *Star quarterback of a great team. Girls all over me.* He chuckled to himself at the thought of what his wife, Dolores, might say to that. As he turned the corner to the parking lot, a young girl stood stiffly by his police car. She certainly looked as though she had something to say, and she stayed in place like a statue until he reached his car. *Ah ha, I wonder if this is Sandy McKinnon. Who else would look like she had so much to say?*

"Hi, Officer... uh, are you by any chance looking for Suzanne DeMarco?"

"Are you Sandy, by that same chance?"

She giggled at that and answered that she was. "I have been absolutely sick with worry about her. Have you found her? Have you found that scumbag that took her away? I've been up all night worrying. Bruce and I have driven around everywhere looking for her after she left that awful party. I mean, I thought Julius was cool, really cool, but now I think she's been taken advantage of, and worse. And it's all my fault! I should have known. I should have seen through his crazy vibe."

And with this outburst, the tears started flowing.

"One question and answer at a time, Sandy. I think you can help this investigation a great deal. I'd like to bring you down to the precinct for questioning, but I don't have the luxury of time to wait. I think Suzanne is in immediate danger, and I'd like you to tell me everything you can think of right now. Okay with you if we sit in my car and talk?"

Sergeant Dormer knew this wasn't protocol, but he knew he had to get the ball rolling. Because he had been taken off the murder and abduction case, and as Mrs. DeMarco had so adroitly pointed out that her missing daughter wouldn't be police news until it was a twenty-four-hour case, he damn well knew he had better get moving on this investigation.

"Let's start with your friend Suzanne. How did you two meet?"

And then the answers came in a wave. It was much the same as he had heard from the principal. Sandy had moved here her sophomore year from New Mexico and hated every minute of Paisley Falls. She and Suzanne had fallen into a friendship out of mutual misery. Suzanne had lost her best friend and withdrawn from everyone at school. Sandy was angry at her parents for separating, causing her mother to relocate out of her own selfish need to get away from her gallivanting husband, Sandy's high school tenure be damned. The two girls invented games to keep them preoccupied and separate from other kids their age.

"What exactly do you mean by games?" asked Dormer.

"Well, I discovered an old Civil War diary my mom had lying around the house—of my relatives, I guess—and we read a few pages of it every day after school. I mean, no one else at our school did anything like this. They were all into gaming and websites; we could not have cared less. We were not online babes. Suzanne even invented a game where we went to visit graveyards, especially to see tombstones of those who had died in the Civil War period. Suzanne cared about it much more than I did, but I thought it was cool too."

"Did Suzanne ever talk to you about suicide?"

"What? No, no. I mean *really* not."

"Did the two of you ever see a film called *Elvira Madigan*?"

"Who?"

"Sandy, was your friend Suzanne unhappy with her life at home?"

"Well, nobody's friends with their parents, Sarge—may I call you Sarge?"

"It's Sergeant Dormer, Sandy, and you're doing great; just a few more questions." And with that, Sandy filled in all the blanks about Julius and their meeting at the mall, as well as Bruce Bonsford, a seemingly innocent chauffeur for Suzanne, and Sandy's boyfriend. He got an earful about the awful high school blast-out party that he had intended to investigate, but didn't think it would lead to anything and, most importantly he thought, Suzanne's parents and their relationship and reaction to Suzanne's disappearance.

"I mean, I went over there, Sarge, I mean Sergeant... uh... Dormer, at two o'clock in the morning to tell them that Suzanne had been driven off into God knows where by this lunatic."

"Lunatic? I've never heard you describe him this way before."

"Well, you know," confided Sandy, "maybe he wasn't as much of a lunatic as her mother."

"What does that mean, Sandy?"

"It means that, in spite of it all, maybe Julius offered her more love than she ever got at home. And that's why kids split, don't you think?"

Sergeant Dormer was silent a long time before he replied.

Tragically, he thought Sandy's observation was right on the money. Families didn't spend enough quality time together. Even parents who loved and worried about their kids were increasingly working two jobs to make ends meet, and relationships suffered because of it. Even the animals in a family suffered. No doggie walks meant peeing on the carpet, followed by punishment when people came home exhausted to find it. Lonely kitties with automatic feeding dishes and self-cleaning litter boxes lingered on windowsills with heads parting the curtains every time a car pulled up, hoping. Multiplying that times a thousand also meant that kids got glossed over while cell phone and video games babysat them. Meals were grabbed, not savored. It seemed like people were working just to pay the bills, not to have a little extra. Most good people loved their children and tried to do their best to put food on the table for them, but they were up against so much more than they could ever comprehend. The lure of drugs, of fantasy lives, of the unending sophistication of the internet, of the demand to be more than just ordinary, was flooding all their senses.

There was a growing underground addiction to anything that could get you more of a high, and some of the good things like being the best on the football team were mixed in with being the best in America's Got Talent competitions, where children developed adult voices to perform outrageous songs and earn the Golden Buzzer from the judges. *This is a measure of success for a nine-year-old child?* thought Dormer as he sat listening to Sandy, who wouldn't have understood one word of what he was thinking.

What were we all worshipping more than showing our kids that we loved them and that they were truly special? He agreed with Sandy's simple little sentence. Yes, he thought, not feeling loved is why kid's split. And it was harder to get through to them by example, not merely words, more than he ever realized.

"Sergeant—Hey, I'm sorry. I didn't mean to go running on about—"

Sandy brought him back from the silent commentary running through his head. He shook her hand and said he would be in touch with her as soon as he heard anything. He told her he might need to get in touch with her again, and then he slowly backed out of the high school parking lot and headed back to the station to get an appraisal of the ongoing situation in Paisley Falls. So many conflicting thoughts swirled in his brain. What had Sandy called Julius? A lunatic? And she implied that Suzanne's mother was even more of one. What would a lunatic do to a person who was looking for love? Annihilate them, possess them, or both?

Cautiously, he made his way back to the precinct, aware that he would have to be most careful not to step on anyone's toes. Then his plan was to track down the car rental agency and try to follow the route the car took that had swept Suzanne out of Paisley Falls and plunged her into a world of darkness. One of these lunatics—no, maybe both of them—had left more clues than they realized.

CHAPTER TWENTY-FIVE

EDDIE THE JUNKIE, as LJ fondly called him, was a pretty simple no-brainer. Julius hung back and let LJ do most of the talking. He pretended to be cozying up to Suzanne in the truck while LJ talked business with Eddie. Eddie didn't say much, being a man of few words, but he was good buddies with LJ, and he knew he owed him money from a stash a while back. The junkyard was huge; stuff was stacked layer upon layer going back years. Ancient cars, farm equipment that had seen better times, a yard of yesterday's rusted-out refrigerators and stoves, and a trove of Sears's finest once upon a time. Eddie was the only man on the job. It was his yard.

"Why you wanna squash up a perfectly fine Camaro? It still looks good to me. He walked over to the vehicle, checking out the body.

"A little dusty, that's all." He checked the license plates. "I can see that it's a rental."

"Well, Eddie, I can't pull nothin' over your eyes. Yep, it's a rental. That and a couple more reasons are why my friend and I need to ditch it. You know you owe me, but I'll still make it worth your while."

LJ pulled out a couple hundreds from his pocket to show Eddie he was putting his money where his mouth was.

"Well, that's a pretty girl you got in your truck. That her boyfriend, or are you two sharin'?"

"She's just a party girl, Eddie, and we gotta get outta here. Can I trust you to make this compact disappear?"

Eddie's mutt, Screwball, came up to sniff the back of the trunk while they were talking.

"Well, yeah, I guess if Screwball there don't eat the car first." He laughed as he shooed the dog away from the Camaro. "Seems like it's worth more than just a couple of hundred, what with the compactor and all. And what if someone comes sniffin' around about a stolen rental car connected to you?"

LJ didn't hesitate to pull out a few more bills while giving Eddie a look that said this is all I'm giving you. "You know you owe me a favor, Eddie. Remember that stash a while back that you didn't pay for?"

Eddie looked away and down at the dirt. He was hoping LJ wouldn't bring that up. "Well, yeah, I do but, like I said, this looks like a special situation, right?"

The two of them were used to playing cards together.

"Okay, buddy, I'm in a generous mood. Let's make it an even grand to make this baby disappear. You've got nothing to worry about with the police; it can't be traced here or to me. That jerkoff in the truck with the ass is the one who has to make this go away. If you do it right, no one will find out where it went. 'kay?"

He pulled out the wadded-up bills and made it look like it was all he had left, handing the money over to Eddie one bill at a time like it was his last dime. "Do it now, 'cause we've gotta split. The sooner the better, and let's party soon, brother."

They high-fived each other, and then LJ moved quickly to the truck. The three made dust as they sped out of Eddie's dump as the rusty sign with "Eddie's Dump'n Depot" scrawled on it started swinging in the wind.

Eddie stood there a few minutes watching the truck hastily disappear. "I wonder what they're up to, Screwball," he said to the dog, who was busily sniffing the back of the trunk like he'd found a wounded animal.

"Let's go see what's got you so riled up," he said and grabbed a crowbar to lift open the lid.

"*Woowee!* That's a smell! Somethin' sure went on in there."

Screwball agreed as he yelped and jumped with excitement.

"Well, let's not jump to any conclusions, boy. I'll go ahead and crush this sucker, but not before I claim the body parts."

With that, Eddie did what he was born to do. His greasy hands lovingly found the engine block, heads, pistons, and valves. Like he was stroking a lover, each part became his own.

CHAPTER TWENTY-SIX

SUZANNE WAS BEING jostled back and forth between the two of them in the front seat of the truck as it made its way down the dusty road. She didn't know where she was or who she was with, and a great part of her didn't care. In this, her current world, she felt no pain; on the contrary, her world was a glorious sunrise creeping over a majestic mountain. She knew she kept reaching her hands up to try and touch the sunrise, but something kept slapping them back down. This angered and frustrated her, and she flailed her arms helplessly as the dark forces kept holding her back. She heard voices, but they sounded like they were several tunnels away. Words like "can't" and "don't" wafted in and out of her consciousness. The voices didn't want to let her go. She had to get out of their seeing eyes. She felt that huge pairs of eyes were looking down on her, trying to prevent her from lifting up.

Yes, she thought, *up, up to the twelfth floor, the thirteenth floor. She was going up to Fantasyland. And her little sister, Bethy, was waiting on the other side. All she had to do was open the elevator door, and she'd be there where wonderful surprises were waiting.*

But the huge eyes were watching. They didn't want her to go up there. They told her it was an illusion; it was not time for

Fantasyland just yet. "Wait" they said, "the time will come when it is right. Don't let go just yet. We have even better surprises in store," they said. The blackness of a secret star enveloped her instead, and she fell limp, succumbing to its numbness.

"Has the plane got enough fuel?" asked Julius as they neared the little airport where the Cessna 320 was stored.

"Yeah, but that ain't our problem. Getting to the hanger, loading her up, and taking off in broad daylight could be tricky."

"Why? Planes come and go all day long in little airports."

"Protocol. I need to check in with the control tower. We've had some run-ins in the past. It'll be all right, but they might check on the number of passengers I've got. We need to make her look more together, but not so much that she squeals on us."

"Well, one thing's for sure, we can't wait to take off any longer. This has got to start happening real fast."

Julius was beat himself, but he had to get back to the action at the port in Long Beach. The cargo containers were due in today, and without Dino there to supervise, the truckers waiting for their loads would be clueless and skittish about the deal if it wasn't handled properly. It was bad enough that he and not Dino would be the one to meet them. Right now, timing was everything, and he knew he couldn't leave LJ to his own devices. He knew LJ needed a fix. He could smell it when that happened. There'd been too much stress and quick decisions made. Little John would soon need to calm down. If there was a delay in taking off, Julius knew LJ would find the opportunity to take a hit, even if he was flying a plane. Ego took over for LJ, and he'd feel that he could do anything. Time to step up the game.

"Let's not take time to socialize, LJ. Just get to the hanger, turn the transponder off, load us up, and wait until the control tower closes. They won't notice you if you don't make a big deal out of it."

"Julius, you can't fuck with airport regulations. They'll report us!"

"LJ, where are all your past glory days? How about our runs into Mexico, buddy? And ditching the body of that snitch into Puget Sound? Those were the days, bro. Have you lost it?"

"No, no, of course not," whimpered LJ.

"And the money, bro. Fifty grand more just for flying a plane for a couple of hours," Julius added. "I know I can trust you to go all out for me, because I can promise you so much more." Julius gave his friend a reassuring little pat on the back. "You're smart enough to succeed in this business. After things settle down when we get back, I'd like to set you up as chief of foreign operations. A guy with your smarts and this sweet little twin engine, you could troll Mexico for a couple of chicks a week and bring them back to headquarters for training. All those Mexican chicks are just waiting for any chance to get into the States, and with your charm…" Julius knew he wasn't laying it on too thick; he needed whatever fairytale charm he could toss out to LJ to get him going.

"Oh… oh… oh God!" With that, Suzanne threw up all over the truck and passed out.

Dreaming and then waking, Suzanne was no longer sure of anything that was supposed to be real. Here, in the cold steel trap of the cage, she had no idea how long she had been here. Days? Minutes? There were two men who had put her here: Julius and some other man. She remembered planes and flying but had no idea whether it was a real trip or an imagined journey. She was cold and completely nude. Sad too, because she knew this wasn't a nightmare that she might wake up from. This was real, and it was nowhere that she belonged.

∽

"Ahhh!" she cried out.

"Baby, bark, okay? Just bark for me, and you'll be fine. I believe in you, baby."

"Oh my god, Julius. How long have I been in here?"

"I told you to bark, baby. I don't want to have to keep punishing you, but I will," said the steely, even-toned voice that she knew all too well. "If you bark first, then I will let you ask a question. Only one question, and then I answer, and then you bark again. Understand?"

Somehow after a long while, a pathetic sound came from her lips. "Arf."

"That's good, baby. What is your question, princess?" He gently laughed as though he was a master giving a treat to his dog.

"I'm cold and I want food!"

"That's not a question, baby," scolded Julius. "Now bark."

"Arf," choked Suzanne.

"What's your question, baby?"

"Can I have some food, please?"

"After you say you're sorry for hitting me so badly in the car."

"I'm sorry."

"Say arf, arf for me."

"Arf, arf," sobbed Suzanne.

"Push the empty bowl in front of you to the edge of the cage."

She did as she was told, nudging it slowly with her chained hand. It was a round tin bowl, and there were two of them. The other one was filled with water. Since she couldn't pick up either bowl with her hands, she knelt on all fours and had to lap up the water with her tongue.

"I didn't say drink yet, baby, so stop right now or no food."

Suzanne stifled the sobs coming up in waves from her throat and moved her head out of the water bowl.

"Good girl." Julius might have patted her head at that point. He reached into the cage from the side and poured a cup of kibble into the bowl.

"That's all you get for now. In a little while, you'll get something better if you're good."

Suzanne sniffed at the bowl only to discover that it was dog food. She retched and spit out what she had taken in her mouth. From somewhere in the blackness of this den, she heard him laugh and then shuffle out the door, leaving her to make the best of this snake pit in a pigsty.

Julius locked the door to the cage room, listening to her moaning, and reveling with the thought that soon she would be ready. His elephant training theory never failed him. There was just a string left now, he thought. Maybe tomorrow he would give her a room with a bed and clean white sheets and a lock on the door. Let the customers come and enjoy. Oh, the money she would make.

On the third day, he brought her a small mattress and a blanket. It was like he had given her a luxurious suite. She now had some solid food to eat and had learned to always bark first before expecting any conversation or granting of requests. The cage was big enough to hold a small urinal in one corner. It was larger and stronger than any dog kennel she had ever seen. *Specially made*, she thought. But today, on the third day, she had another request.

"Arf, arf. I have to go number two," she told Julius when he came in that morning with her food.

"Ah, I was wondering when we would get to that."

"Arf, arf. It's pretty painful, Julius."

Suzanne's hands were no longer chained, and she could sit up now, but she quickly switched back to all fours posturing like a dog and giving a poor doggie look with her eyes that said, *Help me. I'm suffering!*

Naturally Julius had no feeling or concern for her situation, but he was unusually gentle in his response.

"Are you constipated, you poor thing? Do you need an enema or suppository?"

Suzanne tensed at the tone in his voice. "Arf, arf," she hurriedly answered. "I just need to go to a bathroom and go... privately."

"Yes, my little doggie. I know you need to go poo poo, but doggies just go on the ground in public. I'll put some newspapers down in the cage for you."

"Oh, please!"

"Bark!" he commanded.

But Suzanne didn't bark, she howled. And the sound came up from deep in her bowels as they emptied onto the cage floor. She howled again and again, crying out with the anguish of a wounded animal, and she fell sideways screaming with pain and misery.

"Why, why, why?" she screamed out. "Why are you doing this?" She became hysterical as she tried to avoid the shit that had escaped from her body despite her best efforts to control herself.

"Now look at the mess that you're going to have to clean up." Julius might have been reprimanding a child for spilling Kool-Aid on a kitchen floor. "'Why?' you ask, you fucking cunt?

You need to learn how to shit in public, because it's going to be asked of you. You got that? You are going to be asked to perform, and shitting on demand is an art."

Julius was filled with a fury that he could hardly contain. Spittle escaped from his lips, and his eyes looked as though they might explode. His disgust for her and the smell of her excretion overtook every emotion in his body. He shook with venom, appalled at the mess this girl had become in his training ground. Her very being, as compliant as it was, threatened to overtake him, and his need to control her became paramount to everything else. How could this total piece of nothing be so much stronger than him? She was ninety-five pounds of filth, and the sooner he got her out to the marketplace the better.

Why wasn't her training going better? What was he doing that wasn't working? He needed her to be broken quickly, or else he was going to have to kill her. LJ had already wanted that done. If she couldn't be incorporated into the stable soon, he'd dump her. *Probably should have done that right from the beginning,* he thought. Even Dino hadn't liked the time he'd spent wooing her, and her friend Sandy only meant more trouble, as he was sure she would keep trying to find her friend. What had seemed like a good idea was fast turning into a total waste of his energy and trouble for his empire.

She had seemed like such a good idea, different somehow from the other girls. They were just workhorses, moneymakers with cheap looks and no class. This chick had class. She could bring him better money than anyone else if she would just get on board. Maybe he should bring in some of the girls who were already trained so they could bust her ass and set her straight. *No*, he thought, *I want her different from the rest. I want her to be the queen of my stable. She's going to be one hell of a bottom bitch when I get through with her!*

Julius had been lost in these thoughts when he finally focused on Suzanne, who was cowering in a corner, staring at him.

Shit, she's probably going into shock. I'd better ease up on her. He took a long breath, matching her stare as if to say, "to be continued, but you will be tamed," but as he focused more astutely on her posture, he saw a change that he took to his advantage. She really wasn't cowering; there was strength in her presence, calmness in her limbs. She held his gaze and carefully phrased her next question. Without barking first, she said, "Get me some paper towels so I can clean this mess up."

Julius smiled and without a word he slowly left the room, gently closing the door behind him. He knew without question that a corner had been turned and that Suzanne might have been a risk worth taking after all.

CHAPTER TWENTY-SEVEN

SERGEANT DORMER HAD tracked the blue Camaro to the Elite Car Rental Agency in downtown Paisley Falls. He'd known Rick, the car rental agent, for several years, and their kids went to the same high school together. He had to be careful not to mention that the state police had taken him off the case of the four girls and the murder of Dino Hu, because he was hoping that he'd be able to glean a little information from Rick. He knew he was overstepping his boundaries and, despite what Suzanne's parents thought, he knew Suzanne's life was in danger. He figured Rick might not be aware that he was no longer on the case, and he hoped that he could provide him with any little tidbit of information that might help.

"Some crazy shenanigans this is about the murder of some criminal by Muslims and kidnapping kids, for God's sake. Andy, what's happening to people? It's these foreigners. We've got to get them out of our country!"

"I know, Rick. It seems like we're living in very troubled times."

Andy stepped into the tiny dusty office and waited until Rick finished up with a customer.

"I'm trying to figure out what this guy Dino was doing renting a blue Camaro from your agency. If we could find the car, we could solve the case. Got any recent history I can take a look at?"

"Well sure, Andy, but the state police have beaten you to it. They showed up early this morning with a court order demanding all the records. Don't you guys talk to each other?"

"Yeah, I figured they'd stopped by already. I'm doing special detail for a missing person," he explained. "A fifteen-year-old girl from Paisley Falls apparently drove off in it with her boyfriend and disappeared last night. Thought you might have had someone asking for information about who stole this car."

"Yeah, I got a call yesterday from a trooper who stopped a young guy for an infraction and wanted to know if the rental was legit."

Dormer perked up at this news and tried to sound casual as he asked what name the trooper had given Rick.

"Was an Italian name. Julius something," he answered, scratching his head. "And the car for sure wasn't rented to anyone named Julius, just Dino Hu."

"Did the officer say if a young girl was in the car with him?"

"No, I don't think so; can't really remember. He did mention that the guy seemed a little nervous, impatient maybe, and hung around the trunk of the car, gesturing to it a lot. But we didn't get much said, because the all-points bulletin came out for all police available to go to the abandoned cotton mill. That's when they found this Dino guy murdered. Head cut off, for Christ's sake. And then the four girls. I can't believe it. What's happening to people?"

After getting Rick to give him the name of the arresting officer, Andy quickly left the rental agency, promising to get the families together for dinner; Dolores's turn to cook. Rich laughed at that and said the diplomatic thing to do was to have potluck at one of their houses; maybe they could flip a coin just to keep it fair. Andy laughed and made his way back to his patrol car, as he was being paged.

"Sergeant Dormer, please report to the home office. A young girl, Sandy McKinnon, says she has some urgent news for you."

"Did she say what it was about?"

"She said something about remembering a car. I think she said a red Corvette.

CHAPTER TWENTY-EIGHT

NADINE HINES WAS becoming more and more of an annoying problem for Dr. Wilson. He'd been careful, very careful, to keep her out of the town's eye, lest Stephanie hear the slightest rumor. He really didn't give a shit about his wife, but her imposing and wealthy father meant keeping any gossip out of sight and above board. Some strings had been pulled, and the appearance of Nadine at the emergency room had been gratefully yet mysteriously erased from the hospital records. He expected the state police to question his absence at the examination of the four young girls, and he suspected that Nurse Powell had seen him walking out with Nadine, but she didn't say anything to him the next time he saw her. She had looked troubled, though, he thought, and had glanced away as she passed him in the hall, trying to look preoccupied with some duty. Dr. Wilson knew better.

She knew.

So what? he thought. She was the least of his problems. That little slut Nadine had been asking for things: new clothes, fancy restaurants. Where the hell could he take her without being seen? Her latest request, and he really had to laugh at this pathetic ploy, was to be put up in an apartment as his mistress! They had been having some violent fights lately. All of a sudden, she said she wanted out, that she couldn't take it any longer. Her earnest little face with those clouded empty eyes had implored him to let her go. She promised that no one would ever know they had been together. She understood that his reputation and career could be destroyed if anyone ever found out. How he laughed and laughed at her.

And then he beat her to a pulp.

Now the crazy bitch had come full circle. She demanded that he keep her in style. It was as though the beating had had no effect on her. The fearful little waif that he had vanquished had been replaced by this distant and shrill replica of a falsely endowed feminist. She actually thought she had strength.

He had been giving her drugs lately that he'd been pillaging from the hospital coffers. They would placate her, he knew. She was becoming dependent on them and, with the right overdose, getting rid of her might end up being a most natural occurrence. He let her wail and scream and ball herself out, and then he gently injected her with enough fentanyl to send her respiratory system into the next universe.

He'd been seeing her in the seedy little hovel that she called home, and he was careful to erase his presence. Placing her in the bathroom with the needle still stuck in her arm, he arranged the body to look like a suicide. In reality, he thought, this *was* a suicide for her. She'd been a loser for so long that killing her was just doing her a favor. Time for him to move on to better and different things. Sex with young girls just wasn't enough lately. He wanted, no *needed*, younger meat, much younger, something stronger, to turn his life around. Something to make him feel strong and powerful again; he was afraid to admit it, but every time he thought of it, he grew hard with agonizing lust. It was just a tiny secret at first, playing with his mind, but he knew he had to try it, to taste the actuality of it.

He breathed a sigh of relief as he let himself out of her shack and felt the cool night air sweep all sense of heaviness away from him. The great thing was that he felt no shame for anything. Every event in his life had been completed with a purpose. Now he was going on to the next big thing. His god had created a pathway for him.

≪

"Andy, as long as I've been working at Paisley Falls General, I've never seen anything like this," whispered Nurse Powell in the stairwell of the hospital's basement. "The records for Nadine Powell's visit to the ER have been erased, as well as any evidence of any examination from the doctor on call that night, Dr. Wilson. I've let some indiscretions slip by, I admit. There are rumors about his infidelity, but I tell myself it's none of my business. But when the state police come in here and wipe his slate clean and take you off the case, then my back is up."

"Helen, I can't tell you how much I appreciate your support. How'd you hear, by the way, that I was no longer involved in the case?"

"I don't need to tell you that this is a small town, Andy."

"Yeah, but I'd love to know the first person who told who what before it started on a chain of rumors."

"All I know is that Sylvia—you know, Sylvia that works at the CVS on Holston?—she heard two state cops… uh… policeman, sorry Andy, she heard these two guys laughing and talking about how their boss was pussy whipped by Wilson's wife and her father, one of the richest men in the county. She said that they said whatever the father wanted done got done, no questions asked."

Dormer wondered why the father of a daughter whose husband was cheating on her would want to protect him, but he didn't want to fan the flames in a discussion with Nurse Powell. He had to stay under the radar, but everywhere he was looking, he was uncovering more puzzles than answers.

After talking with Sandy about the alleged red Corvette, he was more confused than ever. He checked out the Elite Car Rental Agency, and Rick said there was no way they carried a rental car like a red Corvette. "Would be stolen in a minute," ventured Rick when Andy questioned him about it. Dormer checked every rental agent in the state, but no one had a red Corvette for rent. There were no stolen red Corvettes in the area. Andy carefully checked databases for any stolen Corvettes, but he knew he had to be careful not to raise the eyebrows of the state police who mysteriously wanted to keep him out, not only of this murder investigation, but also away from any of the activities of one of the town's prominent physicians. He did understand the mentality behind covering up Dr. Wilson's indiscretions from that family's point of view. But what if anything tied the murder of a felon by unknown assailants to the capture and release of four underage girls to the disappearance of a fifteen-year-old abducted by a professional playboy?

As quietly as he could, he moved forward with his investigation, always hoping to find out what had become of Suzanne DeMarco... before it was too late. He also realized that before he could find Suzanne, he must first find Nadine Hines.

It wasn't hard to trace Nadine's whereabouts to the Loosey Goosey Saloon. The town regulars, who holed up at the place, were eager to tell their stories about Nadine. Each one perched upon the well-worn leather stools recited his story, and as soon as one finished, the next one began. The musty beer-soaked atmosphere lent itself to nostalgic renditions of town lore.

"Well she was on her way to becomin' a pro, that's for sure, Andy, not that I had anything to do with that, no sir," volunteered Buggy, a local who was nicknamed for his bulging eyes and insect-like hands.

"We knew she waited outside for anybody who would bring her a beer, and she'd paid her way too," laughed Louie, the town's official drunk. "Not that I had anything to do with supplyin' a minor, that is."

"Well, I'm not here to accuse anyone of breaking the law, but it seems as though she's disappeared. I thought maybe some of you might know about that."

No one had officially declared Nadine missing, but her disappearance at the hospital, not only of any record of her admission but also leaving with Dr. Wilson, meant something was very wrong. Ironically, Suzanne's parents had not bothered to file a missing person's report either. *What was going on here?* thought Dormer. Looking at the motley group before him, he decided that they were willing to talk but not really reveal anything. They quieted down and looked as though they had all mutually agreed to shut up and not say anything more. Time to stop squealing on the local townsfolk. Dormer continued on, however, to ask about the mysterious red Corvette.

"Anybody know anyone who drives a red Corvette?"

But the smiles had stopped, and the relaxed demeanor of afternoon bar life suddenly came to a halt. Dormer sensed the presence of someone else in the room and turned to see the state police officer who had replaced him. Detective Woodard filled the doorway with his six-three frame. Both hands on hips, feet spread apart, he made everyone in the room sit up straighter. Dormer felt the tension and his temperature rise.

"Sergeant, may I have a word with you outside? At ease, folks, I didn't come in here to disrupt your day." He chuckled on his way out.

Dormer turned and left the bar with his tail between his legs and was angry with himself for feeling that way.

"Dormer, I'm going to get right to the point. You've been taken off this case, Sergeant… or should I call you Detective?" The sarcasm wasn't lost on Dormer.

"Well, it's just that I—"

"You don't have the authority to go seeking out information on your own. That's our business now, and unless you'd like to be relieved of duty, you'd better follow orders. Do I make myself clear?"

"I was only following up on the disappearance of Suzanne DeMarco. I wasn't trying to interfere with the state's investigation of the cotton mill murders or the abduction of the four teenage girls. I just—"

"Like I said, get off this case. You are not a detective; you are local police. When and if we need you, we will call you. Don't make this harder for me, Sergeant."

Dormer felt like punching the guy out, but he nodded in agreement as the senior officer backed off and got out of his face. He could see out of the corner of his eye that the guys in the bar had all moved to the corner window where they could see what was going on. Just as Woodard was about to get into his patrol car, he turned back and asked Andy Dormer a question that made his heart stop.

"You've got kids, right? Daughters? Go back home and take care of them, Andy. Let us handle the rest before it's too late."

Sergeant Dormer stood there stunned as he watched the other policeman drive off. Was that a threat? *Take care of what?* his mind screamed. His anger had reached the boiling point. These bastards we not going to stop him from doing what he knew was right. If he was going to protect his own two daughters, the only thing to do was find out what happened not only to Nadine Hines but also to Suzanne DeMarco.

Move on, he thought. *Time to check out that nine-one-one call from a local farmer who had seen a couple fighting in his field.* Without skipping a beat, he jumped in his car to follow the next lead on the trail of finding out what had happened to Suzanne DeMarco and to do, in his mind, the right thing.

CHAPTER TWENTY-NINE

STEPHANIE WILSON'S CORVETTE was snuggly parked in her private garage. She'd sent Julius out the other day to have it cleaned and serviced after they'd been fucking in the back seat all night long. Stephanie was no bimbo. She'd graduated from Bryn Mawr with a 4.0 average. The salutatorian of her class, she delivered the salutatory speech on female achievement redefined for the twenty-first century with gusto. She'd met Fred in graduate school and, although her family thought she could do better, she'd admired the "Arrow Collar Man" look he ascribed to. He was just so tall and blonde and good looking. Together they appeared to the world as the perfect couple. Getting on the plane for their honeymoon to Europe, a female passenger had remarked that they were "quite the handsomest couple on board." Willowy and yoga fit, Fred had said he wanted to marry Stephanie because he wanted tall, athletic children, and she was the perfect body type.

Moving to Paisley Falls and having the children, and then settling into a suburban lifestyle held the same staleness for Steph as it did for many young well-educated, beautiful women who wanted the life and then found it vacuous. She went along with it until, sitting in Lucy's Nails one day getting a mani and pedi, she overheard two women talking about the escapades of the town doctor—the new, cute one who couldn't keep his hands off women. It didn't take much for Stephanie to figure out his passwords and codes to click onto the incredible world of his pornographic rapaciousness. It took even less time for her to find a lover. Shopping in the mall one day, she came across this beautiful, seductive man who kissed her lips with his eyes upon first looking at her. He'd do, she thought. He was delicious.

He practically creamed in his pants when he saw her car. It was a ZO6 convertible, tomato red and practically pulsating.

He explained to her that he was in town on a business trip and would love to take her to dinner. The rest, as they say, is history. She loved being temporarily swept off her feet, and he loved being the gigolo who did it. Nobody was fooling anybody, so it was just fun. When he asked her to borrow the car a couple of times, she was glad to oblige. She halfway hoped someone in town would see him driving her car and wonder who *that* was. And was that Mrs. Wilson's car that that guy was driving?

Julius disappeared as suddenly as he had appeared, and it didn't really matter to Stephanie. She filled her days with tennis and golf and workouts with the new hunk at the club who showed her what sit-ups meant when he was hovering his cock one inch above her pussy. She had a great life. She wanted for nothing... until the state police came looking for her red Corvette.

Sergeant Dormer didn't get to Stan Beaufort in time. By the time he got there, the old timer who said he'd seen a fight between two people who had driven off in a hearse was probably just hallucinating. Edna had placed him in a facility after his report to 911, and Stan didn't take to being in a facility. After one afternoon of being force-fed lunch and complaining that it was way too much food, he couldn't control his bowel movements. They didn't come soon enough to change his diapers, so he up and died out of protest.

Sergeant Dormer stood in the field where Stan had sworn this event had occurred and looked around trying to ascertain what had occurred there.

Edna, Stan's wife, stood tearfully beside him trying to explain.

"I thought it was just another one of his hallucinations, Officer. I had no idea there was any truth to it. The week before he had called in to nine-one-one saying one of his cows had gone off into the sunset or some such. Those people have enough to contend with without his crazy stories. I never dreamed that putting him in a facility where he'd be cared for would kill him." She was off on another crying jag.

"I'm so sorry for your loss, ma'am," Dormer managed to say. He was otherwise consumed with being in the field and looking at it from the same angle as the farmer might have. "Did he say what time of day this might have occurred?"

"Well, I know it was early. He gets up early to milk the cows."

"And he spoke about two people fighting. They must have come from somewhere. From that road, perhaps?" Dormer pointed to the dirt road running alongside the farm. "Does that road connect to the major highway?"

"Yes, it does," answered Edna, pointing in the direction of the major highway. "Anybody coming here would have turned off about a half a mile down from here. But nobody lives past us on this road, and we didn't need a hearse for any dead bodies."

"I don't think he saw a hearse, Edna. I think he saw a dark car and associated some harm or danger with it. What he witnessed probably seemed like murder, or at least a life-and-death struggle."

"Lord almighty, Officer, why is everything so scary now?"

"I don't know, Edna. I wish I had an answer for you, but I just don't know any more myself."

While he had been traveling to see the Beaufort farm, a call had come in from dispatch. Nadine Hines had been found, an apparent suicide, a drug overdose. Dormer knew in an instant that it wasn't suicide. Why hadn't he been summoned to go and investigate a local town murder? And there was still no word from the DeMarcos on Suzanne's disappearance. Five days had passed and so much had happened.

Suddenly, he saw something white in the distance, something that didn't look as if it belonged to the grassy landscape. It waved and flickered in the wind, almost calling him to come over and pick it up. As he came closer, he could see that it was a piece of fabric, a torn piece of cloth, part of a blouse, he thought.

As he picked up the flimsy article, he thought of Suzanne, so fragile herself and in much danger of blowing away in the wind. Maybe there was no way to help Nadine Hines anymore, but there was still time to find and save this young girl from a lifetime of slavery.

He had to proceed very carefully now, under the radar every step of the way. Even his wife mustn't know everything that he was doing. He knew he was up against something bigger than he could comprehend, but finding Suzanne also meant keeping his daughters, Julia and Catherine, safe—and that mattered more than anything else in the world to him. He was a proud father and a good police officer. It was important, *vital*, that he contribute his part in making the world whole and right again. He didn't think Suzanne had run off with this guy. He was pretty sure, from all the evidence he had seen so far, that she was being trafficked.

Christ, it was right in front of his face, with the four young girls being abducted. They were supposed to have been shipped somewhere until something had gone very wrong with these two guys' plans. Over and over in his head, he tried to figure out why the state police didn't want him involved. Who was paying them off? He knew he had to keep his mouth shut and find out the truth. *Someone needs to say something about this*, he told himself. This is going on in this country every single moment in every town in every hotel. After it hit Paisley Falls, Dormer knew it was just as much an epidemic as heroin, and like heroin, it was just as dangerous an addiction.

Nice neighborhoods didn't mean anything; even older people were trafficked and used as indentured servants to clean the houses and hotels that people expected to be clean. Nobody looked at these invisible people. *Humans are not objects!* his being shouted. They cannot be sold. Everyone deserves dignity, and he was going to do his part to make this scourge end… or die trying.

He tucked the piece of cloth into his pocket, said goodbye to Edna, and made his way to an unmarked car. Cautiously, he looked around before getting in. He was going to the next city south, toward LA. He'd check out each little town on the way for any information that could prove important. As he drove away, another car parked farther back on the side road and under an embankment started up and began a slow but deliberate tail.

CHAPTER THIRTY

Evan DeMarco's second anxiety attack proved to be far more serious than the first. This one was a real, bona fide heart attack that landed him in the ICU and on a ventilator. A frantic Rhonda called 911 after he had thrown up his breakfast and collapsed on the floor of their bedroom while clutching his chest. Their younger daughter, Bethy, had just gotten back from camp. When she came into the room and cried, "Hi Daddy!", Evan thought at first that it was Suzanne. He jerked up in surprise, ready to embrace her. When he discovered his mistake, he became so distraught that he heaved up all his breakfast and misery in one giant heap of despair. It seemed to Evan that things weren't going to straighten themselves out anytime soon. In every corner that his mind turned, he only felt an increasing sense of unease. Things were walling him up inside a box. He felt like a small but intrepid spider, capable of climbing out of any confining space, as long as there was an exit. But there was no exit from this trap, and so he burrowed down into the darkest recesses of himself; his only recourse was to hide from the fear that ate at his soul.

Rhonda was worried about her daughter, but she was consumed by the condition of her husband. She knew him well.

How he ate, how he slept, how he obsessed about Suzanne. She couldn't help that she wanted him all for herself. Oddly, she didn't mind the presence of Bethy in the family. She was no threat to Rhonda. She was a child who fit in the family. Suzanne didn't. She never had. Rhonda had moments of clarity when she realized that her hatred of Suzanne was morally wrong. She knew it would have actually been a blessing if her hatred for her older daughter had been pure and unadulterated. Then there would have been clearly defined lines in their relationship. They would have been sworn enemies, ready to do battle. Instead, when Rhonda ever allowed herself to define and clarify her confusing feelings towards Suzanne, she realized that those feelings were passive aggressive, hidden and disguised as something else.

Jealousy?

Maybe.

Still in justification for herself, she claimed a maternal, protective posture. She needed to shield Evan from mistakes he might make, a consequence of the seductive quality that oozed from Suzanne. Rhonda knew that this was not a conscious effort on her daughter's part. She could see that, in spite of her resentment towards this child, there was no malintent. It was her daughter's natural state and one that her mother longed to strangle. Even as a child, Suzanne's otherworldliness existed in a rarified state. Her feet touched the ground, but the essence of her soul floated dramatically forward and preceded her every move and thought. *She's so special*, thought Rhonda. *She's out of our league. Much better for the family that she's gone.* And Rhonda devoutly hoped that this was true.

⊰

Julius and Little John lucked out with the Port of Long Beach.

There had been a delay in the shipment of cargo due to a strike by the International Longshore and Warehouse Union (ILWU) Local 13, which lasted two days, long enough for them to cover their tracks and get back to business in LA and short enough to still save the lives of the twenty-two illegal immigrants stowed away in one of the cargo vessels.

The truckers, who normally would have been skittish with any kind of delay or change in plans, waited patiently for the deliveries, which would pay them well for their patience. All systems were go, and after being introduced to the finances behind the business, LJ was looking more and more like a probable partner and fill-in for Dino Hu. The Thailand partners took a bit of a hit with the disappearance of Dino, but Julius wanted to work a new angle anyway. With LJ's Cessna Skyknight, they could squeeze six girls a day into the plane and make daily flights into Mexico. They could rake in a fortune and improve and diversify their stable.

Julius felt better than ever before. There was a constant and unbelievable demand for more and more trade. They needed more bodies to work the circuits. They were getting over three hundred calls in three minutes for girls, and this was just from their internet advertising. Life for Julius had never been better.

And Suzanne?

Suzanne had learned to scrape out a tiny part of her soul and save it for her own private self. She knew this had to be a secret or he would steal it from her and force her to sell even that part of herself to strangers. She had learned from this horrendous experience to become a survivalist, a strength she never knew she had until everything was taken away from her.

Julius was amazed at her progress. By applying the elephant theory and caging her, treating her like an animal totally dependent on him, he had uncovered a gem. And when she was hungry enough, weak enough, depressed enough, broken enough, he slowly began to show her love. He claimed that she was special, like no other girl. He said they'd make a million dollars in six months, and she'd never have to work again. He told her that in order for her to feel whole again, she needed him to fulfill her life. With his guidance, he assured her that she would get everything she desired in life, the same kind of attention little Suzanne had longed for back in Paisley Falls. Now she would become a star. The star of his stable. The magic word was "obey."

"Obey," he said. "It's how the magic all starts."

CHAPTER THIRTY-ONE

IN THE DAYS that followed the murder and abduction of the four underage girls in Paisley Falls, several unusual events occurred. The four girls' families were paid a substantial sum for the traumatic experiences the girls had survived. The two alleged Muslim terrorists were never found and were believed to be a prank carried out by some town locals. Any theories of a transnational gang were poo-pooed as hearsay. The murder of Dino Hu, a known felon, was investigated and eventually dropped, a cold case put aside to be investigated at a later time. Sergeant Dormer was put on unpaid leave for unauthorized interference with a state matter. He eventually left the police department and became a private eye. He never took his eye off the case of Suzanne DeMarco, however, and knew he had to keep a low profile in order to keep investigating. The death of Nadine Hines was officially ruled a suicide, but Stephanie Wilson suspected that her husband had something to do with it and divorced him. She drove off with her two kids in the red Corvette and moved in with her parents, dumping the two kids with them, and then taking off for an extended vacation in Europe.

A confused high school girl named Sandy wondered why

everyone had stopped trying to find her friend Suzanne. It was like she had just disappeared off the planet. She knew Suzanne's parents were struggling with Mr. DeMarco's heart attack, but didn't they care about what happened to their daughter? Sandy hoped each day that passed that she would see Suzanne turn up, but she knew better. Something was very wrong. She talked to her boyfriend, Bruce, about it, and they started to plan their own investigative team. Where, they asked, would someone like a Julius character take Suzanne?

"They went to LA, don't you think, Bruce?"

"Yeah, and if he's a pimp, like I'm sure he is, he's gonna make her pro."

"You mean a ho. You gotta learn the language."

"Well, anyway, let's go find her."

"Bruce, that's the best idea I've heard so far."

Somewhere in a little bungalow in North Hollywood, Suzanne sat with a group of girls drawn together by their common profession. Sitting next to her and getting high was a black woman of generous proportions. Six feet tall, Luscious Lilly, as she was called, passed the joint to Suzanne. As Suzanne took the joint, she couldn't resist asking Lilly how she could get out of this.

Luscious Lilly let out a big belly laugh and answered, "They ain't no gettin' out, sugar. Theys only getting in."

PART TWO

THE BOTTOM BITCH
TWO YEARS LATER

CHAPTER ONE

SUZANNE LOVED THE tattoos being etched on each side of her inner thighs very close to her crotch. After one was done, she gently caressed it as though it were a piece of gold jewelry she had just received from her boyfriend. Julius had encouraged the idea of dollar signs right next to her pussy. As the tattoo artist looked up, their eyes locked in appreciation of the work at hand.

"What a treat for the johns, baby," he declared, and everybody laughed like this was the newest fun fad. "You're going to make me so much money, honey. We're going to retire on an island in the Caribbean and drink champagne and eat lobster."

She thought it was ironic that he mentioned eating, because they had gone through a severe restriction program on food. He told her that eating was a problem in her profession and that starving was part of becoming sexy for the part she was going to play. Julius knew enough about Suzanne to realize that, on some level, she liked the drama. Back in the first of the cage days, she had grown belligerent, screaming at him that she could no longer stomach the garbage he was throwing at her. He laughed when he remembered her, righteously shouting, "I'm not an animal!

You can bet the police are looking for me! My father is looking for me! They will hunt you down!"

"Well, nobody's come around yet," he had answered.

She yelled out a retort, still fighting, her punching gloves still on. "Where am I? How far away from home? Or am I right next door? Where have you taken me?" Tears were flowing now, and her voice was sounding hollow and more desperate. "Stop giving me these drugs," she had sobbed. "I don't want them! I can't eat, I can't sleep! This is a nightmare!" And then finally the pleading. "Let me go. Please just let me go. I won't tell anyone. Please." And when she was met with the usual stony silence, her fury made one last attempt to strike out at the snake's head rising to meet her gaze. "I hate you! I hate your fucking guts." This was followed by the usual ranting and collapse. "I'll do whatever you want. Why am I still alive? How can I ever survive this? Why was I born to be treated like this?"

Julius had often wished he had filmed these training episodes. They would be invaluable tools for future clients and become a teaching point to refine his techniques.

But those days were behind them now, and Julius was so pleased with how far Suzanne had come in learning the tools of the trade. Almost two years had passed since he first requisitioned her for his stable. She had done her training time like a champ. Bused among LA, San Diego, Sacramento, and San Francisco, she had learned how to keep her ass going. He put her in with the more experienced ones at first. They were the ones who were the best teachers. He spent some money decking her out after she had proved herself worthy of a better place on the ladder.

He wasn't very surprised that no one had come after her. Chicks like her got lost every day. They disappeared into the woodwork. He had hundreds of contacts, more than he could even think of supplying. He and LJ were just beginning to touch the internet. That was a goldmine. They were creating their own webcams, where even pregnant girls got fucked on cam. Move over Friends and Sex Cams, "Daddy's Tool Chest" offered cam girls from all over the world signing up at various sites to perform any act one can fantasize and more. The Asian chicks cost less, as did the Eastern European girls, especially in impoverished regions, so Julius easily ditched Dino Hu's Asian connections with Thailand and the cargo ships and went into distribution with various internet sites that asked no questions and made no appearances. Julius had decided that the shipping angle was too dangerous anyway. Several girls had died on the shipment that was delayed in Long Beach two years ago. The truckers were skittish about making anymore pickups, and the Thai connections were asking all kinds of questions about the disappearance of Dino. Julius was telling the truth when he said Dino's death had been horrific.

"I'd never seen anything like it. His head was offered up like it was on a platter," he said to Dino's brother, Big Bobby Hu, when he was confronted. "I had to hightail it outta there, Bobby. I swear I couldn't stick around to find out why."

Big Bobby stood silently listening to Julius's tale and glared ominously at his description of his brother's head. When Julius finished with a final quaver in his voice, Bobby just grunted and turned to leave without another word.

Poor Bobby, too bad, so sad, Julius thought, laughing to himself. He didn't need the Hus anymore. LJ and his Cessna 320C were moving along according to schedule, picking up a ton of Mexican chicks, along with all the local traffic coming out of LA: chicks looking to break into show business, runaways, and addicts. Shit, they had more than they could handle, which never could explain the hold and fascination that Suzanne had over Julius.

Maybe it was because she needed Julius to eat, to breathe, to live. She had finally bonded so willingly with her new support system. It was an amazing transformation. Her eyes glittered with love and lust for his every word. She was his; her soul belonged to him. She would die for him and kill for him, and this made him feel like a god. He could ask her to do anything, and she would obediently grant his wish. Sure, other girls he could command, but nobody was like Suzanne. He wasn't in love with the slut, but he lusted after the total possession of a human being. No one had ever seemed so willing in the end to throw herself away. He was greedy for the constant affirmation of that.

Still, he had to constantly drill her.

"If you eat that much again, I'll cut you bad. You know that. Now puke, dammit!" He'd had a bucket ready, especially in the early training sessions when he knew she wasn't really seasoned yet but pretending to be so that he would let up on her. "You are not smart, bitch. You eat too much and you're bloated. You think you're something special to the world, but you're not!"

"Oh, Julius, I don't think that at all. Please don't punish me anymore."

"Repeat after me, 'I will be a great blow job when I'm done with training.'"

And she would repeat his phrases with mind-numbing obedience.

"I demand the best from myself, and I love getting fucked in the ass! I expect to be a role model forever, teaching other girls how to suck cock and to love swallowing every last drop."

"That's good, baby, now swallow." Julius's cock was always ready for a demo.

Afterwards, when he would let her rest from the training sessions, she would force herself to gag and vomit up what she thought was all the rest of her life. Slowly, Suzanne became integrated into the business. She learned to please Julius by turning over her life to him. What he wanted her to become, she embraced mechanically. Nothing could ever be wholehearted, because she knew her heart would have to be extracted from her. Living to please him meant that she could survive.

In answer to his demands, she lustfully became addicted to sex—sexual acts of all kinds. This was where she could excel now. If she hadn't been special enough or powerful enough to make her way in life as Suzanne DeMarco, then she could become a magnificent whore. Everyone would desire her. She hadn't been able to please her mother or her father; all she had ever heard from them was that she wasn't special or gifted in any way. She wasn't capable of succeeding at anything. She knew her mother especially thought of her as a wasteful dreamer living off the blood of others. She would show them. All of her fury at the limitations her parents had placed on her now became her reason to reinvent herself. Not special or talented or extraordinary? She would show them.

Julius became her savior. The massive, shrouded door he held open for her allowed her to not only fall like some hapless Alice into a tunnel, but also, like Alice falling, she had the ability to see her own loneliness from afar. At times she would feel the pressure of being trapped inside her own body, and the trap would begin to feel like layers and layers of debris. At these times she pretended she was back in her old room hiding from herself behind closed doors. These feelings, combined with Julius's limitless capacity to inflict pain, brought her unwittingly to the closest she had ever come to ending her life just so she could get a good night's sleep. It was as if Julius and her mother had somehow bonded together in some invisible world to annihilate her free spirit. This force had a black hole quality. Whatever went into the black hole stayed in the black hole, and there was a mysterious quality to its analysis of this situation. Nothing left the black hole without express permission. The things that got trapped inside became a food bank for the black hole. These things were meant to be savored, except when it needed to refresh its exhausted victim. Like some vanquished hummingbird that had had its wings plucked by some sadistic beast, Suzanne was only spared when the pain obviously overtook her.

CHAPTER TWO

HE HAD PAID a lot for this girlfriend experience, and he wanted his money's worth. He knew it was going to be a good acting job on her part, and he'd heard great things. He didn't care, he just wanted to feel her desire for him, fake or real, and to taste sex and with it the promise of romance. She was beautiful and she was available. He could taste her in his mind and wanted to feel her everywhere, crazy with desire. He suited up so that he could fuck up. That's all there was to it. Pay4Play was the only way. What was the matter with fools who had no pleasure in life? Married fools with wimpy dicks who let their wives walk all over them and steal all their money were losers. He tied his shoelace, zipped up his fly, opened the bathroom door, and went in to take all the pleasure he could from the object that lay on the bed spreading her legs before him.

Suzanne had to admit that she was getting tired of performing the girlfriend experience. She had come to enjoy the pure lust of sex, devoid of not only any love, but also filled with contempt and hatred for the object—her. She had come to think of herself only as the last sex act she had completed. There was no more Suzanne DeMarco. She was an expertly crafted machine now.

These stupid shits who wanted to pretend they had real girl-friends were pathetic. The actress in her rose to the occasion, but behind her mask was always a thinly veiled attitude of distain.

As a misty rain fell on the dilapidated streets of a San Francisco suburb, this current john wanted to kiss. He'd fucked her in the room of a fancy hotel, and now he wanted to talk and walk in the rain. Seriously? Suzanne shivered in the cheap red chinchilla coat wrapped around her skinny frame and thought the kiss would never end. It was almost like he was posing for any passersby. They both smelled awful from the sweat of sex, and the rain didn't help. She wanted to shut him and the rain out of her mind, but the sky wasn't cooperating. For a brief moment, she fell prey to the thought that he was handsome and that they might be an actual couple strolling through a park. She knew better instantly and wanted to kick herself for the slip. She heard all the old admonitions clanging in her head saying "beware, don't go there." As they walked over a covered bridge holding hands and pretending to be lovers, she felt the taste of defeat and depression overtake her as she looked at him with pretend love and then at the mirrored reflection of herself in a pool of water that the rain had made. He kissed her again, and it tasted bitterer with each lingering moment. *I so want it to end*, she thought. *I want to go, but go where?*

Gratefully, the kiss stopped, and they detached from each other, each body begging to go its own way. He looked lost and tried to turn out of her line of sight. He couldn't separate fast enough and paid her the money, abruptly walking away and leaving her in the shadows of a false promised land. How she felt betrayed for being so gullible, for letting him lead her on.

How much hurt can I stand? she wondered. How much honor is lost trying to pretend they were anything other than customer and client? It was exhausting, this pretending to be someone's girlfriend. It was a shallow waste of time, but then she reminded herself: This wasn't a waste of time in Julius's world, and her life was in his hands now.

Sometimes she slipped up in her own mind, she knew that. There was still some dark recess where little Suzanne huddled in a corner and tried to breathe. "Ha, ha," she laughed and tried to shrug it off. At least Julius didn't know the crevice where little Suz had buried herself. If he knew, he would destroy it. Some part of her brain clicked off with this struggle of knowledge. She wanted to help the little girl with the broken doll bandaged with green tape, but she became terrified and returned to her bottom-bitch status, hurrying back to ground zero and Julius's cave where a spider was weaving a nest.

≪

"I thought after two years now you would have known better." Julius was waiting for her, sitting in his "master chair" facing the door when she returned.

"What do you mean?" Immediately, Suzanne became afraid as she looked into the menacing hard stare that decimated her thin, cold frame.

"You know its money first, bitch!"

"What? You mean you were following me? You were there?"

"I've got eyes everywhere, honey. You know that."

His icy words made her flinch. The punishments were what she dreaded most.

"Well, he was into the girlfriend thing and didn't want to pay in the room—"

"Shut up! He could have run off without paying, and you know what that means."

Her trembling hands grabbed at the money in the wrist bag he made her wear. "No, here, here it is!" Suzanne fought back tears as she thrust the crumpled bills forward.

Julius took the money and threw it across the room in a rage. "I've trained you very well, haven't I?" He shoved his face right up against hers and wrapped his fingers around her neck.

"No, Julius. Please!"

"Down on your knees!" He began scattering tacks all over the floor. "No dinner for you. No shower for you. Now crawl, damn it! Crawl all over these fuckin tacks until your knees bleed. Always get the money first! You got it?"

His voice rose to a furious pitch and the spit spewing from his mouth fell on her tears as she began a rote journey of numbing pain.

"Faster, bitch!" he yelled, and Suzanne began speeding up, looking like a busy little ant colonizing.

As he continued screaming orders like a sergeant with new recruits, the mole around his neck pulsated with increasing blood flow. The spider's web that had been tattooed around it seemed to grow as the queen mother engorged in anticipation of eating the male that she now regarded as prey.

She had stopped crying at this point and moved gingerly over the tacks, showing very little emotion. The pricks became less intense, and she immediately disconnected from the pain. She was more and more able to disengage to avoid feeling anything. It was easier that way. Crawling over the tacks and watching them get moist with her blood, she became someone else watching herself. When at last he hollered out "that's enough," she couldn't stop, but kept on going, a little bug in a routine for survival.

He finally yanked her off the tacks and threw her a towel to clean up. Disgusted, he left her to fend for herself. The ramshackle railroad apartment they rented in the inner Sunset area of San Francisco had four pallid rooms. The squalid neighborhood sheltered hookers and junkies, with a few token bars for the alkies. Suzanne had learned to call it home, like all of the other temporary apartments they rented throughout California. From this location, it was easy to zip into the Regis or the Hilton for a job. She was running into nasty competition from some of the working girls from other districts, and pimps were honing up on her, threatening to kick her ass out of there. She would have to talk to Julius about this when he calmed down. Right now, all she wanted to do was get to her room, which was the last one on the left. Julius was in the front one. LJ, when he was there, holed up in the second, and the third room was occupied by a newbie in training. Cleaning duties were performed by her. She went by the name of Lulu, a young Chinese girl that Julius saved for special occasions. Suzanne never quite understood Lulu's role. She wondered why she wasn't out on the streets like the rest of them. She was quiet and always kept her head down. As Suzanne walked past her door, she noticed that it was open a crack, and then the downcast face that was Lulu's poked through.

"You okay?" she whispered.

"Mind your own business, bitch."

"I have medicine to help clean up your knees." The door opened an inch wider as Lulu beckoned for her to come in.

"I can do it myself. I sure as hell don't need any help from you!"

"Hey, girls!" shouted Julius like some recalcitrant prison guard. "Did I ever tell you to talk to one another?"

Lulu swiftly shut her door, and Suzanne finished the walk to hers, firmly slamming it, knowing she risked further punishment for her obstinacy, but Julius was strangely quiet, as though he were preoccupied with other things. He had no time to micro-manage their insidious squabble.

He was on the phone with LJ and in a foul mood. "Where the hell are you? I expected you back tonight with the girls!"

"Hey, bro, I know. Got held up at the airport in San Diego. Well, it didn't work, so I had to cut them loose. We had been partying pretty heavy, and they didn't even know where they were or that they were in any danger yet. Nothing went wrong, Jules, I just couldn't get them across. Everything's cool, no citations, nothing."

"You wouldn't know if somebody *was* writing you up, you fool. Best lay low for a while. Don't come back here for a few days."

"Yeah, sorry man, I'll be more careful next time."

"Don't fuck up again or I'll have to replace you." His hollow laugh and the true intent of that sentence made its way across the phone line.

"Hey, dude, you sound like a Nazi," said LJ. "I can get back over there with the Cessna in a few days by taking a different route. I'll make it up to you, bro. See ya."

"See you later, you bastard," sneered Julius.

LJ cut off his cell and slammed it down. He hadn't been anywhere near Mexico in the last week. He'd flown into his little hometown to look after his dog and his house, like he'd been doing off and on for the past two years. Julius didn't need to know about it. He didn't need to know about the plan Junkyard Eddie and he had concocted either, the one that would make them both a lot of money, more money than he'd ever see from Julius and his schemes.

Somebody else was watching that little shack in the woods that LJ called home. Sergeant Dormer had managed to track down the blue Camaro to the little hamlet of Leverton. Staying well under cover and out of the state police's limelight, Andy Dormer had stealthily pursued the trail that Julius and LJ had left. In the two years that had passed since Suzanne's disappearance and Nadine's murder, Andy had been "let go" by the local police force. His wife, Dolores, had grown angry at his obsession with these cases and filed for divorce. Heartbroken by this development, he shouldered his grief but could not let go of his need to make things right. If he could find Suzanne and bring Dr. Wilson to trial for the murder of Nadine, he would be able to restore justice, which in his mind had been given no chance anymore.

His two teenage daughters were now sixteen and eighteen. The older one was going off to college. He couldn't believe it, and how was he going to pay for it? Both thoughts collided in his mind. More than anything, he needed the world to be safe for them. His health had suffered as a result of his obsession. His blood pressure was off the wall, and that girth around the middle he had been fighting was winning day by day. Too much reliance on fast food and endless cups of coffee, a PI's staple, he thought. If only Dolores could understand that he was doing the right thing, that he had to do something good before his own life ended, she'd forgive him and take him back. How he longed to go back home and feel the comfort of his wife and daughters surrounding him. They had suffered from their parents' arguments, pulling away from him to support their mother, but really just bouncing back and forth between their mother and father, wanting them to stay together. They didn't, or couldn't, understand his need to solve these problems. Andy realized that it didn't matter anymore what anyone thought about what he was doing. He simply had to finish this mission, even if he died trying.

He knew that he was also driven by his hatred for Julius and the kinds of men who did these things to women and children. He needed to understand what really made them tick. Once he figured that out, he'd be better able to fix it. The last time he saw Dolores, she'd been crying over his choice to leave her and the kids.

"You don't even know this girl, Andy. She's not your daughter. What about your own kids?"

"You don't understand," he had pleaded. "Bringing this bastard to justice *is* saving my kids! Stopping monsters like him and Wilson takes a lot of courage, not just from me, but maybe I can start a whole movement of people who will join forces worldwide to stop these tragedies from destroying people's lives. Suzanne and Nadine represent thousands of girls who are trafficked and made to feel like objects, less than human. It's something I have to do, Dolores, or else it will destroy me."

"That's another thing, Andy; going after people like that Dr. Wilson puts all of us in danger. You know how influential that family is in this town."

"Yeah, I do, and I'm not going to let people like them bully me."

"Bigger forces than you have tried to shut you up, Andy! What about the state police taking you off the murder case at the plant two years ago? I can't go on like this, Andy. They'll kill you if you get too close to anything. Why can't you understand that?"

"Baby, I do understand that. It's a risk I'm willing to take."

They just stood facing each other at that point, looking beyond each other's eyes and focusing only on the resolution they wanted to hear from the other.

Andy had left then without another word, leaving his two daughters crying softly in their rooms. He shed a tear, remembering that time as he sat in his beat-up grey Honda watching and waiting for LJ to come back home and feed his dog.

CHAPTER THREE

"Evan, honey, wake up. It's time for your bath."

In the two years following Suzanne's disappearance, Evan DeMarco's health had steadily declined. His heart attack, suffered when his younger daughter suddenly returned home reminding him that his older daughter was irreparably lost, left him partially immobile and on a ventilator for three months. Once off the ventilator, he was put into an assisted care facility where Rhonda would visit daily to attend to his needs. She made sure he was turned every six hours, and she bathed him daily. If she wasn't a caring and devoted mother, she made up for it by being a doting and compassionate wife. Now that Suzanne was out of the way, she had Evan all to herself. The only catch was that Evan was no more than a completely dependent cripple. There were times that Rhonda agonized about this feeling that her lack of affection for Suzanne had warranted this punishment. *I've been a terrible mother*, she would lament. It wouldn't last long, however, as she would always return to her devoted spousal state. Bethy, their younger daughter, was very low maintenance. She could take care of herself.

"Evan, wake up, dear. Bath time."

This was met with a disinterested groan, as Evan wanted nothing more than to be left alone. "Aaah, Rhonda, goddamn it, leave me alone!" He turned his face away from her, as if to protect himself from her daily invasion of his body. "When am I gonna get out of here? I wanna go home. That's all I want. Is that too much to ask? I just wanna get out of here." He struggled to make some attempt to get out of bed but was hopelessly weak and incapable of doing it.

The same thing might well have been said about Suzanne, hundreds of miles away. She too was hopelessly weak and unable to get out of the terrible bed her life had become.

If Evan blamed Rhonda for Suzanne's disappearance, he never accused her. At first, they had spoken heatedly about it. As time went on, the discussions were less desperate and much more infrequent. Evan had welcomed the questions from Sergeant Andy Dormer, but was sidelined by the state police's refusal to take her disappearance seriously. Of course, they considered it a missing person's case and would do everything possible to find her. There were so many instances like this of young girls seeking the glamour of Hollywood and nightlife. He was led to believe she had purposely run away from home. If it was of her own free will, argued Rhonda, who were they to stop her? Never mind that she was only fifteen, some bad seeds ran away to escape the responsibility of growing up, and now at eighteen she was legal. So, Evan became lost in his own failing health, too weak and confused to justify his own thinking, and more than ready to be guided and controlled by Rhonda's logic. It was easier to give in to Rhonda than to fight an uphill battle and pay the cost of reprisal, so they played the fake game of "everything's all right and, who knows, maybe she'll come back when she's gotten it out of her system."

Days turned into weeks and weeks into months, and one day Sandy, Suzanne's best friend from high school, came to visit Evan. Sandy had purposely picked a time when Rhonda wouldn't be there so she could talk openly to Evan about his lost daughter.

"Hi, Mr. DeMarco. It's me, Sandy. Remember? Suzanne's friend from high school?" she added.

Evan had been asleep and half-opened a bleary eye toward Sandy. He couldn't seem to place her at first, but after a moment his eyes came into focus and he struggled to sit up.

"Sandy, yes, I... remember... is Suzanne with you? Is she here?" Evan started trembling and reached his hand out to grasp Sandy's. He shook her hand up and down as if to validate his words. Sandy wouldn't have shown up unless Suzanne had come back.

"Well, uh, not exactly, Mr. DeMarco, but that's what I've come to talk to you about. I think Suzanne was kidnapped. I know you and Mrs. DeMarco think that she's run away, but I saw the guy she was with, and he was older, much older than us and not from around here."

Evan was beside himself at this point, squeezing Sandy's hand. "Yes! Yes, Sandy, I agree, I agree! I don't know why Rhonda's so convinced she's run away on purpose. My little girl would never leave me. Why are you here, Sandy? I thought when I saw you..." His voice trailed off and he started sobbing. He released Sandy's hand, trying to wipe away his tears.

"I don't know if you've heard, but that sergeant who was investigating got taken off the case and everything else that happened in Paisley Falls the night Suzanne disappeared."

"He came by to see us after she disappeared and wanted to see her room and everything," sputtered Evan, trying to sit up. "He acted like he was still active. What happened?"

"Some people think that the state police are trying to hush something up and that Sergeant Dormer was getting too close for comfort. You know about the Nadine Hinds thing, don't you?"

"Hi, Sandy. What brings you here?" Rhonda said, barging into the room like her own personal space had been violated.

"Oh," Sandy blushed, "I just wanted to pay Mr. DeMarco a visit."

"He's in very delicate condition, Sandy. Too much excitement isn't good for him. Maybe you should come back another time and let me know first so that I can prepare him."

She took Evan's face in her hands and soothed his forehead. "Now, now, dear, calm down. We'll see Sandy again next time." Turning to glare at the girl, she shooed her away while closing the door with her foot.

She knows something, thought Sandy. *Only thing is, I know more than she does.*

The truth was that Sandy knew where Suzanne was, or at least she thought she knew the territory that Suzanne was traveling. She had gone into LA to do her own detective work, telling her parents that she was applying to a business college, and staying with Aunt Betty who needed help anyway. She received free boarding in exchange for cooking meals. In her spare time, she started looking.

She began walking the Hollywood streets. It took her a while to catch on to why cars would pull up next to her and roll down the window on the passenger side. They didn't ask questions; they just pulled up sharp, looked, waited, and then drove off. Finally, it dawned on her that this was the way johns picked up bait. She laughed at herself for being so dumb, but she kept on asking the trade or ladies of the night if they knew of a pimp named Julius. A few of them laughed at her and asked if she wanted to join the union. "Cute number like you could earn a bundle," they said. Forget that pimp, as they could set her up with their guy, a real winner who took care of his girls. Sandy nodded and took it in stride but kept looking. She even hit a few shelters for recovering girls, and there she got some leads about a pimp who sounded just like Julius.

"He's a real bad dude, girl; don't get mixed up with the likes of him," one girl told her at the Hope for Change House. "You cross him and he'll kill you as soon as look at you." She looked as though she had been beaten to near death. Old bruises inflicted over and over that refused to heal littered her face and arms. *Arms that had gotten very used to needles*, thought Sandy as she thanked the girl for the lead about the whereabouts of Julius's camp in LA. She prayed that the Hope for Change House would help the young girl who looked like a lost soul sailing away on a ghost ship.

She started hanging out in the neighborhood where she thought Suzanne and Julius might be, but knew it was important that Julius not spot her. She realized that he knew what she looked like, and even though she tried to blend into the seedy neighborhood, she worried that she probably stuck out too much like a kid from the sticks. One good thing about LA, she reasoned, was that there were a lot of young kids looking to get their start in movies or modeling out here, so looking like you were green and from out of town was the "in" way to look.

She wondered if she might run into that detective from Paisley Falls who had been kicked off the murder case back home. She knew he was the only one who cared about what happened to Suzanne, and she had heard that he was still pursuing any leads.

Paisley Falls, she laughed to herself. That town seemed like a million miles away from here. The silly simple life that she and Suzanne led seemed so long ago, like in a history book, reading that journal about that Civil War soldier, and putting up with the dumb boys in high school. She had to admit she still liked Bruce, although he had lost interest in finding Suzanne and stayed behind. All of their lives seemed so plain and simple compared to this.

Recently, things had begun to change at school. There were a lot of school shootings going on in the country, even some in their state, and there was talk of teachers being armed with guns to protect the students. Some older boomers were beginning to call her generation the new hippies. She laughed as she remembered that her grandmother had been a hippie—a mother in the revolution, she once declared to Sandy. She liked the free spirit that her grandmother, self-named Daisy Ray back in the day, professed to be. They might have been leading a revolution against the establishment, thought Sandy, but her generation was fighting against themselves, because the people who wanted to destroy them were their own kind. *Kids killing kids*, thought Sandy; *there's no safe place anymore.*

Maybe I'm just chasing up a blind alley, she thought one rainy afternoon as she stood in a 7-Eleven on a corner street in Silver Lake. The Hope for Change girl had said she thought Julius and his gang hung out in this neighborhood. She was getting weird glances from the Iranian cashier who seemed impatient for her to be on her way. Out of the corner of her eye, she saw a man with a limp hurry up some apartment steps and slam the door, impatient to get inside. There was something about the way he rattled the door as though he was trying to pull it apart and that limp. Julius had a limp, she remembered, and he was tall and dark and well-dressed. This man didn't fit the neighborhood, she noticed. Everyone else was dressed casually in jeans and T-shirts, and this man seemed impatient and in a hurry.

She waited a minute more and stepped outside the little grocery. In the misty rain she saw the same man appear, this time with two young girls in tow. One was oriental and the other was younger, very fragile looking, and blonde. Suzanne! She was sure of it. The way she held her head, as though out of touch with everything around her, was so like her friend had been. She wanted to scream out and run toward them, but she dared not. She didn't want to blow it for Suzanne, and Julius could have a gun and shoot both of them on a whim. If she could just get closer. She had to be sure.

She glanced back at the Iranian guy inside, hoping she could pop back into the store and use the window as a place to hide and look out, but he was looking at her like he wanted to call the cops. She saw Julius look up and glance her way, and she abruptly turned the other way and walked in a different direction. Unfortunately, walking was not a usual practice in LA. Everyone drove a car to the 7-Eleven, so she purposely wandered up to an old Ford Wrangler and pretended to be getting inside. The Iranian guy was really watching her, so she had to be careful. She leaned in against the driver's side and fiddled with her purse, like she was looking for her keys, turning her head ever so slightly to keep track of Julius and the two girls down the street. It looked as though they were getting into a car, more like being shoved into a black van. She quickly memorized what she could see of the license plate, but it was too far away to be sure. How could she make contact with Suzanne before they drove away?

Just as she was considering running down the street after them, she heard a voice behind her say, "Can I help you, miss?"

She turned around to see a young, very cute guy gazing down

at her between sips of a large coffee. He was smiling, but his eyes were cautious. Sandy looked him up and down and liked what she saw. He had that five o'clock stubble that made guys look so available, and his baseball cap casually turned around still revealed a healthy crop of sandy blonde hair. She felt like she was looking at Brad Pitt. *He's probably going to think I'm nuts*, she thought, but she made up her mind in an instant.

"I'm in a little bit of a bind, and I wonder of you can help me out," she stammered, batting her eyelashes and producing a smile that she hoped would melt his wariness.

"My girlfriend is just getting into a car down the block, and I don't have time to run after her to give back her cell phone that she's forgotten she loaned me last night. You'd think she'd have missed it by now. If I don't get it back to her before she leaves, I'll be killed!" Sandy added a kind of helpless laugh to punctuate her dilemma. "I hate to ask, but would you mind driving me just a half a block down there. See that black van pulling out?" She pointed with one hand, leaning slightly toward him with her body. "If I could catch them before they leave, you would be doing me and her huge favor. I don't normally get into cars with strangers," she added, hoping this added credence to her sincerity, "but you look like one of the good guys." She added another big smile, which she hoped would seal the deal.

"You're right about one thing, miss: it's not such a good idea to get into cars with strange guys." His big blue eyes lit up with another smile as he opened the door of his old Wrangler. "Get in, and let's see if we can catch them."

He held the door open as she scooted inside, glancing surreptitiously at the Iranian clerk who was busy with another customer. She pointed again at the black van that was now pulling away from the curb. He honked his horn to try and get the driver's attention. Sandy stuck her head way out of the window and gave it all she had with one cry, "Suzanne!" she screamed, looking straight into the vacant eyes of her best friend. What she saw terrified her. What had happened? It was Suzanne, she was sure, but the person in front of her had morphed into someone, if not something, else. Her shriveled appearance with straw-like hair that lay in thin wisps around her face was dirty and forgotten looking. If Suzanne recognized Sandy, she gave no indication of it.

Sandy waved and cried, looking at her old friend who seemed to have aged twenty years since she last saw her. If at first Suzanne seemed not to care that someone in another car was seeking her out, her next reaction was that of paralyzing fear. She shook her head in a "no" kind of way and put her bony hand up next to her mouth to shield a scream.

Julius jerked the car around into the next lane to avoid any further contact with the Wrangler, while giving Sandy a wild, uncomprehending look. As he sped off to get away, he kept glancing into the rearview mirror until he realized who he was looking at. He made a notation of the Wrangler's license plate and disappeared into a few dark alleys until he felt no longer pursued by the vehicle.

Sitting in the dark of the alley, he slowly turned to the back seat where the oriental girl was holding a sobbing Suzanne. The spider mole on his neck was twitching, and his hand reached back with a solid punch to each girl's upper body. He pounded them again and again with one fist as the other held the wheel. Spurts of blood began flying everywhere, some landing on his neck where the mole was pulsating, giving it the surreal appearance of being alive and sucking the vein in his neck like some famished Dracula.

"My name's David, by the way, and you are?"

"Uh, Sandy. That's my name. Sandy."

The cutie-pie guy she was sitting next to seemed to swim distractedly before her eyes. She couldn't get away from the terrible image that she had seen. Suzanne had looked so ashen and emaciated. Sandy was frightened by what she had seen. Not that she hadn't suspected that Suzanne would look different, but the death-like mask she had witnessed on her friend's face had been terrifying. For the first time since she had begun this journey to find her friend, she was afraid. What had he done to her and what might he still do?

"I guess that guy sure didn't want her to have that cellphone. Ya think?"

Sandy sat numb, not saying a word.

"Look, I don't know what's going on here, but it looks like a lot more than you can handle. I've got to get going myself. Can I drop you somewhere?"

No response.

"Okay then. Again, my name's David and here's my number." He offered her a card that said "Trail Blazing Printers" with his name on the side. It said David Hargrove, along with a phone number. "Call me anytime."

With that, he leaned over her to open the passenger door of his Wrangler and gestured for her to get out. As she got up to go, he casually put his hand on her shoulder as if to reassure her that he meant no harm and was ready to help her if he could.

"Take care." And with that he was off, leaving a dazed Sandy standing on a street corner wondering what to do next.

CHAPTER FOUR

LJ AND JUNKYARD Eddie were making plans for a move into the porno business without the help or knowledge of Julius. LJ and Julius had been having some problems getting along, and getting away from Julius had been LJ's plan all along. Besides, they'd been having some major problems with Bluepage. The website was devoted to offering up human beings (mainly teenage girls) for sex. It was being glitched by the FBI so that prospective buyers were being arrested after they'd signed up for an afternoon delight. The biggest haul came from the Fantasyland Hotel in Anora, where a family might come to visit the amusement park, the mother and children taking off for the day while the father booked a date with some tweenies for lunch instead.

LJ had flown the Cessna into the local airport in Leverton, and Junkyard Eddie picked him up. Together they stopped at the junkyard, where Eddie showed LJ the parts from the Camaro that he had salvaged before he tossed it.

"That car sure had a history, LJ. You know anything about that?"

"Whatever happened in there was none of my business,

Eddie, and none of your business either. Why'd you save these parts? I thought we paid you to junk it."

"Well, there was nothing wrong with this stuff, but the rest of that car was somethin' else. I would not have wanted to experience what happened in that trunk, LJ."

"That's all behind us, Eddie; it's been over two years now. Nobody's come lookin' for it, right?"

"True enough. But I took pictures—"

"Don't try to railroad me, Eddie. Let's just focus on the plan to make more money than either of us have ever had."

"Okay by me," Eddie said.

"First of all, we keep everything in cash. We'll use the drug money I get from hauling coke in the Cessna's wheels to pay the cast and crew. We don't need any paperwork to slow us down. We can sell the movie to a distributor and get a valid, taxable check in return. Then we'll sell the movies twice: once on the black market and once on paper for a huge inflated price. This way we can launder even more money and keep things growing."

"Where we gonna get this cast and crew, LJ? Leverton's a pretty tight little town."

"Don't you worry about that, Eddie. Julius has got a flock. Nothing I'd like better than to tap on that stock."

"Playin' with fire there, LJ. That man's mean."

"Mean, but not smart. He's got a flaw, and I know just how to take advantage of it. Now let's go see my dog. You been takin good care of him?"

Eddie nodded, but when they got in the truck he said, "We better take the back roads. I think somebody's watchin' your house."

⤔

A blinding rage tore through Julius as he drove the two girls back to the house they had just left. It had taken him a while to recognize her, but he knew it was that dense, lame girlfriend of Suzanne's. Had she been spending the past two years looking for this bitch Suzanne? Why did he still call her Suzanne? he wondered. Why not just stupid bitch? *Nothing is going right anymore!* he shouted to his own brain.

He clawed at the mole in his neck as though it might give him an answer as to why his world was coming down on him. What would his mother tell him to do? *The spider bitch*, he laughed to himself. He needed something to calm himself down. His anger was stifling. He hated anything addictive, because it showed weakness. He thought he might vomit if he couldn't subdue this monstrous tide of anger. No, not anger. When he faced it, he felt fear. Realizing that behind the rage and anger lay fear catapulted him back into even more rage.

Suzanne sat in the back seat holding a sobbing Lulu as Julius made a vicious U-turn and headed back to the apartment. She was surprised by the feelings that had come to the surface. Sandy had come looking for her. No one else had seemed to care where she had gone. She had been allowed to disappear, and that made her feel so small, like a good wind might come and blow her away. She had given herself to Julius as he had demanded, and that had driven the emptiness and loneliness of her old life away, but seeing Sandy's worried face had been so comforting. She thought it odd that she would even care about anything or anyone in her past life. All that was over, and Julius had promised a new, exciting life full of promise if only she would do exactly as he said. Her subconscious prompted her to see a dark rock in a quarry. She gave into the image for a moment and saw that the rock glowed and stood out from the rest. The more she looked at it, she could feel layers and layers of skin-like tissue fall away. The menacing rock seemed to be hissing at her, tearing off the layers of tissue that clung to her until she stood before it naked and aware.

"Oh," she said and took a breath. Lulu had stopped crying and was staring at her from a corner of the back seat. For that brief moment, Suzanne felt human... again. She thought about the old Civil War diary she and Sandy had found. It had been such fun to read it aloud. She remembered her room and the old dresses and water pitchers she used to keep and fantasize about. And her green doll! The doll she loved but didn't take care of, leaving it outside in the wind and rain so that it fell apart. There had been so many times in the past two years when she had agonized over not having saved the doll—she knew it represented her own life, her own failures. She deserved all the bad things that had happened to her. She felt in her heart that she had not been worth saving, but somebody else felt differently. It was a featherweight drop, but the last layers of tissue came down with a thud. *I wish I could find a way to talk to her, but I'll probably never see her again. And Julius would kill me for sure.* She let the thoughts drift away from her. She couldn't find Sandy again, and it didn't really matter anyway. Better make do with what she was given.

"Hey, honey, let me out here tonight. I can make a killing in this neighborhood." She knew he wouldn't, but she had to try.

"We go by the plan, Suzanne. Aren't you getting ahead of yourself?" He was staring at her in the rearview mirror, calculating. "You don't leave my side, remember, baby? Leaving my side in the wrong way means something very bad."

"I understand. I really do. You never have to worry about me."

"Good, baby." He reached behind and touched her face so

gently, as if to make up for the slaps he had whipped her with just a minute ago.

She warmed up to his touch and purred contentedly like a cat.

Lulu watched and slowly smiled, her eyes locking with Suzanne's.

≼

Paisley Falls had never been the same after the grisly murder of a convicted conman and the abduction of four teenage girls held prisoner and then released by two unknown assailants. The suggestion that the assailants had been Muslim terrorists had been laughed off by the state police who were called in to investigate. That the local police, particularly the town's most trusted servant, Sergeant Dormer, had been booted off the case, was widely debated in hushed circles. Paisley Falls didn't take much to outsiders. It was damned rude, said the patrons of the Loosey Goosey Salon, who had witnessed the showdown between Detective Woodard from the state's finest and its local pride, Sergeant Dormer. Many felt it had been unnecessary to shame him in public. Conversely, the murder of Nadine Hines, a local favorite, at least to the patrons of the Loosey Goosey, was considered a serious crime, because everybody knew who did it and also who covered it up. Since the four teenage girls had not been harmed and their families had been substantially reimbursed for the trauma it caused their children, no harm no foul was the consensus. After all, the con was killed and the children were saved.

End of story.

Or was it?

Dr. Frederick Wilson and his gorgeous, flaunty wife,

Stephanie, had had a very public falling out. Eventually, Stephanie had figured out what everyone in Paisley Falls already knew: That Dr. W was playing house with a minor, admittedly a real loser, but a minor nonetheless. Poor Nadine, the townies whispered, didn't deserve to be labeled a suicide, and a druggy no less. What she wanted out of life was just to be loved. She was a hapless victim of a pariah who felt that he could get away with everything because he had married into the right family. It was Stephanie's family who had paved the way for Frederick to accomplish his medical degree and his residency at Paisley Falls General. Stephanie's father, Roy, a steel magnate who had ties with Saudi Arabian oil, gave his daughter and his new son-in-law everything within his power. If Stephanie wanted to live in Paisley Falls, so be it; Roy saw to it they got the house of their dreams just to get the ball rolling. Generous trust funds for their two adorable children followed suit, but things came to a screeching halt when Roy found out about Nadine. It was early in the game when he did.

Long before Nadine met her end, Roy had had a little talk with his son-in-law. "Stop what you think you're getting away with or I'll cut off your balls" was the gist of their conversation, but Dr. Wilson was in too deep with Nadine, and he had fully explored every fetish he had online and with prostitutes and humans of every age and gender he could find. He was an addict, and he didn't care. It wasn't wrong for him to live out his fantasies, it was his privilege. Frederick deferred to his father-in-law but secretly continued his violent relationship with Nadine. Then Stephanie found out. The town was abuzz with the saga of the red Corvette and the sashayings of the doctor's wife and a gigolo from out of town. Wilson didn't care and considered it tit for tat, until Roy put the squeeze on him again.

"You'll lose your fuckin' job so fast and any chance to get another. You'll never see your children again, and you'll be penniless to boot. I can ruin you in a second, buddy, you know that. Get rid of her!"

But he couldn't.

He wouldn't.

Or at least he wouldn't until he damn well felt like it.

Killing Nadine had been the easy part, but continuing on board at Paisley Falls General had become monotonously unpleasant. In the two years that had passed since Nadine's death and the murder at the cotton mill, things had gotten worse for Dr. Wilson. The ER nurse—that Powell woman—barely spoke to him anymore unless it was necessary. He was shunned at the Loosey Goosey, not that he cared anyway. Stephanie had packed up and left the kids with her parents and traipsed off to Europe in a huff. She'd found out about everything, not only about Nadine, but also about the porn and the black sites that provided his more prurient interests. He'd been satisfying himself by putting plastic bags over his conquests and asphyxiating them almost to the point of death, but he found himself inexplicably off the hot seat after getting rid of Nadine.

After the initial questioning by the state police, there had been a straightforward and unquestioned decision of suicide by overdose. He was pretty sure his father-in-law had bought off the incident, but he'd wondered if the police had just become so distracted by the murder and the abductions at the cotton mill that they'd forgotten. After all, Nadine had been part of that haul with the four other teenage girls. She was the only one who had managed to escape; he had to hand it to her, she was ingenious. Too bad she had become such a bore.

It annoyed him somewhere in the farthest part of his

well-structured cognitive faculties that he wasn't satisfied enough from his sexual conquests. He was left hungry, always wanting more, probably the price to be paid for going after what most people only dreamed of. He'd had to go underground in this miserable small town, placating himself by watching snuff movies where sluts got bashed in by baseball bats. He laughed as he remembered their bewildered faces as the guys in their supposed porno films surprised them by yelling "strike one" and then bashing in their heads. That was followed by "ball one," which was straight up the ass, and "strike two," but by then they were already unconscious with blood flowing everywhere. By "strike three," they were dead and the thrill was over.

The handsome Dr. Wilson, whose looks had taken on a ghostly pallor, walked the streets of Paisley Falls late at night, as was his custom after a night shift, brooding over the thoughts that swirled frantically inside his curdling brain. It was really no surprise at all that he found himself turning a familiar corner into a dark alley one night and coming face to face with two men brandishing knives. It wasn't much of an effort on their part to take him down, with one holding him and the other administering kicks and punches. When he was subdued enough by the beating, the older of the two raised his knife and plunged it deeply into the heart of the astonished Dr. Wilson.

"That's for my daughter, you motherfucker!"

"This one's for my sister, you bastard!" the other one said. "May you live in hell forever!"

They disappeared into the darkness, leaving the lifeless body of a bewildered soul, eyes open, beckoning in the light of a new life.

CHAPTER FIVE

WHILE SERGEANT DORMER had been sitting it out at LJ's in Leverton, he got a call from his old pal Sid on the force back home in Paisley Falls.

"Guess who just got knocked off?"

"God, it could be anybody back there; it wouldn't surprise me anymore."

"Wilson just bit the dust. Couldn't have happened to a nicer guy."

"They get the perp?"

"Not yet, nobody's in a hurry. They found him in an alley. The usual walk home, several stab wounds, beat up first. Looks like it coulda been two guys. Nobody saw nothin'."

"Good old-fashioned revenge. Nothing like karma to take care of the bad guys."

"How you holdin' up? Dolores and the kids all right? Paisley Falls misses you, bro."

"Yeah, I miss them too. Keep me briefed on the Wilson thing, will ya? Give my love to Doris."

Dormer needed to think. He had so wanted to pin the Nadine Hines murder on Wilson. Everybody knew he had done it. If he went back now, he could track down Wilson's assailants. Find the motive for such a killing, not that he didn't already suspect it. Everyone knew that Wilson lived a perverted life using whatever and whomever he could for his own selfish pleasure.

Dormer knew, however, that there was a lot more going on in Paisley Falls than just the murder of the town sicko. Wilson had been involved in something that the state police had been trying to cover up for over two years now. His mind kept going over and over the murder of that conman two years ago at the plant. He knew Julius had been his partner. He also knew that they had been kidnapping girls for their trafficking business. Dormer knew there had been trafficking concerns in Paisley Falls, particularly in the hotels and big-box warehouse chains. Forced laborers from Honduras had flooded the underground labor force, and he had worked to get it cleaned up, but everywhere he started digging he only scratched the surface.

He knew everyone thought he was crazy to go rogue. Alone you were anybody's handicap, a thought that came to him just a moment too late, as he had gotten out of the car to relieve himself when LJ and Eddie came up behind the car and bopped him one on the head with Junkyard Eddie's handy tire iron.

When he came to, the boys had him hog-tied, bound, and gagged. He cursed himself for having been so careless; he was getting sloppy. He was tired and it was beginning to show.

"And you an officer of the law trespassing on other people's property. Well, shame on you!"

Junkyard Eddie was having a ball waving the Sergeant's wallet and ID in front of him.

Andy Dormer knew that he'd been had. His head was bleeding from where they'd hit him. He felt like an idiot for letting himself be caught.

"Well, I've been wanting to talk to you, Little John… or LJ. Which is it?"

LJ stood quietly in the back of the room, in no mood for humor. He knew his connections with Julius were what brought this out-of-town copper to the rural community of Leverton. He figured the fuzz was from Paisley Falls. In the two years after he had hooked up with Julius, he had heard plenty about the death of Julius's partner, Dino, and the thwarted kidnapping of the teenage girls. He'd also wondered why no one from Suzanne's family had filed a missing person's report or tried to find her. Not that he cared, but he wondered just the same. His mind started to put some of the pieces of the puzzle together, all of which might begin to explain this guy's presence on his property.

"I think you're barking up the wrong tree, mister. What the hell are you doing here? What gives you the right to sit up here on my property?"

"I think you know why I'm here, LJ. If you would untie me, we might be better able to communicate."

"I. Said. Tell. Me. Why. You. Are. Here."

"Does the name Suzanne DeMarco mean anything to you?"

LJ thought to himself, *Do I need a lawyer?*

"Look," said Dormer. "I'm not on the force anymore. I'm just a private dick looking for a lost girl. You're not in any trouble. I'm not going to arrest you. I just want to talk. Understood?"

LJ knew better, but he was sick of Julius's game. If he could turn on Julius, maybe all of what he had done would be lost in the shuffle. Be nice to this guy and gain some points.

"Okay, Eddie, lets untie him. Just so you know, we've got your gun and your wallet, and we know you're an ex-cop."

Dormer rubbed his aching arms in relief when the plastic ties were loosened. He felt all of his fifty-seven years right at the moment. His head was throbbing; he put his hands up to the wound that was oozing blood on the back of his head.

He started in.

"Two years ago, and yes I was on the police force as a sergeant, several things occurred in Paisley Falls that involved Julius Conaforte, Suzanne DeMarco, and Dino Hu. Do any of those names mean anything to you?" Of course, Dormer knew they did, but he had to ask.

"How much do you know about Julius?" asked LJ.

"Enough to put him away for quite a long time," said Dormer.

"Suzanne passed through here about two years ago. She and Julius were on their way to LA."

Junkyard Eddie gave a knowing little laugh that was not lost on Dormer, who couldn't help but notice the nervous tick that took over Eddie's face.

"Eddie's Dump'n Depot, right?" Dormer turned to Eddie to verify what he already knew was true.

"I think I'd better get back to the yard. Screwball needs dinner right about now."

"You didn't happen to spot a blue Camaro in the yard around two years ago by chance."

"Can't remember that far back."

"I've traced the car to here, boys. If you help me, I can assure you I can help you." With that, Dormer stood up to shake himself off.

"How about a shot of whiskey all around?" LJ asked.

Julius must have been having a feeling in his bones that his network was about to come busting wide open. The nightmares with Bluepage.com seemed to have no end. The Federal

Communications Act had started interfering with who could post what on Bluepage. All of a sudden, he was being fined for what the shit asses were printing, albeit for his use. He claimed he was only an innocent bystander and insisted that he was not part of any of these nefarious ads. The fact that they were calling his number for sex referrals, however, was screwing him up royally. Not only that, but the Port of Long Beach and the port truck firms that hired the truckers he had depended on two years ago to transport his human cargo were having legal battles with each other going back over two years when he was still in business with Dino. The truckers were being interviewed about the losses they incurred while listed as independent contractors yet having to defer to the truck firms' schedules and regulations. Interviews brought up all kinds of back stories about what cargo was shipped where. Dangerous stuff!

And how he missed Dino!

Many, many times he had wondered what exactly had happened in the little shit town of Paisley Falls to screw up their schemes so royally. So Dino and he were in somebody else's territory, so what? Why not a slap on the wrist and get out of town. Why such a grisly murder and the whole Muslim show?

He'd kept an eye on the proceedings after the murder, making sure he stayed out of the picture. He was grateful but bewildered by the hush up. It seemed to have gotten thrown under the rug by the state fuzz—lucky for him, but still uncanny. Dino's people hadn't forgotten about him either. He felt their presence hanging over his head. He felt like he was walking on eggshells with what should have been a steady multi-million-dollar business. As for LJ, he didn't trust him at all. He was disappearing for too long a period of time and coming up empty. Making excuses. And now, to top everything off, this thing with Suzanne and her stupid friend, which could mean big trouble. He knew that small-time sergeant—what was his name? Dormer!—had a jones for finding Suzanne. Why? Even her own parents could not have cared less about her.

As he drove the girls back to their apartment, he vowed to change things, do things differently. He needed to start looking ahead and looking out for himself. *Himself*, he savored that word. *What a nice word*, he thought. A nice comforting secure feeling assuaged his troubled nerves. The only thing that mattered was *himself*.

৵

"Change of plans, girls," he said when they had gotten back to the apartment. "You're not going out tonight. We're leaving. Get moving. Pack now."

The two girls scurried up the steps of the temporary home they had in LA. Not being told where they were going was usual for them. They tossed the few garments they had into cheap weekend bags, and, as if by rote, they were done in five minutes flat.

"Move your asses downstairs. This is because of that idiot friend of yours, Suzanne. Lulu, lock that door of yours."

Lulu quickly brought up the padlock to the door that barricaded it from the outside. The other doors each had sliding locks that closed the girls inside until they had performed their duties, but Julius wanted to make sure no one had entry to Lulu's room. LJ was due back with a shipment of new girls to be trained. Julius didn't want anyone learning something they shouldn't. The three of them raced out to the car parked out back in an alley. Julius shoved the girls inside, glancing around quickly before getting in and speeding off.

What he didn't know was that he had an unknown visitor in the alley. Sandy was lucky that she hadn't been seen. She hadn't expected them back so quickly. As soon as she had been dropped off, she had scurried back to where she thought the apartment was, in order to glean any information she could about what kind of a setup they had and maybe contact a neighbor for information.

The car had barreled into the alley, and Julius, Suzanne, and the other girl had hurried out, with Julius pushing them to go faster. They disappeared into the apartment. Sandy just had time enough to duck behind a garbage can, hoping she hadn't been seen. She thought the Chinese girl had looked in her direction, but she couldn't be sure. She hoped that the girl was a friend and wouldn't turn her in. As she sheltered there wondering what to do next, she saw the three of them appear with luggage that was quickly flung into the trunk of the van. Then they were off again. This time, the Chinese girl clearly turned around from the back seat and gazed in her direction.

Well, I can't follow them on foot, she thought. *At least now I've got the license plate number and make of the car.*

She had no idea how the information could be of use to her, since she couldn't follow the car, but she hoped that her newfound friend, the cute guy that had tried to flag down Julius's car, would feel like helping her. She fished around in her purse and pulled out the card that he'd given her. "David Hargrove," it said. *Nice name,* she thought, hoping that he was as reliable as he seemed. She walked to the corner where the 7-Eleven was to wait for the next bus. As she stood there, she could see the Iranian clerk staring at her through the store window. Laughing to herself, she thought, *He probably thinks I'm a hooker.*

Lulu and Suzanne were quiet in the back seat as Julius sped through the streets of LA trying to get to the freeway before rush hour. They both knew the next place was scheduled to be a stop in Sacramento, but they usually traveled late at night when traffic was lighter. After a quick stop at an ATM to make a cash deposit, they were on their way. Julius was nervous about the deposit, usually made late at night to avoid being seen or attract attention. Because of the change in plans, he had no choice. He said nothing more to the girls as he went about his business, but when he was out of the car making the deposit, Lulu whispered to Suzanne that she had seen her friend in the alley as they drove off.

"Really?"

Maybe this was the start of some kind of miracle that would change her, thought Suzanne. For such a long time she had felt no hope. It had become easier to live without it. So many times she had simply shut down any of her wishes or desires just in order to survive. What she thought or wanted didn't matter anymore. She was an object whose directive was to blindly obey. Objects worked, performing whatever they were programed to do, like the elephant object she had been trained to be. Her obedience had allowed her to graduate. No chains were binding, no strings were attached, and she was free. It's just that the freedom weighed her down so much that she was drowning from the pressure of it.

Lulu whispered again in her ear just as Julius was walking back to the car. "We'll talk again tonight when I can escape from my room. I can help you find your friend."

In the two months that Lulu had been on board, she had talked to no one. Julius had kept her locked up most of the time, and Suzanne had seldom run into her, except for that night in the San Francisco drop when her door had been open and she had offered to fix the wounds on Suzanne's knees after the usual punishment for breaking the rules. He had screamed at them not to talk to each other. Still, Suzanne had wondered about the unusual treatment that Lulu was being given. Maybe tonight they would have a chance to talk.

They both fell asleep after a while, hungry and exhausted by all the excitement and danger that the day had brought.

CHAPTER SIX

THEY DIDN'T GET to Sacramento until six a.m. The streets were dark and empty, and the shack they had here wasn't much more than a pit stop. Here, girls were bused by van into unsuspecting neighborhoods, and johns were brought to a designated house. The neighborhoods were neat and tidy, and everything was run well under the official radar of police and neighbors. Since it was already six a.m., it was too late for a setup with johns. He could put the girls out on the street, but it looked dead out there, so he gave them the night off. Besides, he was exhausted and so tired lately. He simply didn't want to be bothered with anything. After making sure they were securely locked in, he disappeared into his own room and buried himself under a pile of dirty sheets and worn blankets.

"Lights out and shut the fuck up," he shouted from his bedroom.

Lulu emerged on tiptoe from her bedroom. She had somehow managed to slide the outside lock from inside her door, nudging it slowly with a paper clip till it glided open. Once carefully across the hall, she slid open Suzanne's lock and motioned for Suzanne to leave her room and come join her. She held her finger silently to her lips as she gestured that Suzanne follow. Once inside the tiny room, she soundlessly pushed aside a small dresser that hid a makeshift hole in the wall, revealing an entrance to a boarded-up closet. They both crawled inside the dark hole that Lulu had managed to light with a candle. Here, Suzanne sat incredulously as Lulu began the story of her life and how she had come to be a part of Julius's stable.

Lulu had been born in the tiny fishing village of Yumingzui in the eastern province of Shandong, China. The little village supported itself by harvesting fish, sea cucumbers, and abalone, but fell victim to pollution, overfishing, and rising sea temperatures brought on by global warming. As her impoverished family struggled to pay bills, barely subsisting on what little food they had, Lulu was prostituted at the age of two in nearby wealthier provinces, not because her parents didn't love her, but because they had no food. Reluctantly, her father took her around to local meeting houses, and she was passed around in basements where men gathered for whiskey and cigars. He begged them, as he sold her, not to hurt her but only to feel and kiss her private parts. Even as he turned to leave, he could only pray that they not harm her too much. By the time she was four, she had experienced everything there was to know about sex. She developed an aversion to any yogurt or milk products, because it reminded her of semen. A charity group had rescued her by the age of five, and she was unable to speak at all until she was ten years old. Traumatized by any contact with men, she was kept in a quiet room attended by female nurses who fed and comforted her.

Her grandmother, who she adored but knew only when she would be occasionally returned, found her in this halfway house and wanted her to come back to the family, but she became violent at the thought of leaving the only home she had ever known.

She also feared her father would push her back into the same nightmare. Her father, however, had since committed suicide in disgrace, and the family was once again left in a perilous state. Her grandmother assured her all was safe for her return, and she hesitantly reunited with her family.

Her mother, Yansee, cried with joy upon seeing her again, and for a while all was good. One night, a man came to the house promising her brother and uncle huge amounts of money to fish on his great yacht. The uncle and brother agreed to sign on as fishermen, but once on voyage, they became indentured servants forced into slave labor.

Strange men came to the house and took the unprotected women away. They were put on cargo ships with other immigrants and shipped to America, courtesy of Dino Hu and Julius Conaforte. Finally arriving in the Port of Long Beach two years ago, Lulu's mother and grandmother were found dead in the ship's galley and tossed overboard. Lulu survived and ended up a by-product of Julius's slave trade. At first, she was forced to work in hotels as a maid by day and hooker by night for the hotel's clients. After Dino's murder and the relationship with the Hu family fell through, Julius and LJ began their lucrative business using the 320C Cessna Skyknight as their new motif for business. Lulu became part of Julius's stable and was also used for special projects.

As Suzanne sat stunned, listening to Lulu's story, she couldn't help but notice how innocent Lulu looked. Her beautiful and unblemished skin glowed in the candlelight, and her eyes were feverishly brilliant. She was so childlike, mused Suzanne, who realized that both of their childhoods had been ripped away from them. She thought there couldn't be anyone who had seen a more sordid side of humanity than herself, until she heard

Lulu's story. For the first time in a very long time, Suzanne felt tears streaming down her cheeks—tears that came not from her own pain and suffering, but ones that flowed for someone else's utter sorrow and misery.

"I can help you find your friend," Lulu said as though she were transitioning from one grocery list to the next. "Julius sets me free at some times to go into hotels and warehouses to make sure that the 'help' are doing all that they should."

"Why, Lulu, would he trust you not to run?"

Knowing Julius as Suzanne had experienced him, the last thing he would ever do was let somebody go free to do anything. *Maybe she's had the elephant training technique,* she thought. But no, Lulu's wounds seemed inflicted way before she met Julius.

"Because my brother and my uncle are what is called indentured servants," continued Lulu. "Julius told me they will be killed, and their bodies will be thrown overboard to the sharks if I ever disobey him. That is why I am given certain tasks and certain privileges."

Suzanne had never thought of stepping out of bounds. She had been programmed to operate solely within the rules that had been defined by Julius. Exceeding the limits set by him were dangerous waters to her. She marveled at Lulu's courage; maybe she hadn't been as severely instructed as Suzanne. *No,* thought Suzanne, *she was pushed beyond her limits to come out on the other side of survival.*

"How can you do it, Lulu?"

"Give me your parent's phone number. I can sneak away from the hotel to at least make a phone call."

"Oh," laughed Suzanne. "I don't think my parents care anything about what's going on with me. You'll probably scare them off. The most you'll get from them is 'well, if you're telling the truth, have Suzanne call us'."

Lulu wasn't the least bit phased by this, but she understood the cynicism. "Your friend's phone number? Perhaps I should have asked for this first."

"Lulu, it won't make any difference."

"You're not going to say something like 'nobody cares about me' are you?"

"No. I think Sandy cares about me as much as anybody ever has!" shouted Suzanne.

Lulu raised her hands to quiet her, lest Julius hear them and find the hidden location.

"But it's not enough," Suzanne whispered. "I'm here now. This is reality." Startled by a sound, Suzanne wanted to crawl out of the dark hole that Lulu had created.

"It's just the wind," cooed Lulu.

There was nothing Suzanne feared more than being discovered by Julius in this newly found hiding place. Gathering herself together, she left the little hole in the closet and returned to her quarters, resolutely closing the door on any further conversation. After a while, Lulu crept out of her room to fasten the lock on Suzanne's door. Then she used the paper clip she had used to open her own lock to secure her door again... to keep the rats out.

Rhonda was at her wit's end with her husband. Ever since Suzanne's friend Sandy had meddled with Evan's state of mind regarding their older daughter, she hadn't been able to calm him down. Now he was constantly unnerved and depressed—as if he hadn't been that way already. *Why does he constantly have to*

bring her up? she wondered. The girl had been headstrong and determined to go her own way; far be it from her or Evan to stop her. Anyway, now she was eighteen and of no concern to them. Rhonda knew she sounded like a heartless old hag, but she didn't care; besides, she put on a concerned and sorrowful face whenever needed. Underneath it all, she knew that she fooled no one and did very little to hide her indifference. A few of her friends had called, worried about what had happened, but she shined them on. Surprisingly, Bethy, her younger daughter, had said very little about Suzanne's disappearance. She quietly resumed her presence as the silent younger sibling, neither trying to fill the gap that Suzanne's absence had created or reinventing a new place for herself.

Bethy seldom visited her father in the convalescent home and barely nodded to her mother's comings and goings. She increasingly spent more time at the mall wandering in the big empty spaces created by store closings. She would stand in front of each empty storefront and try to remember what it had been. Since so many of the stores had moved and left directions to new locations, it was easy to remember what they were. Cindy's Clothes had been the place she had first shopped for school with her mom, and Happy Nails was the shop where the owner's daughter had been abducted. The owner and her family had sold the place and moved away, but now the shop stood empty, the new owners setting up somewhere else. She remembered all the publicity that had happened about that.

The little girl, Kim Su, had never recovered from being abducted and stuck in a cage without any clothes. Bethy wondered what it would be like to be put in a cage without any clothes. *I guess it would be like being an animal at the zoo*, she thought. The whole town had been upset about the murder of a criminal and the abductions. *Abduction.* What a funny word. Everybody in town had worried about their children. Bethy had wondered about her older sister and why her mother tried to shut her up whenever she asked about Suzanne. She had been abducted like the others, but it was something her mother didn't want to talk about and definitely something her father couldn't even face.

She turned her thoughts back to the mall. It was rumored that the mall would officially close in two years and become office spaces. Bethy looked at the play horses and ponies that she used to climb up to ride on in the children's area. It was a little wonderland where all the kids played. It was like the Fantasyland that her older sister had made for her. She didn't want it to end. She danced around the tiny kiddie park, singing to no one, "I don't want Fantasyland to stop. Keep going and going and going please!"

The three of them sat around LJ's kitchen table, belting down shots of Jack Daniels. Dormer was nursing his, not wanting to lose focus on his prime objective. There was no love lost for LJ or Eddie, but he focused on the fact that their common enemy was Julius. The enemy of my enemy is my friend, so the saying goes. LJ sat a little apart from the cop turned private eye, watching every move Dormer made. He was cautiously optimistic about the outcome of this meeting, and Junkyard Eddie was just getting drunk.

"How come a cop like you, so far from home, comes to stake out a place for one girl who passed through here over two years ago?" LJ looked at Dormer like he thought he was crazy, but he was curious. "How you makin' money? Don't you have a family? Is the girl a relation?"

"I'm glad you're asking, LJ. It shows you have some backbone."

"How so?"

"I think that underneath that tough exterior you might care about what happens to that girl."

"Well, you think wrong, mister. I was the first one to fuck her right over there on that couch behind you."

Dormer wanted to get up and punch his face into a pulp, but he sat tight, his eyes the only thing that betrayed his rage. "Where is she now, LJ?"

"Well, she sure ain't in the back of that Camaro no more, that's for sure," Eddie interjected.

"Shut up, Eddie. Maybe you should go back to the junkyard and tend to business."

"Eddie, what became of that Camaro? Still there in the yard or broken up for parts?"

Eddie was teetering on his feet, and he glanced uncertainly from Dormer to LJ. "Well, I-I better be getting back."

"Dormer, you know what happened to that car."

"I just want Julius, LJ. The rest of it isn't necessary, unless you don't come clean with me. Then all of it gets dug up, and you and Eddie here are looking at some heavy-duty jail time. Now, let's start at the beginning and don't leave anything out."

"Hello, Mr. Hargrove, David? I met you the other day at the Seven-Eleven? Remember me? You know, the cell phone and my friend?"

"Sandy, I sure do. Where are you?"

"Oh, kinda near that Seven-Eleven again. Ha, ha."

"Still waiting for your friend to return? That might take a while."

"Well, yeah, I guess. I'm a little worried about her. I'd like to ask your advice about something."

"Ask away, Sandy."

"I have the license plate number on that car—"

"Really? There was no time to write anything down."

"Uh… well, I went back to where I thought they lived and—"

"Thought? I thought you *knew* where they lived. And why do you need to get a license plate number? Is your friend in danger?"

"I think so. Yes, definitely, she's in a lot of danger."

"Then you should call the police, Sandy, and give them the license plate number."

"I'm afraid of doing that."

"Why?"

"I think the person she's with will kill her. I think she's in way over her head. She may not want to leave him, and he in turn might want to kill me."

"I think you're in a lot of trouble, Sandy. Playing Nancy Drew is harder than you realize."

"Oh, David, I know." Sandy sobbed. "Can you help me please?"

"I'll meet you, even take you to dinner, but I'm not sure I can help you at all."

They met at a local diner near David's place. Turned out he lived nearby the 7-Eleven.

"That's where I go to get my morning fix," he said, laughing.

Sandy blurted out the whole story, telling David everything right from the beginning. How they'd been best friends in high school and the sudden appearance of a stranger from out of town who started showing up around school seemingly infatuated with Suzanne. Then there were the unbelievable stories of four underage girls locked up in cages naked at a closed-down cotton mill and the gruesome murder of a gangland criminal. This all coincided with the disappearance of Suzanne and the dismissal of it by her mother followed by her father's heart attack.

"What a mess. You must have been traumatized by all of this."

"I guess I was. Nothing like this had ever happened in tame little Paisley Falls."

"So you immediately flew into action to save your friend." David was looking at her intently. His eyes were full of concern and curiosity. "What did the police do?" he asked.

"Oh, that's another whole story." Sandy was off again, explaining the whole jumble of events that left the local police out of the picture. "The state police took over, David! They kicked Sergeant Dormer off the case, and nothing got solved after that. The murder at the plant is still a cold case, and the four teenage girls who were never physically harmed are back with their parents like nothing was ever wrong. And Mrs. DeMarco! She's a trip, really. It's like, well, Suzanne is just a runaway; she'll come back when she's ready—or not!"

"What about Suzanne's father?"

"Mr. DeMarco is… well… he's frail. He's in a convalescent home right now. He had a bad heart attack after Suzanne left—or was kidnapped. I don't know anymore." She trailed off, lost in her own thoughts, trying to figure out if she was making any sense at all.

"How old are you, Sandy?"

His question startled her. "Eighteen, why?"

"This is an awful lot to take on single-handedly. Where are you staying? How do you get around in LA without a car? What do your parents think about you taking off like this? Why is it you seem to be risking your life to save your friend? Isn't this a police matter?"

"Whew, that's a lot of questions. You're not a cop, are you?" Sandy knew better, but no one had ever made her face the reality of what she was doing so much. "Okay," she stammered. "I'm staying with an aunt who lives in LA. I've told my parents I'm trying to get into a business college."

"So the staying with the aunt is the true part," David replied, laughing, "and the trying to get into a business college is the false part. Right?"

They both laughed at this, but David was serious.

"Why?" he said.

"She's my friend. I care about what happens to her."

"The danger, Sandy, is that you risk losing your life. Do you have any idea what you're up against? Human trafficking. Yes, I do think your friend has been kidnapped and is now a sex slave. It's one of the most flourishing crimes in the world right now. You are up against some very dangerous people that wouldn't hesitate in a second to take you right out. The sex trade is big, big business in this country. Hell, it's taken over the drug trade. Drugs you sell once, bodies you can sell over and over. There's so much money to be made! Christ it's amazing that you haven't been abducted yourself. I suppose you started by canvasing the streets of Hollywood and talking to girls in the trade. Do you have any idea how dangerous that is?"

"Well, I guess I hit a nerve. What makes you so sure you have all the right answers?"

"Oh, come on, look around you at the world we live in right now. Every political and social movement has another movement inside it arguing for its right to not exist. Gun laws are supposed to protect people's right to bear arms, but within that concept is the actual pillaging of people by maniacs who are able to purchase firearms and use them to kill innocent victims just for a lark. Free speech is our constitutional right, yet Bluepage can print any kind of garbage they want to appeal to any prurient assholes who go for it, and millions—and I mean millions—of underage children are bought and sold to do their bidding every single day.

"I'm a printer. Sandy. Do you know how many missing-children flyers I've done or brochures I've printed about human trafficking? Have you ever heard of the Soroptimists or N2 Gives? They're combating a worldwide problem and something that exists in all fifty states here. It's a one-hundred-fifty-billion-dollar-a-year industry.

"I'm sorry, I don't mean to lecture you or sound like your parents, but the innocence in this world that is plundered and destroyed for someone's sexual fantasy sickens me. It's not just bodies that are sold, Sandy, its human souls. After the pleasure of their sexual perversion, the utter destruction of their victim's soul is what they crave the most, and then, like the end of any addiction, the thrill is gone and on to the next."

"David?"

"Sorry, Sandy, it's just—"

"I know... I think you're wonderful. We can do this. Together. I need you. Will you help me?"

CHAPTER SEVEN

JULIUS WOKE LULU up first. One of the local hotels here was
having trouble with a group of Honduran workers who were
refusing to work twenty-four-hour shifts. The hotel manage-
ment had preferred to turn a blind eye to the workers they hired
through Julius's company, Make a Bed Inc., laughingly created
by Julius and LJ one night when they thought of all the unmade
beds their hookers had slept in. "How many do you think we
have, LJ?" Julius asked, laughing.

"All the johns' beds in America, Jules!" said LJ.

All the Restful Sleep Hotel chain wanted, it told Julius, was a
staff that was available 24/7. Each hotel employee hired through
Make a Bed Inc. was expected to clean, make up, stock, and
refurbish all the hotel's fifty rooms as needed for each twenty-
four-hour period. They were expected to be on duty for fifteen
hours a day and on call for the nine hours they were off duty. On
call could mean pretty much anything from cleaning up vomit at
three a.m. to giving blow jobs to customers requesting "a visit."
Tips were at the discretion of the buyer.

Julius used two Honduran women for the maid's job and
one man, an eighty-five-year-old Honduran, for the day/night

cleanup job. He was the father of one of the two women who had to hook it at night to pay for their servitude. His daughter was older but had severe back problems that prevented her from doing anything extraneous, so a fifteen-year-old, his granddaughter, did most of the cleaning all day long and the sex slave work all night long. They had been an easy pick up at the Mexican border.

Honduran immigrants were being denied access to the United States, and LJ, in one of his Cessna flights, had an easy pick from the hordes of people who were willing to do anything to get into the US. The old man had been slacking off on his duties, and the hotel had put several calls into Julius to *fix* the situation. What annoyed Julius the most was that they expected him to fix *everything*. Couldn't they police this crew on their own? So, he and Lulu got off to an early start as this needed to be addressed ASAP.

Suzanne knew the minute they were gone. With a shock, she realized that when she left Lulu's room last night, she hadn't been able to close the sliding lock on her door. She hadn't even paid attention to that. If Julius saw it, there would be hell to pay. She crept out of bed and tried to open the door, but it was locked. Lulu must have done it either this morning when she left or last night after Suzanne had stormed out. If Julius had seen it unlocked, she wouldn't still be lying in bed; she'd probably be crawling around on a bed of tacks crying her eyes out.

She thought about Lulu's story last night and couldn't get over how powerful it was. Lulu had more courage than anyone she had ever met. Suzanne felt so cowardly next to Lulu. She acknowledged that her own story was weak and sad, filled with self-remorse. A part of her disavowed all that she had become, even though Julius praised her for becoming so good at selling and using her body. There were also many perks, which all centered on pleasing Julius, however. When she had time to think is when she felt the emptiness.

In the beginning, when she'd been let out of the cage and put into her first room with a bed, she thought she'd died and gone to heaven. It was just a cot really, she recalled, not an actual bed, but it was so nice not to be sleeping on that jagged floor with a rag for a blanket and dog dishes for plates and, worse, no clothes. There was nothing at all to shield her from Julius, and that had been his plan. She knew better than to believe anything else. It was all a plan to change her into what he wanted her to become, and when she was finally changed, molded really into the selling tool that he desired, how he showered love on her. It had felt so good to finally be approved of, to be considered special.

She had begun to need more drugs to fulfill her duties. They felt so good and empowering, allowing her to do more, become more than she ever knew herself capable of being. But on free times like this, lying in her bed in a Sacramento pit stop, the nagging thought that this was all wrong spread throughout her mind and body like a plague. *How can I get out of this?* She let her mind think the thought: *I'm in a trap and have no one to turn to.* Maybe if she prayed hard enough, her captor would just let her go out of the goodness of his heart. She laughed at that, knowing even before she thought it that it was an empty joke. Vaguely, she remembered her parents. Her mother, she knew, could not care less about her whereabouts. Actually, she knew Rhonda cared, albeit guiltily, about her physical wellbeing, but the fact that she was out of her life must be a great relief for her mother—more time to be with the only one she cared about: her husband.

Dad… she let the memory of him fill her mind. What had become of her father? She knew he loved her, if only because he treated her as an extension of himself. Still, why wasn't he searching for her? The only glimmer of hope was seeing Sandy. What had made Sandy come all this way to try and find her? Why had she cared so much when her own family cared so little? Her thoughts were interrupted by a loud banging on the door and the slashing zing of the lock being slid back.

"Enough sleeping there, sleeping beauty. Up and at 'em."

"LJ? Where have you been?"

"Pack a bag, Suzie Q. I'm getting you outta here."

LJ told Dormer almost everything about his current relationship with Julius. He briefly mentioned their previous collaboration with drug smuggling but left out the fact that he was currently involved in a human smuggling partnership with Jules. He had been unpleasantly surprised when Julius showed up on his doorstep two years ago with a girl in his trunk. He hadn't wanted to get involved with the bastard again, because he never really trusted him and knew that any partnership that involved money would become a nightmare, but Julius was begging. He offered a huge amount of money to fly the two of them back to LA.

"How much money?" asked Dormer.

"A hundred grand."

"Really?" said Eddie. "You never told me you got that much. All you gave me was a grand!"

"Sounds like you got screwed, Eddie," said Dormer.

"Well ya, if I'm gonna be prosecuted for grinding up a car that I didn't even know was part of a crime scene."

Dormer and LJ each looked at Eddie like they wanted to get up and punch his face, each for his own reason: LJ, so he'd just shut up, and Dormer because he was such a goddamned liar. Shifting his gaze back to LJ, Dormer continued his questions.

"So, you're no longer involved with Julius? It was just a one-time thing?"

"You tell me," said LJ. "Apparently, you've been tracking me for quite a while. Why?"

"I traced the Camaro to here. One of the local farmers called nine-one-one and reported a fight between a young girl and a man in some pasture. I followed the nine-one-one call to the farmer's house, hoping to find him or some clues, but he had since passed away, and the only thing his wife could do was show me the field where the alleged fight took place. Looking around the area, I spotted a piece of material. It was a torn piece of clothing, which I had checked for DNA, and, sure enough, I think you know who that torn piece of blouse belonged to. Leverton was the next town down the pike, and Julius had stopped at the local gas station to ask directions. Bingo! That led me to you!"

LJ and Eddie looked at the cop turned private eye like there was no place else to hide. Eddie protested again that he didn't have any idea that he was committing a crime and didn't want to be considered an accomplice. Dormer assured him that he was.

LJ said nothing but looked long and hard at Dormer. Then he finally said, "I've got your gun and your wallet. Eddie here could make your car go away real fast."

"Now just a minute," said Eddie, "I'm not getting in any more of your trouble. No way."

"People back in Paisley Falls know where I am, what I'm doing."

"Really? Must make your wife and kids real happy. Bet the state police would love to get you out of their hair too. Shut up, Eddie, you're already in way over your head. Look, Dormer, I know where she is. I know where to find Julius. What do I get in return?"

"I don't turn you in to the state police. I forget we ever met. I don't buy it that you're not currently in some kind of business with him, because you're seldom here. I feel sorry for your dog, because Eddie here doesn't come around much. I think you're a thief and a coward and a slime ball to have taken advantage of that underage girl. I could have you prosecuted right now," Dormer said, "but I won't if you give me the whereabouts of Suzanne and Julius."

"Deal," said LJ. "But tell me one thing, why is it so important for you to find her?"

"I don't know if someone like you would ever understand. I want the world to be safe again. If I can set something right one case at a time, then I will have done something good. We live in a disorderly universe. I want to change people's behavior. That girl deserves something better than what evil bums like Julius are offering. My own girls are the reason I'm out here busting my ass. I'd give my life for them to always have a safe haven and feel loved."

Dormer was surprised at his own show of emotion. He knew he was tired physically but even more fatigued by the internal fight that ate at him. Somebody had to stand up for good, and it was always a struggle against the insurmountable greed and evil in the world. His wife had often chastised him for taking on so much. Why, she wondered, did he think it was his personal duty to save the whole world?

As if on some fateful cue, his cell phone rang. Dormer answered it. When he heard what was said, he paled. "All right, I'm coming." He looked up, dazed by what he had just heard, and against his better judgement said, "My youngest daughter is missing. They can't find her."

This was becoming a day of surprises for Suzanne.

"What? Julius will kill you, LJ!"

"That's not for you to worry about. Let's get going. Where is Julius, by the way?

"Out with that Chinese girl, Lulu. What exactly does she do, LJ?"

"Oh, she ah… tends to another side of the business."

Suzanne played innocent, not wanting to divulge the fact that Lulu had revealed her life's story last night in a secret meeting. LJ would tell Julius, no question about it.

She had gotten over her fear of LJ. That fifteen-year-old girl who had gotten raped in his cottage two years ago after nearly being beaten to death and stuffed into the trunk of a car wasn't fazed by much now. She leaned back in the single bed and spread her legs provocatively.

"Want a freebie? I guess Julius wouldn't mind." She knew she didn't care anyway.

"Uh no… I think I'll take a raincheck. Let's get moving. How long ago did Julius and Lulu leave?"

Suzanne had never seen LJ so nervous before. She knew Julius was having arguments with LJ. The walls were paper thin, and she often heard Julius cussing him out over the phone. LJ hadn't been around much, and the internet business with Bluepage was backfiring, not enough girls to safely fill the quota of an ever-expanding business spied on night and day by the cops, the Feds, and conscious-awareness groups all over the world. Julius wasn't taking the time, either, to go out and personally recruit.

Suzanne felt flattered that she was probably the one girl he had spent the most time romancing and personally training. *I am his bottom bitch*, she thought proudly. When Julius sometimes talked with her about the business, he told her of groups like COYOTE (Call Off Your Old Tired Ethics)[4] that was doing great work normalizing prostitution. They represented hookers who were happy doing what they were doing and wanted all the religious bigots to stop telling women what to do with their bodies. Julius was all in favor of happy hookers. The world needed to know that fucking well was a practiced art that would never go out of style. Johns wanted—and needed—a break from the dull and ordinary, overweight wives who were no longer capable of giving good head and whose tired pussies were a turnoff. They really needed pros to take all of the anger and tension they had to release. They were sick of the selfish bitches that bled them for dinners and drinks and then wouldn't put out. The world was growing more complex and dangerous every day. Relieving tension was actually medicinal. Sure, sometimes things turned violent and chicks could be roughed up, but that was part of the job, wasn't it? Suzanne came to understand from these conversations that violent and punitive sex was all part of the job, although she had heard from other girls about International Whores' Day on June 2 of each year that honors sex workers and recognizes their often-exploited working conditions. Her daydreaming mind often went there, thinking that someday she might even be an activist for hooker's rights.

"Well, if I knew more about what he was actually doing, I'd have a better guess of what time I think they'd return," she said, still not moving.

Suzanne had returned to the present reality, and her goal was to find out more from LJ about what was actually going on in

---

4   Ibid

Julius's circuit. All she knew was that the usual smooth and routine comings and goings were getting out of whack. Something was wrong somewhere, and she didn't know if it was Julius or LJ, but she knew that she had to find out.

"Did he go to the hotel with Lulu?" asked LJ.

"I don't know where they went. Is she hooking at the hotel here?"

"The less you know the better, Suz. Now get up and move your ass."

Suzanne knew better than to do anything without Julius's permission. She stayed where she was and was caught off guard when LJ whacked her across the face and pulled her up from the bed.

"Now get dressed, and I mean now. We're going somewhere." He yanked her up and threw her against the wall, his giant fists pulling up her chin tightly against his face. His teeth clenched, and with a churlish smile he whispered, pressing his lips to hers, "I'm giving you a second chance, Suzie Q, now let's get the fuck outta here." His hold on her felt strangling, and she panicked when his grip grew tighter around her neck.

Something about LJ's intensity scared Suzanne, not that she hadn't been around violent men before. Julius had been brutal and trained her well, but she had developed instincts. When to trust and when not to trust had become her mantra. It was her survival instinct that told her that LJ had become a caged animal—driven by what she didn't know. All she did know was that she had better do whatever he said. Obedience kicked in the way it had been indoctrinated in her. Like any subservient beast, she immediately began to dress and pack. As if by rote, she stood ready in a matter of minutes, while LJ said, "Good, good, baby."

They left the tiny apartment without another word. He

pushed her into the Mazda Miata he had left idling in the alley, and they sped off, Suzanne thinking only that the end of her life lay near. As they turned out of the alley, Julius and Lulu pulled up, and Julius, recognizing the familiar car, immediately got out and stood in the alley staring after them, rage and wonder filling his eyes.

CHAPTER EIGHT

DORMER DROVE BACK to Paisley Falls doing ninety miles per hour almost all the way. The winding back roads gave way to the flat monotony of Interstate 5. Even as he made it home in record time, his mind forced him to slow down and take a while longer to digest and embrace what this homecoming was really all about. He kicked himself a million times for displacing his priorities. His family should have been number one. Why had he neglected what was so important? He knew the answer. He and Dolores had raised their two daughters to be intelligent, thoughtful people. They were not girls who did impulsive, stupid things. Suzanne hadn't been so lucky he knew. She had retreated into an imaginary world inside her own room in order to survive with parents who seemed to be unaware or didn't care that she suffered. No wonder she fell for a monster like Julius, someone who had cultivated the art of milking another's insecurities for his own gain. He couldn't stand to see so many young people in the world so wrongly guided, thoughtlessly neglected by absent parents or no parents at all. Families were dying, he knew, and so many were dysfunctional.

He wondered about the rash of killings that were taking

place in schools by kids and the possible connections between the trafficking of teens and all these senseless acts of violence. He thought it meant they were searching for some kind of escape from reality. Opioids were out of control, with more and more deaths each year. He understood that it was pointless for him to think he could fix every kid in the world, but he was obsessed by his need to try. In the process, he had neglected what mattered to him most—his youngest daughter, missing since yesterday.

He knew the statistics: One in three young people is solicited for sex within forty-eight hours of running away or becoming homeless in the US. Had she run away? Impossible, she knew better. Dolores had been hysterical and angry on the phone. If he had been there, she said, none of this would have happened. It had been impossible to get a clear answer from her as to Catherine's whereabouts. She had been writing some kind of term paper on the four girls who went missing in Paisley Falls two years ago. She contacted one of the girls and apparently set up a time to meet her. Dolores had seen the texts and heard the cell phone call. When she questioned her daughter about it, Catherine had grown very defensive and stormed out. "She hasn't been *back*, Andy, and now it's been twenty-four hours."

"All right, I'm coming," he had said in front of LJ and Eddie.

All hell had broken loose with that phone call from home. He couldn't think clearly. All he could do was try to stall for twenty-four hours while he at least got home to find his daughter. God, he hoped nothing had happened to her. His mind raced as he floored the car, driving like a maniac. *Huh*, he thought, *if I were a cop, I'd stop me for endangering the lives of the cows along Interstate Five!*

He had quickly set up the terms of the deal with LJ: twenty-four hours to get Suzanne and Julius to a location where they could easily be apprehended by Dormer. He told LJ he'd call him in a few hours to set the location, and once LJ had secured both Suzanne and Julius, he was to give Dormer a call. If he didn't hear back from LJ within twelve hours, he would contact the state police, who would love to hear about drug and human smuggling with LJ's Cessna 320C Skyknight at the Mexican border.

He left without another word, hoping he hadn't jinxed the deal and have to start all over again. He had been so close. He wasn't sure what he would find or how much support he would get when he returned to Paisley Falls. As he turned off the freeway to greet the little town he had called home for more than forty years, he was met with a roadblock of police car and fire truck sirens. *Well, they can't be heralding my homecoming*, he thought.

Julius was bewildered. As he gazed at LJ's retreating Mazda, he realized that he wasn't exactly snapping into action. There was always a delayed pause now between his senses and correspond-ing action. There had been two figures in the car, which meant Suzanne was with LJ, and that wasn't supposed to happen.

Julius had issued Lulu the whip at the hotel, and she had given all three employees a taste. They wordlessly agreed to any and all of the enforced conditions they were told they must meet, or all of their families would be punished back in Honduras. They shouldn't forget that their benefactors, the people at Make A Bed Inc., were responsible for their freedom in the United States.

Confused and beaten down, they were unaware of the fact that 68 percent of trafficking victims globally work in forced labor and are exploited in agriculture, construction, and domestic work. A look of utter despair crossed the face of the eighty-five-year-old grandfather as he was beaten into servitude. Even as he begged for the release of his fifteen-year-old granddaughter from nightly prostitution, he knew no mercy would be given. His tiny family had been deceived into believing in the American dream. As many Americans in their own homes were beginning to realize, they too had been hoodwinked into believing that their savior was out there making America great again.

"How did LJ know I was in Sacramento?" Julius asked Lulu when he returned to the apartment. Lulu was sprawled out on the bed in her room. As she lay on the small bed, her eyes fell upon the hole in the closet that she had failed to adequately cover with the dresser. If Julius saw the opening she had created where she and Suzanne had talked last night, he would extract an explanation and learn more than she would ever want him to know.

"Don't you remember he called to tell you he was coming to check on the Make a Bed agreement with the hotel? He'd gotten some flak from them about the Hondurans. The hotel thought it was a bad idea to fly them into the local airport."

"Why didn't the hotel contact me? I'm the one running this organization."

"Take it easy, Julius. You asked the hotel to deal with LJ; he's the one smuggling them in with the Cessna."

But Julius had already pulled out his cell and was calling LJ for an explanation. When he got no answer and was sent to voicemail, he flung the cell phone across the room. It landed right by the dresser, inches away from the hole in the closet. Lulu rushed to pick it up, but not before Julius noticed the crack.

"What the hell is this?" he asked as he pushed the dresser away and saw a hole in the closet that was large enough for people to crawl through.

"Rats," said Lulu, but not before Julius had grabbed the whip and slashed her repeatedly across her body, carefully avoiding her face.

⤙

"I'd really like to break into that apartment," Sandy said as they drove back to her aunt's place after dinner. Sandy couldn't believe how lucky she had been to find a guy like David. He knew so much about human trafficking. He seemed to understand what had happened to Suzanne and why it had happened. Sandy had always known that Suzanne was a very fragile girl who lived a great deal of her time in an imaginary world where she finally could be in charge and in control of all the elements around her. It had always been as if Suzanne couldn't function in the haphazard world of the present. The disruption of everyday life always seemed like chaos to her. Sandy remembered her high school poetry, which always reflected some kind of sadness and regret that she wasn't a stronger, better person. *I hope I find her before she kills herself,* thought Sandy as they drove in silence back to where she was staying in LA.

"How nice it is to be in a car instead of a bus," laughed Sandy, needing to change the topic that was engulfing her mind. "I never really knew how hard it was to get around LA without a car."

"You're really nuts, you know that? That'd be breaking and entering for one thing, not to mention there may be a whole trove of people coming and going in that place."

David wasn't about to let her change the subject that was on *his* mind. He was questioning his own thinking about getting involved with such a treacherous situation. Because he had printed so much material on the subject of human trafficking, he knew how much danger Sandy was putting herself in. He knew that you didn't mess around with these kinds of people.

"Sandy, I think we need to take the information you have about your friend's disappearance to the police. I can't in good conscience let you get any more involved with this than you already are. You've seen what a vicious character this guy is. Let the police handle this."

"Oh, I don't know. I've come this far, David. Look, I promise I won't try and break into their apartment, even though it looked as if they were going away for a while. Remember I saw them get into the car with luggage, like they were going someplace else? Don't they do that? Travel each night from one city to the next?"

"Yes, it's called 'working the circuit.' The girls might be moved each night from LA to Sacramento and then to San Jose or San Francisco."

"Why so much movement? Wouldn't they get more customers if they just stayed in one place?"

"That's not what these pimps want, Sandy. Staying in one place could encourage relationships to form. The girls are purposely kept isolated and definitely not allowed to bond with anyone except those in charge. These monsters control every aspect of their girls' lives. I'm afraid your friend has been beaten, starved, and tortured more than you could even imagine."

"This is it, right here, David. This's my aunt's house. You've really helped me a lot. I can't thank you enough. I'll call you tomorrow after I get a good night's sleep." With that, she leaned over and kissed his cheek.

"Sleep well, kid. I'll talk to you tomorrow."

David pulled his car up to a little one-story bungalow, and Sandy got out and waved goodbye. He stayed until she got up the walk to see that she got in, but Sandy waved and pointed to the backyard as the way she would enter. After one more final wave, she turned and blew him a kiss as he drove away. Then she scurried through the yard and made her way into another street where she hurried to the corner to catch a bus.

She really liked David, but she wasn't going to let the chance go by to find her friend. She knew if the police were involved, this Julius character would probably try to kill Suzanne rather than give her up. She also felt that, by this time, Suzanne must be so brainwashed that she might try and kill herself rather than be taken alive. Something about the way she had looked in the car when she stared right into Sandy's face as they drove away haunted her. It was as though she was possessed by someone else. *If evil spirits do exist, then I think they've gone and taken her over*, she thought. *Time to find an exorcist.*

But her timing couldn't have been worse, and it was a choice she would come to regret.

CHAPTER NINE

As Dormer pulled up to the roadblock, a familiar face waved him down.

"Andy, it's good to see you. How long's it been? A coupla years, my God!"

It was Sid, his old partner from when he was on the force. They high-fived it from the window of Andy's car.

"What's going on here, Sid? Why all the lights and sirens?"

"A girl was found murdered here last night. The body was dumped in the ditch. Apparently, the crime was committed elsewhere."

Dormer's heart froze. If anything happened to Catherine, he would never forgive himself. He struggled with words as his mind tried to grasp what Sid had just said. If it had been Catherine, Sid would immediately have tried to protect him, shield him from any information. Sid knew Catherine; their kids had played together since first grade, and if it had been Catherine, Sid would have said it differently.

"Looks like a teenager. Hey, Andy, what's wrong? You okay?"

"My daughter's been missing for twenty-four hours. It's not her? Sid, please tell me it's not Catherine."

"Oh my God, Andy! They don't have an ID yet, but I don't think it's her."

Andy had gotten out of the car and was walking rapidly to where he could see the body. Sid rushed down to escort him to the crime site. With a rush of relief—he could tell that it wasn't his daughter. He nearly fell to the ground with relief.

"Well, look who we have here, Sergeant Dormer. Andy, it's good to see you. As you can tell, you couldn't have come back at a better time."

"What... what do you mean, Chief? I don't understand."

"This girl here? She's one of the four teens you found two years ago. Remember they'd been wired together and told a weird story about being abducted and put in cages and witnessing a murder? You brought them into Paisley General. The town had never seen anything like it. You pursued the murder of that gangster and tried to figure out why the girls had been abducted in the first place. Then the state police came up here and shut down you and everybody else involved with this case. You never gave up on the abduction of that DeMarco girl either. We could use a good man like you, Dormer. We want you back."

Dormer let those words sink in. It felt good to be wanted back into the fold. He had always resented his dismissal by the state police and felt slighted by the lack of support from his team. He said he'd think about it, but a family emergency called him back home.

"We know Dolores called in about Catherine's missing. Don't worry, we'll find her, Andy."

Andy looked again at the slender figure now covered with mud and lying forgotten in a ditch. He tried to remember the four girls. He studied the swollen figure before him. She appeared to have been strangled, her face purple and bloated, and she looked sad, as though she already had lived a forgotten life. He remembered her as the girl who thought she was meeting a talent scout at Starbucks to become a star in a music video. *They all want to be special*, he thought.

He turned away as the forensics team began to do their work on her, but he turned back suddenly, as if struck by something familiar. Around her neck was a locket that Catherine sometimes wore. *No, it couldn't be*, he said to himself, but as he examined it closer, there was no doubt in his mind that it was Catherine's.

Suddenly, all his plans of apprehending Julius took a back seat. He couldn't think of anything else but finding his daughter.

After some brief goodbyes, he promised to be in touch as soon as he could. Quickly, he jumped into the grey Honda that had been his refuge for almost two years and headed home.

Dolores was silent when he came in. The house looked tired and empty somehow. He could feel the loneliness caused by the absence of two people who used to be part of the family, three now that Catherine was missing. Julia, their older daughter, was off to college at Chico State.

Dolores looked exhausted. Andy wanted to rush over and grab her in his arms, but he held himself back. Better take it slow. She was sitting on their old worn couch that had gotten them through two kids and twenty years of marriage. He came and sat down beside her, taking her hand in his. She didn't pull back—that was a good thing—but she made no move to hug him either.

"Dolores, tell me what happened."

"You've been gone a long time, Andy."

"When did Catherine leave? Was she with anybody?"

"I think she's in real trouble, Andy. Those girls who were abducted four years ago and that murder at the cotton mill… these things have never gone away from this community. And you taking off, chasing after that DeMarco girl, spending money we don't have. It's no wonder our daughters felt abandoned."

"One of those four girls was found murdered and dumped in a ditch today, Dolores. I need you to tell me what happened."

"Oh my God, was it Shelby? They became friends. Catherine left with her yesterday. What if something's happened to her? Oh my God!" With that, Dolores collapsed on his shoulder, great sobs shaking her.

"Honey, we have a lot of time to make up. My focus is on you and the kids now, but in order to help, I need you to tell me what the hell happened yesterday. Please, just start from the beginning. Please."

Rocking his wife gently in his arms, he realized just how much he had missed her and their children. He'd got caught up in something that had obsessed him for the better part of two years.

"I wasn't crazy about the new friendship with Shelby," said Dolores. "The girl was too street wise. Even though she had learned her lesson with that episode when she thought she was going to star in a music video and instead ended up in a cage like an animal, she still pushed her limits."

"How on earth did they meet? That girl wasn't from around here."

"Catherine was doing a term paper on human trafficking in school—they're starting early to teach kids about this kind of stuff in class. They also have police drills on terrorist attacks and psychological profile studies of adolescents with anti-social tendencies. What kind of world are we living in now, Andy? I don't understand it and it terrifies me."

"How did she get in touch with Shelby?"

"Some YouTube thing Shelby made. She's become her own social media star after all. In it, Shelby talks about what it was like to be stripped of all her belongings and stuffed in a cage with no way to get out and no clothes, no cell phone, nothing. They were given dog food, Andy, and water bowls like some animal." Catherine wanted to interview her in person, and they went off a couple of times. When I found out that they were going to the cotton mill where this all happened, I went ballistic. I put my foot down about going there and she bolted."

"Did you tell the police that's where they were going?"

"Yes, of course, but there's been no trace of them, and now you're telling me Shelby's dead. What on earth could have happened to Catherine?"

"I'll be back."

Andy prayed that no harm had come to his daughter, but he knew that a lot of the answers to all kind of questions lay in the secrets at the old abandoned cotton mill. He knew without a doubt that he would find his daughter there.

CHAPTER TEN

"LJ, JUST PLEASE tell me where we're going."

They had left Sacramento in a hurry. LJ was hell bent on getting out of town fast, and he kept glancing in the rearview mirror, half expecting to see Julius in pursuit. They were heading north, Suzanne noticed. *On to the next location so soon?* she wondered. No, this was not Julius's plan.

"He'll kill us both, LJ. What's going on?"

But LJ kept driving, his mind in another place. Suzanne wondered if he was high on something. That always pissed off Julius, when he took drugs. *He never minded getting me high,* she thought. At first she'd hated it, and now she depended on it, especially when it came to performing.

"LJ, hook me up with what you're on. At least then I can relax and kick back knowing I'm going to be offered up for slaughter." She laughed, a hollow shrill sound even to her ears, but LJ paid no attention to her. The cell phone on the seat kept ringing and ringing. LJ wouldn't pick it up; she knew it was Julius. Once she reached for it, but he pushed her hand away.

"Leave it alone, Suzie Q. You're on a new adventure."

"Adventure? Uh huh, that's what my life has been all about, one fuckin' adventure after another."

LJ looked sideways at her, thinking about what she had become. She'd recently turned eighteen, but looked thirty easy, maybe forty. *Her looks are shot*, he thought. He knew he had contributed to her demise, but he didn't want to go there. All he really wanted to do was deliver her to Dormer and then get outta Dodge. Not exactly deliver in person, but put her in an easy location for him to find. By the time Dormer found her, he'd be long gone. He was done with Julius and all his bullshit. He and Eddie had a great new gig with the porn stuff, and they'd picked a new location in the country where he was sure no one would find them. He just needed to get this done and done quickly.

"You don't always have to be in the business, Suz. There are other things you could do."

That elicited a raucous laugh from Suzanne. "Thanks for the career boost, LJ. You were the first."

"Sorry about that. I *am*. I mean, you were too young, and you were beat up pretty bad back then. I felt like I had to bring you back to life. Sounds crazy, I know. You're just so damn help-less, so unconscious about who you are. You're a pretty girl who doesn't know she's pretty or doesn't care that she is. It's like a wasted quality with you. God gave you looks and you say 'what for?' Don't you know that animals like Julius eat that stuff up? That's how he preyed on you. You know, it's kinda funny. Julius, in his crazy, screwed-up way, is in love with you. Sickening, isn't it?"

"If that's love, please give me hate, at least that's something I understand."

"Don't you ever wonder why you're never with any of the other girls?"

"Well, it's not that I don't put out. I work my ass off."

"But not with a lineup of whores. You're different; you're special."

"So what's with Lulu?" she asked, changing the subject. "She's the only one I ever see anymore."

"She's into something else, a different line of business."

"Yeah, she's something else."

"What do you mean?" asked LJ.

Suzanne didn't want to get into how she knew Lulu's story. No sense making trouble for herself. If LJ told Julius that she knew all about Lulu's life, she was sure they would both be punished.

"Nothing. Can we stop for some food? I'm starving."

"You can eat later. Let's get this done."

Suzanne was so tired of having everything decided for her, being trussed up for strange men, and herded from place to place like cattle. She had been trained to suppress all emotions, but suddenly she didn't care. She could never have explained the overwhelming sense of defeat and the huge welling up of tears that shook her thin frame.

LJ was moved in spite of himself. She hadn't asked to become a prostitute; it had been thrust upon her, so to speak. Suddenly, he wanted to tell Suzanne everything. Screw Julius.

"Lulu has a special purpose. She's in charge of disciplinary action for the immigrants who don't get with the system. You've heard about the cargo shipments we used to get in Long Beach? Well that fizzled out, but Lulu was among the ones we smuggled off our last delivery."

"I know."

"What? There's no way she would have told you that. The rest of her family would have been killed. Besides, you two are kept away from each other. There never would have been a time for you to talk."

"Well, there was, last night."

"When? Weren't you locked in right away?"

"Lulu found a way to communicate, and she told me about her life. I'm hungry!"

"Well then, you know all about the hotel and the immigrants and the smuggling."

"Oh?"

"Yeah, it's one of the reasons Julius and I are splitting up. I really don't care that she beats them with a whip when they don't do what's expected of them, but I draw the line at babies."

"What do you mean?"

"They're fucked up and perverted, those two. She cons women into giving up their babies, and they're used as sex toys. Disgusting, right? That's not all of it. They're also used for organ parts—big demand overseas, in this country too. It's a fucked-up, crazy world, right?"

Lulu sat stone-faced as Julius repeatedly landed blows on her body with the whip. She barely made a sound. Her silence was a heavy contrast to the vocal theatrics Julius was dishing out.

"You fucking bitches! I'm sick of all of you! You know better than to try and double-cross me, Lulu!"

It was obvious that he derived some kind of sadistic pleasure in beating the life out of her. Lulu was certain that he was out of control. It was terrifying most of all to see the way the spiderweb tattooed on his neck around the tiny black mole moved maliciously, almost as though it was going to envelope the spider and eat it. She had to stop him before he killed her. With a feigned calm resolve, she raised her hand and said, "I've made a tunnel."

The whip stopped in midair. Her words hit Julius like a cyclone. He gave her one astonished look and stepped back, stumbling.

Incredulously, he formed the words he spat out at her in a stupor. "To get out?"

Lulu thought he was about to cry. He looked like a spoiled bully, surprised when he discovers that everybody he's beaten doesn't like him.

"No, to bring them in."

Julius put down the whip and ran to the little dresser, shoving it aside. He stooped down to investigate at first, seeing nothing but old pillows and blankets left in storage. Then, pushing them aside, he could see out into the street.

Lulu got up and managed to move in closer to him, shaking with each step. She was badly hurt but trying not to show it.

"There are a lot of poor, desperate people in this town: immigrants who need a place to hide, desperate people looking for drugs. I can lure them here. There is no end to the people who need hope and the promise of anything to enrich and fulfill their lives. This is a place where they can come and hide and feel safe, at least temporarily. It won't take much to capture them. We can't do this for a long time, Julius, but for a while we can clean up on the fools who have nowhere else to go. I can get children. I can get organs. This is for you. Can't you see that?"

Julius turned to look at Lulu, and through his mind's eye he was seeing his mother at her ingenious best. It was a novel idea, like she would have thought up. "It's ingenious, Lulu. No one would ever know it's here."

"That's right, Jules." She lay back down on the bed, knowing how he would want to thank her.

Julius stepped forward, unzipping as he came. "Make room for me, baby," he said as he lowered himself onto her. As he did so, her eyes fell upon the black spider mole now at rest, no longer threatened by itself.

Humm, she mused, *time for a visit from a black widow.*

❧

David tried Sandy's cell phone several times, but it always went directly to voicemail. He couldn't deny that he was worried. A million things could happen to her in LA, especially given that she was hell-bent on digging up pimps and rescuing victims of human trafficking. He had to admit that he admired her strength and courage, but her foolishness made him weep.

After the second day of not hearing from her, especially since he had offered to give her some of the literature he had printed on the subject, he decided to go back to her aunt's house. As he pulled up to the little house on the quiet street, he already knew just by looking that she wasn't there. He got out of his car anyway and went to knock on the door. The occupant was a tiny old man who lived alone and had never heard of Sandy McKinnon or her aunt.

❧

Sandy did make it back to her aunt's house, way across town from where she had been dropped off. Two transfers and three buses later, she let herself in and quietly crept to her room to think. If the girls were being caravanned to the cities that David had mentioned, then Suzanne wouldn't be back in LA for a while. *What was so wrong with breaking in? Nobody was there.*

She wished that David hadn't been such a fuddy-duddy about the whole thing, scaring her off like that. She knew Julius was a criminal, but Suzanne wasn't. Her friend needed help; of that she was certain. As she turned out the light, she fell asleep, exhausted yet energized by the plot she was forming in her head.

The next morning, she headed back to the now-familiar neighborhood. *Better not go near that 7-Eleven*, she thought. Wouldn't do to run into David, the place where he gets his morning fix. He'd probably be suspecting something by now. She casually walked by the apartment a few times like she was on her way to somewhere else. Everything looked quiet. The neighborhood had a blue-collar feel about it. Most families were out of their houses by nine a.m.—off to work most likely. No one seemed to pay any attention to her.

She walked up to the brownstone building and tried the front door. Not open, but a panel of buzzers with names and apartment numbers were on one side of the entryway. She couldn't see any names in one of the spaces and figured that was the place. How could all these other people live in this apartment building and not know what was going in there? She pushed the first button a couple of times, but there was no answer. The second buzzer was answered by a gruff voice who said he didn't want to be hassled, but the third time was the charm. A tentative buzz issued and she pushed herself in.

Apartment 4F was three flights up and no elevator. *At least I'm getting my exercise*, she thought. As she took each step, she wondered what she would find, if anything. She had no idea how she was going to get in the apartment, but she knew she would try.

As she rounded the last flight of stairs, the door to one of the apartments slowly opened. At first no one was there, and Sandy realized that was probably the person who buzzed her in. *Oops, what am I gonna say?* she wondered. An older woman poked her head out, and as she did so, her cat came out to greet Sandy. The small woman appeared to have had a stroke on one side, as one arm hung limp. She spoke with a slight slur and murmured that she thought Sandy was the Vons grocery with a delivery.

"Tito, come back in here. That's not the grocery boy." Then she added to Sandy's surprise, "You're not going up there, are you? Are you one of them?"

Meeting Norma was one of the luckiest breaks Sandy ever could have had. Staring in utter surprise at what the old lady said, she realized that any excuse for ringing her buzzer went right out the window. After introducing herself and explaining her mission to save her friend, the door opened wider and she was ushered in.

"My name's Norma and this is Tito. Welcome to our little abode."

Sandy looked around at the humble but charming apartment. Books were piled everywhere, and pictures of what looked like generations of family crowded the little space that was left on end tables. A lovely wedding picture of a young and beautiful Norma with her husband sat next to the TV. An off-white sectional sofa that had seen better days was placed near a window overlooking the street.

"Make yourself comfortable while I make us some tea," she said, leaving Sandy to wander around the little living room to look at pictures and peruse books. *Millennium Prophecies: Predictions for the Coming Century*, by Edgar Cayce. *I wonder what century she's in*, thought Sandy. Other books included *The Bible Code* and *The Singularity is Near: When Humans Transcend Biology*.

Wow, she's a heavy reader, thought Sandy. "You're into some pretty interesting books, Norma," she said, hoping she was speaking loud enough to be heard in the kitchen.

"Yes, well now I have the time to read and speculate about what I think is going to happen to the world," she answered, coming back into the living room struggling with a large tray. "Can you set this tray down on the coffee table for me, dear? Since the stroke, I've had trouble doing much of anything."

Sandy took the tray of tea with two porcelain cups, a creamer and sugar bowl, and a tiny plate of sugar cookies to the coffee table and the two sat down to chat.

"Yes, I've known for quite some time what's been going on upstairs, but I thought it was a sex cult. Human trafficking! You say your friend is blonde?"

"Yes, she's eighteen now and has always been thin, but she looked emaciated when I saw her in the car."

"Well I know the one you mean. There are only two girls upstairs and two men, although one of the men hardly comes around anymore. The man who stays there makes a lot of noise sometimes. He seems like a violent man when I see him in the hallway, and I keep my distance."

"That's probably Julius," nodded Sandy. "When I met him two years ago back in Paisley Falls, I thought he was scary even then, but he didn't waste any time getting to know Suzanne. He came around our high school, just magically appeared one day driving a red Corvette. He said he'd graduated from Paisley Falls High and was in town on business. What business in Paisley Falls, I wonder?" Sandy said and laughed.

"Anyway, after she disappeared and her father had a heart attack, I knew I couldn't give up on my friend. Her mother doesn't even seem to care, and the police acted weird about the whole thing, because a murder took place in town the same time she disappeared. Everyone thought she had just run off. It's just me and Sergeant Dormer—"

"Oh, so the police are involved," interrupted Norma.

"Well that's just it, Norma, he—I mean Sergeant Dormer—was kind of shut down by the state police, taken off the case of the town murder and told that unless her parents filed a missing person's report they weren't going to do anything about it."

"But you're saying that this sergeant hasn't lost interest in the case. Is he still working it?"

"Well, not in any official capacity. I mean, I haven't seen him in two years, but I understand that he's become a private investigator and is still pursuing leads."

"My goodness, young lady, you sound like a detective yourself. It's remarkable what you've uncovered so far. This is very dangerous business. Don't you think the LA police might be interested in what you've found out?"

"Yeah, well, maybe. How much are they going to believe from someone like me when her own parents don't even think she's in danger? I don't have proof of anything. Maybe her parents were right, maybe she just ran off with the guy. I need evidence, evidence I might very well find if I could get upstairs to see what's in that apartment. You say they live right above you?"

Sandy looked around the place, seeing the front window overlooking the street. She got up and walked over to it and looked up. She saw only a thin ledge and shut windows.

"Not that way, silly," said Norma. "Since they left yesterday, that means they won't be back for four nights," she continued. "That's their usual routine."

"That makes sense," said Sandy. "They've got their regular stops in the cities they've chosen."

"Well, I've got a back balcony where I keep the garbage. There's a fire escape that goes straight up to their porch. I've got a key from an old neighbor friend of mine who used to live there. Honey, if you've got the gumption, I've got the means!"

Tito let out a loud meow as he wound his way around Sandy's legs. As if on cue, he led the way to the kitchen and scratched on the door.

CHAPTER ELEVEN

THE ABANDONED COTTON mill looked foreboding in the late afternoon sun. Pieces of faded yellow tape from the two-year-old crime scene hung forlornly around the old building that had seen better days. Originally built in 1883, it was the largest cotton mill west of the Mississippi River. Hundreds of Portuguese workers had manned the plant producing a variety of finished products such as comforters, drapery cloth, towels, and mops.

In 1917 the plant was rebuilt, and in both World Wars it was a major supplier of tents, parachutes, and fabric for the military, but the building was shuttered in 1954.[5] Many attempts had been made to designate it a national landmark, but there was a lot of red tape in the way. Some of the town's inhabitants had former relatives who had suffered in a fire that led to the eventual closing of the plant. There were claims that improper fire escapes and no ventilation had led to the needless death of many workers trapped by the flames. The relatives of those killed wanted a memorial erected, honoring those who died. Others

---

5 The Cotton Mill is based on the description of The California Cotton Mill in Oakland California built in 1883 and converted into Cotton Mill Studio Apartments.

in the community wanted to revive it and turn it into shops and artist spaces, with no memorial needed. Let's move on with the future, the town's mayor had argued. Why waste this valuable land on an empty grave site? And so the building stood, dangerously empty and decaying.

Since it had become the site for a gruesome, unsolved murder and a bizarre kidnapping, nobody wanted to touch it. Nobody but crazy teenagers and druggies, thought Dormer as he made his way up to the concrete steps. The massive doors hung tight and were locked. He walked around the perimeter of the building, looking for anything that looked like a clue. What were his daughter Catherine and her new friend Shelby looking for up here?

He started calling out her name as he walked. Both his daughters had been taught that this abandoned building was a dangerous place. Shelby might have encouraged her, he thought. She probably made it sound glamorous and dangerous to Catherine. If she'd already publicized her captivity with a YouTube video, she undoubtedly relished the attention it got from other kids who knew firsthand about the incident.

His mind raced back to the night two years ago when he had first found the young girls wandering in the street at two a.m. They were naked, wired together by wrist ties, and obscure messages written in blood were smeared across their bodies. Why weren't they cold and shivering? He remembered the calm, robotic motion the girls made as they walked. They seemed impervious to anything. They had been drugged he assumed, high on something that made them forget about the chill in the night. They seemed hypnotized. Drugs. It had to have been drugs that were kept here, hidden here.

The two out-of-town thugs who made the mill a temporary

hideout for their catch of young girls were probably unaware of the junk that might have been kept and hidden. But by whom and for how long? Maybe Julius and his partner had found the stash and started using and distributing it. Someone had found out and had to take action quickly. He remembered something coming over the wires about a transnational gang. Here in Paisley Falls? How ridiculous. But when you think about it, how clever. A place where you think you'll never get found out.

The two factions in town were still fighting about what to do with the building, so the property stayed vacant and unused. Surely the police would have searched every nook and cranny of it looking for any evidence they could find. Unless… unless the state police intervention prevented that. They'd certainly gotten rid of *him* quickly enough.

Suddenly, he stumbled upon something in the dirt around the grounds of the building. It looked like one of Catherine's shoes. He started shouting her name loudly now, frantically searching the area when he heard some noise in the bushes nearby. He ran to the area and saw a terrified Catherine hiding in the underbrush. She was covered in dirt and had some bruises around her head, but Dormer was grateful that she appeared to have no broken bones.

"Oh, honey!" he cried. "Are you all right?" He quickly examined her face and body for bruises and contusions. When he was satisfied that she was all right, his mind raced to the possibility of other psychological or physical traumas. "Did anyone hurt you? Oh my God, did anyone force themselves—"

"Dad! No! Nothing like that! I just—" She broke off crying and huddled into his arms. He cradled her and rocked her back and forth as he had done so many times in her short life. "I've just been so silly, Dad. It's all my fault, it really is." She broke off sobbing, and the father in Andy felt his blood begin to boil.

"Start from the beginning, honey, and tell me who did this to you." He tried to calm himself a bit for her sake, but he was ready to kill whoever who had hurt his child.

"I know you're mad at me for coming here."

"We'll deal with that later. I'm guessing you had a real good reason for disobeying your mom and me."

"Well, probably not good enough for you, but for me it was a chance I couldn't pass up."

Of all the possible sentences that Andy Dormer might have heard come out of his daughter's mouth, he never expected that one. Still, he held his breath and urged her to continue.

"I was doing this term paper on the cotton mill murders. It's the two-year anniversary, remember? Well, I thought I'd do a paper on the history of the event, especially since you found the girls. That had a lot of credibility, Dad, the fact that you were involved in it."

"Okay, but why come here?"

"Well, this is where it all happened. This is where that guy was murdered and where the girls were kept in cages. Nothing is more important than the scene of the crime. I shouldn't have to tell *you* that."

Dormer looked up. He thought he heard a sound coming from inside the building. "I'm calling the police. Let's get you out of here."

"No! Dad, no! Don't call the police." Catherine was immediately hysterical again, and Dormer wondered what she had been through.

"Catherine what exactly is going on here?" he asked sternly, reassuring himself that his Colt .45 was snuggly tucked in its holster.

"If you call the police, Dad, they'll kill her!"

"Who?"

"Shelby, Dad. She's the recruiter!"

❧

Suzanne tried to process what LJ was telling her. Lulu was prostituting babies and selling organ parts? All the admiration she had felt for Lulu's plight suddenly vanished. Of course, she was under Julius's control, but how could she? She had been a baby herself when she had been molested. How could she wish that on other innocent children? *It's what we experience, it's all we know. For her it's normal.* Suzanne knew the answer. She felt a stab of pain for someone who had been so hurt and abandoned, so completely disregarded. *Just like me*, she thought, *I have become so disregarded.* She wondered for a moment if she had brought that on herself. Perhaps all her life she had set herself up to be shunned. *No, wait a minute*, she said to herself, *I didn't ask to be abducted, raped, and forced into this nightmare. This is not my fault!* But what if some tiny piece of you somewhere boxed your own self into a situation that had no exit? She didn't think she had the courage to answer that question. If she did answer that question, she didn't think she was capable of withstanding the answer.

LJ was driving straight toward Leverton, figuring that was the best place to drop off Suzanne. Dormer had wanted a twenty-four-hour window, and instinctively LJ had gone to Sacramento where he knew the girls would be. Their schedule after San Diego was LA then Sacramento and finally San Francisco. He had talked with Julius the night before, and they had quite an argument. Julius was paranoid—and rightfully so. LJ chuckled at that. Julius didn't think LJ was doing his job picking up recruits in the Cessna.

"Where's my six chicks a day, asshole?" muttered Julius on his cell when he and the girls were on their way to Sacramento.

"You wanna be my ambassador at the border? Maybe ICE will give you a fuckin' medal for taking the load off them. I have to watch myself and stay out of sight for the time being. It's just temporary, Jules, till I find another way to get the job done."

But that hadn't pleased Julius. Nothing would, reasoned LJ, so he was moving on to better territory.

Dormer was giving him a chance to exit this handicap with no questions asked. He'd be free to fly the friendly skies in pursuit of his own interests, but driving Suzanne to Leverton wasn't the safest bet for him. *Yeah, what am I doing? It's too close to Paisley Falls and Dormer! Better make it a bit harder for Dormer to get to Suzanne.*

And with that, LJ turned around right in the middle of Interstate 5 and headed back to LA. He figured he'd make it in about five hours, and then he'd give Dormer a call about the location. What he didn't know was that that was just about the time Norma, Sandy, and Tito the cat would be making their entrance.

David kept telling himself over and over that what Sandy was up to was none of his business. After all, he barely knew the girl. He was annoyed about the brush off with the fictitious story of the aunt and the supposed house in LA. He knew the wisest thing to do was to just let it go, but something about the girl touched him. She was spunky, bright, and so vulnerable. He knew that she genuinely liked him, but ultimately saw his presence as a hindrance. That bruised his ego, but he found himself driving to that location in Silver Lake, just to see if he could spot any sign of her. He knew she'd be there, staking it out like the little detective she was. She just didn't seem to comprehend that she could be in a whirlwind of danger.

He cruised past the apartment building, slowing way down to take a good look. He thought he saw a girl look out of an upstairs window. She leaned out and peered upward as though she were trying to gauge how to get into the apartment upstairs. He didn't get more than a one second glance at her, but he knew it was Sandy. Somehow she had maneuvered her way into someone's apartment and was calculating her chances of getting into the place where she thought Suzanne was being held against her will.

"By this time," David muttered under his breath, "her friend is a willing participant in everything she's asked to do. She just doesn't know she's a victim. That's the tragedy of it," he mused as he gazed up at the unsuspecting Sandy, who appeared to be contemplating her next move. Before she could spot his Wrangler, he quickly drove into the alley behind the apartment. There, he shut off the engine and just sat in his car.

I should go up and get her, he thought. *No, I should just start the car and get out of here. What kind of a risk am I taking?* "Fuck it," he said. "She'll get herself killed." He thought about it another minute, and then he called the police.

～

Sandy and Norma made their way up the back fire escape with Tito leading the way like he'd been up the stairs many times before. Sandy spied the brown Wrangler that she thought might be David's and froze in her tracks. Suddenly, the car started up and drove down the alley. Sandy couldn't be sure if he'd seen them or not. He wasn't looking up at them, and if he had seen them, he surely would have waved or yelled at them. *What is he doing here anyway? Is he going to be a problem?* God, she hoped not. She needed to have some answers; she felt she was so close to finding Suzanne, or at least finally putting an end to this amazing story. Something told her she was close to disrupting Julius's world and rescuing her friend. If what David said was true and human trafficking was becoming a worldwide epidemic, then there was going to be one victim less in the mixture.

An out-of-breath Norma leaned over her shoulder and gave Sandy the key that she knew would unlock the back door.

"Can't move the way I used to after the stroke," she murmured. "One of my dearest friends lived up here for many years. She traveled a lot and gave me the backdoor key to check in on her apartment while she was away, put the garbage out, and get the mail, stuff like that."

"Why didn't she give you the front door key instead?"

"Because she didn't want a lot of people to know she was gone, a very mysterious woman who kept a low profile."

The key was old and a bit rusty. It was obvious that the lock hadn't been turned in a while. After a few tries the door finally creaked open and all three of them entered the musty and sparsely furnished enclave. The kitchen had a cardboard table set with four mismatched chairs around it. Grimy countertops held a toaster and an old Mr. Coffee machine with traces of old coffee sitting in it. The cupboards were all closed, and one was locked and bolted. The fridge was an old fifties model, and Sandy opened it to find mostly bottled water and a smelly, half-opened container of yogurt.

"Well, Vivian had it charmingly furnished when *she* lived here," said Norma as they made their way down a hall to the bedrooms. There was no living room, and it was obvious that the former living room had been cordoned off into two rooms with locks and bolts on the doors. There were also two bedrooms with bolts and locks on the doors as well.

"I've never seen an apartment quite like this," said Sandy. "Every room in the place has a lock and a bolt on the door. You can't go from one room to the next without unbolting something."

"What were they trying to keep inside these rooms?" asked Norma.

"Girls," said Sandy. "Did you ever notice a lot of guys coming up and down those front stairs?"

"Now that you mention it, there was a lot of activity at times. But, like I said, once they'd leave in a group, they'd regularly be gone four or five days before they'd return. Like clockwork. I never did get the feeling that someone lived up there. It seemed more like a place to crash before you moved on."

Sandy tried one of the doors, but it was locked by a key, as were all the other doors. The only place they had any chance to explore was the kitchen, and that didn't hold much. Startled by a loud crash, they found that Tito had wandered down the dark hallway and was meowing from another entryway. He had found the only bathroom and had knocked over the tiny wastebasket where a mouse had been rousted from his home. Some dirty towels hung on the rack above the dingy bathtub, and the cabinet beside the sink held what looked like used syringes. The water in the toilet looked grey, as though it hadn't been cleaned in quite a while. A dingy shower curtain hid the dirty rings around a chipped and broken claw-foot tub.

"Oh, Vivian kept this bathroom beautifully, not filthy like this!" cried Norma. "She always said that bathrooms were like rooms you lived in. She wouldn't have allowed a mouse in here.

No way!" Norma shook her head in disbelief and scurried out of the bathroom. "Yikes, let's get out of here!"

"I don't think these people have much interest in keeping this apartment as a living space. You were right when you said they just came here to crash, and of course," Sandy added, "to do business."

It was then that they heard another kind of noise: the sound of the front door opening.

⊷

Julius caressed Lulu's pristine face. Her chiseled features were so dramatically framed by the thick, long, dark hair that hung beyond her shoulders. Every caress the two of them gave each other appeared on the surface to look like love, but it was the kind of act that no genuine lover would express to another. It wasn't even lust. It was a rehearsal for the next event in their lives that would lead them into their real orgasm, the exploitation of the most vulnerable, the most innocent.

"Does anybody else know about this little project of yours?" whispered Julius as he stroked her breasts.

"Who would I tell, Jules?"

"You are my amazing little Asian friend. No wonder so many men want to fuck you. Under every layer of you is another woman contradicting the first; you're sexy, then ugly, then evil. Deliciously decadent is what you serve up for dessert."

His laugh made a shrill, raucous sound as he got up from the bed. He was feeling older than his years, and his limp was acting up. Ever since that encounter with Suzanne two years ago when he had forced her into the trunk of his car and she had attacked him with a tire iron, his body had never completely healed. *That little bitch*, he thought as he hobbled across the room. It was time to be done with her. She'd lost her looks, and her sullen personality was a turnoff to johns. As much as he'd tried to beat her into submission, it seemed as though he could never totally control her. *Like trying to tame a wild horse,* he thought.

Lulu had so much strength, yet she was a woman he could dominate. She could corral these immigrants in hotels working for him to do her bidding. Relentlessly cruel. He laughed to himself. She had no choice but to work as his own personal tyrant. How Julius loved the juxtaposition of that. She was a beaten-down bad ass. His favorite kind.

"Let's get up and get packed. I want to get out of here tonight."

"On to San Francisco?" she asked.

"No, I want to get back to LA. LJ's planning something. That's where his plane is. The way he took off earlier with Suzanne makes me think something's not right. He won't answer his cell, and he owes me plenty. Get your ass up and let's go."

Lulu struggled up from the messy bed. Her legs were bleeding where Julius had beaten her with the whip. She staggered up and wiped herself with her dirty T-shirt lying on the floor.

"Let's go! Get your ass moving!" Julius hollered.

She knew she didn't have much time. She blocked the hole in the wall that led to the outside with the blankets and rags that had previously been used to successfully camouflage it. Then she put on the clothes she had come with and turned out the light in the tired and dingy room. She thought it was odd that the room has a forties kind of faded wallpaper of pink roses. Patches of it were peeling off the walls—perfect for the young children that she would introduce into the business. They'd feel right at home in a room that had no future.

CHAPTER TWELVE

RHONDA DEMARCO HAD heard that Andy Dormer's daughter was missing. She'd heard the news from the nurses at the retirement home where Evan now lived permanently. His health had been on a steady decline in the past year. Rhonda didn't have much hope that he would recover enough to ever return home. She and her younger daughter, Bethy, lived two solitary existences. Bethy kept mostly to her room, just the way Suzanne had. They each had their dinners at different times. Bethy wasn't eating much; she was on some paleo diet or something.

Rhonda would wander the empty house late at night, sometimes going into Suzanne's room, which remained untouched, and just stand there looking at the chenille bedspread and the 1860 portraits of women wearing the fashion of their time. Sometimes Rhonda would light the candles that adorned each bedside table and sit on the bed and cry. She hadn't wanted life to turn out this way. She was alone and losing her family. Had she wished this upon herself? she wondered. If this is the bed she made, I guess she'd better lie down in it. She thought that was how the saying went.

When she'd heard that Sergeant Dormer's youngest daughter

went missing, she wondered if he would return to look for her. Of course he'll comeback; it's his daughter! *And when he does show up, I'm going to be right there in his face asking about the whereabouts of my own daughter!* She remembered being amazed that he had actually quit the force to go out and look for Suzanne. Of course, he had pretty much been kicked out of the police force, some kind of power behind that from the Wilson family. That doctor had gotten away with murder, and his rich wife's family had hushed things up. Not that any of that really mattered to her, but she was curious to see if the sergeant had come up with any information on her daughter's disappearance.

She couldn't believe that she actually missed her. Really what she missed was the interaction of the four human beings that used to live in this house. For better or worse, they functioned as a family. Now, the loneliness of her existence was the only task there was to manage. If Suzanne really wanted to come back home, she would, she reasoned. Rhonda knew that she hadn't been kidnapped. That was ridiculous, and it had greatly upset Evan. Now, Rhonda had no one and, as usual, it was Suzanne's fault. She was going to corner Dormer and demand that he tell her all that he knew.

Helen Powell had also heard that Catherine Dormer was missing. She had run into Dolores Dormer at the supermarket, and Dolores had just broken down right there in the store crying, distraught. *The absence of her husband has been very hard on her*, thought Helen, who had been the emergency nurse on duty that night two years ago when the four young girls were brought in. She had personally attended to Nadine Hines that night as well. She hoped and prayed that the Dormer's daughter had not met the same fate as any of these girls. She had read and heard much in the two years that had passed about the epidemic of human trafficking and how prevalent it was now in the United States.

Transnational gangs were switching from drugs to trafficking people; it had become more lucrative. Human beings could be sold over and over. Drugs didn't have that kind of resale value. She understood why Andy had suspected that Suzanne had been trafficked and why she had become a symbol for him of something to be solved. She knew how idealistic Andy was about the world and how much he wanted to change it and make it a better place. A lot of people had thought that Andy Dormer was a fool to take off without a job and abandon his family on some pursuit that even her own family didn't take seriously. That was part of it, thought Helen. He was so angry that the DeMarcos didn't even care about the mysterious and unexplained disappearance of their fifteen-year-old daughter. She hoped that when she ran into her friend that she could give him the kind of support he needed. For her, Andy Dormer was the light in the ever-increasing darkness that was creeping over the world.

"Let's start over, Catherine—preferably while we're walking to the car," said Dormer as he gathered up his daughter. He feared what her explanation of Shelby being a "recruiter" was and, more than that, he didn't want to reveal that it was Shelby's body that the police had just discovered. Getting her out of this location was the only thing on his mind at this point. Since it would upset her if he called the police right now, he decided to put that off until later. Her safety was the only thing that mattered anyway.

"Let's just get to the car and go," he said as he hurried his daughter to his car.

"There's so much I have to tell you, Dad. So much more has happened, you know!" She was so excited to get the words out that she started shaking. "I mean about the two masked men and the murder of that gangster and the four girls in cages," she said. "So much more that you don't know about."

Another sharp noise jolted both of them. Dormer was sure he wasn't mistaken now—there were sounds coming from inside the cotton mill. Scraping sounds, like chains being dragged across a concrete floor.

"Catherine, let's just go!" Dormer practically threw her into his car, and they started off, tires squealing in the dust.

"This is former Sergeant Andy Dormer with the Paisley Falls Police. I want to report some suspicious activity at the cotton mill over on the east end of town." Andy was wasting no time putting in a call to the police as he and Catherine sped quickly back to their home.

"Dad, please!"

"I recovered my daughter, unharmed at the site, but heard indistinguishable noises coming from inside the plant. It's my understanding that it's still abandoned. Am I correct, Officer?" he asked the sergeant on duty taking the call.

"Oh hi, Andy. Great that you have located your daughter. I'll pass that information along. Yes, the cotton mill is not officially occupied at this time, but you know as well as I do that it's a druggie hangout. We're investigating this latest murder victim as it relates to abduction two years ago."

At this point Andy's daughter let out a scream. "Oh no! Please tell me it's not Shelby!"

"Excuse me, Andy, was that your daughter?"

"I'm afraid it was," sighed Andy. "I'll talk to you later." As Andy pulled up into their driveway, he turned to his hysterical daughter. "Try to keep it together for your mother. We'll find out what happened later. Catherine… ?" But she was inconsolable and sobbing on the floor of the car.

"Oh my God," Dolores said as she came running out of the house when the car pulled up. "You've found her! I know you've found her!" Yanking open the door, she fell to the ground embracing her daughter, both of them crying on each other's shoulders.

"I want to hear the whole story, Catherine, from beginning to end. Don't leave anything out," said a weary, tired but relieved Dormer as he ushered his family into their home.

"Andy, Helen Powell is here. She stopped by to offer any help she could when she heard that Catherine was missing."

Dolores wished that Helen wasn't here right at this moment; she couldn't hug her daughter enough, and it was too emotional a time for them to sit down and talk, but Andy seemed relieved to see her.

"Helen, you were on duty that night when the four girls were brought in. What do you remember about a girl named Shelby?"

"Oh, Andy, I certainly remember that night, but the details about the girls are a bit vague. Was she one of the older girls, the one who wanted to be in a music video?"

"Yes!" cried Catherine. "She's the one I met and interviewed at the old cotton mill."

"You mean recently?" asked Helen.

"Does anybody want coffee?" Dolores asked, wringing her hands, not knowing what to do anymore.

"Everyone sit down. There's a lot to talk about." Andy knew he had to get control of the situation. "Time is very important right now. First of all, Catherine, I'm sorry to tell you, but your friend has been found dead, probably murdered. I was stopped by the police when I first entered town. They were examining a body, and I feared it was you. I asked to see it. Sorry, honey."

"Oh no," sobbed Catherine, and Dolores rushed to grab her from falling. "It's all my fault."

"Honey, please, tell me exactly why it is your fault. You were writing a term paper on the cotton mill murders. That doesn't explain why you felt it necessary to go there. Why did you say Shelby was the recruiter? I need some answers now."

Andy sat down beside his daughter and, with her mother on the other side, a visibly shaken Catherine began her story.

"Shelby wanted to be famous. That's why she made the YouTube video. She was more mad than scared that the murder and the assassins were hushed up two years ago. I can't believe that she's really dead."

It didn't seem like Catherine would be able to stop crying anytime soon.

"How did you and Shelby become friends, honey? She's older than you, and don't you go to different schools?" asked Nurse Powell, suddenly remembering that night in the emergency room when the four terrified girls were brought in.

"I saw the YouTube stuff along with everybody else at Paisley Falls High," explained Catherine. "The murder is still big news, because it was never really solved, and since my dad was the lead investigator, I thought I had a special angle in getting the story," said Catherine, sounding like the news reporter she had recently decided to become.

"It was easy to find her, and once I told her who I was, she was excited to meet me. We met after school a few times, remember, Mom?"

"Unfortunately, yes. I was never really comfortable with that girl, seems like she's been around a bit."

"Mother, please! She agreed to tell me everything she had gone through at the cotton mill," continued Catherine after giving her mother a look. "She asked that I meet her there so we could 'take a tour,' those were her words, of the spot where the murder had taken place."

"And you agreed to such a thing?" Dolores was beside herself with worry and anger—she wasn't sure which emotion was going to take over.

"Oh, Mom, I knew if I told you, you never would've let me go. I had to take a chance to get the story."

"All right, let's get on with the story." Andy was losing patience.

"You're right, I should have known something would go wrong. Anyway, Shelby and I have been hanging out for a while. Actually, we got to be pretty good friends, and she loved a necklace of mine, so one day I just took it off and gave it to her."

"Yes, I recognized that necklace," said Andy.

"You mean she had it on her when she—"

"Yes, Catherine. What possessed you to give it to her? I haven't known you to give away your belongings to just anyone."

"You haven't really known Catherine in the past two years, Andy," Dolores offered.

That stung Andy, but his wife was right. He had let his family go.

"The necklace was meant to be a gift, but Shelby said it was so pretty that it was going to become a symbol."

"What?" shouted Andy.

"A sign or a symbol to the secret patrol that controls the mill, letting them know that a new girl was ready to join."

"Join? Join what?" Even as he shouted out the question, part of him dreaded the answer.

"The cotton mill girls, Dad—one-hundred-percent certified organic cotton."

Dolores let out a shriek and covered her mouth to stifle a scream. Helen moved over to hug her.

"Tell me, please, what the cotton mill girls are," Andy prompted.

"Well," continued Catherine, hesitating over each word as she continued, "they're girls from all over the world who are, you know, virgins."

"Jesus Christ," said Andy.

"The cotton mill has lots of floors and places where bales of cotton were kept in the old days," said Catherine, now sounding like she was giving a book report. "When the girls are brought in, they lie down on white pillows of cotton, and, well, after they're... uh... given to the men, they bleed, you know, after they've done it, and the red shows up on the white cotton. That's why they wear white cotton underwear. And then they're certified after that."

"This is disgusting," said Helen.

"Why in the hell did you go there, Catherine?" Andy asked, visibly shaken. "Did you want to join, for God's sake?"

"What got into you, Catherine?" sobbed her mother. "Did you think it was some kind of a cool thing to do?"

"NO! Mom, honestly I just went there to get the story, but after I was there, I realized that I was being recruited! Shelby said nobody from around here gets recruited because it would cause suspicion, but since I had asked and had connections, she thought I'd be perfect for the organization, uh, so to speak. After the girls prove they're virgins, they're sent on to Europe or Saudi Arabia to live luxurious lives with princes or heads of states."

"And you believed this!" cried Andy, becoming more and more upset with every word Catherine spoke.

"Dad, the minute I got the message, I tried to run. Shelby started to close in on me and demanded I join right then. She had my necklace and tried to give it back to me, but I ran. When I got out of there, two guys jumped on her, and I don't remember anything after that."

Nobody said anything for a couple of minutes.

Finally, Andy asked. "Why did she want your necklace?"

"I'm not sure, but she said she wanted to give it back to me. It was somehow important that I get it back."

"Why, Catherine? Why do you think she wanted it in the first place?"

The necklace wasn't any work of art. It was a simple pendant hanging on a fake gold chain. The medallion was a plain, small, imitation gold coin. It was seemingly innocuous to anyone who might have glanced at it. To Catherine, it was only a symbol of a win in a volleyball tournament.

"Well," said Catherine, "she said it was a symbol, so I think that it meant some kind of goal was accomplished."

"Yes," said Andy. "It meant that the girls were one-hundred-percent certified organic and moved on as the next shipment of goods."

"Odd," said Helen almost to herself. "one-hundred-percent certified organic should have meant they were virgins."

"I think it's a class system," said Andy. "It means they're the next best thing, innocent and relatively untouched, and still very worthy for a whole new type of customer."

The room grew silent now, except for the sounds of Andy's sobs as he sat with his face in his hands, crying as if his guts would spill out. He didn't notice that the cell phone in his pocket kept ringing, a timely beacon portending another disaster about to happen.

⤚⤙

LJ gingerly inserted the key in the lock of the apartment, hoping to dump Suzanne there as quickly as possible and then get the hell out. He never, ever expected to see two strange women confronting him with totally bewildered expressions of utter panic.

"Ah!" cried Norma, quickly hiding behind the electrified Sandy, who was bracing herself for the next move in this never-ending drama.

A reluctant Suzanne came in behind LJ, not aware of the coming turn of events. Seeing Sandy standing in front of her caused Suzanne to suddenly feel dizzy. She staggered and fell upon LJ's shoulder, and an "Oh my God" escaped her lips before she fell headfirst onto the floor.

"Who the fuck are you two ladies, and what are you doing in my apartment?" asked LJ quickly while drawing his gun out of his pants.

"Suzanne!" cried Sandy as she rushed toward her friend, only to be smacked down by a bewildered LJ as he tried to regain control of the situation.

Sandy cried out again from the floor after sustaining the punch. "Suzanne!"

Suzanne did not want to get up and face her friend or her life, which at that point kept relentlessly repeating itself in front of her eyes. All the things that she had been or had done kept flashing before her eyes. Some good things emerged looking through this kaleidoscope, like the time she helped a friend who was dying of leukemia, but everything about her life at home with Rhonda, Evan, and Bethy just looked like macaroni and cheese bits on parade. The macaroni and cheese bits flipped about as though they were frenzied by design. Was this her brain on overload? Suzanne couldn't process Sandy's presence in her current world. Her immediate counter response was that she would die if she acknowledged her friend, and that her friend would die as well if she acknowledged *her*. Comprehending all of this, she stayed on the floor, wishing only for a way out of any conflict.

"I'm going to ask you two once again: what the fuck you are doing in this apartment, and how did you get in?"

LJ pulled up Sandy by the back of her blouse and shoved her against the wall, jamming the gun against her chest.

Norma shouted, "Leave her alone! I've got the backdoor key."

Incredulously, LJ turned around to look at the old lady, and Sandy took the opportunity to bite his hand.

"Ouch! You little bitch!" LJ backhanded her once again. "Jesus, I ought to shoot you both right now."

"LJ, please leave them alone. It's not their fault," Suzanne cried out from the floor.

"Christ, it's a good thing Julius isn't here, Suz, or you'd be dead by now."

"Just let them go, LJ!"

"I'll do what I fuckin want, bitch," he said, and then kicked her hard in the groin. She howled in pain and tried to scoot away from him. "This is all your fault!" he yelled.

"No!" cried Sandy. "It's my fault. Suzanne never expected me to be here. Norma was someone I used to find a way to get in. She's just an old lady who lives downstairs. Let her go!"

Caught off guard, LJ stepped on Tito's tail as he struggled to regain his balance after kicking Suzanne. This roiled the cat so much that he jumped headlong up onto LJ's leg, screeching all the way as he ran up his leg and landed his claws right onto his groin underneath his shorts. LJ dropped the gun and howled out in pain. As the gun hit the floor, it went off, sending the bullet through the door.

Violent pounding ensued at this point, and a male voice could be heard shouting, "Open up! Sandy, are you all right? It's David!"

CHAPTER THIRTEEN

JULIUS'S SIXTH SENSE was up. How on earth had Lulu pulled off creating a hole in the side of their apartment? How much crap was happening behind his back? Was LJ in on this? Did Suzanne know about Lulu's plans? And where was LJ disappearing to? The Cessna Skyknight flights had all but stopped. Bluepage was becoming more and more of a problem than it was worth with all the government red tape, and he desperately needed the business acumen of his old partner, Dino Hu. The Daddy's Tool Chest sex cams were guaranteed money, but he missed the pleasure of actually training the girls.

He had loved the excitement of getting new meat off of the cargo shipments as they came into the Port of Long Beach. The slave labor that he had procured in hotels and restaurants was paying off, but it wasn't enough. Suzanne was the problem, he thought. She'd never fulfilled his expectations the way he had expected. He'd wanted her to be the star of the motion picture he was directing, the famous madam with an impressive list of clients, the bottom bitch, an example for young hopefuls everywhere on how to turn a trick. He'd taught her superbly and given her everything she needed in order to make it. The cage had worked like a charm. Didn't she now do everything he asked without any prompting? Just as with the elephant training, she no longer needed chains or cages or even a rope, not even a string. She was his to do his bidding, but it wasn't enough. *She* wasn't enough. He had to kill her. Get her out of his system. He'd get Lulu to do it while he watched.

"I think this new idea in Sacramento is going to pay off bigtime," said Lulu.

"Who asked you to think?" answered Julius. "Try LJ's cell again."

She punched in the numbers, and then said, "It went to message."

"Fuck!" He pounded the steering wheel with his fists.

Better the steering wheel than my face, thought Lulu as they battled traffic on the I-5.

LJ was in a panic. The man on the other side of the door kept pounding on it and saying the police were on their way. The fucking cat had creamed his balls. This chick from hell had kicked away the gun and was screaming at the top of her lungs. Suzanne was curled up in the fetal position against the wall, and the stupid old lady was backing away from him and heading toward the kitchen where the back door was.

"Get moving, lady." He shoved Norma so hard she almost fell over. "We're going down to your place right now."

LJ was wheezing and out of breath, struggling to manage his three-hundred-pound frame in all this conflict. He jammed Norma through the back door and they hastily scrambled down the rickety back stairs. Upstairs, the two girls were left alone for a moment and they stayed put, rigidly staring at one another. It might have been a moment that lasted a lifetime, but in fact it was only a second before Sandy managed to jump up, run to the door, and unlock the multi-bolted door to let David in.

Once inside, Sandy fell into his arms sobbing as he tried to hold her and, at the same time, reach to pick up the gun lying by the door. He grabbed her up. as only a man surprised by love would, and held her close while his arms never failed to protect her. They were lost for a moment in each other's passionate embrace. Overwhelmed by the realization of his feelings for her, she had no idea how brave she had been because for that moment all she could fathom was his love.

Suzanne gazed at her friend with such envy and longing. How she wished she were her. *She and I are eighteen years old*, she thought. *But I am eighteen and twenty-eight and thirty-eight and fifty and on and on. I am over with, Sandy, but your life is just starting, so fresh.*

She wished she could get up, but her body felt glued to the floor. She felt like a puddle of nothingness. Sandy broke her embrace with David to come over and kneel beside her friend.

"I'm so very glad to see you again, Suzanne," she whispered. Tears fell from her eyes as she took her friend's face in her hands. "We have to get you out of here now."

With all the strength she could muster, Suzanne suddenly sat upright and, in pleading yet strong tones, insisted that Sandy leave as soon as possible. "I'm not leaving without you, Suzanne. Besides, the police are on their way."

"Not exactly," said David. "I was going to call them and realized that I had no proof of anything, except your breaking and entering. It was just a bluff to get in the door. We had all better get out soon before that buffoon comes ambling back in."

"Someone much worse may be showing up, and I don't want either of you in that kind of danger."

"Suzanne, I know who it is. It's that guy Julius, isn't it?"

"He's much worse than you could ever imagine, Sandy. He'll kill all of us if he finds anything wrong. Just go, please go."

Sandy stared at the friend she no longer recognized. What kinds of horrible things had happened to her? Things that had obviously shaken her soul. *She seems marked for life, but I won't abandon her*, thought Sandy.

"Get up please, Suzanne. We can get you some help. Please let's just go."

"I can't go back home; you know that. Nothing's there."

"Your dad's been sick. He's in a rest home now. He loves you, Suzanne."

"I don't believe in anything now, least of all anyone loving me. I'm so happy you've found someone, Sandy, but there is nothing left for me anymore. Leave me in peace."

As she fell back on the floor, David swooped down and picked up her wasted body. "She doesn't even weigh ninety pounds," he said. "Let's get the hell out of here, Sandy. My car's parked out front."

But as they hurriedly ran down the stairs, they found LJ waiting at the front door, along with two others: Julius and Lulu. All three looked up expectantly like onlookers at a wedding waiting for the bride.

Julius had been the last person LJ wanted to run into. He had been avoiding his calls, desperate to get Suzanne placed in a location that Dormer would accept and be on his way. All he wanted right now was to get to his Cessna and fly out to parts unknown. He and Eddie would hook up later as planned. Getting caught by Julius's wrath was not anything he had wanted to risk. As he labored down the stairs coming from Norma's apartment, his mind kept rehearsing get-away scenarios.

Julius looked livid, a state that was becoming his norm. He took one look at LJ and his lips curled into a snarl. "Where the hell do you think you're going?"

"Police, man, let's get the hell out," was all LJ could think of.

"What happened upstairs, LJ? Why are you here instead of picking up girls with your stupid plane?"

"Julius, man, things are really tight right now. No time to talk. Let's move."

For some reason, Julius didn't care. He didn't care anymore about being pressured or bothered. He did care about revenge, however, and his hatred for LJ and someone else he ranked in the same deceptive category: Suzanne. She had become the reason for his failure as an entrepreneur in the world of human trafficking.

Julius, with unperceived strength and dexterity, grabbed the bumbling LJ by the throat and choked him into submission. LJ succumbed, either by fact of his weight or loss of confidence, and fell to the ground, where he stayed. It was at this moment that the trio appeared at the top of the stairs. One group looked up and the other looked down, each bound by an obligation to destroy each other. David, at the top of the stairs, had the gun and he waved it forcefully to the group below.

"I'll shoot anybody who tries to stop us," he declared, but there was hesitation in his voice, and Julius picked up on that instantly.

"I think you have some property of mine," Julius said and laughed, gesturing to the tight grip David had on Suzanne's body. "You're not going anywhere with *her*."

"Julius, if the police catch us here—" Lulu began.

"Shut up! That's not what's important here. Who...who the

fuck are you?" A sign of recognition crossed Julius's face as he turned his gaze to Sandy. "Ah, yes, well look at you, my little dimwitted high-school friend. You've been tracking Suzanne for how long? Is this the same idiot you were dating in high school? I think not."

He turned his steely gaze back onto David, who was standing firm at the top of the stairs. He didn't move down, however, and Julius took the opportunity to take a step up.

"I said let go of my property and no harm will come to you."

"Hey, asshole, don't you notice a gun when you see one."

David fired shots as he ran down the stairs still carrying a limp Suzanne. Sandy followed in tow, a tour de force plowing through the group. Lulu fell in the sway, but quickly pulled out a knife, stabbing Suzanne as she passed.

Suzanne cried out in pain, but David and Sandy pushed through. Sandy threw a punch that startled Lulu, and in the stumble, Sandy was able to grab the knife. She thought about plunging it into the woman but decided against it. David, sensing her impulse, shoved her body away from Lulu and propelled all three of them toward the front door of the building. LJ tried to block their departure with his massive frame, but something inside of him, some weak spot that harbored a sense of moral courage, allowed the party to disembark, thereby disavowing him of any wrongdoing. He hadn't really wanted to fuck Suzanne in the first place. How was he to know that she was so young, virginal, and so damned vulnerable? Julius was the bad guy here, wasn't he?

In the recesses of LJ's mind, he recalled one of his favorite books, *The Portrait of Dorian Grey*. Just like Dorian, he unconsciously reminisced, any discrepancies would only be recorded on the portrait of his soul, to be reckoned with at some later time.

Unbelievably, at that moment Norma burst down upon the crowd. LJ had thrust her in a closet buffeted by a dresser, shoved hastily against the door to keep her sequestered, but Norma, propelled by some adrenalin rush, had forced her way out of the closet and, grabbing an ancient samovar from one of the shelves in her living room, came charging down like Theodore Roosevelt, screaming, "Believe you can and you're halfway there!" as she hurled the Russian urn haphazardly into the crowd below.

The shock of seeing her disoriented them all, and Suzanne, in a flourish, grabbed the knife from Sandy and thrust it deep into the side of LJ, screaming, "You didn't have to do it, but you did!" Just as suddenly, her screams subsided as David whirled her past with an astonished Sandy by his side. They both pitched a sobbing Suzanne inside David's Wrangler and sped off. Destination unknown.

Uncovering a crime of this magnitude in a small town like Paisley Falls meant moving through layers and layers of complicated data influenced by social status, money, and hidden corruption. *Are the police in this town complicit?* wondered Andy. He wasn't sure who he could trust. After Catherine had finished her story, he asked that she not repeat it to anyone. He also asked Helen if she would not repeat any of what she had heard, and without hesitation she pledged her allegiance.

"For now, this story stays with just our family and our trusted friend," he said, hugging a tearful Helen who silently nodded.

"You know, Wilson's family and the state police have a part in this, Andy. How are you going to fight forces like that?"

Dolores fought back tears of rage while gripping her teenage daughter as though she alone could shield her from harm.

"I know a lot about what goes on at the hospital," admitted Helen. "More goes on than you realize, Andy. Sometimes patients are brought in… well, at first we don't know how to diagnose them. They've got cuts and bruises, and when we ask them to explain how they got them they become strangely silent. I've been going online and taking classes in how to recognize beatings. That is," she continued, "different kinds of beatings, sustained beatings, covered up by people who know how to beat up victims regularly without it showing. Not that that hasn't been something we've seen for years. We have, of course, dealt with the abused wife or child, but there's a new kind of victim." She hesitated as though she even doubted her own observations. "Someone who claims they're not a victim. It's like they've been beat up but clearly want to be patched up in order to get back into the ring again. And believe me, there are people waiting outside to take them back."

"How many cases have you seen where you've felt it was a human trafficking incident?" asked Andy.

"Well, you know there's never been any formal training in how to determine that it's a result of trafficking, but now that I've become more aware, and definitely after hearing Catherine's story, I'd have to say it's probably more than usual."

"What kinds of wounds are you seeing?" persisted Andy.

"It's not something that's necessarily physical, Andy. It's a whole set of circumstances that don't seem to add up."

"Example?"

"Well, the other day a female of about eighteen or nineteen was brought into the ER, and her escort claimed she'd had a heroin overdose. Well, this girl wasn't comatose, she was crying hysterically. Obviously, she seemed terrorized by something, and there were scratches all around her neck. Nothing about her appearance or demeanor suggested an overdose. I asked the guy who brought her in if he would leave the room while I examined her, and he said that wouldn't be necessary. Then he asked if I could give her a sedative to calm her down. I wasted no time telling him how ridiculous that was if she indeed had overdosed. Honestly, I don't know what they wanted. They left without seeing a doctor. It was just a strange occurrence."

"Are these local girls, Helen?"

"Well, some, but more frequently they're from other parts of the country, some foreigners too. But they're almost always accompanied by someone who does most if not all of the talking. Of course, I've charted what I've seen, but since Dr. Wilson's no longer there, no one seems to be paying much attention to these things."

"Are you telling me Wilson noted incidents where he felt the patient was abused by a trafficker?"

"Sounds crazy, right?" Helen replied, shaking her head in disbelief. "Especially after what happened to Nadine. We all think he killed her, although no one can prove it. Sometimes I think it's become a company policy, if you will, to routinely dismiss any suggestions of trafficking. In the course of any day there are always accidents, broken bones, contusions that can often appear deliberate but also can be dismissed as accidental. I'm not a detective, Andy, although at times like this I wish I were."

They were interrupted by a phone call from the Paisley Falls Police Dept. It was Sid, Andy's former partner. In a town like Paisley Falls, population 1,350 in 0.89 square miles, the police force had consisted of only two people when Andy had worked with them. Now there were six officers, and apparently all six had been called to the cotton mill east of town.

"We checked everything out, Andy. We went over the whole area with a fine-tooth comb. There's no sign of any activity going on there, except for one thing."

"What's that, Sid?"

"Some kind of necklace that says 'one-hundred-percent certified cotton.'"

CHAPTER FOURTEEN

As the Wrangler sped off into the city, Sandy, who was sitting in the back seat with Suzanne, checked the knife wound Suzanne had sustained.

"It's a miracle we're all even alive at this point," she said.

"It's just a superficial scratch."

Pausing for a moment to look closely at her friend, Sandy tried to gauge what to say, what to ask. Suzanne was limp, eyes expressionless. "Oh my God, Suzanne, I don't even know how to comfort you."

Tears welled up again in Sandy's eyes, knowing that it was impossible to say anything that would get through to Suzanne. She seemed at once helpless yet fiercely self-sustained. Since she remained unresponsive, David chimed in from the front seat, focusing on the problems at hand.

"Now I think we should go to the police."

This created quite an arousal from Suzanne, who said emphatically, "No!"

"You're in shock, young lady, and your friend here has been risking her life to find you. We know you're scared. It's obvious you've been through hell. Let us try to help you."

David was trying his best to sound mature and responsible, but Suzanne surprised them both when she screamed, "No, no! Take me back to him right now." She frantically grabbed at the door handle, which might have swung open if Sandy had not grabbed Suzanne's arm in time. "I don't want to be with you! Take me back to him, you fuckin' assholes!" She began punching the back seat, slamming her fists at no one.

David quickly glanced back to see if her seat belt was fastened. It wasn't. "Sandy, fasten that seatbelt. Quick."

But as Sandy reached over to fasten the belt, rush hour traffic took over and cars all around came to an abrupt stop. Suzanne took that opportunity to fling open the car door and run madly into the oncoming traffic. As she ran haphazardly from car to car, begging anyone she could see for a ride, she was apprehended by a motorcycle cop. It was then that Suzanne continued her tirade claiming that she had been kidnapped by the very two people who had tried to save her.

"Thank God the police are finally involved," said David, too weary at the moment to get out of the car and explain the issue.

"I'm very afraid for Suzanne, David. This guy has become her addiction, her fix. Without him she might die."

"Goes both ways, Sandy. With him, she will surely die."

"Hey, you two! Out of the car now! Hands behind your back! This girl says you kidnapped her!"

CHAPTER FIFTEEN

LJ WAS BLEEDING profusely from the knife wound that Suzanne had inflicted. Lulu was looking for something to stop the bleeding, but Julius had become enraged and shoved her away, grabbing LJ by the throat.

"You worthless son of a bitch, I'll kill you. Where the fuck have you been? You're conning me, and you should know better, pal."

"Hey, man, I'm hurt. I've gotta get to a hospital."

"Don't touch him, you bitch," Julius hollered at Lulu. Let him bleed out. I could not care less." Julius stood up, wanting to be done with it all, and noticed that Norma had disappeared.

"What happened to that old bitch? Where in the hell did she go?"

"That's Norma" said Lulu. "I've seen her sometimes in the hallway passing. She lives on the third floor."

"Oh, what a big help you've been, Lulu. So glad you're attentive to all the tenants living here." He backhanded her, which sent her sprawling to the floor once again. "We've got to get out of here." He turned and paused to look down at the hapless LJ. Jeeringly he added, "Let's get to your little plane. You've got it all readied to go, I'm sure. Don't worry, we'll stop on the way for a Band-Aid," he laughingly said. "Oh," he started before turning back to Lulu, "what's her name again?"

"Norma," whispered Lulu.

"Norma, dear, one word to anyone or the police and you're a dead woman is that clear?" No answer. "I know you're listening, darling, and I can assure you that if you contact the police, I will know it was you and will come back and remove your head from your body. Do I make myself clear?"

There was a muffled growl coming from behind Norma's door on the third floor. It could have been Tito the cat answering with a battle cry, but Julius had never seen the cat and assumed that the sound was coming from a terrified old lady.

"Good, let's get the fuck out. Lulu, help him walk to the car."

"He's bleeding bad, Julius."

"Shut up! Wrap him up with the blankets we've got in the car and let's go." Abruptly, he tripped over the samovar that Norma had wielded when she had come cascading down the stairway. "God, what theatrics! Mother would have loved it!"

He touched the tattoo on his neck in fond remembrance of her, and the little spider inside the web seemed to quell with desire.

Upstairs, Norma was preparing to go on a journey of her own.

The officer listened patiently as David tried to explain the situation while rush-hour traffic surrounded them at the corner of Vermont and Los Feliz Boulevard. The officer tended to believe David's story. Nonetheless, he hauled all three of them into the Rampart Community Police Station. The one girl seemed to know her alleged captors and appeared to be strung out on drugs.

David and Sandy were coherent and were not resisting arrest. They weren't officially charged, but all three were cuffed and put in the back seat of the backup that had arrived.

"I understand, sir," the officer said to David. "This whole business deserves some serious investigation. I appreciate your cooperation in coming down to the station."

The cop was a young man who looked tired and dusty at five p.m. on a hot LA day. Drugs, human trafficking, and kidnapping were all part of the everyday LA ritual. He hoped that the young couple was really trying to save the battered girl. Nothing would surprise him though. It never did.

Once the three of them were tucked in the police car, Suzanne started shaking uncontrollably. Sandy, who was next to her, began to reminisce about their times in high school, as though no time had passed. "Remember that time, Suz, when we were walking down the hall before first period and Ed Eastman smiled at you and you didn't even see it so I nudged you and told you to smile in his direction and wave your hand and you automatically did it? He gave you this big grin back like he thought you noticed him, but you just kept on walking as though it was my duty to tell you when people were smiling at you. Ha ha! It was so funny! Those were the days, huh?"

"It *was* your duty," Suzanne said.

"What?" Sandy asked.

"You were the only one who knew how dead I was inside. You knew that nothing mattered about life to me, even then."

"Oh my God, Suz. Oh my God."

When they reached the station, the cop sat them down on a bench in the back. "Can we start from the beginning here? First of all, young lady, what's your name?"

"Suzanne DeMarco from Paisley Falls, Officer," volunteered Sandy.

"I'm asking this young lady. I'll get to you later."

"Oh, sorry; it's just that she's not feeling well."

"We'll let her be the judge of that."

But Suzanne was silent. She had quieted down and was no longer hysterical. Her eyes, however, darted back and forth frantically, trying to find some way to escape. She was still cuffed, and her hands twitched nervously as she tried to pull them out of the restraints. As far as she was concerned, this was just a prelude to another cage. No one here was a friend. She had to get back to what she knew, to where she belonged. *Say anything!* her mind urged her. Try to sound normal, just make it out of here. *Julius will protect me*, she reasoned.

She shifted slightly in order to hide any blood coming from the knife wound. She knew her dark clothes would camouflage the blood. Hiding her wounds had become just another trick of the trade.

"Yes, Officer, my name is Suzanne, formerly from Paisley Falls, California. I'm eighteen years old and of sound mind and body. My home is here in LA now." She smiled, feigning confidence, and feeling her imprisoning control take over.

"What's that new address, ma'am?"

Suzanne laughed inwardly at that one. She had no idea what the address was. She was just used to going there and then moving on. Addresses had no meaning for her.

No one said a word. David and Sandy exchanged glances, but both cast their eyes downward and away from the interrogation. David nodded silently to the cop and gestured toward another room where they could talk privately, but the cop wasn't budging.

"So I'll take that as no current address," he said, jotting that down in his report.

"Do you know these two people?" he asked, pointing to Sandy and David.

Suzanne hesitated. She wanted to say nothing. Maybe saying nothing would make them go away. She didn't want to be saved. She knew she would never go back to Paisley Falls. The very idea seemed completely absurd.

"That's my friend, Sandy. I knew her in high school. I don't know him," she said pointing to David. "I have no idea why they're here in LA trying to get me to go with them. I haven't done anything wrong. I'd just like to go home."

"She was kidnapped, Officer, two years ago in our hometown and forced into prostitution! It's human trafficking, Officer. Can't you see that?" Sandy burst into tears at this point, tired and exhausted by the chase and the effort.

"Suzanne, are your parents still living in Paisley Falls? Did they file a missing person's report when you were allegedly abducted?"

"You'd have to ask them that, Officer. I have no idea."

The cop shook his head at the frail and battered young woman before him. He didn't think he had the right to hold any of them. The girl was eighteen and legally, at least, doing what she wanted to do with her life. It appeared that the two girls knew each other and that the couple was trying to intervene in order to save her life. But it was her life to save after all. No one else had that right.

After a brief interview with David and Sandy, he explained that he had no legal obligation to hold her. He emphasized the fact that they had no legal control over her either. He ran a background check on one Suzanne DeMarco and came up with nothing. After offering Suzanne the opportunity to see a social worker, or take her to a hospital for an examination, he explained the function of several halfway houses in LA that took in and counseled victims of human trafficking. Did she want to take advantage of these services? He knew what the answer was going to be. He saw girls like this frequently. They never wanted to leave their pimps. It was always the same, and he couldn't understand why they never seemed to care about or value their own lives. *What a waste*, he thought. But that was all the time he gave it. It was just another day in LA, a city full of a million problems. *Can't solve them all*, he reasoned.

Background checks on Sandy and David provided nothing, and he instructed them to leave her alone or risk being arrested for battery.

Out the door of the precinct, all three went into the bright LA sunshine. Sandy and Suzanne stood facing each other on the sidewalk, just an arm's length apart. Suzanne moved first, slowly and tentatively putting her arms around the crying Sandy.

"Don't cry, Sandy. I'll be all right. I really will. Thank you. I mean it, for trying so hard to find out what happened to me. I'll never forget that."

With that, Suzanne turned and started walking down the boulevard, looking for cars that she knew would stop to pick her up.

Sandy stared at the retreating figure as she slowly disappeared in the fray. Left in a state of numbness and shock, she felt an anger rise up inside her. All the time and money she had wasted trying to rescue someone who no longer wanted to be saved. She'd lied to her parents, lied to her aunt, risked her life, and taken advantage of people. All she could think of was what a loss this was. She clutched at David's shoulder as they stood together in the hot LA sun watching a lost soul wander away from them. Feebly she called out, "We could find you a safe house!"

But Suzanne heard, "We can find you a safe place." *There is no safe place*, answered Suzanne in her mind. *This is where I belong now. This is the safest place I can find.*

CHAPTER SIXTEEN

LJ WAS SWEATING profusely in the back seat of the car. His heavy frame was doubled over in pain, and a look of sheer panic distorted his features. Lulu, normally ambivalent to anyone else's pain but her own, was unusually solicitous about his wound. Wrapping blankets around his midsection and applying pressure, she whispered words of comfort. "I'll get him to take you to emergency. Don't worry."

"So how bad is it, fuck face?" Julius asked Lulu. "Can you stop the bleeding, or should I just pull over and shoot him." Julius was glaring at the two of them in the rearview mirror.

"If he's dead, he can't fly his plane out of here, and we'll be stuck in LA with the police after us."

Lulu had a point, but that didn't make Julius feel any better. Everything was falling apart. How he wished he could go back to the old days with Dino. Everything had soured after Dino's death. It was as though his luck had turned. That macabre murder, Dino's head on a platter. They'd had a great business going with the truckers hauling ass with some great product fresh off the cargo containers from Thailand. Those were the easy days: training sessions with the cage and the pleasure of seeing their identities dissolve into nonexistence. Every bitch he had ever trained had turned into pure gold.

Except Suzanne.

How he hated her now. She brought trouble, but when he thought about it, she always had. That episode in the trunk of the car when she had nailed him, he still wasn't over it. It had made his limp worse than ever, and it had turned LJ against him. He didn't trust Lulu either. He'd like to dump them all and just start over.

He was so consumed with these thoughts that he wasn't aware at first of the hypodermic needle that stung his neck. *Was it a bee sting?* he wondered. But before he could decide anything more, he was swaying on the road, and a nimble Lulu had hopped into the front seat, guiding the steering wheel and pushing his foot off the gas pedal.

"What's wrong, Julius?" asked Lulu as she put a reassuring hand on his shoulder. "Let me take over the driving. I think you might be having a stroke."

She had deftly located the "chick pack" that they kept in the car. A syringe filled with a tranquilizer, duct tape, wrist ties, and blindfolds were neatly packaged and stuffed into a side pocket for easy access.

"Whas happen? What di you do?" Julius drawled as his mind slowly came to a grinding halt.

"Easy, easy there, my dear," cooed Lulu. "Let's pull over now. Slowly, easy does it."

"You bitch," he managed before he passed out.

Lulu took over driving the car without much of a fanfare. It was still rush hour in LA, but the transition to her taking control had been practically seamless.

LJ picked his head up from the back seat. He was getting

weaker by the minute, his flaccid face a mass of sweat. "Why are you helping me? Or should I ask, are you helping me?"

"Yes, I will get you to a hospital. I want you to be okay. Julius was going to kill me, I know that. Saving you means you flying us out of here to Canada or Mexico. Do you understand?" Now it was her turn to glare at him from the driver's seat.

He was fading fast, but he managed a smile and mouthed "no problem" as he lost consciousness. Lulu turned on the GPS and found a hospital within two blocks. She pushed Julius's limp body over to the passenger side and propped him up so it would look like he was asleep or drunk, and then she quickly pulled over, signaling a left turn. The bright red emergency sign of a hospital greeted them ahead as she quickly sped up to enter. Lulu parked haphazardly and assumed a panicked look as she rushed to the left rear of the car and opened the door. Frantically she called out, "Quick! Somebody help me! My husband has had an accident!"

Two aides standing outside the building for a smoke rushed to assist her, and together they lifted the lumbering giant onto a stretcher. No one paid attention to the other passenger in the car when he stirred slightly and opened his eyes briefly before falling back to sleep.

LJ had lost a lot of blood. They rushed him into emergency surgery. Lulu was met by two of the hospital police who maintained a routine stay there.

After one look at Lulu and listening for thirty seconds to her wild tale of an accident while her alleged husband was mowing the lawn, the two cops took her into a private room for questioning. Since she had no identifying papers, there was no way to do a background check. Subsequently, they determined that she was an illegal alien and placed her under house arrest.

John Toomey, aka Little John, aka LJ, had a crumpled-up driver's license as well as a pilot's license and a dubious history of drug abuse and smuggling narcotics. A background check of his home in Leverton showed a police presence there that led to an inquiry about any information former Sergeant Andrew Dormer might have, which led to a phone call.

Andy, who had been totally caught up in his own circumstances, was concerned about the whereabouts of Suzanne DeMarco, which led to another check of local police activity. One Suzanne DeMarco had recently been picked up by the Rampart Police Station and then released, whereabouts unknown. Since the van that Lulu and LJ showed up in was illegally parked, blocking the ER entrance, the two cops went to inspect it for possible stolen property. There they discovered a groggy Julius, who didn't know how he had gotten there in the first place. After hauling him into ER for a possible drug overdose, they ended up arresting him as well.

Julius Conaforte was a well-known drug smuggler, human trafficker, and gangster with a long rap sheet of multiple felonies. Lulu couldn't help smiling at the crazy situation she had put the three of them in. She knew LJ would have died if she hadn't gotten him to a hospital, but the truth was, she didn't care about him. She knew she'd wanted to use his plane to escape, but her own sense of reality knew better than that. Some unconscious part of her knew the jig was up. It was all over and it didn't matter. Maybe she had wanted it to end; that part was true. Trying to hold onto something that never had any good end except financial gain was exhilarating but exhausting—not that she cared either about the countless lives she had ruined. Some lives are meant to be sacrificed; hadn't hers been?

Some faint stirring of concern went out to her brother and

uncle, but weren't they doomed to a life of servitude anyway? Was that her fault? Each person must look out for himself. That lesson she'd learned before she could walk. She would get out of this eventually but knew she would have to disappear into another underworld. One in which she could no longer be found by Julius.

In her head, she began singing a nursery rhyme, one of her many "fathers" had sung while molesting her. A fat old American grandpa, who had retired on the ancient Chinese island where she was born, had hidden his guilt at his deeds with a wholesome fatherly demeanor. "Three Blind Mice," he would sing. "See how they run," as his fingers ran up and down her little legs. "They all ran after the farmer's wife," as he pulled down her panties. "She cut off their tails with a carving knife. Did you ever see such a sight in your life, as three blind mice." She had been comforted by that rhyme but was always slightly nauseated by the memory of what came after.

Suzanne was eventually picked up by someone cruising by in a car. Not a john, but a Good Samaritan who could tell just by looking at her that she was injured and about to faint. He dropped her off at an urgent care facility, but didn't stick around, as he had no details to provide.

"Honey, what's your name?" a pleasant grey-haired physician's assistant inquired.

"Suz…. Please, I'm fine. I just want to go home."

"Okay, sweetie. Have you got a phone number? Somebody we could call to pick you up?"

Suzanne was stumped by this and murmured the only phone number she could think of—her parents' number in Paisley Falls.

"Oh, gosh, don't call them. They don't care."

"Oh, but I'm sure they do. Honey, are you on anything? I need to get a blood sample from you. You just lay back on the table now and catch your breath."

But Suzanne wasn't being cooperative and started to struggle. "No! Don't! I don't want anything! Leave me alone!" She struggled to get up from where she sat but fell back.

"Loni!" the nurse called out. "I need some assistance in here."

As the two of them struggled to subdue Suzanne, she begged for them to let her go, just as she had when first being introduced to the cage. The memories flooded back, and she cried, cajoled, begged, and threatened, as she once had done when trying to survive for months like a caged animal. "Please, please don't keep me in this cage any longer! I'll do anything you ask!" she screamed out to the astonished nurses.

"Loni, here's the number she gave. Go call these people and tell them who we found."

"What's her name?"

"All I got was Suz, but if these people know her, that's enough."

The DeMarcos still had a landline, and when the call came through, it was Bethy who picked up the phone. "Hello?" she said, more like a question than a statement.

"Hello, this is urgent care in Los Angeles calling for a woman here at the clinic going by the name of Suz. Is this person familiar to you? Is she a member or friend of your family?"

Bethy stared at the phone for a long moment. "No," she finally said.

Her mother called out. "Who was that, Bethy?"

"No one," she said as she placed the receiver back down. "Just a robo call."

CHAPTER SEVENTEEN

It was the second time in thirty minutes that Sid called Andy Dormer. This time it was to tell him that Suzanne DeMarco had been brought into the Rampart Police Station in Echo Park with a friend, also from Paisley Falls, Sandy McKinnon, and a man named David Hargrove. The LA police let her go because they said they had no reason to detain her. Andy felt a flood of emotions overtake him on this already extremely emotional day.

Suzanne's high school friend had found her. An eighteen-year-old girl with no professional detective experience had managed to do what he had failed to do, track down Suzanne. After kicking himself for not finishing the job and then hating himself for abandoning his own family, he became furious with the police for letting her go. Certainly, Sandy would have verified the fact that she had been kidnapped, that she was a victim of human trafficking. The problem was that her parents hadn't seemed to give a damn about her. No one had filed a missing person's report. The state police had moved in to take over the investigation of the murder at the mill and the abduction of the four teenage girls. Suzanne had just become an afterthought. It was time, he thought, to pay another visit to the DeMarco household. He knew that he had to confront Rhonda DeMarco about her feelings for her daughter. and he hoped that Evan DeMarco was still alive enough to care.

As he drove back into the older section of town where the DeMarcos lived, he passed by the high school that Suzanne and Sandy had attended. It was Saturday afternoon, and the football team was playing one of their rivals, a small town twenty miles north of Paisley Falls. He recalled that one of the abducted teenagers had come from there. He had always known that no place on earth was free of crime and there were people intent on doing evil to others all over the globe. Maybe he was naïve to think that abducting young children and enslaving people didn't happen anymore, at least not in these little hamlets, not in his town, in his neighborhood. This stuff was supposed to happen in LA, New York, Chicago, big cities where crime was a fact of life, not out here in the boondocks. He had let his town down. He had wanted to keep his side of the street clean, and it was with a new sense of powerlessness that he realized he couldn't protect them all, and he would better serve the community if he stopped trying to solve the whole world's problems. The DeMarcos were, however, one problem that he wanted like hell to get to the bottom of.

He rang the doorbell, but no one answered the door. He thought he heard shuffling and something sounding like a cane or a walker being dragged across the floor. There was a flutter from the window blinds being pressed down and released, and then a grunting noise as the locks on the door began clicking. The door opened so slowly that he felt like he was in a Halloween horror movie. A shriveled Rhonda DeMarco appeared at the screen door and tried to focus on who it was she was looking at.

"You're that detective or whatever who tried to find Suzanne, aren't ya? Any luck?" she cackled.

She must have aged twenty years, Dormer thought as he looked at the wasted figure before him. Disheveled hair framed the grey pallor of her skin, and Jack Daniels smelled like her best, perhaps only, friend.

"May I come in, Mrs. DeMarco? I'm formerly Sergeant Dormer with the Paisley Falls Police. We did speak a couple of times about two years ago when your daughter went missing. I understand that you and your husband never filed a missing person's report."

At the mention of that, Rhonda bristled. "Formerly sergeant? What? Were you kicked off the police force? I don't see what our private business has to do with you."

Dormer felt it was useless to explain to her that he had become a private detective who had continued to look for her daughter. Instead, he decided to give her what he suspected wouldn't be very good news.

"Suzanne has been located in LA. She was apparently found by her high school friend, Sandy." Just to lay it on a bit thicker he added, "They'll be coming back to Paisley Falls soon."

Whatever response he might have expected from Rhonda DeMarco, he wasn't prepared for what he got.

"Evan! I've got to go and protect Evan!"

"Is he here? I'd like to have a word with him."

"Here? He hasn't been here for almost two years. He's in a rest home. He can't even move. I go take care of him every chance I get. And who do you think takes care of me? No one, that's who. If he sees Suzanne again it might kill him. I've got to make sure she doesn't come near him. All she's ever been is trouble. I don't want to see her again, and she mustn't ever go near him.

Can't you arrest her before she gets back in town? I'm sure she's done plenty of illegal things. She's probably a full-fledged whore by now. Do your duty and get her out of here."

Dormer felt his temper rise. Worse, he imagined hitting her. What an insensitive piece of garbage. No wonder Suzanne had left home. What kind of environment had this been for a young girl? He couldn't help but think of his two young daughters who were loved and appreciated and praised. To try and thrive under this kind of a rock must have been beyond depressing.

He remembered finding that little booklet in Suzanne's bedroom when he was investigating her disappearance, thinking it might be a possible connection to the teenage abductions. The pamphlet that glamorized suicide, Elvira Madigan style.

He couldn't think of any reason to stay and smell any more of her fetid breath. Disgusted, he turned to leave, but a young girl appeared in the doorway. Of course, he thought, it's the younger daughter. She didn't look anything like Suzanne or even have the same manner about her. She stared vacantly at him, but then her eyes focused as though she'd made a decision to say something.

"They called."

"What? Who called?" barked her mother.

"Some place in LA. They said they had her there and asked if I knew her."

"What did you say?" asked Dormer, even though he knew the answer before she gave it.

"I just didn't want her to come back, that's all. It's so much more peaceful now.

❧

As Dormer closed that awful chapter in his mind, another

troubling epoch presented itself. Where in the hell was LJ? Had he gotten away? Dormer had been so distracted the last twenty-four hours that he had forgotten the agreement they'd made. Obviously, if he had ever had Suzanne in the first place, she wasn't with him now, but it didn't sound like she was out of danger yet.

He looked at his cell phone records and saw that LJ had called. A garbled message about locations made no sense. He decided he'd make a plea to his previous pals at the police station to run a check on all phone calls that had come through to the DeMarco household, praying that they still had a landline. It should be easy enough to trace the origin of the phone call that Bethy answered. He had to return to the station anyway.

He now knew the story behind that necklace they found. Sid had sounded sincerely baffled by the object. Were the local police innocent of any knowledge about what went on there? He simply didn't know who to trust. All of these things dredged up the past that had involved Dr. Wilson and poor Nadine Hines as well as the state police cover-up of the murder and the abductions. He'd have his hands full; the only thing he was really sure of was that he had to proceed with caution. Someone or some group wanted him out of the loop.

He remembered the scene in front of the Loosey Goosey with Sergeant Woodard and the distinct warning he got about endangering his family. "How dare him," murmured Andy. Woodard had even mentioned his daughters and the need to keep them out of danger. Had Woodard been in on a deal even then about turning the cotton mill into an international brothel? The local police had to have had some knowledge about this. It was too big an operation to go unnoticed.

First things first. Dormer shook himself to pay attention.

His family came first from now on. Uncovering the mystery of the cotton mill came second. Finding Suzanne came third and nailing LJ to the wall came fourth. Last but not least, was busting Julius and his enterprise wide open. He knew that uncovering and exposing all of these things would automatically help to solve the murder of Nadine Hines as well. Dormer thought again about the priority of what he had to do, and without further hesitation, he turned his grey Honda around away from the police station and headed home.

Since Lulu had committed no crime and claimed she was seeking asylum, she was released on her own recognizance and assigned a court date. She headed back to the Sacramento apartment where she had begun her underground business of body smuggling. She talked her way back into the Make a Bed Inc. agreement with the Restful Sleep Hotel chain as a full partner, explaining that Julius was on an extended business trip and would not be available for many months. Of the three Honduran workers employed at the hotel, the old man had died and needed replacing ASAP. Lulu had anticipated his demise and had already recruited an illegal who had made his way via underground to the secret tunnel that she had created in the side of the apartment. The new mandates at the border made illegals more desperate than ever, and the imaginative and industrious Lulu resolved to find a way to enslave them all.

While recovering from surgery, LJ managed to persuade a young nurse's aide that he would fly her to the moon and give her all the free cocaine she wanted if she could help him find a way out of the hospital without notifying the cops. He had no idea whether Dormer was on his trail. Obviously, he had failed to keep his end of the bargain, and he was afraid to contact Eddie, lest his whereabouts become known to Dormer. Junkyard Eddie had all the money they'd managed to scrounge for their budding career in the porn-movie industry hidden in rusty car parts at the Dump'n Depot, but LJ, who had never really trusted anyone, had always kept a secret stash of cash in the inside rim of the Cessna's wheels. Going back to Leverton was simply out of the question. He still had the Cessna, and his *new girlfriend*, the cute nurse's aide, had a car, and that was all they needed at the moment.

She couldn't help giggling as she dressed him in her brother's clothes, which were a bit tight on LJ's generous frame. He had lost weight with his bout in the hospital, but it had done little to shave his physique of any bulk. Still, he managed to get out of the hospital one dark night with her help. A quick drive out to Long Beach where the Skyknight was stored and they were on their way to Canada, where LJ still had some contacts. He couldn't believe how easy it was to get away. He felt as though he had rid himself of the virus that was Julius. He should have done this a long time ago. There was nothing better than to start all over in life, a clean slate, a wide blue sky before him.

Julius was sentenced to ninety days for a variety of offenses. Basically, anything the judge could find to imprison him. He had certainly done time before, but he was feeling especially unhinged of late. He wasn't having the luck his mother had promised him as her legacy. Nightmares had returned, and the dream about the house with too many rooms that he had wandered aimlessly in came back to haunt him. Now as he tried to flee from one room to another, each door slammed shut and locked. Once he managed to pry it open, a bigger lock would automatically appear sealing him in. The mole on his neck itched constantly, and he scratched it till the little tattooed web around it bled. He had insisted on seeing the prison doctor, convinced that he might have a melanoma, but he was laughed at and his pleas disregarded. "Get it checked when you get out of here, asshole. What do you think this is, the Mayo Clinic?" It wasn't long before word got out that he was in the hole.

Bobby Hu heard.

Bobby had never gotten over his baby brother's death, and he held a great deal of resentment for Julius. He had never wanted Dino to hook up with him in the first place. Dino had had a great head for business, organizing Asian girls in motels and moving them between locations in nine counties. Those chicks had brought in more than three hundred fifty thousand dollars a month. He sure as hell didn't need Julius. How come *his* head hadn't been decapitated? He never bought the feeble explanation that Julius had offered two years ago, some story about some fuckin' Muslim impersonators knocking Dino off. For what? That was bullshit, and Bobby had bided his time.

A friend in prison owed him a favor, and the timing couldn't have been better. Julius had not only caused his brother's death, he had fucked up a huge business enterprise at the Port of Long Beach. Now you couldn't smuggle a cockroach into the Port of Long Beach without causing a police riot. Bobby put out a request to his party, and the deed was done quietly and efficiently.

Julius started choking in the mess hall one day, and before any of the guards could get to him, he was dead. He didn't know what happened at first. The food had tasted strange and very salty, but all of a sudden, his throat was burning up and he couldn't swallow. "Help!" he had cried to the guy next to him, but he got no response.

Flaccidly, he stared into the cold, grey eyes of the bald man sitting there who betrayed nothing—not pity, not anger, just duty bound—a guy who had an assignment. Julius panicked when he realized that this was it. This was the end. His mind, as he became delirious, kept bouncing back to Suzanne, to the last time he saw her. His eyes filled with blood as his body began to rupture internally.

Gasping, he fell to the floor in a pool of vomit and blood. He held fast to an image of Suzanne as he held her by the neck and squeezed, unaware that he was squeezing the life out of his own neck as well. Screaming in agony, he tried to tear out his own throat right where the spiderweb was. As he began tearing at his own flesh, he thought he saw his mother standing over him laughing. "No, no stop!" he cried to this monstrous image as his mother helped him tear off bits of skin from his body, her eyes shining as she skinned him alive Then it was over, and he was gone, collapsed on the concrete floor, his face frozen with a look of hatred and loneliness.

"Needed a Heimlich maneuver," his fellow inmates said. Too bad it came too late. Word had it that he knew he'd been poisoned and the only word he uttered as he fell to the ground was "Suzanne."

CHAPTER EIGHTEEN

"WAKE UP. WAKE up, Suzanne." Someone was shaking her shoulder. She opened her eyes and didn't recognize anything around her. Dazed, she tried to sit up but realized that her wrists were bound to the bed she was lying on.

"Where am I?" She banged her foot against a metal bar and struggled to break free of the restraints and get up.

"Don't worry, honey, you're safe. You're in a halfway house. You were scratching yourself so much that you got violent when anybody tried to help you, so they had to restrain you. They'll take 'em off if they can see that you're better." The kind lady smiled, revealing a toothless mouth and a lot of charm.

Since the urgent care facility couldn't find anyone to claim Suzanne, they had taken her to New Chances, a nonprofit geared to helping victims of human trafficking recover. Suzanne opened her bleary eyes as she tried to focus on who was talking and what she had said.

"Have I been drugged?" Suzanne asked, pulling at the bandages that bound her to the bed. "I need to get out of here right now. How long have I been here?"

"You came in here yesterday afternoon, honey, and you slept

it off pretty good. Don't know what you was on, but you look all better now. Let me get someone."

She shuffled off, leaving a panicked Suzanne picking at her wrist ties, trying to sit up.

Desperation was welling up in her. Every routine she had come to depend on in the last two years was being broken. Julius would kill her for sure if he knew where she was. Why wasn't he looking for her? Why wasn't he here?

Sandy! She remembered seeing Sandy, her high school friend. Had she dreamed that or was it real? She remembered being thrown in a car with Sandy and someone else and that she had stabbed LJ. It was all flooding back to her now, being carried down the steps by that man with Sandy, the fight that ensued, seeing the menace in Julius's eyes.

The words "wake up, wake up" clicked in the recesses of her mind. Wake up to what? Another endless day of johns and Julius? She couldn't take one more day of it, and she couldn't stop it either. The last thing she wanted to do was wake up.

Another woman came bustling into her small room. It wasn't a hospital room; it looked more like a teen's bedroom, with bold-colored walls and a bookshelf with an equal amount of books and stuffed animals. Pretty pictures of landscapes and ocean views decorated the small room. *Another person trying to save me,* Suzanne thought cynically. She couldn't wait until she could get up and get out.

"Suzanne DeMarco, how are you feeling today?"

"What the fuck! How in the hell do you know my name?" Suzanne looked up at the motherly figure standing before her. How she detested motherly figures; worse were women with motherly attitudes. A badge on the front of her blouse identified her as Margaret Perron, Director of New Chances.

Smiling right through Suzanne's foul mouth, she continued. "Believe me, it wasn't easy. You have no identification on you, no driver's license, no history of one, no cell phone, no credit cards, nothing. You were picked up yesterday by the local police with two other people, one of those was supposedly a personal friend who identified you as Suzanne DeMarco from Paisley Falls, California. The police had no cause to hold you, thank goodness," she added, smiling. "So, you apparently left the station on foot and were picked up by a nice gentleman who dropped you off at an urgent care facility. Any of this making sense to you?"

Groggy still, she shook her head, trying to put things in place. So, meeting Sandy had really happened after all. She vaguely remembered the staff at the urgent care and a bunch of needles with more drugs and blood tests. They had asked a lot of questions, like where she lived and where she was from. What had she told them? She couldn't remember.

"They placed a call to a number you had given them, but the party there said they'd never heard of you."

Suzanne tried to pretend she hadn't heard that, but the tears burst out of her.

"Okay, okay, easy now. Just breathe. We might have called the wrong number. Maybe the one you gave us was incorrect, honey." She cradled Suzanne's head as she felt the young girl give herself over to great heaving sobs.

"No… ha!" she cackled. "I'm sure you called the right number," she managed to blurt out. "It doesn't matter. I don't have any family I want to go back to anyway."

Margaret seemed ready to handle that response and she pointed to a slogan that adorned one of the walls of the room.

It said:

FAMILY ISN'T ALWAYS BLOOD.

It's the people in your life who want you in theirs.

The ones who accept you for who you are.

The ones who do anything to see you smile.

The ones who love you

NO MATTER WHAT.[6]

"For now, just keep your eyes on that slogan. Keep reading it over and over. I don't know exactly what you've been through, but that journey is over. You're safe here. I know you don't feel that way, but you are. No harm will come to you here."

Something about the way the director was talking to her made Suzanne feel calmer. Her big, brown eyes gazed directly at her. There was no malice, no jealousy in this mother's demeanor.

Margie, as the staff fondly called her, had seen so many young girls come through here so lost, alienated from the person they had been before. So many of them had been duped by someone who made them feel special, as though they were the only one. If only she could go back in time with each one of them and show them the truth about themselves and their seducers: people, drugs, illusions, expectations, pressure from social media, money. Margie didn't know it, but she shared the same dedication to serving justice in the world as did Andy Dormer, Helen Powell, David Hargrove, Sandy McKinnon, and countless others. It was the same old battle between good and evil, as it always had been. She, like all of them, felt an instinct to never give up. It was a lifetime commitment, one that was accepted without argument.

---

6   Author Unknown. "Women Working Dare to Live Fully," WorkingWomen.com, Retrieved from the World Wide Web, July 10, 2019, https://www.womenworking.com/meme/family-isnt-always-blood/.

Suzanne was absolutely stunned. If Julius found out, she'd be back in the cage for months. She didn't know quite how to react. She was terrified and relieved at the same time. In her own mind, she placed the restraints upon her body that Julius had once bound upon her. She felt the imaginary chains come down upon her wrists and ankles; she ate the dog food from the dog dishes because it was familiar food. She begged to be let out of the cage as she took comfort in its confines. She lay still with deadly patience, waiting just as she had done on her very first night in the cage, praying for dawn to come, and it was in this trance that she rested on day one of her rescue.

"Leave her alone," Margaret said to the others as she closed the door to her room. "She has to rest for quite a while. If she calls for anything, go in the room and tell her she is loved. Then come and get me."

Dormer may have been done with Rhonda DeMarco, but he wasn't finished with the case. Once home, he sat down to dinner with his family. The dining room table that had held so many dinners was an extension of the kitchen. Farm table white with four round-backed chairs, it had served for many years as the gathering for family therapy sessions. His older daughter had come home from the community college where she was a freshman majoring in photography, so happy to hear that her dad was back. Dolores had made his favorite dinner: pot roast (her secret recipe) with new potatoes and glazed carrots, a salad with fresh tomatoes and red onions, and a nice bottle of red wine to go with the meal.

God, it felt good to be home again.

Dolores was less frosty than she had been when he first came back. He knew he had to give her time. He had to give all of them time to get over the fear that he might leave again. He was never going to. There was plenty to do in Paisley Falls.

They sat around the dinner table and talked about their lives in such a simple, loving way. Andy realized how lonely he had been and how much these three people meant to him. He was coming to the realization that he had shut down a great portion of himself in order to succeed.

Looking back on the past two years, he realized he'd failed to find Suzanne, but it was a good thing Sandy had. She was probably the only person in Suzanne's life right now that could get through to her. Still, the thing on his mind was talking to Evan DeMarco. My God, what had happened to him? Next on his list was contacting Sandy McKinnon and finding out when and if Suzanne would be coming home. He had the feeling that Evan, at least, had missed his daughter and would love to see her again. Instead of keeping these thoughts to himself, he shared with his family all that had happened, meeting Rhonda and Bethy, and the sad and tragic mentality of a family that had never really loved or understood Suzanne.

After dinner, he put in a call to the McKinnon family, asking for Sandy's cell number. He got an ear load from Mrs. McKinnon about her daughter's whereabouts and the danger that she thought her daughter had gotten into.

"Sounds like she's got herself a nice boyfriend, but she never brought him around to her aunt's house in LA where she was staying," she said. "We had kind of a fight yesterday when I called. She probably doesn't want to talk to me anyway."

"Why's that?" asked Andy.

"Well, she and her boyfriend had found Suzanne all right,

but the girl didn't want to go with the two of them. Sandy said Suzanne just walked away."

"And they let her go?"

"What were they supposed to do? Chain her down? It's still a free country, Andy, even though it doesn't feel much like it anymore."

⁕

Sandy felt like she had been hit with a steamroller. It had been a few days since they had seen the retreating figure of her friend making her way down the boulevard. Nothing David said made any difference. She had failed to rescue Suzanne. Enough said. Job over. What's next?

"I know it's not the outcome you wanted, Sandy, but you can't control someone else's life."

"The life she has now is not the life she wanted. She fell headlong into a nightmare. I feel like I'm going crazy trying to pull her out of it."

"She's not your responsibility. Isn't it time you started looking out for yourself?"

"Well, I don't know how you'd feel if you saw someone cutting their wrists right in front of you. Would you try to keep someone from committing suicide?"

"Of course I would, but this is a little more complicated than that. Sure, if she was standing on the edge of a bridge getting ready to jump off, I'd try to talk her out of it—"

"Or maybe the only way you could save her is by grabbing her before she jumped."

"That's a big risk," he said. "She could fall before you succeeded."

"I've got to keep trying, David, because to me she is cutting her wrists right in front of me *and* getting ready to jump."

"You're chasing a firestorm, Sandy. Nothing you do will ever be enough for her. Can't you see that?"

Sandy's cell rang right at that point. She listened to what was being said, nodding her head as though she agreed with the caller. When the call ended, she shared the contents with David. "That was that private detective who started looking for Suzanne when I did. He's back in Paisley Falls and traced a call to her home from an urgent care facility in LA where she got dropped off by someone who had picked her up."

If Sandy had been discouraged by the recent events, she wasn't now. She shook her hair back and straightened up as though a heavy weight had been lifted. Confident of her own actions, she turned to David. "Care to join me?"

There was an awkward moment, and then David came to her and took her hand. They left together without another word, arms entwined around each other.

～

Evan was staying in Restful Days, the wealthier section of Brook View Manor in Paisley Falls. It was situated right on the river, near an elegant little manufactured village that smugly referred to itself as a town separate from Paisley Falls, although it had no post office. A few choice restaurants dominated the little enclave where Stephanie and the late Dr. Wilson used to dine. Some elegant boutiques dotted the landscape, catering to the soccer moms who visited between yoga sessions and after-school practice drop-off and pickup. Dormer thought it was an odd place for a rest home and also a bit pricy for the DeMarcos.

After he had found out where Evan DeMarco was housed,

he inquired about his daily schedule. Not wanting to run into Rhonda DeMarco again, he informed the staff that he needed to have a private meeting with their patient and wondered if Mrs. DeMarco had any kind of regular schedule. Yes, she did, one of the day nurses said when he called, sounding annoyed when she told him.

"She manages to come in here every morning around ten and disrupt whatever it is we're doing, Mr. Dormer. Any way you could get her to stop?"

Andy laughed and made some small talk, reminding them that he had no clout since he'd been taken off the police force, but all that was about to change.

"We're all so glad to hear that you're coming back. The state police never did solve that crime. I'll distract Mrs. DeMarco if she shows up when you're here. Come in around three. She's usually gone by then. She doesn't come back again until dinner time, when she insists on feeding him and criticizing the food."

Dormer made arrangements to see Evan DeMarco the next day. When he showed up at three p.m. to have a chat, he couldn't believe what he saw. It had been only two years since he'd seen Evan at the hospital when he'd had a heart attack and once later in their home, but the changes in him were remarkable and devastating. Like his wife, he had aged horribly. Shriveled and lifeless, he lay in his bed barely able to pick up his head. He showed no recognition of Andy and had no response to the questions regarding his daughter Suzanne. At the mention of her name, his eyes flickered slightly as if he had wanted to say something important. He raised his hand up and pointed upward in one violent jerk. Then he sputtered and fell fast asleep in a fantasyland of his own making. Sadly, Dormer turned to leave, when something on the old man's bedside table made him take a closer look.

There, crumpled up and hidden under a piece of tissue, was a pendant necklace with the inscription "One-hundred-percent organic cotton. Made in the USA."

CHAPTER NINETEEN

"SID, ARE YOU telling me that there was no noticeable sign of activity when you inspected the cotton mill the other day?'

"Just what I told you, Andy. We found a necklace, nothing expensive. A pendant. Some kind of cheap chain with a round piece of metal hanging on it with the inscription 'One-hundred-percent organic cotton. Made in the USA.'"

He was describing exactly what Andy had found on Evan DeMarco's bedside table. "Where is this necklace now?" asked Andy, hoping it was still at the station but fearing it was not.

"State police were notified about this and came to collect any evidence we found for their records."

"Doesn't that sound suspicious to you now? Everything about the way the investigation of that murder two years ago and the abductions of those girls has been mishandled and covered up. Why is that?"

"Our hands have always been tied, Andy. You know that. Stephanie Wilson's father controls the police all over the state. I have to admit, though, your finding another necklace besides the one we found at the mill is pointing to something strange, out of the ordinary. Maybe this is something that shouldn't be reported at this particular time."

"I couldn't agree more, Sid. For now, this is just between us."

Andy decided not to tell Sid about what his daughter had found out from her encounter with Shelby. The whole thing sounded wildly improbable, although Andy had learned that anything you can possibly imagine about human trafficking was conceivably a sad reality somewhere in the business of enslaving humans.

It was no surprise either that Roy Barber, Stephanie's oil-rich father, had some interest in controlling or manipulating the police. Sid had filled in Andy on the details of Dr. Frederick Wilson's death, and it was rumored that Roy had had a hand in hiring the two guys who knifed him, although they were both connected to victims of Wilson's perverted leanings. Dormer wondered how the sophisticated Mrs. Wilson was doing after her husband's death. He made a mental note to pay her a visit, but first on his mind was tying this necklace to the bizarre organization that Catherine had described.

He was also worried that if Shelby had been killed after telling Catherine about the organization and failing to recruit her into it, that Catherine would be next. Andy mentally went over the details of the murder of Dino Hu at the cotton mill two years ago. The young girls had described two men, allegedly Muslim, who had killed Dino, released them from their cages, wrote symbols with blood on their bodies, and sent them on a walk through town, naked and tied together with wire, in the early morning hours.

His mind raced back to that morning at two o'clock when he had found them walking while he was on patrol. What a dizzying sight it had been. All young teens seduced by online chats or kidnapped in malls when their parents weren't looking. The minute he had started asking questions, he had been silenced! Could this 100-percent cotton club have been in the making back then? When he put Roy Barber into the picture, everything started to make a different kind of sense.

Roy had oil and steel ties to the biggest corporations in America: oil with Middle Eastern ties and steel with American-made steel used in buildings all over the US. The appearance of two Middle Eastern men in a small town like Paisley Falls was enough to ring all kinds of warning bells already sounding throughout this country about the supposed danger of foreigners infiltrating our borders. It was enough of a sensation to call in the state police to quell the fears of a small community, which had never before witnessed such a thing.

Could the whole thing have been a distraction for what was really being planned at the mill? No wonder the town's plans for revamping it into a shrine for the victims who had perished in the fire a century ago or turning it into art galleries had been stymied. But how on earth would anyone be able to keep it a secret? This town was too small to have no one notice something so incredibly out of the ordinary. Could he really trust Sid? Could he really trust anyone?

Suzanne continued to drift in and out of sleep for the next few days. Slowly, she came to accept where she was, defining it only as being away from Julius. At first this was met with blinding fear that somehow he would find her and kill her. She took little comfort in the reassurances from others that she was safe. The slogan on the wall, the stuffed animals, and brightly colored walls didn't appear inviting to her, but rather menacing, challenging her to return to a former life she never really understood anyway.

Stripped of her identity as a prostitute, who she had been before, she felt unrecognizable. It always had struck her as funny that she never quite knew what she looked like. It was only when someone took a picture of her and showed her that she had any idea of her physical appearance. *Oh,* she would think gazing at the picture, *this is how I look. This is me. I have no connection to this person.* She was terrified that someone would come and take a picture of her now. She knew that she'd never be able to face it.

Margaret Perron, the director of New Chances, had been taking care of young women like Suzanne for years. A survivor herself of sex trafficking, she had packed her bags one day and with the aid of a cross-country bible toting trucker who had picked her up hooking at a truck stop saying only that he wanted to save her from sin, helped her escape from her pimp and start a new life. He had been able to hide her with a series of Christian families in several different states, always picking her up and moving her along his truck route so that she was never in one place for too long.

Margaret had been in constant fear, not that her pimp would find her, but that he would kill her family as he had threatened. When that didn't materialize, she moved herself to a big new city to try and start a better life. Even though she had never been very religious, the good people she had met along the way had connections to a halfway house and a small community of people working together with dedication to reinvent themselves and restructure their past. New Chances had come to her at a special time in her life when she thought suicide would have been her only choice. She understood Suzanne all too well and was determined to pay it forward the only way she knew how.

"Good morning, Suzanne. Did you sleep well?" Margaret asked, knocking before entering her room. She smiled at the subdued girl struggling to sit up in bed.

"Yes, I slept. I don't know how *well* it was, but I did it. I finally slept."

"It's hard, isn't it, to put your life back together… afterward?" Silence filled the room at that point, neither one wanting to take a step further into the conversation.

Finally, Suzanne answered. "I guess I don't see myself in an *afterward* kind of position," she said, still attempting to sit up and making some effort to comprehend the person and the newness of the situation.

"It's a different kind of place, this place," Margaret continued. "Everyone's been where you've been. No one's going to ask anything of you right now. We all have our private and unique version of hell. We all have our stories. Join us as you are. There will be no questions asked. When you're ready, though, we'll be here." Margaret smiled at Suzanne, hoping to get a smile in return, but none was forthcoming. *That's okay*, she thought. *This can't be rushed.*

Margaret left the room then, willing to wait and not expecting any reply. She knew this was a girl who needed time to heal. At her own pace.

≪

David and Sandy met Margaret Perron in her office before seeing Suzanne. Margaret wanted a complete rundown of Suzanne's family life before she had been trafficked. Sandy filled her in about their daily activities in the small town. She knew that Suzanne had been unhappy at home. Both her parents were heavy drinkers, especially at night, and often the two girls would escape to the mall, as it was the major social outlet for the teens of Paisley Falls. Sandy spoke of Suzanne's obsession with the Civil War era and the fun they had reading the diary of one of Sandy's ancestors who had fought in the Civil War. Suzanne, explained Sandy, was a shy and rather introverted girl who wrote lots of poetry and locked herself in her room at home a lot. This guy, Julius, had swept her off her feet, making her feel like a movie star with his red Corvette.

"Did he sweep you off your feet as well, Sandy?" asked the director. "Was he someone you also found attractive?"

"I guess I was pretty impressed with his style, and definitely his red Corvette, but no. I mean, I had a boyfriend, and I felt good about Suzanne being appreciated. She didn't get much positive feedback at home."

"Tell me more about that. Was one parent more affectionate than the other?"

"Well," stammered Sandy, "I guess I'd say her father was the more positive one toward Suzanne, but he was awfully critical of her. He threatened her quite a bit, and that scared her, but she felt he loved her just the same. Her mother was an entirely different story. I think she was jealous of Suzanne and felt that her husband paid too much attention to his daughter. It was just a weird kind of situation. I mean, Suzanne wasn't beaten or anything, but I don't think she felt she had a place in the family. She thought she was expendable. You know, like if she disappeared the family wouldn't miss her at all. So, in a way, running off with Julius made sense."

"Did she run off, Sandy? Is that why there wasn't a missing person's report filed?"

"Wow, how did you know that?"

"There is no record of one filed. It seems strange to me that no report was filed."

"I know! It seemed strange to me too, but her mother claimed that she ran off with the guy, even though I knew she didn't!"

"How did you know for a fact that she wasn't a willing partner in this? Did she call you?"

"No, I had her cell phone. It was in her purse when she left the party."

"So, you've had no communication from her in the two years since she left, but you feel certain that she was kidnapped."

"But this creep Julius is a gangster—"

"Did you ever learn his last name?"

"No but…" Sandy was bewildered by this line of communication. "Why are you even asking?" she stammered.

"Look, Sandy, I can see that she's been battered and beaten up by her experiences. When she first arrived, she was delusional and claimed she was being held in a cage. She's terrified now that this Julius will come here and kill her. These are typical behaviors from someone who has been trafficked, but we'd like to catch this guy. We'd like to shut him down, and we don't have a single piece of evidence to go on. We don't know where she was kept or any of the places she was stored for business. We don't have the names of any associates he might have had and no access to any other trafficking he might have been involved in. We can—and we will—take care of Suzanne here. There's no doubt about that, but we need more information about all that's happened in the past two years. We want to nail this guy and any others we can find along the way. If her parents can't or won't help, is there anybody else who can?"

"Yeah," chimed in David, "that private detective that's been chasing her for two years. Sergeant Dormer."

Andy Dormer sat for some time with all the information he had, trying to put all the pieces together. His daughter was temporarily safe and had seemingly uncovered a bizarre plot to extort young girls for prostitution. So far, two necklaces had been found that had been allegedly modeled after his daughter's necklace for some kind of ritualistic initiation into a secret club. One was found at the cotton mill and the other on the bedside table of Evan DeMarco. Rhonda DeMarco had been overtly hostile at the mention of her older daughter's return, and her younger daughter openly admitted that she didn't want to welcome her back either. Dr. Wilson had been killed, and there was a possibility that his father-in-law, Roy Barber, had not only hired the killers but controlled the investigation by the state police. Was he also involved in the two-year-old murder of a gangster trying to hone in on his drug trafficking as well? The one thing he was thankful for was that Suzanne had been found and was safe, at least for the moment. He had to hand it to her friend Sandy for her persistence in not giving up. He knew that he had to tie up loose ends with LJ, but it took a back seat to all the other pressing problems.

His thoughts were interrupted by a phone call from Rick, his old friend from the Elite Car Rental Agency.

"Hey, Andy, learned you're back in town. Glad to hear it. We've all missed you."

"Rick, how you doin'? How's the car rental business? Any surprises?"

"As a matter of fact, yes, Andy. I just got a call from some junk depot guy in Leverton who swears he's got a blue Camaro with some registration papers in the glove department that say the car belongs to us. I'm pretty sure this is the car that was stolen two years ago. I remember a state trooper calling me back then to ask who it was registered to. Apparently, he had stopped the guy for a traffic violation. I looked it up and learned it was rented by a Dino Hu. I remember it was funny that the trooper said a Julius Conaforte was driving it. Anyway, this guy says he doesn't want any part of stolen property, and I said, 'Then why'd you take two years to call us?' He said he had it sittin' around the yard and wasn't paying attention, but he knew who dropped it off and just wanted to report it."

Dormer wondered why Junkyard Eddie was turning on LJ. He let that sink in for a moment.

"Hey, Andy, you still there? Doesn't this have something to do with the abduction of that girl you were investigating?"

"Yes, Rick, that was the stolen car all right."

"Well, just for the heck of it, I looked up the records for a Julius Conaforte, and he had quite a sheet. The interesting thing is that he was just recently doing time in an LA jail."

"Well, that's right where he belongs," said Dormer.

"Yeah, I'd sure like to get my hands on him but…" Rick's voice drifted off into the background as Dormer let all this sink in.

"What? Sorry, Rick, did you say he's in jail?"

"Much more than that, Andy. The guy's dead. They say it was an inside job."

CHAPTER TWENTY

SANDY DIDN'T HESITATE to put in a call to Sergeant Dormer. After all *he* had called *her*!

"The thing is, Sergeant Dormer—"

"Sandy, technically I'm no longer a sergeant."

"Okay, well anyway, she's in this place called New Chances. It seems really nice. They could really use your help. I guess Suzanne's a difficult case. You know, I lost her the other day. She just walked away from me, and I'm scared to talk to her again. I guess I really don't know how to talk to her now. Anyway, they could really use your help. I mean they need to know what you know. You know what I mean?"

Andy thought that if they knew what he knew they'd flip!

"I guess I'm pleading with you, Sergeant... uh... Mr. Dormer, to come back to LA and talk to these people and help Suzanne. I know that all the work you did these past two years gave you some insight into what's going on, and that could help. Please... one more time?"

Dormer knew that if he could tell Suzanne that Julius Conaforte was dead that would either help her or send her into an abyss. It might be worth a trip to LA to try and help her recovery process, but things in Paisley Falls were unravelling. It was the call he got next while on his cell that made the deciding factor. While talking to Sandy, he got a call from Sid. "Hold or accept" flashed on the screen. He told Sandy to hold on while he took Sid's call. Afterwards, he got back to Sandy.

"I'll be there as soon as I can."

Sid had called Andy to tell him about a frantic phone call from a hysterical Rhonda DeMarco. Bethy, her younger daughter, had disappeared. Rhonda had found a note on the teen's pillow in her bedroom. In it, she simply said that she wanted to find her sister to ask her something. Rhonda had telephoned the station in a rage, saying that Dormer had told Bethy where Suzanne was and had helped her to leave home.

"I know you're not officially back on the job here, Andy, but do you think you could stop by the DeMarco house and calm this woman down?"

"I wonder how she finds it in her to blame me for the problems with every single member of her family. Yeah, I'll stop by there on my way to LA. Suzanne DeMarco is in a halfway house there, and they're asking that I help them. I'll be glad to finish this business once and for all. Sid, I trust you'll keep an eye out for the young girl. She can't have gone far. It's what? Three in the afternoon? I hope to get on the road to LA before rush hour. I'll let you know what I find out."

With that, Andy threw a few supplies into his Honda and said goodbye to his wife, promising that this would be the end of his quest to find and help the tragic runaway that had consumed his life for two years.

"I should be back by tomorrow night, Dolores. Hopefully this younger daughter of the DeMarco's will be found locally.

I have no idea how a thirteen-year-old could make it to LA in just a couple of hours. God, I hope she didn't try to hitchhike."

"I just wish you didn't feel so obligated all the time, Andy. I thought you'd had enough of this."

"This could have been our daughter, Dolores. I do feel obligated… to do my best always, but don't worry. I mean it. I will be back."

He left then without turning around to wave. He never saw the tear that unraveled its way down his wife's face.

Rhonda DeMarco had been drinking. By the time Andy Dormer knocked on the door, she had finished the bottle of Jack Daniels and lashed out at Andy with a litany of insults she had been rehearsing for his arrival.

"'Bout time you showed up here," she blurted out, staggering across the kitchen floor. "Now the second one's gone as well. What'd you tell her?"

"May I see your phone, Mrs. DeMarco?"

"My phone? What's my phone got to do with anything, asshole?"

She was weaving so badly that Dormer thought she might pass out any minute. He ignored her and went to the landline phone on the kitchen counter. There he was able to pull up the history of phone calls received and made within the past few days. He found the call Bethy had received from the urgent care facility in LA, and the same number was repeated just yesterday. He didn't want to have to tell this woman anything, but he calmly explained and showed her the two times these numbers were on her call list.

"You can see—well, when you're sober maybe you can

see—that there are two times in the past few days that this number was received by this household. Yesterday it was dialed out. Did you make this phone call, Rhonda?"

But Rhonda was so far gone she had passed out on the floor.

"No, I guess not," he said.

He dialed the number and got the urgent care facility that had called a few days ago asking Bethy if she knew anyone named Suz. Dormer wondered why she had said no in the first place. He explained to them that a young teenager might be coming there looking for her older sister Suzanne. If she showed up, would they contact the following people: him, Andy Dormer, a private investigator working on this case, CA license # 21784; the local police; and, reluctantly, he added her mother, Mrs. DeMarco of Paisley Falls.

ᴅ

"David, I don't think it's such a great idea for you to be in on this meeting with Suzanne," said Margaret, sitting at her desk across from the couple who had done so much to help this fragile girl. "It's only because she could view you as just another john or a pimp that wants to own her. She's got history with Sandy, and we're hoping to reestablish that friendship so she has someone to trust from her past. This is nothing personal. I hope you know that."

"I've got no problem with that, and I should get back to my printing business. I've got a living to make." He smiled at Sandy, who blushed back at him.

"See you later, babe. Call me, and I'll pick you up." As he stood up to leave, he turned back to Margaret and reached out to shake her hand. "Thanks for all that you do. I mean that. I live for the people who make a difference in this world."

She smiled back at him. "So do I."

Sandy got up and walked David out. "I'm a little scared of this," she said. "I don't quite know what to expect."

"Take it easy on yourself and go slow with her. It sounds like she has a long way to go before…" His voice trailed off.

"Before what, David?"

"Before she's capable of being normalized, I guess. I think she's been traumatized way beyond these past two years. From what you've said, Suzanne has never really been a happy person. She's always had trouble."

"Well, yeah, I guess. I mean, I never realized that she suffered. I don't know how to deal with that. I was just her friend, not her therapist."

"Sounds like what she needs right now is just that, Sandy: a friend. See you later."

He left then, and Sandy stood for moment outside the door wondering how she would handle the situation inside. Once sitting back across the desk from Margaret, the director wasted no time getting to the point with Sandy.

"Do you think Suzanne was molested at home?"

The question took her by surprise. "No," she said after a while. "It was more like her mind wasn't allowed to be her own. I'm not sure if that makes any sense, but I always had the feeling that she almost wasn't allowed to think her own thoughts, and that was why she locked herself in her room and wrote so much. The writing allowed her to express herself when talking to people didn't feel safe."

"Why could she talk to you?"

"I was a different kind of loner, I guess. I mean, when I first moved to Paisley Falls in the middle of the school year, I knew no one. I had no friends, and people were different than I was used to. Suzanne had lost a friend to a tragic disease, and she had no one. I guess we just glommed onto each other."

"I think you're right on the money with your perceptions about Suzanne, Sandy. She may have pushed you away when you first found her in LA because now the two of you have nothing in common. Whoever she was before she got trafficked no longer exists. She thinks of herself as merely an object, no different than her last sex act. That's a typical reaction to this kind of trauma, but most of the time it's life in the family home that starts the problem. Molested by an uncle or grandfather or father, a young girl starts off perceiving herself as the one who caused the molestation, that something she did or said caused it. That it was her fault, and she becomes ashamed of herself. That she's been a bad girl. In talking with you and Suzanne, this doesn't sound like her at all. She's not typical, at least not in that respect. She is also terrified of drugs. Most girls we see here come in so hopped up that they need weeks of detox before they're straight enough to talk. I can see, of course, from one look at her arms that she's been hit with a lot of stuff, but it seems to have been forced on her, or so she says."

"We didn't take drugs. It just wasn't our thing. I honestly don't know why, since everyone else did. We were just different, I guess."

Sandy wondered where all this talking was leading. She almost wished she'd left with David. Trying to fix Suzanne was not something she really wanted to tackle.

Sensing her nervousness, Margaret backed off a bit. "Sandy, I don't expect you to fix Suzanne. What's wrong? What is it?"

Sandy was crying, tears were rolling down her cheeks. "It's just… I don't want to lose my friend," she sobbed. "When I first found her after looking for almost two years, I couldn't believe what I saw. She was unrecognizable. It was like a whole part of her was cut out. I didn't really know who I was looking at. The horror coming out of her eyes wanted no part of me either. I don't know if I can do this. I'm tired, you know? I'm exhausted from trying so hard to be a savior. She's safe now, that's what matters most. I don't think I can do anything more to help her."

She didn't get up out of her seat, however, and Margaret came around to where she sat and put her arms around her. "You are helping her now, Sandy, just by caring enough to be here. We both know she has no family to speak of. Whether you admit it or not, I think you're all she's got."

Neither one of them had noticed the man standing in the doorway listening to the conversation.

Sandy looked up first, a surprised look crossed her face. "Oh, it's you."

"Yes," said Andy Dormer, "and look who I've found along the way." He stepped aside to reveal a young thirteen-year-old teenager named Bethy.

"I want to see my sister," she said. "I've got something very important to tell her."

CHAPTER TWENTY-ONE

THE ROOM WAS dark, and Suzanne was dreaming. The little room in the halfway house that she now considered home had been darkened to help her sleep. She didn't know if it was night or day, but that kind of thing didn't frighten her anymore. She liked that they had drawn the curtains on the closed windows. She could just make out the outlines of the little stuffed animals on the shelves. One little teddy bear in particular seemed to smile and nod at her, its little button eyes telling her that everything was going to be okay.

In her dream, she saw Lulu running on a vast desert plane of sand. Suzanne saw herself trying to catch up with her, but she could never run as fast as Lulu. Lulu was definitely running toward something; it seemed like it was the edge of a sunset that she was chasing, but as she got nearer and nearer to her, she saw that what Lulu was running toward was Julius. He loomed large in the sky like the sun, and he was sinking into the horizon like the sun would do at the end of a day, or a lifetime of days. She started to yell at Lulu to stop running. She knew that if Lulu kept on, she would disappear into the diminishing form that was Julius. She yelled and screamed for Lulu to stop before it was too late. Suddenly, she felt a presence in the room, and then someone was shaking her, ending the dream.

She woke up to Margaret's pressure on her arm and her gentle voice telling her to wake up. "It's just a dream, Suzanne. Wake up. There's someone here who wants to see you."

"No, no! I don't want to see him! No! Tell him to go away!" Suzanne struggled to get up, pushing the bedsheets out of the way.

"No, honey, don't worry; you're safe now. Your little sister has come to see you."

"Bethy? Bethy's here?"

"Bethy and your friend from high school, Sandy. They're both here because they love you, Suzanne. They want to see you whole again."

"Oh, oh my God. I can't."

"Yes, you can, Suzanne. You have to."

The door slowly opened and someone she hadn't seen in two years walked right up to her bedside. "Hi Sister Sue."

It was Bethy, who had grown taller and was three years older.

"Oh my goodness, you're so tall!"

"I'm thirteen now, Suzy. I came all this way to tell you that I've just gotta get a message to you."

"Oh." Suzanne giggled. "That's that old-timey song you used to sing from one of Dad's old records," she said, referring to the ballad by the Bee Gees in the late sixties.

As a small child, Bethy had been fascinated by her father's old record albums. "I've Gotta Get a Message to You" was one of her favorites. Suzanne had always felt that it conveyed some kind of desperation on Bethy's part that she wasn't being understood or listened to.

"That's the song they play all the time at the Restful Days assisted living facility where Daddy is now. Can you come home now, Suzy? I miss you so much. I came all this way to get this message to you." Her younger sister buried her face in Suzanne's neck and cried for her to come back home.

"Bethy, what do you mean? Why is Dad in a rest home?"

"After you left, he had another heart attack. He was always so worried about you leaving. One day I came home from school and said "Hi, Dad" so loudly he thought it was you. That's when he had the attack, and Mom couldn't take care of him anymore, so she put him in the Restful Days assisted living facility. I don't think it's a very restful place, Suzy. Every time I've visited him, he seems more upset than ever. He always asks me when you're coming, and Mom gets angry at him for even asking. He's going to die, Suzanne! Without you and him, I'll have nobody. Please, please come back."

"Where's Mom, Bethy?"

"She's not there. She never was. Dad and I need you back, Suz. Only you can save him if you try. 'I second that emotion,' to quote the words of another golden oldie."

With that, Sandy entered with a flourish, pirouetting her way across the room, and Margaret, standing in the background, slowly raised the room lights and opened the curtains to reveal daylight.

"Some important people in your life, sweetie," said Margaret.

"You've got to get them out of here, do you understand?" shouted Suzanne.

"They can't ever be here when Julius—"

"Julius is dead, Suzanne." Andy Dormer stood in the doorway and delivered the news. Suzanne shrunk back in horror as the effect of those words bore down on her.

Julius dead? How she had prayed for that day. She didn't know how she was supposed to feel. "How?"

"Some gangster had a grudge and settled the score while he was in prison."

"And LJ?"

"At large. He was apparently wounded in a fight."

"Yes, I know," said Suzanne.

"He left the hospital with one of the nurses' aides and managed to get to his plane and fly off to parts unknown, but not for long. I'm on his trail, and I won't stop till I've got him."

For Dormer, it was a pledge he would not back down on, even though it brought him once more into jeopardy with his family.

"There's a lot we have to talk about. Things that are happening in Paisley Falls and so many other towns in this country and the world. I need everyone's help in this room. We've got some big problems to tackle."

All the women in the room turned to look at the rumpled figure of a man who looked as though he had the weight of the world on his shoulders. No one spoke for a long moment; it was Margaret who finally whispered, "I think we're in."

"I'm going home," said Suzanne. She got out of bed holding her sister's hand, as Sandy, choking back tears, looked around for the closet that held her clothes.

Margaret and Andy left the room, and then Andy proceeded to fill the director in on all the events he had learned since this investigation had begun. "I know how crazy this sounds, but there's an old cotton mill in Paisley Falls," he said, walking down the hallway.

"Nothing sounds crazy to me in the world of human trafficking," said Margaret. "Everything that can possibly be imagined is unfortunately a reality somewhere in this nightmare. Believe me, it's my life's purpose to end this," she said.

"You've got a friend here," said Andy.

∽

Back in Sacramento, in the tiny apartment that had been converted into a hiding place for immigrants, Lulu smiled, holding another baby in her arms ready for transport.

LIST OF REFERENCES

Books:

Malarek, Victor. *The Johns: Sex for Sale and the Men Who Buy It*. New York: Arcade Publishing, 2009.

Ivy, Pimpin' Ken and Karen Hunter. *Pimpology: The 48 Laws of the Game*. New York: Simon & Schuster, 2007.

Newspapers:

Alejandra Reyes-Velarde, "Owners of Senior and Childcare Centers Charged with Trafficking," *Los Angeles Times*, September 7, 2018.

Editorial, "Congress' Pursuit of Backpage.com is Risky," *Los Angeles Times*, March 6, 2018.

Lara Powers, "Trafficking Nonsense on Facebook," *Los Angeles Times*, April 4, 2017.

Patt Morrison, "Sex-Traffic Cop, Melissa Farley," *Los Angeles Times*, November 18, 2015.

Interviews:

Lieutenant Marc Evans, LAPD officer-in-charge of Human Trafficking Task Force Operations, Valley Bureau

Detective Eric Hooker, Long Beach Vice Investigations

Detective Sheriff Judith Porter, Ventura County Sheriff's Special Crimes Unit, Human Trafficking Investigator

Sergeant Dante Reese, LAPD assistant officer-in charge of Human Trafficking Task Force, Valley Bureau

Dr. Allison Santi-Richard, emergency medicine physician, Los Robles Hospital, Thousand Oaks, CA

Countless stories from survivors at Soroptimist International Community Awareness Events

Websites:

Forever Found. "What Can I do to Fight Human Trafficking?" Last modified 2019. http://www.foreverfound.org

Polaris Project. "Human Trafficking Cheat Sheet," National Human Trafficking Resource Center. https://polarisproject.org/

Soroptimist International of Oxnard. "Stop Human Trafficking and Sexual Slavery." http://oxnardsoroptimist.org/

US Immigration and Customs Enforcement, "Human Trafficking PSA." Last modified April 13, 2014. https://www.ice.gov/video/human-trafficking-psa-full-version

Women Working. "Family Isn't Always Blood." Last modified 1/1/2019. https://www.womenworking.com/